HOST

Doctor and author Robin Cook is widely credited with introducing the word 'medical' to the thriller genre, and over twenty years after the publication of his breakthrough novel *Coma*, he continues to dominate the category he created. Cook has successfully combined medical fact with fiction to produce over twenty-eight international bestsellers, including *Outbreak* (1987), *Terminal* (1993), *Contagion* (1996), *Intervention* (2009) and, most recently, *Cell* (2014).

www.robincookmd.com

'Forensic pathologists and doctors-turned-detectives do battle against epidemics, lethal illness and drug-related deaths, the causes of which are far from natural . . . you'll find yourself completely hooked'
Daily Mail

'Likeable heroes, a compelling medical mystery and growing suspense – the result is a highly entertaining read. Commercial fiction, at its best, is pure entertainment. But Cook, like Michael Crichton, offers readers a smart dissection of contemporary issues that affect us all'
USA Today

'Gripping . . . terrifying'   *New York Times*

'Strikes a deafening chord of terror'   *Washington Post*

'Holds you, page after page'   Larry King

ROBIN
COOK

HOST

PAN BOOKS

First published 2015 by G. P. Putnam's Sons,
a member of Penguin Group (USA) Inc, New York

First published in the UK 2015 by Macmillan

This edition first published 2016 by Pan Books
an imprint of Pan Macmillan
20 New Wharf Road, London N1 9RR
Associated companies throughout the world
www.panmacmillan.com

ISBN 978-1-5098-0072-8

1 3 5 7 9 8 6 4 2

A CIP catalogue record for this book is available from the British Library.

Printed and bound by CPI Group (UK) Ltd, Croydon, CR0 4YY

*For Cameron, an exemplary boy
who is fast becoming a man—find your
passion, son, and have a great life!*

HOST

PROLOGUE

The following private journal entries were written by the late Kate Hurley, a thirty-seven-year-old, physically fit (played lots of tennis and was careful about her diet), moderately compulsive, third-grade elementary school teacher and doting mother of two boys, aged eleven and eight. Until her death during a horrific home invasion, she lived with her family at 1440 Bay View Drive in Mount Pleasant, South Carolina, across the harbor from Charleston. The house stands in a relatively secluded wooded section at the very end of the road. She was married to Robert Hurley, an aggressive personal-injury lawyer.

Saturday, March 28, 8:35 A.M.

It is a dreary, gray day as I look out the window of my hospital room in the Mason-Dixon Medical Center. Hardly the spring weather we all expect. I haven't been good about writing in my journal over the last six months even though doing so has always been a great solace for me. Unfortunately I have been exhausted at night and much too busy getting the boys and myself ready for school in the morning, but I will make an effort to change. I could use the consolation. I am in the hospital, feeling sorry for myself after a dreadful night. It had started promisingly enough as Bob and I had met Ginny and Harold Lawler for dinner on Sullivan's Island. They all had fish, and in retrospect, I wish I had done the same. Unfortunately I had chosen the duck, which was prepared on the rare side and which I would later learn from the emergency room physician probably had been contaminated, most likely with salmonella. I began to feel strange even before finishing the entrée, and it got progressively worse. While Bob was taking home the babysitter, I had my first episode of vomiting—not pleasant! I made a mess of myself and the bathroom. Luckily I was able to clean it up before Bob returned. He was sympathetic but tired from a busy day at the office and soon turned in. Since I still felt horrid, I parked myself in the bathroom and threw up several more times, even after I thought there was no way there could be any more food in my system. By two A.M. I realized I was weak and getting weaker. It was then that I woke up Bob. He took one look at me and judged that I needed to be seen by a doctor. Our health plan directed us to the Mason-Dixon Medical Center over in Charleston. Luckily we were able to get Bob's mom to come over to be with the kids. She's been a lifesaver on a number of occasions, this being one of them. At the emergency room, the nurses and the doctors were great. Of course I was mortified as the vomiting continued and bloody diarrhea began. I was started on an IV and given some medication, which I'm sure they explained, but I don't remember. They also advised that I be admitted. I felt so out of it that I didn't object, even though I have always feared hospitals. I also must have been given a sedative, because I don't even remember Bob leaving or my being transferred from the ER to a hospital room. Yet a few hours later I do remember partially awakening when someone, probably a nurse, came into the dark room and adjusted or added something to the IV. It was as if I were dreaming, because the person appeared like an apparition, with blond hair and dressed in white. I tried to talk but couldn't, at least not intelligently. When I awoke this morning I felt like I had been run over by a truck. I tried to get out of bed to use the bathroom but couldn't, at least initially, and had to call for assistance. It is one of the things that I dislike about being in a hospital: you're not in control. You have to give up all autonomy when you check in.

The nurse who helped me said that a doctor would be by shortly. I will finish this entry when I get home to talk about how this episode has made me realize how much I take general health for granted. I had never had food poisoning before. It is much worse than I had imagined. In fact it is god-awful! That's all I can say.

Sunday, March 29, 1:20 P.M.

Obviously I already have failed to follow my resolution about writing in this journal more frequently. I did not finish yesterday's entry as I promised myself because things did not go as I had planned. Soon after I had written the above, I was visited by one of the hospital's resident physicians, Dr. Clair Webster, who noticed something that I hadn't, namely that I had a fever. It wasn't a high fever, but it was a change, since I had a normal temperature the night before. Although I didn't realize it, machines were recording my pulse, blood pressure, and temperature continuously, which was why I hadn't seen anyone during the night except for the person who had adjusted my intravenous. Even my IV is being controlled by a small computerized device. So much for the human touch in the modern hospital! Dr. Webster said my temperature had started rising about six A.M. and that she wanted to wait to see what it did before discharging me. I called Bob to let him know about the delay.

As it turned out, it was more than a delay, as my temperature did not return to normal but rather proceeded to climb all day and all night up to 104° F, so here I am still. And there have been some further complications. Right after Bob and the boys left from their afternoon visit yesterday (the boys were not supposed to visit because of their ages but Bob snuck them up to the room) I started to get very achy, and now I understand what people mean when they say they have joint pain. Worse than that, I have begun to have some breathing problems, and as if that is not enough, when I took a shower yesterday, I noticed I had a slight rash under my arms, and under my breasts, that are flat, tiny red dots. Luckily they don't itch. The nurse said I had some on the whites of my eyes also. All that brought the resident doctor back. She said that she was confused because the symptoms were suggesting I might have typhoid fever, and she insisted I be seen by an infectious-disease specialist. So he came by and examined me. Thankfully he said it wasn't typhoid and gave a number of reasons, chief of which was that I didn't have the right strain of salmonella. Still, he was concerned that my heart had speeded up while I've been in the hospital. To check this out, he called in a cardiologist, a Dr. Christopher Hobart, who examined me as well. My room was like a convention center, with all these doctors coming and going. Dr. Hobart immediately ordered a chest X-ray because he thought I was having some fat embolization! As soon as I had a chance I looked up *fat embolization* online (thank God for the Internet) and found out it is globules of fat in the bloodstream, a condition usually seen in patients with severe trauma, including broken bones. Of course I haven't had any trauma except emotional, so the cardiologist concluded it was from severe dehydration. But since I already had the intravenous line, he said there was no need for any further treatment, especially since my breathing seemed entirely normal. I was pleased about that, but, I have to say, all this has made my hospital phobia skyrocket. I read something about hospital complications a few months ago in the *Post and Courier*, and what was going on with me seemed similar and was making me really anxious. The only thing that was wrong with me when I came in Friday night was food poisoning, and now I was supposedly having fat embolization. I called Bob and told him how I felt and that I wanted to get out of this place and come home. He advised me to be patient and that we would discuss it later, when he comes to visit, after his mother comes over to the house to watch the kids. I will finish this entry after Bob and I talk. On top of my other symptoms I'm having some trouble concentrating.

Monday, March 30, 9:30 A.M.

Once again I failed to write in the journal, as I had planned after Bob's visit. My excuse was feeling spaced out. That's the best way I can describe it. I had written yesterday at the very end of the entry that I was having trouble concentrating. It got worse. I don't even remember all that Bob and I talked about when he was here, although I do remember that he, too, got upset about all my emerging symptoms, demanding to talk to the doctors who had come to examine me. Whether he did or not, I don't know. And I don't remember much else that he said, although I do remember that he was going to call Dr. Curtis Fletcher, our old family doctor, and get him involved.

I vaguely remember getting agitated after Bob left, worrying that I was getting worse and not better. That got Dr. Webster back, and she prescribed a sedative to calm me down, which certainly did. The next thing I remembered was again waking up in the middle of the night. This time it was with someone doing something to my belly that felt like a needle prick. Maybe it was the same person who had adjusted my IV the night before. I'm not sure. When I awoke this morning, I wondered if it had been a dream until I found a slightly tender area on my abdomen. Are some sedatives given there? I will try to remember to ask. My fever is down slightly, although still above normal. More importantly, I don't feel so spaced out, and the achiness is much improved with ibuprofen. Maybe they will let me go home. I hope so. My dislike and fear of hospitals have not improved. They've gotten worse.

10:35 A.M.

I am back writing! I am very upset. I am not going home. Dr. Chris Hobart just returned with bad news. He said he had ordered an albumin test yesterday, which turned out to show that the albumin was okay but that I had another blood protein that was way up! He said I was developing a monoclonal gammopathy, whatever the hell that is. I have yet to look it up on the Internet. I hate it when doctors talk as if they don't want you to understand. I know this sounds paranoid, but I think doctors do it on purpose. To his credit, he did say that the elevated protein was probably not a problem, but he wanted me to have another consult with a blood specialist, meaning I wasn't going to be discharged.

3:15 P.M.

The blood specialist just left, promising to return in the morning. If her visit was supposed to calm me down, it didn't work. My worst fears about hospitals are coming to pass in spades. This new doctor is a blood cancer doctor! An oncologist! I'm now terrified I'm going to come down with something like leukemia. The doctor's name is Siri Erikson, which sounds Scandinavian, and she looks it. All I can say is that I want to go home! Unfortunately I still have a high fever, and Dr. Erikson said it would be better for me to stay another few days to see if they can find out what is causing my temperature to go up, or, at the very least, let it come back to normal.

But I'm really anxious. Everything that is happening is convincing me that hospitals are not safe places to be unless you really need them, like I suppose I did Friday night. It seems that the longer I stay here, the more problems I get. I will talk to Bob about all this when he comes to visit after work. On the plus side, my GI system is getting back to normal. My diet has been upped to normal foods, which I am tolerating fine. I just want to get out of here and get home with Bob and the boys.

4:45 P.M.

Bob expects to be here around six P.M. In the meantime I put in a call to Dr. Fletcher, our old family doctor, which Bob had forgotten to do after he said he would. I remembered seeing the GP for a physical about two months ago, when Bob and I were toying with the idea of getting some life insurance. The examination had included some basic blood work, and I wondered if it included blood proteins. At the time I had been told everything had been normal. When Dr. Fletcher called me back to commiserate about my bout of food poisoning, he told me that the blood work he had done did include a blood protein screen. He confirmed it had been normal. When I told him about possibly having a protein problem now, he was surprised, although he said such a problem can start at any time but usually only involving people much older than I. His advice was that the test should be repeated, and I told him that it had already been ordered. As far as getting him involved in my in-hospital care, he said he couldn't do it. He said that he did not have privileges at the Mason-Dixon but would be happy to talk to any of the doctors taking care of me if they wanted. I thanked him and told him that I would suggest it. Needless to say, I'm disappointed with what's going on, and I have decided, no matter what, I will check myself out of the hospital tomorrow as long as Bob is okay with the plan.

7:05 P.M.

Bob just left. Unfortunately I've gotten him really upset. After telling him what I had learned from Dr. Fletcher, that my blood proteins were normal a few months ago, he wanted to sign me out of the hospital immediately. Strangely enough, his emotional response made me hesitant about leaving, especially since I had been told that it would entail signing out against medical advice. Finally I was able to convince Bob that we should wait at least until the morning, when I would be seeing Dr. Erikson again. After all, blood problems were her specialty, and I wanted to be reassured I didn't have something really bad, like cancer.

Now, lying here at the mercy of this place and listening to the sounds drifting in from the corridor, I wonder if I should have let Bob check me out no matter what I needed to sign. To make matters worse, I have just noticed what might be a new symptom: my belly feels slightly tender. Or at least I think it does when I press deeply. But maybe it always feels that way. I don't actually know. Maybe I'm being overly melodramatic and even a little paranoid. I'm going to ask for my sleeping pill and try to forget where I am.

Tuesday, March 31, 9:50 A.M.

I just hung up with Bob. I'm afraid I have ignited a firestorm. I told him that Dr. Erikson had come by with the news that the protein abnormality, or gammopathy, in my blood was real, and the level was even slightly higher than in the previous test. When she saw how upset I became, she tried to backtrack and calm me down. But her reassurances fell on deaf ears. Not after reading what I had on the Internet about blood protein abnormalities. As soon as she left, I called Bob and, bursting into tears, I told him what had happened. He told me to start packing my things because he was coming in to sign me out. And that was not all: he said he is going to sue the bejesus out of Middleton Healthcare, the corporate owners of the Mason-Dixon Medical Center and thirty-one other hospitals. When I asked why, he told me he'd pulled an "all-nighter" doing research using his inside channels (he actually pays informants at area hospitals to find out about difficult cases so he can contact the patients directly). He said he had learned something disturbing concerning Middleton Healthcare hospitals that he needs to follow up further and will explain when I get home. Meanwhile, he wants me out of the Mason-Dixon Medical Center pronto (his word). He said that the Middleton Healthcare hospitals had excellent stats in relation to hospital-based infections, but when it comes to a discharge diagnosis of a new, unsuspected blood-protein abnormality, like I supposedly have, their numbers are off the charts. He believes that he may have stumbled onto a class-action lawsuit that could make his career. He said that his intuition was telling him that Middleton was doing something strange, meaning some sort of corporate wrongdoing, and he intended to find out what it was and do something about it. We talked for quite a while, with him doing most of the talking. I have to admit I progressively felt a bit betrayed. His main interest had morphed from my problems and mind-set to a lawsuit supposedly in the public interest.

After I assured him I would be ready when he got to the medical center, and we disconnected, I stared out the window, feeling particularly lonely and worrying that Bob's state of mind was going to cause problems for us over the long haul. We had to use Mason-Dixon Medical Center, as it was the only area hospital in our insurance network. The problem is, when Bob gets started on something like this, involving a major lawsuit, he is like a dog with a bone. I can't imagine why Middleton Healthcare Hospitals would see more blood-protein abnormalities than other hospitals. It doesn't make sense. Does Bob think they are drumming up business? I can't imagine that could be true! But his aggressiveness about the hospital gives me a bad feeling, especially since the doctors and nurses really did help me when I was in need on Friday night. What if the boys need hospitalization in the near future? Could Bob jeopardize that? What I do know, and know better than anybody else, is when Bob says he is going to sue somebody, it happens. I suppose I can hope that once I am home I can calm him down, and we all get back to normal.

BOOK 1

1.

Spring in Charleston, South Carolina, is a resplendent affair, and by the beginning of April, it is always well under way. The azaleas, camellias, hyacinths, early-blooming magnolias, and forsythias, as if competing for attention, all contribute to the riot of color and fragrance. And on this particular day, as the sun prepared to rise, there was the promise that it would be glorious for almost everyone in this scenic, historic town. Everyone, that is, except for Carl Vandermeer, a successful young lawyer who had grown up in nearby West Ashley.

Most mornings, regardless of the time of the year but particularly in the springtime, Carl would be part of a sizable group of joggers who ran along the Battery, which was located at the southern tip of Charleston's peninsula. The Battery fronted that portion of the expansive Charleston Harbor formed by the confluence of the Cooper and the Ashley Rivers. Lined with restored nineteenth-century mansions and boasting a public garden, the Battery was one of the city's most attractive and popular locales.

Like most of his fellow runners, Carl lived in the immediate and charming residential neighborhood known to the locals as SOB, the acronym for "South of Broad." Broad Street was a thoroughfare that ran east to west across the Charleston peninsula between the two rivers.

The reason Carl was not jogging this beautiful spring morning was the same reason he had not been jogging for the previous month. He had torn the anterior cruciate ligament in his right knee during the final basketball game of the past season. He and a half dozen other athletically inclined lawyers had formed a team to play in a city league.

Carl had always been into sports through high school and Duke University, where he played Division 1 lacrosse with considerable renown. Having made it a point to keep himself in shape even during law school, he thought of himself as generally immune to injury, especially since he was only twenty-nine years old. Throughout his athletic career he had never suffered more than a couple of sprained ankles.

So the knee injury had come as an unwelcome surprise. One minute he was perfectly fine, having played the entire first half of the game and scoring eighteen points in the process. With the ball in his possession, he had faked the fellow guarding him to the left and then went to the right, to drive to the basket. He never made it. The next thing he knew, he was sprawled on the floor, unsure of what had happened. Embarrassed, he got right to his feet. There was some discomfort in his right knee, but it wasn't bad. He took a few steps to walk it out and immediately collapsed a second time. That was when he knew it was serious.

A visit to Dr. Gordon Weaver, an orthopedic surgeon, had confirmed the diagnosis to be a torn anterior cruciate ligament. Even Carl, a complete medical novice by choice, had been able to see it on the MRI. The bad news was that he'd have to have surgery if he wanted to play any kind of sports. Dr. Weaver said the best operation involved diverting a portion of his own patellar tendon up through his joint. The only good news was that his health plan would cover the whole deal, including the rehab. His bosses at the law firm where he worked were not thrilled about the necessary downtime, but missing work was not what bothered Carl. What bothered Carl was that he had a particularly strong distaste for anything having to do with medicine and needles. He had been known to pass out from merely having blood drawn, and he didn't even like the smell of rubbing alcohol because of its associations. He had never been hospitalized, but he had visited friends who had been, and the experience had freaked him out, so going into the hospital that morning for surgery was going to be a challenge, to say the very least.

The irony of his embarrassing and secret medical phobia was that his steady girlfriend for the last two years, Lynn Peirce, was a fourth-year medical student. She often made him light-headed with her stories of her daily experiences at the Mason-Dixon Medical Center, where Carl was scheduled to have his surgery in a few hours. She had been the one who had recommended Dr. Weaver and had explained in agonizing detail exactly how Carl's knee was going to be repaired.

It also had been at Lynn's insistence that he request that his operation be Dr. Weaver's first case on a Monday morning. The rationale, she explained, was that everyone would be fresh and on the ball, meaning there would be less chance for mistakes or scheduling problems. Carl knew that Lynn meant well with all this, but her comments only made him even more nervous.

Lynn had offered to spend the night as she had on Saturday night to make sure Carl followed his pre-op orders and got to the hospital on time, but Carl had begged off. He was afraid she might end up innocently saying something that would make him even more worried than he already was. But he didn't tell her that. He said he thought he'd sleep better alone and reassured her that he would follow his pre-op instructions to the letter. She had accepted gracefully and said that she'd come visit him in his hospital room as soon as he came back from the PACU, or post-anesthesia care unit.

Carl had never mentioned his medical phobia to Lynn for fear that she, at a minimum, would laugh at him. Nor did he let on how anxious he felt about his upcoming surgery. To preserve his ego, there were some things better left unsaid.

Carl let the alarm ring unabated for a time out of fear of falling back asleep. He'd slept poorly and had had trouble getting to sleep the night before. His instructions from Dr. Weaver's nurse were to have nothing by mouth after midnight except water and to take a good, hot shower with antimicrobial soap when he got up with particular attention paid to his right leg. He was supposed to arrive at the hospital no later than seven, which was going to be a rush, since it was already six-thirty. He wanted it to be a rush, thinking he'd have less chance to think, but here he was, not even out of bed and already anxious.

As if sensing his distress, Pep, his nimble eight-year-old Burmese cat, awoke at the foot of the bed and came up to rub her wet nose against Carl's stubbled chin.

"Thank you, girl," Carl said, tossing back the covers and making a beeline to the bathroom. Pep tagged along as always. Carl had saved the cat at the end of his undergraduate senior year at Duke when one of his classmates was going to abandon her at the pound after graduation in the hope that it would be adopted. Carl couldn't abide by the plan, considering it a possible death sentence. He took the cat home for the summer, became hopelessly enamored with her, and ended up taking her along to law school. Frank Giordano, a close friend and fellow basketball-playing lawyer, who would be arriving shortly to drive Carl to the hospital, had volunteered to take care of the cat by coming to Carl's house and making sure it had food and water until Carl's homecoming in three days. Everything was in order, or so Carl thought.

As Carl Vandermeer eased into a hot shower, Dr. Sandra Wykoff leaped out of her BMW X3. She was in a hurry not because she was late but because she was enamored with her work. Unlike Carl Vandermeer, she loved medicine so much that she had not taken a real vacation in the three years she'd been on staff at the Mason-Dixon Medical Center. She was a board-certified anesthesiologist who had trained across town at the older Medical University of South Carolina. She was thirty-five years old, a workaholic, and relatively recently divorced after a short marriage to a surgeon.

From her reserved parking spot on the first floor of the parking garage, she avoided the elevator and took the stairs. It was only one flight, and she liked the exercise. The state-of-the-art operating rooms of the medical center, which was built just after the millennium, were on the second floor. In the surgical lounge she gazed up at the monitor displaying the image of the operating room's white board. She was assigned to OR 12 for four cases, the first being a right anterior cruciate repair with a patellar allograph by Gordon Weaver under general anesthesia. She was pleased. She particularly liked Gordon Weaver. Like most of the orthopedic guys, he was a gregarious fellow who enjoyed his work. Most importantly, from Sandra's perspective, he didn't dawdle and was vocal if there was more blood loss than expected. To her, such communication was important, but not every surgeon was as cooperative. Like all anesthesiologists, she knew that she was the one responsible for the patient's well-being during an operation, not the surgeon, and she appreciated being informed if anything occurred with the surgery that was out of the ordinary.

Using her tablet PC, Sandra typed in the patient's name, Carl

Vandermeer, along with his hospital number and her PIN to access his nascent EMR, electronic medical record. She wanted to look at his pre-op history. A moment later she knew what she was dealing with: a healthy twenty-nine-year-old male with no drug allergies and no previous anesthesia. In fact there had been no previous hospitalizations for any reason whatsoever. It was going to be an easy, straightforward case.

After changing into her scrubs, she made her way into the OR proper, passing the OR desk commandeered by the extraordinarily competent OR supervisor, Geraldine Montgomery. On her right she passed the entrance to the PACU, which used to be called more simply the recovery room. The pre-operative holding area was on the left. There was a lot of frenetic activity in both rooms. A bevy of nurses and orderlies were preparing for the soon-to-begin and inevitably busy Monday-morning schedule.

As a generally friendly although private person, Sandra greeted anyone who caught her eye, but she didn't stop to chat or even slow down. She was on her usual early-morning mission. She was eager to check out the anesthesia machine she would be using for the day, something all anesthesiologists and nurse anesthetists were required to do. The difference was that Sandra was more conscientious than most and couldn't wait to start.

Sandra worshipped the newer anesthesia machine, which was essentially computer driven. In fact it was the expanding role that the computer played in anesthesia that had attracted her to the specialty in the first place. As her father's daughter, Sandra was also attracted to most everything mechanical. Her father, Steven Wykoff, was an automotive engineer brought to Spartanburg, South Carolina, from Detroit, Michigan, by BMW in 1993. The fact that computers were destined to become more and more involved in medicine was the reason she went to medical school. It was during her third-year surgery rotation that she was introduced to anesthesia, and she was captivated from the start. The specialty was a perfect blend of physiology, pharmacology, computers, and mechanical devices, all of which suited Sandra just fine.

Entering OR 12, Sandra greeted Claire Beauregard, the assigned circulating nurse, who was already busy setting up for the case. But there was no conversation. Sandra stepped over to her trusted mechanical partner, with which she was going to spend most of the day. It bristled with varicolored cylinders of gas, multiple monitors, meters, gauges, and valves. The machine, like all the equipment in the relatively new hospital complex, was a state-of-the-art computer-controlled model. It was number 37 out of nearly 100 total. The number was on a sticker on the machine's side, which also included its service history.

From Sandra's perspective the apparatus in front of her was a marvel of engineering. Among its many features was an automatic checklist function that satisfied what the FDA required before use, akin in many respects to the checklist required in a modern aircraft before takeoff to make certain all systems functioned properly. But Sandra did not turn on the machine immediately to initiate the automatic checklist. She liked to check the machine the old-fashioned way, particularly the high-pressure and the low-pressure systems, just to be 100 percent certain everything was in order. She liked to physically touch and operate all the valves. Her hands-on inspection made her feel much more confident than relying on a computer-controlled algorithm.

Satisfied with what she found, Sandra rolled over the stool that would be her perch for the day, sat down, and pulled herself directly up to the anesthesia machine's front. Only then did she turn on the machine. Spellbound as usual, her eyes stayed glued to the monitor as the apparatus went through its own automated checklist, which included most of what she had already done. A few minutes later the machine indicated all was in order, including the alarms for trouble, such as changes in the patient's blood pressure and heart function or low oxygen levels in the blood.

Sandra was pleased. When something was amiss, even a minor thing, she was obliged to contact the Clinical Engineering Department, which serviced the anesthesia machines. She found the technicians to be a weird bunch. Those she had had interaction with were all expat Russians with varying fluency in English, most of whom seemed like the teenage computer nerds of her youth. She particularly did not like Misha Zotov, who had sought her out in the hospital cafeteria to engage her in conversation the day after she'd gone down to the department to ask a simple service-related question. He gave her the creeps, even more so by calling her at home a few days later to ask her to have a drink with him. How he'd gotten her unlisted number she had no idea. Her response was to fib and say she was in a committed relationship.

With the anesthesia machine ready to go, Sandra then began checking her supplies and pharmaceuticals with equal diligence. She liked to touch everything she might need so she would know where it was. If there was an emergency, she didn't want to search for anything. She wanted everything at her fingertips.

W ant me to park and come in with you?" Frank Giordano asked Carl as he turned into the Mason-Dixon Medical Center a few minutes after seven. They had been driving in silence. Initially Frank had tried to make conversation as they started northward up King Street, but Carl wasn't holding up his side. Frank guessed that Carl was stressed out about his upcoming surgery, especially after Carl admitted he was as nervous as hell before they had started out.

"Thanks, but no," Carl said. "I'm a little late, which I hope means I'm not going to be sitting around." It was clear he was agitated.

"Hey, man," Frank said, "you got to relax! It's no big deal. I had my tonsils out when I was ten. It was a piece of cake. I remember being told to count backward from fifty. I got to about forty-six and the next thing I knew I was being awakened, and it was all done."

"I have a bad feeling about this," Carl said. He turned to look at Frank.

"Shit, man, why are you going to go and say something stupid like that? Be positive! Look, you got to get it done, and you got to get it done now so, come next December, you're good to go for the next basketball season. We need you healthy."

Carl didn't respond. There was a line of cars backed up under the porte cochere. People were getting out with overnight bags. Carl guessed they, too, were arriving for surgery. He wished he could take it all in stride as it appeared others were doing. He glanced at his cell phone. It was now almost five after seven. He had meant to arrive exactly on time so there would be no sitting around.

"I'll get out here," Carl said suddenly, opening the passenger-side door as he spoke. He climbed out.

"I'll have you at the door in thirty seconds," Frank said.

"I don't think so. It will be faster if I walk." Carl slammed the car door and opened the trunk. He lifted the backpack containing his essentials and slung it over his shoulder. "Don't forget about the cat!"

"No worries," Frank said as he, too, alighted from the car. He came around and gave Carl a quick hug. Carl didn't respond, just looked him in the eye when his friend stepped back. But when Frank raised a fist, Carl followed suit. Their knuckles touched in a fist bump. "Later, dude!" Frank added. "You're going to be fine."

Carl nodded, turned, and negotiated the small tangle of cars waiting to get closer to the front door to disgorge their passengers. As he entered the hospital he remembered reading Dante's description of hell in civilization class at Duke.

A pink-smocked volunteer directed him down the hall to surgical admitting. Carl gave his name to one of the clerks seated behind a chest-high counter.

"You're late," the woman said with a mildly accusatory tone of voice. She had an uncanny visual resemblance to Carl's sixth-grade teacher, Miss Gillespie. The association made him feel as if he were going back to an earlier stage in his life when he truly wasn't in control of his fate. Carl had been an irrepressible twelve-year-old and had clashed with Miss Gillespie. The clerk picked up a packet of paperwork that was on the desk in front of her and handed it to Carl. "Take a seat! A nurse will be with you shortly."

Although similarly as bossy as the clerk, the nurse was significantly more congenial. She smiled when she asked Carl to follow her back to a curtained-off area where there was a gurney made up with fresh sheets and a pillow. Draped across it was the infamous hospital johnny. After checking his picture ID and asking his name and birth date, she put a name tag on his wrist. Once that was done, she told him to put his valuables in a zippered canvas bag that was also on the gurney, take off his clothes, put on the johnny, and lie down. From the inside, she pulled the curtain around to allow privacy. She watched as Carl picked up the johnny and tried to figure out how it was supposed to be worn.

"The opening should be in the back," the nurse said, as if that were going to solve Carl's confusion. "I'll be back shortly when you are done." She then disappeared through the curtain. It was apparent she was in a hurry.

Carl did as he was told but had trouble with the johnny, particularly in terms of figuring out how to secure it. One tie was at the neck, the other at the waist, which made no sense. He did the best he could. No sooner had he gotten onto the gurney and pulled the sheet up around his torso than the nurse was outside the curtain, calling to ask if he was finished.

Back inside the curtain, the nurse then went through a litany of questions: Did you eat anything this morning? Do you have any allergies? Do you have any drug intolerance? Do you have any removable dentures? Do you smoke? Have you ever had anesthesia? Have you had any aspirin in the last twenty-four hours? It went on and and on, with Carl dutifully answering *no* over and over until she queried how he felt.

"What do you mean?" Carl asked. He was taken aback. It was an unexpected question. "I feel nervous. Is that what you are asking?

The nurse laughed. "No, no, no! I mean do you feel well right now and did you feel normal during the night. What I'm trying to ask is whether or not you feel like you might be coming down with something. Have you had any chills? Do you feel like you have a fever? Anything like that?"

"I get it," Carl said, feeling embarrassingly naive. "Unfortunately I feel fine health-wise, so there's no excuse not to go forward with all this. To be honest I'm just anxious."

The nurse looked up from her tablet, where she had been recording all of Carl's responses. "How anxious do you feel?"

"How anxious should I feel?"

"Some people find the hospital stressful. We who work here don't because being here is an everyday event. You tell me, say on a scale of one to ten."

"Maybe eight! To be honest, I'm really nervous. I don't like needles or any other medical paraphernalia."

"Have you ever had a hypotensive episode in a medical setting?"

"You'll have to translate that into English."

"Like fainting?"

"I'm afraid so. Twice. Once having my blood drawn for some tests in the college infirmary, and once trying to give blood in college."

"I'm going to note this in your record. If you'd like, I'm sure they will give you something to calm you down."

"That would be nice," Carl said, and he meant it.

The nurse took Carl's blood pressure and pulse, which she remarked were normal. She then had a conversation with Carl about which knee was to be operated on, and when Carl pointed to his right knee, she made an X with a permanent marker on Carl's thigh, four inches above his right kneecap. "We want to be sure not to operate on the wrong knee," she said.

"Me too," Carl responded with alarm. "Has that ever happened?"

"I'm afraid so," the nurse said. "Not here, but it has happened."

Holy fuck, Carl thought. Now he had something else to worry about. As nervous as he felt, he wondered if he had been wrong in discouraging Lynn from coming by to at least say hello before the procedure. Maybe he needed an ombudsman.

D r. Wykoff, the patient is in the CSPC," Claire said, coming back into OR 12, referring to the center for surgical patient care, an extra-long name for the patient holding area.

"How about Dr. Weaver?" Sandra responded.

"He's changing. We're good to go."

"Perfect," Sandra said. She stood and picked up her computer tablet. "How are you doing, Jennifer?" Jennifer Donovan was the scrub nurse, who was already gowned, gloved, and setting out the sterilized instruments. It was 7:21 A.M.

"I'll be ready," Jennifer said.

As Sandra walked back down the central corridor, she checked Carl's EMR and noticed the admitting nurse's entries. There were no red flags for trouble. The only thing she picked up on was that the patient was unusually anxious and had a history of several hypotensive episodes in the past associated with drawing blood. In Sandra's experience she'd come across a number of men with such a phobia, but it had never been a problem. People rarely fainted when lying down. As far as she was concerned, anxiety was par for the course. That's why she liked midazolam, or Versed, so much. It worked like a charm, relaxing even the most skittish patients. In the pocket of her scrubs she had a syringe with the proper dose, according to Carl's weight.

She found Carl Vandermeer in one of the pre-op bays of the

CSPC. She couldn't help but notice that he was a handsome man with dark, thick hair and startlingly wide-open blue eyes. Except for his apparent anxiety, he was the picture of health. The thought went through her mind that working with him was going to be a pleasure.

"Good morning, Mr. Vandermeer," Sandra said. "I'm Dr. Wykoff, I will be your anesthesiologist."

"I want to be asleep!" Carl stated with as much authority as he could muster under the circumstances. "I went over this with Dr. Weaver, and he promised me that I would be asleep. I don't want an epidural."

"No problem," Sandra said. "We're all prepared. I understand you are a little anxious."

Carl gave a short, mirthless laugh. "I think that is an under-statement."

"We can help you, but it does require me to give you an injec-tion. I know you don't like needles, but are you okay with getting one? It will help, I guarantee."

"To be truthful, I'm not excited about it. Where will you give it?"

"Your arm will be fine."

Steeling himself, Carl dutifully exposed his left arm and looked away to avoid seeing the syringe. After a quick swipe with an anti-septic wipe, Sandra gave the injection.

Carl turned back. "That was easy. Are you finished already?"

"All done! Now I want to go over with you the material the ad-mitting nurse recorded."

Rapidly Sandra asked the same questions about Carl not having had anything to eat since midnight, about allergies, about drug in-tolerance, about medical problems, about previous anesthesia, about removable dentures, on and on. By the time Sandra got to the end, Carl's attitude had completely changed, thanks to the midazolam. Not only was he no longer anxious, he was now finding the whole situation entertaining.

At that point, Sandra started her IV. Carl couldn't have cared less and watched her preparations with a sense of detachment. It helped that she was extremely confident and competent with the procedure. She always made a point to start her own so she could trust it. She used an indwelling catheter rather than a simple IV. Carl never stopped talking through the process, particularly about his girlfriend, Lynn Peirce, who he said was a fourth-year medical student and the best-looking woman in her class. Sandra diplomatically let the issue drop.

A few minutes later Dr. Gordon Weaver appeared to have a few words with Carl, including which knee they were going to work on. He checked that the X that the admitting nurse had made with the permanent marker was on the proper thigh.

"You people are really hung up on which knee," Carl joked.

"You better believe it, my friend," Dr. Weaver said.

With Sandra guiding in the front and Dr. Weaver pushing from the back, they wheeled Carl down and into OR12, stopping alongside the operating table directly under the operating room light. Somewhere en route Carl had drifted off into light sleep in midsentence, again reminding Sandra why she was so fond of the midazolam. Only much later would Sandra question the dose she had given in the process of reviewing everything she had done. Sandra, Dr. Weaver, and Claire Beauregard moved Carl over onto the operating table with practiced efficiency.

When Dr. Weaver went out to scrub, Sandra pulled the anesthesia machine close to Carl's head. This was the part of the case that she liked the best. She was center stage and about to prove once again the validity of the science of pharmacology. Anesthesia was a specialty marked by extreme attention to detail; periods of intensive activity, like what she was now beginning; and then long segments of relative boredom, which required dedicated effort to stay focused. Whenever she thought about it, the analogy of being a pilot came to mind. At the moment she was about to take off. After that had been accomplished she would be in the equivalent of midflight autopilot and have little to do besides scanning the monitor and the gauges. It wouldn't be until the landing that she'd again be called upon for intense activity and attention to detail.

Since there were no specific contraindications to any of the current anesthetic agents, she planned on using isoflurane, supplemented with nitrous oxide and oxygen. She had used the combination in thousands of cases and felt comfortable with it. There was no need for any paralyzing drugs because a knee operation didn't require any muscular relaxation like with an abdominal operation, and she wasn't going to use an endotracheal tube. Instead she would use what was known as a laryngeal mask airway, or LMA. Sandra was a stickler for detail in all aspects of her life but most specifically for anesthesia, and had never had a major complication.

Like all anesthetists who are specially trained nurses and anesthesiologists who are specially trained doctors, Sandra knew that the ideal anesthetic gas should be nonflammable, should be soluble in fat to facilitate going into the brain, but not too soluble in blood so that it could be reversed quickly, should have as little as possible toxicity to various organs, and should not be an irritant to breathing passageways. She also knew that no current anesthetic agent perfectly fulfilled all these criteria. Yet the combination she intended to use with Carl came close.

The first thing that Sandra did was to set up all the patient monitoring so that she would have a constant readout of Carl's pulse, ECG, blood oxygen saturation, body temperature, and blood pressure, both systolic and diastolic. The anesthesia machine would monitor the rest of the levels that needed to be watched, such as oxygen and carbon dioxide levels in inspired and expired gases and ventilation supply variables.

As Sandra positioned the monitors, particularly the ECG leads and the blood pressure cuff, Carl became conscious. There was no anxiety on his part. He even joked that with everyone wearing masks it was like being at a Halloween party.

"I'm going to give you some oxygen," Sandra said as she gently placed the black breathing mask over Carl's nose and mouth. "Then I will be putting you asleep." Patients liked that comfortable metaphor rather than what Sandra knew anesthesia really to be: essentially being poisoned under controlled and reversible circumstances.

Carl didn't complain and closed his eyes.

At that point Sandra injected the propofol, a fabulous drug in her estimation that was unfortunately made infamous by the Michael Jackson tragedy. Knowing what propofol did to arterial blood pressure, ventilation drive, and cerebral hemodynamics, Sandra would never give the drug to someone without appropriate physiologic monitors and a primed and ready anesthesia machine.

In the induction phase, Sandra was now in her most attentive mode. With an eagle eye on all the monitors she continued to use the black breathing mask to allow Carl to breathe pure oxygen. In the background she was vaguely aware of Dr. Weaver coming into the room and putting on his sterile gown and gloves. After approximately five minutes, Sandra put the breathing mask aside and picked up the appropriately sized LMA. In a practiced fashion she inserted the triangular, inflatable tip into Carl's mouth and pushed it into place with her middle finger. Quickly she inflated the tube's cuff and attached the tube from the anesthesia machine. The immediate detection of carbon dioxide by the anesthesia machine in the exhaled gas suggested the LMA was properly seated. But to be sure, Sandra listened to breath sounds with her stethoscope. Satisfied, she taped the LMA tube to Carl's cheek so that it could not be moved. She then dialed in the proper levels of isoflurane, nitrous oxide, and oxygen. The nitrous oxide had some anesthetic properties but not enough to be used on its own. What it did do was lessen the amount of isoflurane needed, which was helpful, because the isoflurane did have some mild irritant effects on breathing passage-ways. She then taped Carl's eyes shut after putting in a bit of antibiotic ointment to protect his corneas from drying.

Sandra watched the anesthesia machine with its readout of all the vital signs. Everything was in order. The takeoff had been smooth. Metaphorically they were nearing cruising altitude and soon the seat belt sign could go off. Sandra's pulse, which had jumped considerably during the induction of anesthesia, dropped back to normal. It had been a tense few minutes, as it always was, yet it provided her a shot of euphoria of a job well done and a patient well served.

"Everything okay?" Dr. Weaver questioned. He was eager to begin.

Sandra gave a thumbs-up as she manually checked Carl's blood pressure yet again. She then helped Claire put up the anesthesia screen, which would be covered with sterile drapes to isolate the patient's head from the sterile operative field. After the screen was in place she sat back down. She was now in midflight.

As he worked during the course of the operation, Dr. Weaver kept up a mostly one-sided conversation with everyone in the room. He talked about what he was doing technically as he fashioned the patellar graft, he talked about his kids, and he talked about his weekend house on Folly Island.

Sandra listened with half an ear, as she imagined the scrub nurse and circulating nurse did as well. Sandra spoke up only once when there was a break in Dr. Weaver's monologue. She took the opportunity to ask how long he thought he'd be.

The surgeon straightened up, paused briefly, and assessed his progress. "I'd guess another forty minutes or so. It's all going smoothly. Everything okay up there with you?"

"Everything is fine," Sandra said. She glanced down at her notes. The machine did the anesthesia report in contrast to the old days, but she kept her own record for her own use and to remain focused. Another forty minutes would put the total time for the procedure at just a little more than an hour and a half, meaning Dr. Weaver was acting true to form. There were other orthopedic guys who would take nearly double his time.

Sandra moved a bit to keep her circulation going and stretched out her legs. She had the option of having someone come and relieve her for a few minutes if she so desired, but she rarely took advantage of the opportunity and wouldn't now, even though everything was going perfectly smoothly.

Sandra heard the sound of the drill start, meaning Dr. Weaver was creating a pathway through bone into which he would thread the patellar allograph. Knowing that the periosteum was richly enervated with pain fibers, Sandra looked up at the integrated patient monitor screen to see if there were any observable changes to suggest Carl's level of anesthesia wasn't what it should be. All the tracings were exactly as they had been throughout the case. She homed in on the heart rate. It was at seventy-two, without the slightest change. But as she was watching, the screen did something she had never seen it do before. It seemed to blink, as if for a split second it had lost its feed.

A bit concerned about this blip, Sandra leaned closer to get a better look as her own pulse ratcheted upward. The idea of losing all the monitors in the middle of the case was not a happy thought. Holding her breath, she watched to see if there was another episode. A few seconds went by and then a few minutes. There wasn't another blink.

After five minutes she began to relax, especially since the tracings on the monitor all stayed completely normal, including the ECG. Whatever it had been clearly hadn't happened again. The only change, and she wasn't even sure there had been a change, was that all the tracings appeared very slightly higher on the screen than they had been, as if there had been a slight baseline or calibration change. But that couldn't have happened, because she hadn't changed anything.

Sandra shook her head as if to loosen imagined cobwebs. Maybe she did need a break. Yet her fear that the possible artifact had been real kept her glued to her seat and watching the patient monitor closely. It was mesmerizing as the tracings raced across the screen, particularly the ECG, with its rapid, repetitive, staccato up-and-down movements.

After about ten minutes Dr. Weaver got Sandra's attention by telling her that he was within twenty minutes from closing the skin. That meant that her second most busy time had arrived. She shut off the isoflurane but maintained the nitrous oxide and oxygen. The second she did so, disaster struck! The blood oxygen alarm went off, making Sandra jump.

Sandra's eyes shot to the monitor. The oxygen had suddenly gone from nearly 100 percent down to 92 percent. That wasn't terrible, but it was a change, as it had been pegged at maximum during the whole case. It was also encouraging that it was now at 93 percent and already heading upward. But why did it drop? Sandra didn't have the foggiest notion. That was when she noticed the ECG had changed, too. At the same moment the oxygen level had fallen, there was sudden tenting of the T wave, suggesting endocardial ischemia, meaning lack of adequate oxygen to the heart. That was not good. But how could it be? How the hell could the heart be lacking oxygen when the blood level hadn't changed but an instant earlier and not by much? This was nuts!

Sandra forced herself to be calm by sheer force of will. She had to think. Something was wrong, that was clear. But what? Quickly she upped the oxygen percentage, cutting back on the nitrous oxide. That was when she noticed the tidal volume was seemingly falling, meaning Carl wasn't taking as deep breaths as he had been. Immediately Sandra dialed in ventilation assist. She wanted to push in more oxygen to get the low-oxygen alarm to turn off.

"Hey!" Dr. Weaver yelled out with alarm. "Both his legs are hyperextending. Is he seizing? What the hell is going on?"

"Oh, God, no!" Sandra cried out silently. She leaped up, snatching a penlight in the process. Pulling off the tape holding Carl's eyelids closed, she shined a beam of light into his pupils. What she saw terrified her. Both pupils were widely dilated and only sluggishly reactive! She felt a sudden weakness in her legs, requiring her to momentarily support herself by grabbing the edge of the operating table. Her fear was that the hyperextension of the legs was something called decorticate rigidity, suggesting that the cortex of the brain, the most sensitive part, was not getting the oxygen it needed. When the cerebral cortex of the brain is deprived of oxygen, the millions of brain cells don't merely malfunction like the heart—they die!

2.

Lynn Peirce and the friends she was sitting with burst out laughing. Unfortunately for her, she had just taken a sip of coffee and ended up spraying a small arc of it onto the table in front of her. She was mortified and couldn't quite believe what she had done. "I'm so sorry," she managed while wiping her lips with a napkin. Michael Pender, positioned directly opposite her, leaped back, overreacting for dramatic effect, knocking over his chair in the process. Everyone laughed even harder, to the point where they garnered disapproving looks from people nearby.

Lynn and Michael were sitting with four other fourth-year medical students in the popular ground-floor coffee shop of the Mason-Dixon University Medical Center. It was an 800-bed hospital, run by Middleton Healthcare, which owned and operated a total of thirty-two hospitals sprinkled throughout the southeastern corner of the United States. The students were crowded around a four-top table, having pulled over a couple of extra chairs for a celebratory coffee break. The floor-to-ceiling sliding glass windows directly next to them were pushed open, allowing warm air from outside to permeate the room, and affording an unobstructed view over the meticulously landscaped hospital grounds.

The hospital was situated in the northeastern corner of Charleston, South Carolina, with a bit of the "Holy City" visible over a row of magnolias that lined the street. It was called the Holy City because of all the churches, and even from the hospital coffee shop, a number of steeples could be seen jutting up from among the historic homes. It was a gorgeous morning, like most Charleston spring mornings, filled with sunshine, flowers, and the sounds of songbirds.

What had made Lynn laugh so suddenly was an off-color joke about an angel who had traded in her harp for an upright organ. It had been told by Ronald Metzner, the jokester of the class, who had a phenomenal memory for jokes. What caught Lynn by surprise was that, although she usually didn't find his jokes funny, somehow this one touched a nerve without her knowing exactly why, and only later would she realize it was because of suppressed tension she was trying to ignore.

Apologizing again to her companions for what she thought was a major faux pas, Lynn picked up her coffee cup and saucer to wipe off the table. She noticed that Ronald had a big, contented smile on his face, obviously pleased with the effect he had had on her and on the group as a whole.

The six medical students, four women and two men, appropriately dressed in their white coats, were hyped up and goofing off. For them, the almost four years of work, doubt, discovery, and challenge were all but over. Just over two weeks previously they had gotten the results of the National Residency Matching Program, so their uncertainty was behind them. They all knew where they were going for the next and, perhaps, most important part of their professional training.

For the final couple of months before graduation the group and several dozen other fourth-year students on the same rotation were supposedly getting their introduction to ophthalmology; ear, nose, and throat; and dermatology. But the rotation was not as organized or as important as had been the case in other, more basic disciplines, such as third-year internal medicine and surgery. They also had no real patient responsibilities, at least not yet. So far there had only been what they considered rather poorly planned and uninspiring lectures and demonstrations in the three specialties. That morning they had decided to skip the lecture to enjoy their sense of accomplishment. Truth be known, they were essentially in a cruise mode until getting their diplomas.

"I never knew you were interested in orthopedics," Karen Washington said to Lynn after the group had recovered. Karen's tone had a slightly captious tinge that only Lynn could detect. Just before the angel joke, Lynn had revealed her residency plans, which she hadn't shared until that moment, and it had come as a surprise for Karen. She and Lynn were both from Atlanta and had known each other from high school and their undergraduate college days at Duke. They had been close friends during high school and their college freshman year, but when they both had decided on medicine as a career, competitiveness had interfered. But it wasn't the only thing that came between them. Financial problems with Lynn's family during sophomore year at college had impacted every aspect of her life, including her relationship with Karen, whose family was particularly well off.

Although Lynn and Karen ended up at the same medical school, their close friendship had never truly revived, as Karen's keen competiveness continued. Instead Lynn had gravitated toward a close, platonic connection with Michael Pender. At one point during the first year of medical school Karen had confided to Lynn that she would have understood better if it had involved romance. Lynn's response was that she was the one who was most surprised to have such a close, nonromantic friendship with a male, although Lynn's boyfriend, Carl Vandermeer, had come in at a close second. Lynn had confided to Karen that Carl initially had a lot of trouble accepting the situation.

It had all started innocently enough and was based on the alphabetical proximity of their surnames, Peirce and Pender. As a consequence, from day one Lynn and Michael had been thrown together for everything that required medical students to pair up, mostly for labs and physical diagnosis. Although never romantic, they became a real team, somewhat like a brother and sister, making sure they had the same rotations, covering for each other, and studying together to the partial and unintended exclusion of others. The result was that Lynn and Michael had been saddled with the nickname "the twins."

"Really? Orthopedics?" Karen continued, with disbelief. "It caught me totally by surprise, as much or more so than if you had told me you were going into urology. I always thought you were sure to become one of those brainy internal-medicine people."

"I don't know why it should have been a surprise," Lynn responded, sensing a bit of the old hurt feelings on Karen's part. "You of all people know that I was always a jock in high school and college, especially with my interest in lacrosse. Sports have always been a part of my persona. But what sealed the deal was doing orthopedics as my elective this fall. It surprised me how much I liked it. To me it is happy medicine, at least for the most part. That's appealing."

"But the surgery," Karen complained with an exaggerated expression of distaste. "It's not like what people expect surgery to be. It certainly wasn't for me. It's like a bunch of carpenters with hammers and saws, banging in nails and then having X-ray come and see where they went. Whereas ophthalmology! What a difference! That is surgery at its best: precise, bloodless, and you get to sit down while you operate." Everyone knew Karen was off to Emory in Atlanta for a residency in ophthalmology.

"To each his own," Lynn said. She was not going to be baited into a comparison of the two specialties.

"And you are staying here?" Karen asked, with continued incredulity. "Actually, for me that was even more of a shock. I thought you were destined for some Ivy League–affiliated hospital, like Mass General in Boston, considering your rank in class." Everybody knew that Lynn was very near the top of the class, scholastically. She and Michael were always neck and neck in the ranking: two peas in the pod in more ways than one.

"I'm going to leave both internal medicine and the Ivy League to Michael," Lynn said, acknowledging her partner's coup. Michael smiled contentedly at the recognition. Everyone at the table knew that few people got a slot at Mass General and Harvard from Mason-Dixon University School of Medicine, whose stated goal was to supply well-trained physicians for South Carolina and its environs, and not for medical academia. "For me, I'm happy staying right here at Mason-Dixon," Lynn continued. "And you should talk, Karen. Emory for ophthalmology! Not too shabby." It was also common knowledge that, academically, Karen was in the top ten of the class as well.

"Everybody knows why Lynn is staying here for her residency," Ronald said with artificial disdain. "Like the angel, she traded in her harp for Carl Vandermeer's upright organ!"

There was another burst of laughter, this time at Lynn's expense, although she too was smiling. She pelted Ronald with a balled-up napkin as he basked in the glory of having again gotten everyone to laugh over the same mildly salacious joke.

"Am I to gather that you and Carl Vandermeer are still going to be an item come graduation?" Karen questioned while struggling to control her laughter. The group's outburst had again attracted disapproval from others in the coffee shop. It was, after all, a hospital.

Most of the class had met Carl Vandermeer through Lynn at various social functions over the course of their four years of medical school. It was common knowledge that Lynn and Carl had first met at Duke when Lynn was a sophomore and he a first-year law student. It had also been common knowledge that over the last couple of years they were seeing each other exclusively. What wasn't known was the long-term seriousness of the relationship. Even Lynn didn't know for certain. As close as they were, Carl was always evasive on the subject.

"We'll see what happens," Lynn said, tossing her long brunette tresses away from her face. She had yet to pull her hair back in a barrette, the way she always wore it in the hospital. What she didn't say was that she felt rather strongly that it better work out with Carl, because the real reason she hadn't applied for a training program in Atlanta or Boston was because Carl was committed to his job in Charleston. From her perspective there was no doubt it was a sacrifice. Truth be told, she had expected an engagement and wondered if it would be coming for graduation. In her mind, it would be a wonderful graduation present. As a competitive, modern woman, Lynn didn't feel she needed love, but, having serendipitously found it with Carl, she wanted it. She also had enough self-awareness to suspect that her eagerness to create her own nuclear family had something to do with losing her father when she was in college. She and her father had been close, and it had been because of his early death that she had decided to become a doctor.

"Any specific plans we should know about?" Karen questioned, needling her friend. When the love affair with Carl had begun back at Duke, Karen had accepted the diminution of Lynn's friendship much more than these last four years when it had expanded to involve Michael. Karen had never lost a girlfriend to a member of the opposite sex with no romance involved. She couldn't help but wonder if there was some element of romance between the two, even if they both denied it.

Lynn responded by holding up both hands, palms toward her. "No ring, no specific plans. Like all of us, I'm going to be very busy next year being a first-year resident. That's job numero uno."

"Hey, everybody," Ronald said, "have you heard the one about the urology transplant surgeon?"

It was now Karen's turn to throw her napkin at Ronald. "Quit while you're ahead, my man!" she said. "I even remember that joke, and it ain't funny because it is based on a pathetic male fantasy."

"It's a good thing we are graduating soon," Michael said. "Ronald is running out of jokes."

"Oh, shit!" Lynn said, catching sight of her watch. "It's going to ten already. I have to go!" She scrambled to her feet and gathered her dishes together.

"You're not going to the ophthalmology lecture and make us all look bad, are you?" Alice Wong, one of the other women, asked.

"Hell no!" Lynn said. "Carl had a little operation this morning, and I want to be available when he gets to his room."

"Really?" Karen questioned. "You never said anything about him having surgery."

"It was his decision," Lynn said. "He didn't want it to be common knowledge."

"Catch you later," Michael said. He fist-bumped with Lynn but didn't get up. He knew that Carl was to be operated on, but he was the only one who did.

"Give him our best," Karen called out to Lynn, who was already on her way to drop off her dirty dishes, as the coffee shop was run like a school cafeteria.

Lynn waved over her head in acknowledgment but didn't turn around. She was in a hurry. She was tense because of Carl, and feared she might have whiled away too much time having coffee. Knowing how fast Weaver was and knowing that the less time a patient was under anesthesia, the shorter the recovery time, she wouldn't be surprised if she got there and found Carl already in his room. She hoped that would not be the case.

3.

Lynn moved quickly toward the main bank of elevators. It was crowded as it always was at that time in the morning, especially on a Monday morning. Lynn was well aware that the hospital, along with Medical University of South Carolina on the other side of town, served as the tertiary-care centers for the metropolitan area, with a population soon to be pushing a million. Charleston was growing, as its manufacturing and biotech base expanded, particularly in the northern suburbs. Boeing was enlarging its 787 assembly plant, and the multinational drug giant, Sidereal Pharmaceuticals, had just announced it was adding a thousand new jobs to its expanding biologics manufacturing plant.

There was another reason the hospital was busy. Answering what was considered a national need, Middleton Healthcare had built a state-of-the-art facility, called the Shapiro Institute, for the care of persistent vegetative state, or PVS, and had physically connected it to the Mason-Dixon University Medical Center. It had been built with a huge philanthropic grant from Sidereal Pharmaceuticals. Although the institute was for the most part self-contained, it did use the center's clinical laboratory and operating rooms when necessary. Although Lynn and her buddies knew little about the establishment, since it was not used for teaching purposes, she did know that patients from all over the United States arrived on a regular basis along with their families and were admitted through the hospital.

During her second year of medical school Lynn and her fellow classmates had been given one visit, presumably to encourage them to refer their vegetative patients to the facility when they went into practice. Their guide was one of the institute's hospitalists, but the tour had been very limited. Its purpose was mainly to impress upon the medical students how computerized and mechanized the place was, and how that made it possible to take care of so many patients with so little staff.

Accustomed to multitasking, Lynn slipped her computer tablet out of its pocket as she hustled along and entered Carl's name to get his room number. When no number came up, she wasn't concerned. She knew how the system worked. On day-of-surgery admissions, a room wasn't assigned until the patient was ready to leave the PACU. That meant that Carl was probably still there. But sometimes during the busy morning hours, data entry for room assignments lagged as much as an hour behind more important data entry. Even without a specific room, she was not going to go to the PACU. It was one of the areas of the hospital that medical students were discouraged from visiting, even when rotating on surgery during their third year. Instead Lynn would head up to the fifth floor, where orthopedic cases were sent after surgery, provided a room was available.

"Excuse me," a pleasant voice said amid the general din. At the same moment Lynn felt a tug on her arm and found herself looking down at an older woman with blue-tinted white hair. At five feet ten inches tall, Lynn looked down on a lot of women. "Can you help me, Doctor?" the woman added when she had Lynn's attention. She was clutching some lab slips.

"I'm not a doctor yet," Lynn said. Lynn was honest to a fault. "But how can I help?"

"You look like a doctor to me even if you are much too young. I need to have some blood work done, but I don't know where to go. They told me at the front desk, but I've already forgotten."

For a moment Lynn hesitated. If she was still going to be in time to welcome Carl, she needed to get herself up to the fifth floor. Yet, sensing the woman's panic, she relented. "Of course I'll show you." Lynn took the woman's free hand and marched her back the way they had come. From the main entrance foyer, they crossed over the connecting bridge into the outpatient clinic building. Once inside, Lynn took the woman to see one of the clerks behind the main check-in desk.

"I will be happy to show this young lady where she needs to be," the clerk said.

Lynn quickly retraced her steps, and after a short wait, boarded one of the main elevators on her way up to five. Unfortunately it was a local, stopping at every floor to discharge or pick up people. Pressed into the back of the car, Lynn tried again with her tablet to see if Carl had been assigned a room yet, but he hadn't. She expected it was going to happen at any moment.

Once on five, she went directly to the main desk. Like the rest of the hospital, the floor could not have been any busier. To add to the chaos, the breakfast trays were in the process of being collected. The nurses who had long since finished report were getting some patients down to surgery, welcoming others back from the PACU, attending to doctors' orders, distributing medications, and arranging transportation to radiology and physical therapy. It was comparative bedlam.

Lynn knew many of the people who worked on the floor from

her monthlong elective back in October. She looked for the head
nurse, Colleen McPherson, with whom she had gotten along well,
but didn't see her. When she asked another floor nurse, she learned
that Colleen was in with a hip replacement patient whom they were
trying to mobilize. Instead Lynn went back behind the desk to chat
with Hank Thompson, the ward clerk. In the hospital hierarchy run
by the nurses, medical students were low on the totem pole, but
Hank had never treated her that way. He was a student at the
College of Charleston and doing his own version of a work-study
program.

Like everyone else, Hank was doing six things at once. He was
on the phone, with a number of people on hold. While waiting,
Lynn pulled up the master list of all the patients on the fifth floor
on one of the monitors. It was organized according to room number.
She ran her finger down all the names, looking for Vandermeer. It
wasn't there. But there were several vacant rooms, so she thought
there wasn't going to be a problem. She was pleased. It was best for
orthopedic patients to be on the fifth floor because the nurses and
aides were well versed in handling the usual problems that had to
be faced by post-operative orthopedic patients, like dealing with
the CPM, or continuous passive motion machines, which flexed
and extended joints immediately after surgery. Lynn knew that
Carl would have one because Weaver used them with all his ACL
cases.

When Hank finished with the people on hold, he started to
punch in the numbers to make another call. Lynn grabbed his arm.

"Two seconds of your time, Hank! A patient by the name of Carl
Vandermeer will be coming to the floor shortly, unless he is already
here. Does the name ring a bell?"

"Not that I remember," Hank said with a shake of his head.
"Who's the doctor?"

"Weaver."

Hank grabbed the master OR list and scanned it. "Yeah, here it is. It was a seven-thirty case." He looked at his watch. "Should be coming up any minute, unless there was a complication."

"It was a straightforward case. First operation. Healthy, young guy."

"Shouldn't be a problem. We have several rooms vacated this morning, and they have already been serviced, so they are clean and waiting."

Lynn nodded and absently played with a paper clip. Hank turned his attention back to the phone. It occupied 90 percent of his day every day.

Lynn knew she should probably head over to the eye clinic. The lecture would be over and patients were probably lined up to be presented and examined by the medical students. Yet she knew she wouldn't be able to concentrate until she was certain Carl was comfortable and all was in order.

Suddenly she stood up. Feeling she couldn't just sit there, she decided she'd go down to the second floor and at least check the OR schedule. There could have been a delay in getting started. What if Weaver had come in late for some reason? What if the OR was short of nurses? There could be millions of reasons why a case could be delayed.

Lynn took an elevator down three floors. Feeling a bit like a fish out of water, she walked into the surgical lounge. It was another one of those places medical students didn't wander around unaccompanied. Like the rest of the hospital, it too was crowded, since the OR was in full swing. Most or all of the lounge-style chairs and couches were occupied by doctors and nurses. All were in scrubs. A TV in the corner was tuned to CNN with the volume turned way down. Most people were reading newspapers, either waiting to begin or taking a quick break in the middle of cases already under way.

Fearful of calling attention to herself and possibly being ordered to leave, Lynn didn't hesitate. She stepped into the room far enough to see the image of the OR white board in the monitor mounted on the wall. She looked for Weaver's name and found it in OR12. He was doing an anterior cruciate ligament, all right, but the patient's name was Harper Landry, not Carl Vandermeer. So obviously Carl's case was over.

Lynn's eyes scanned around the room for a familiar face, somebody, anybody she might know however vaguely from either her orthopedic elective or from third-year surgery. But she didn't recognize anyone. With sudden resolve she went into the women's changing room.

Getting some scrubs, she changed quickly, using an empty locker for her clothes. After tucking her moderately long hair into a cap and grabbing a surgical mask, she checked herself in the mirror. The almost-white surgical hat emphasized her olive complexion, and without the benefit of her thick hair to frame her face, she thought her youthful, angled features and slightly upturned nose made her appear younger than she was. Combined with her height, she worried she was going to stand out like a sore thumb as a first-year medical student who didn't belong. More to conceal her identity than to be aseptic, she put on the mask.

Satisfied, she returned to the lounge. Without hesitating, for fear she would lose her nerve, as Lynn generally followed rules, she walked out of the lounge and pushed her way through the double doors into the OR suite. She had been there before on numerous occasions during her monthlong orthopedic elective and even a few times during third-year surgery, but always accompanied. She had even assisted Weaver as well as a few other surgeons to get a close-up idea of orthopedic surgery. To her, orthopedic surgery was a lot different from what Karen had suggested. It wasn't eye surgery, to be sure, but with newer tools it was considerably more precise than it had been.

Lynn half expected that she would be challenged, but she wasn't.

She kept moving at a good clip with the belief that any hesitation on her part would be a tip-off that she was an interloper. Her destination was the PACU, and she headed directly for it. She pushed through the second set of double swinging doors as if she belonged, but then stopped a few feet inside the room.

For most people, Lynn included, the PACU was a busy, alien world of high tech, which made students feel incompetent. The patients were on elevated beds with side rails. Most of the beds were occupied. There were no dividers between the beds. Each seemingly sleeping patient had at least one nurse, many with a nursing assistant as well. Fresh bandages covered varying areas of the patients' bodies. Clusters of intravenous containers that appeared like plastic fruit hung on the tops of metal poles. The lines snaked down to run mostly into exposed arms, although a few were central lines going into the neck. Monitors were clustered on the wall over the head of each bed, with various electronic blips tracing lines across their screens. Plastic bags hung under the beds for drainage and urine. Several of the patients had ventilators for assisted respiration. The sounds in the room were a mixture of the electronic beeping, the cycling of respirators, muted voices of the nurses, and a low hum of powerful HVAC motors keeping the air in the room clean and cool.

Right behind Lynn, a gurney came crashing through the swinging doors, bringing in a fresh post-op patient and making Lynn jump out of the way. An OR nurse was pulling at the front. In the back was an anesthetist pushing while making sure that the patient's breathing was not being compromised. A nurse from behind the central desk came around to help guide the gurney alongside an empty bed.

As the patient was efficiently moved from the gurney onto the bed, Lynn took a quick loop around the room, trying not to be conspicuous. None of the staff seemed to notice her. Carl was not there. She would have recognized him immediately. There were two people who had had knee surgery with CPM machines to keep their knees constantly flexing and extending. Neither was Carl.

Confused and not knowing exactly what to do, Lynn wandered over to the counter facing the central desk. She assumed she would soon be challenged, but felt it no longer made a difference. If Carl was not in the PACU or on the fifth floor, then where the hell was he? And why was he not on the orthopedic floor? There were beds available, according to Hank. Of course maybe Carl had been finished so soon that it was before the beds on five were ready. Hank had said that they had been vacated just that morning. Lynn felt that had to be the explanation. Yet the ongoing mystery was starting to upset her, fanning the subliminal tension she had felt upon awakening that morning, the same tension that had made her laugh so hard at Ronald's off-color joke about the angel.

"Can I help you?" a voice questioned.

Lynn turned to face a PACU nurse almost as tall as she. The nurse was gowned over her scrubs. She regarded Lynn with a questioning, steady gaze.

"I hope so," Lynn said. "I'm looking for Dr. Weaver's first case. A man named Carl Vandermeer."

"And who are you?" The woman's voice wasn't challenging or truculent, just authoritative.

"I'm Lynn Peirce, a medical student. I did a rotation in orthopedics and scrubbed with Dr. Weaver." It was the first thought that came to her mind. It wasn't a real explanation, but it sounded good.

The nurse eyed Lynn for a moment, then went behind the desk. "The name is not familiar to me," she said. She took a quick look at the PACU log and found it. "He was Gloria's case," she said to Lynn, and then called loudly across the room. "Gloria! What was the dispensation of the Vandermeer case?"

"The neuro consult guys took him to the neuro ICU," Gloria called back.

Lynn reached out and grabbed onto the edge of the desk to help support herself. The neuro ICU! What the hell did that mean? As she turned and fled from the PACU, she tried not to think. The problem was that she had a pretty good idea of what it meant for Carl to be in the neuro ICU.

4.

ynn was in a hurry. It was a way to avoid thinking. Without bothering to change back to her street clothes, she went directly to the main elevators, where a number of people were waiting. To avoid the possibility of getting into a conversation, she avoided any eye contact, keeping her attention glued to the floor indicators above the elevator doors. Nervously she continuously pressed the up button. None of the cars appeared to be moving up or down.

"That's not going to get the elevator here any faster," a woman said. Lynn closed her eyes, hoping that by not responding she would be spared having to try to be pleasant while her mind was in turmoil. There was nothing about Carl being in the neuro ICU that could be good news, and it was difficult not to imagine the worst.

"You are a fourth-year med student, if I'm not mistaken," the voice said, undeterred by Lynn's silence.

Reluctantly Lynn turned to face the woman. As soon as she did, she recognized her as one of the surgical attendings. She was wearing a long white lab coat over scrubs. Lynn assumed she was between cases and heading up to the surgery floor to check on a patient.

Lynn tried to smile in an attempt to be sociable. Her pulse was throbbing in her temples. She wondered if her face was red or pale. It had to be one extreme or the other, as she was experiencing an adrenaline rush. She was aware she was hyperventilating. She nodded. "I am," she said distractedly. What the hell could be holding up the elevators? Still none had moved from the various floors where they had been when she first hit the button.

"Lynn Peirce," the surgeon said, bending forward and reading Lynn's ID hanging from a lanyard around her neck. "Actually, I remember you from your third-year surgery rotation. I'm Dr. Patricia Scott."

"I remember you for sure," Lynn managed. "Your lectures were terrific, especially your slides." Lynn forced another half smile at the tall, elegant woman before returning her attention to the elevator floor indicator. She hoped her anxiousness wasn't too apparent. She didn't want to explain herself.

"Thank you. You must have been paying attention. I remember you did extremely well. I understand you got your residency notification a couple of weeks ago. Considering how well you did in your surgery rotation, I hope you gave surgery some consideration."

"Orthopedics, actually," Lynn said.

"Indeed! That's terrific. We need more women in all the surgical fields, particularly orthopedics, where we are not very well represented. Where will you be going for your training?"

"I'm staying here," Lynn said.

"Wonderful," Dr. Scott said sincerely. "That's super. I'll look forward to having you scrub with me during your first year of general surgery."

"I'm sure I will enjoy that, Dr. Scott," Lynn said, hoping she didn't appear as preoccupied and stressed as she felt. Finally one of the elevators that had seemingly been parked on the first floor began to ascend.

"You can call me Patricia now that you will be part of the house staff. And, for the record, my office is always open if you need any advice. It wasn't that long ago I went through the training gauntlet, and unfortunately surgery is still anachronistically considered by some to be a men's club."

"I appreciate your thoughtfulness," Lynn said.

The elevator's doors opened. The car was jam-packed. Dr. Scott gestured for Lynn to precede her, and both had to literally squeeze in to allow the doors to close. Lynn was briefly tempted to ask Dr. Scott what it meant for a patient to go to the neuro ICU directly from the PACU, but she didn't. The trouble was, she could guess. It had to have been some kind of anesthesia problem or disaster. Yet she still maintained a certain amount of hope it could have been something less worrisome. Could a nerve in Carl's leg have been damaged with the bone drill? As bad as that might be, it was better than other possibilities she was trying to avoid imagining.

By the time they got up to the sixth floor, where neurology and neurosurgery were located, the elevator had emptied considerably. Lynn thanked Patricia Scott before getting off. She walked quickly. She knew where the neuro ICU was located. She'd been there on a few occasions during her neurology rotation and again during her stint on neurosurgery.

Most visitors to the floor were expected to check in at the main nurses' station. But Lynn decided on the spur of the moment to act the same way she had down in the PACU: as if she belonged. Without hesitation she pushed into the ICU directly.

The neuro ICU appeared superficially similar to the PACU in terms of its prominent high-tech equipment, but here patients stayed much longer, sometimes weeks, even months on occasion. There were separate cubicles defined by glass walls, and not all the patients were sporting bandages. There was also less frantic activity from constant arrival and departure. Instead, a kind of heavy silence reigned, broken only by the distant beeping of monitors and the rhythms of the ventilators. A central circular desk was positioned to afford a view into each of the sixteen individual bays. All were occupied. At least half had nurses in direct attendance.

As Lynn glanced around the room she saw that each cubicle had an ID slot with the patient's name printed in bold letters. Almost at once she zeroed in on VANDERMEER, cubicle 8. Slowly she advanced. Carl was supine. She could not see his face. As she had expected, there was a CPM apparatus constantly flexing and extending his operated leg. Seeing it gave her a modicum of premature hope that everything was as it should be, but it didn't last long.

Two people were in attendance. An ICU nurse was on Carl's right, checking the blood pressure by hand, even though there was a BP readout on the monitor. On Carl's left was a resident physician dressed all in white. He was using a penlight and shining it alternately into each of Carl's eyes. It didn't take Lynn long to recognize that Carl was unconscious. She could also see that he was evidencing some low-amplitude myoclonic jerks with his free leg. His free arm and wrist were flexed across his body. The other arm with the IV was secured to the bed rail.

Coming up to the foot of the bed, Lynn looked at the monitor. Blood pressure was normal. The same with pulse and the ECG, as far as she could tell, but she was no expert with ECGs. She could see that oxygen saturation was down a little but still reasonable at more than 97 percent. Carl seemed to be breathing normally. She forced herself to glance at his face, which she could now plainly see. His color wasn't bad, maybe a little pale. The worst part was that it was definitely Carl and not someone else.

As the resident straightened up he noticed Lynn. Slipping his penlight into his jacket pocket, he asked, "Are you from radiology?" Then without waiting for an answer, he added, "We are going to

need an MRI or a CT scan ASAP." Lynn could read his name tag:
Dr. Charles Stuart, neurology. He was a slight man with thinning
hair, small features, and rimless glasses.

"I'm not from radiology," Lynn managed. Seeing Carl unconscious
and possibly seizing was almost too much to bear. "I'm a medical
student," she added. She reached out and grasped the railing at the
foot of the bed to steady herself. As she had in the PACU, she felt
suddenly light-headed. A hospital was a place of tragedy as well as
hope, but this was turning out to be all tragedy. "What is going on?"
she asked as casually as she could.

"It's not looking good," Charles said. "It seems that we are dealing
with a delayed return to consciousness after reportedly uneventful
anesthesia for a routine ACL repair. So far it is a mystery as to why."

"So he hasn't awakened?" Lynn asked, not knowing what else to
say, yet feeling as if she had to say something to warrant standing
there.

"That's the long and short of it," Charles said flippantly. Lynn
didn't fault him. She'd come to learn that it was one of the ways
house officers shielded themselves from the reality of human tragedy, which they were forced to face on a daily basis. Another way
was to become consumed by academic detail, which he then evi-
denced by saying, "He's completely unresponsive to spoken word
and normal touch, except for a slight corneal reflex. On the positive
side, he has retained some pupillary response to light. Seems that the
brain stem is working, but with his decorticate posturing and flex-
ion response to deep pain, it doesn't look good for his cortex. It must
have been a global insult, and we feel it was most likely hypoxic in
origin, despite what the anesthesiology report suggests. It can't have
been embolic, as his deep tendon reflexes are not only preserved but
also symmetrical. The problem is that he has a Glasgow Coma Scale
sum of only five. As you probably know, that's nothing to write
home about."

Lynn nodded. The reality was that she had little understanding of anything the neurology resident was talking about except the concept of an insult to Carl's brain from hypoxia, meaning lack of oxygen. Neurology had been a short rotation and more applied neuro-anatomy than clinical.

"How could there be hypoxic damage if, as you say, the anesthesia was uneventful?" Lynn asked, more by medical-student reflex than anything else. Medical students were expected to ask questions.

"Your guess is as good as mine," the resident said, reverting back to flippancy. "I'm afraid that's going to be the million-dollar question."

The nurse finished checking Carl's blood pressure and headed back toward the central desk. She glanced briefly at Lynn but didn't say anything. Lynn moved alongside the bed where the nurse had been, forcing herself to look back down at Carl's face.

From his expression he appeared to be asleep and totally relaxed, despite the movement of his free leg. It was apparent he hadn't shaved that morning, which was how he looked most Sundays when the two of them awoke. She associated his appearance with intimacy, which was totally out of place in the current environment and circumstance.

Lynn had to fight the urge to reach out and shake him awake, to talk to him, to yell at him to get him to respond and prove the neurology resident wrong about his not being responsive. What made the situation worse was that Carl's face looked so achingly normal, just as it had yesterday morning when she had awakened and had watched him for a time as he slept, admiring his handsomely masculine features.

"Are you one of Dr. Marshall's neurology preceptor group?" Charles asked, watching Lynn from across Carl's bed. It seemed to Lynn that he was sensing something unprofessional about her behavior.

"Yes," Lynn responded without elaboration. She had been in

Dr. Marshall's preceptor group, except it was a year ago. It wasn't easy for her to be deceptive, but she assumed that she would be kicked out of the ICU if she wasn't there for official teaching purposes. The hospital was strict about confidentiality issues, and she wasn't technically family, at least not yet. With effort, she avoided eye contact with Charles for the moment. She could tell the resident was watching her.

Hesitantly Lynn reached out and lightly touched Carl's cheek with her right hand. His skin felt cool but otherwise normal. She was afraid it would feel rubbery and unreal.

"Have you done an EEG?" Lynn asked, falling back into the protective medical-student persona by asking a question. She was suddenly worried that her touching Carl's face might have seemed strange to the neurology resident. She didn't say electroencephalogram because that wasn't how house staff referred to the test of brain function.

"There was an EEG done on an emergency basis. Unfortunately it showed very low amplitude and slow delta background. I mean it wasn't completely flat, but it shows diffuse abnormality."

Lynn raised her eyes, forcing herself to look across at Charles despite her discomfort in doing so. In the most professional tone she could manage to camouflage her roiling emotions she asked: "What's your guess at the prognosis?"

"With a Glasgow score of only five I'd have to say pretty dismal," Charles said. "That's been our experience with comatose patients not involving trauma. My guess is that when we get a brain MRI we are going to see extensive laminar necrosis of the cortex."

Lynn nodded as if she understood what Charles was saying. She had never heard the term *laminar necrosis*, but she very well knew that necrosis meant death, so extensive laminar necrosis must have meant extensive brain death. With some difficulty she swallowed. She wanted to shout "No, no, no!" But she didn't. She wanted to run away but she didn't. Lynn considered herself a modern woman, aware of current-day female opportunity, and she had "taken the ball and run with it," acing high school, college, and medical school. Her approach was to work as hard as she could, and when she confronted problems or obstacles, which she most certainly had experienced, her reaction was just to strive that much harder. But here was perhaps one of the biggest challenges of her life. Here the man with whom she had come to believe she might share her life was possibly brain dead, and there was nothing she could do.

"Hey," Charles said suddenly. "You know what? This is a perfect teaching case to demonstrate doll's eye movement as a test for brain stem function with comatose patients. Have you ever seen it?"

"No," Lynn forced herself to say. Nor did she think she wanted to see it with Carl as the subject, since it would only make his status that much more real, but she didn't think she could refuse without possibly betraying that she was there under false pretenses.

"Then let me show you," Charles said. "But I need your help. You hold his eyes open while I rotate his head."

As if touching something forbidden, Lynn used the thumb and the first finger of her left hand to elevate gingerly Carl's upper lids. She stared down into blankness of his mildly dilated pupils. It gave her an eerie feeling, as if she were violating his personhood. Silently she shouted for him to wake up, to smile, and to talk and say that this whole episode was a sham and a joke. But there was no reaction, just his rhythmical breathing.

"Okay, good," Charles said. He bent over Carl's chest and put his hands on either side of his head. He first rotated Carl's head toward Lynn and then back toward himself. "There, did you see it?"

"What am I seeing?" Lynn asked in a hesitant voice. It was all she could do to keep from recoiling and running from the room.

"Notice that when I rotate the head, the eyes move in the opposite direction." Charles rotated Carl's head again.

It was now easy for Lynn to see that Carl's eyes did rotate as Charles had described, blankly staring upward as his head went to the side.

"It's a vestibulo-ocular reflex," Charles said in a didactic-medical monotone that was all too familiar to Lynn. "It means that the brain stem and the involved cranial nerves are operating as they should. If the patient is malingering, acting as if unconscious, something you will see on occasion in the ER, the eyes move in the direction of the rotation. If the brain stem is not functioning, then the eyes don't move at all. Rather dramatic, wouldn't you say? I could also show you the same phenomena using caloric stimulation, meaning putting cold water into his ears. Would you like to see that as well?"

"This is quite enough," Lynn said. She pulled her hand back, allowing Carl's eyelids to close slowly. She had to get away. To where, she didn't know. As a member of the hospital community and soon to be a doctor, she felt a responsibility in Carl's disaster above and beyond her recommending Dr. Weaver and the Mason-Dixon Medical Center.

"I have all the paraphernalia available," Charles said. "It will only take a second to get it. It's no imposition whatsoever."

"Thank you," Lynn said, backing up from the bed. "I appreciate your taking the time to show me what you have, but I have to go. I'm sorry."

"That's quite all right," Charles said. He stared at Lynn and furrowed his brows. It was obvious he was confused about her behavior. "If any of the other members of your preceptor group would care to see this classic doll's eye movement, I'd be happy to show it to them."

"Thank you," Lynn said. "I'll let the others know."

Lynn fled out of the ICU. Once in the hall, she stopped and took a few deep breaths. It was somehow comforting to be back in the usual commotion of the hospital with patients, nurses, and orderlies passing her. Her heart was still racing. There was nothing she could do to help Carl, and her first thought was that she had to find Michael. She needed an anchor, someone to hold on to during this storm of uncertainty and emotion.

5.

Lynn found Michael in the cafeteria. She had first gone back to check the coffee shop, but he and the others had left. She thought about texting him but had no idea what to say. Instead she wanted just to find him. Maybe she wouldn't even say anything for a time.

Considering the hour, she had decided the cafeteria was the best bet, as the food was considerably cheaper there than at the coffee shop, and Michael rarely missed a meal. As usual the room was crowded with its usual lunchtime rush. It had taken her a moment but she managed to locate him in the food line. She felt lucky he was by himself. The other members of the earlier coffee-shop group were nowhere to be seen. She was glad about that. She wanted to talk only to Michael.

"Hey, Lynn. How's Carl doing?" he asked when he turned to look who had tapped him on his shoulder.

"I need to talk," Lynn said, her voice faltering. "Privately."

"Okay, no problem," Michael said. Knowing her as well as he

did, he immediately sensed her brittle emotional state. He eyed her.
"You okay?"

"That remains to be seen," Lynn said. There was an audible
catch in her voice.

"How about grabbing some lunch and hanging with me?"

"I'm not hungry at the moment."

"Do you mind if I eat while we talk?"

"Of course not!"

"Then let me settle up for these vittles. Then we can sit over
there in left field by the far wall. I see a couple of free tables."

Lynn glanced in the direction and nodded. The cafeteria was as
good as anyplace else in the hospital for a talk with Michael. The
hubbub might actually help her keep her emotions in check.

Although Lynn wasn't hungry, she was thirsty, and she got herself some water before sitting at one of the free tables they had seen
from the steam-table line. The area was farthest away from the windows, which looked out onto a sumptuously landscaped interior garden. A number of tables in the garden were the most popular, and
were the first to fill up when the weather was as good as it was.
Lynn could see quite a few of her classmates outside.

As she sat waiting for Michael to pay, she watched him in the
checkout line. He was a commanding presence and stood out from
the similarly white-coated medical students. The main reason was a
combination of his size and the fact that he was black. In Lynn's
class there were only three African American males along with five
females of color, making up only 6 percent of the class despite the
school's active recruitment efforts. Michael was a muscular man
with a thick neck who Lynn learned had played football at the University of Florida and who had had a shot at playing professionally
had he not set his heart on becoming a doctor. Lynn knew that
the career choice was a debt he owed to his mother. His features
were broad, his skin a dark mahogany, and his hair was relatively
long and worn in what Lynn had come to know was a lock-twist.

Initially she thought they were short dreadlocks but now she was the wiser.

Back on the second day of medical school when Lynn had first spoken with Michael when paired with him for the anatomy lab, she had been mildly intimidated. Not only was he a sizable man, but he seemed to her to have an animus toward her right out of the gate. From their first words he complained about her attitude, so she did the same. During the initial days they merely tolerated each other, and both had to make an effort just to get along well enough to work together.

Lynn had never considered herself racist, but over time Michael had made her see that she had been to an extent, and that racism was unfortunately alive and well in America. Michael for his part learned from her that he was so accustomed to having to deal with patronizing attitudes that he often evoked it. He also came to learn from her that despite fifty-plus years of feminism, misogyny and gender discrimination had not disappeared. Both came to understand that with racism and gender issues, one had to be a member of the oppressed to really appreciate the subtleties and the not-so-subtleties of discrimination that had so influenced their respective lives. Throughout her life, Lynn always felt she had to do a bit better than the men with whom she was competing whereas Michael always felt he had to do much better than everybody.

As Lynn and Michael came to understand they were kindred spirits, they began to appreciate each other's idiosyncrasies apart from race and gender, stemming from their different backgrounds: Lynn, from a middle-class Atlanta upbringing, with two siblings who ultimately fell on hard times; and Michael, from a single-parent household from the South Carolina Low Country, with five siblings who had had to struggle to keep a roof over their heads and food on the table. They also became aware of their similarities besides their being extremely motivated hard workers who strived for excellence. Both had defied stereotypes and had responded to

STEM programs in their schooling, meaning science, technology, engineering, and math. Both early on liked computer gaming and had an interest and facility in coding. Both had aced college. In medical school both were on full scholarships, which was the main reason they were at Mason-Dixon University. Both of them had been accepted at all the medical schools to which they had applied, but Mason-Dixon had had the best offer financially. Finally, although Lynn had been close to her father, she also knew what it was like not to have one.

As Michael approached, Lynn felt thankful for their relationship and grateful to the school for having paired them up. She had never had a male friend like Michael, and valued their relationship, as he had truly expanded her life in so many ways. And now, if the neurology resident was right in his prognosis of Carl's condition, she was going to need Michael's support more than ever.

"Okay, whassup?" Michael said, affecting nonchalance while sliding his tray onto the table. He settled his solid two-hundred-pound frame onto the chair, which squeaked in protest. He picked up his sandwich and took a healthy bite.

For a minute Lynn was unable to speak. She wasn't one to cry often, possibly because of a reaction to the stereotype, and she didn't want to cry now. She felt torn. She wanted Michael's support to avoid the sense of isolation that she was already feeling from the shock of this unfolding calamity, yet she worried that telling Michael about what had happened would make it more real. As a medical student, she knew enough about the psychology of the grief reaction to know that she was still solidly in the early denial stage.

Michael did not press her. He chewed his sandwich and took another bite, seemingly ignoring her. He was content to wait. He knew her well enough to be concerned. Something significant was in the wind, and it had to do with Carl and his surgery.

Lynn took a drink of water and then closed her eyes tightly. When she opened them she let the facts flow out, explaining about

Carl's apparent anesthesia disaster and how she had gone up to the neuro ICU and talked with the neurology resident. She concluded by saying that Carl's Glasgow score was only five and that the neurology resident said the prognosis was dismal.

Michael put his sandwich down and pushed his plate away as if he had lost his appetite. "That's a low Glasgow score."

Lynn stared at her friend. There were lots of times that he amazed her, and this was an example. She had never heard of a Glasgow score, and Michael apparently had, despite the fact that they both had taken the same neurology rotation during their third year. He had a facility to remember facts no matter how obscure. "How do you know about the Glasgow score? I don't think I have ever heard of it."

"Let's just say I had reason. It is a way to evaluate people in a coma. What was the neurology resident's name?"

"Charles Stuart, I think. I don't know for sure. My mind isn't working at full speed."

"I don't think we had him for any part of our neurology rotation."

"I know for sure we didn't. I had never seen him before."

"What else did he say besides the Glasgow score and that the prognosis was not good?"

"He said that he expected to see extensive laminar necrosis on the MRI when they do it."

"I don't know what laminar necrosis is."

"I don't, either, but it is not hard to guess."

Michael nodded. "Did you talk to anyone else, like the surgeon or the anesthesiologist?"

"I haven't spoken to anyone. I wanted to talk to you first."

"Did you look at the anesthesia record?"

"No. All I did was see if it was Carl, and it is. He's in a freaking coma, for Chrissake! And I was the one who recommended the doctor and encouraged him to get his fucking knee fixed here at Mason-Dixon."

Michael reached out and enveloped Lynn's comparatively narrow wrist with his large hand. His grip was firm. "Listen, sister," he began. When they were alone together they jokingly called each other sister and bro, a bit of Black argot that Michael had instigated as a sign of their platonic intimacy and comfort with each other. As a further sign of their closeness, he also treated her to basketball metaphors he'd used with his buddies in high school. "I can tell you right off the top, you are not responsible for whatever happened during today's game. You weren't a player. No fucking way!"

Despite her efforts at control, tears brimmed and some spilled over Lynn's cheeks. She wiped away the moisture with a knuckle of her first finger. "I know I'm going to feel a certain amount of guilt no matter what; I know myself well enough. But what about his parents? They had wanted him to have his surgery over at Roper Hospital. Why did I interfere?"

Carl's father was a lawyer in Charleston like his son but at a different firm and involved in a different specialty. The father's area of interest was litigation and criminal law, unlike Carl's emphasis on real estate and corporate law. His mother was an elementary school teacher. The parents lived in the same house in West Ashley where Carl had grown up. Lynn had met them on numerous occasions, particularly over the last several years, as Lynn and Carl's relationship had solidified. Even Michael had met them for a couple of celebratory birthday dinners.

"The Vandermeers are smart people," Michael said. "And it's easy to see they care for you. They are not going to blame you. No way!"

"I'm not sure I wouldn't if I were them."

"But we're jumping the gun here. We don't really know as an absolute certainty what's going on. Here's my take: Let's hightail it up to the neuro ICU before our dermatology lecture and check out

Carl's chart." Mason-Dixon Medical Center had a fully integrated EMR, but there were still physical charts for inpatients while they were in the hospital. There had been some talk of completely phasing out the charts, but it hadn't happened, at least not yet.

"What will that accomplish?" Lynn wasn't sure she could go back quite so soon. Seeing Carl in a comatose state was enormously unsettling, to say the very least.

"I don't know, but we will have a better idea of what happened. There has to be an anesthesia record in the chart. I mean, there must be some explanation. Come on!" Michael started to get to his feet.

Lynn grabbed Michael by the sleeve of his white coat. "They are not going to look kindly on two medical students appearing without authorization to look at a chart in the ICU."

"Leave it to me," Michael said. "As I've told you in the past, most people think I'm either a token or a Tom. Sometimes it causes problems, but sometimes it helps. This is one of the times it will help. Trust me! Besides, I've done it before."

"In the neuro ICU?"

"Yes."

"When?"

"About three months ago."

"Why?"

"We'll talk about that later. Let's go up there and see Carl and hope to hell Doc Stuart is wrong." Michael got to his feet and tugged on Lynn's arm to get her to stand. To Michael she looked like a deer caught in headlights. He picked up his tray and carried it over to the window. Lynn followed. She appreciated that someone else was making the decisions.

6.

As they ascended in the elevator, Michael glanced at Lynn. She was watching the floor indicator above the door. Her eyes were red and watery. The elevator was crowded, putting a lid on any conversation about their mission. For Michael there was a strange, uncomfortable sense of déjà vu, and he hoped any similarities to the events he was thinking about would be minimal.

When the doors opened on the sixth floor, Michael and Lynn were not the only people to get off. Lynn grabbed Michael's arm to hold him back as the other passengers proceeded toward their respective destinations, most going to the central desk. The place was as busy as it had been earlier.

"We have to have a plan here," Lynn said, lowering her voice so as not to be heard. Several people were standing nearby, waiting for a down elevator. "I got away with going into the ICU earlier because the resident assumed I was on a neurology rotation. You are not going to get away with that. They're going to remember you because you stand out. How do you plan on handling this? You know we medical students are not welcome in the ICU unless we have an official reason."

"I'm counting on not having a problem, provided we don't act hesitant or indecisive."

"What is it you want to do, exactly?"

"Mainly I just want to look at the chart. But we're not just going directly to the desk and grab the chart without checking out the patient. That's not cool. It's not the way it's done. You know what I'm saying? Do you remember where Carl is? That would be a help. We don't want to draw attention to ourselves by acting lost."

"He's in cubicle number eight, I believe, but I could be wrong. My mind's in turmoil."

"All right, here's the plan. We head directly into cubicle eight. Provided it's the right address, we check out Carl's current status. If it's not, we find him, fast! You okay with that? You don't have to do anything. Just hang. I'll do something appropriate to make it look official."

"All right," Lynn agreed, although she wasn't entirely sure her emotions wouldn't take over.

"Let's do it!" Michael said with conviction.

With Michael half a step ahead and moving at a quick pace, they passed the busy sixth-floor central desk and headed for the ICU. At the door Michael hesitated for a split second to glance at Lynn, arching his eyebrow. Lynn assumed he was questioning her mental state, so she nodded. She was as ready as she was going to be.

Michael pushed through the heavy door. Inside was a different world. Gone were the noise of the lunch carts, the babble of voices, and the sense of commotion. In its place were the muted electronic sounds of the monitoring and the to-and-fro cycle of a couple of ventilators. Otherwise a heavy stillness reigned. The patients were all completely immobile.

As he had said, Michael made a beeline for cubicle 8. Lynn's memory had served her well. Carl was in the bed and momentarily alone. The half dozen nurses and an equal number of aides on duty were occupied with other patients.

Michael went to Carl's right, and Lynn to his left. Carl appeared to be sleeping as he had before, save for the jerking of his free leg. Again Lynn had to suppress the almost irresistible urge to reach out and shake him awake. For the briefest moment she felt a twinge of anger, as if Carl were doing this on purpose.

"Deceptively peaceful," Michael said.

Lynn nodded. Tears again threatened. She tried to think objectively about what might be going on in Carl's brain. She watched as Michael took out his penlight. After raising both of Carl's upper lids, he shined the light alternately in each eye. "Pupils are equal and maybe sluggish, but both react. Nothing to 'fatmouth' about, but it is something. At least the brain stem is still working."

Lynn nodded again but didn't speak. As a defense mechanism she thought about the doll's eye movement that the neurology resident had shown her, and its implications.

"Vital signs are normal," Michael said.

Lynn followed his gaze up to the monitor. Everything was as it had been earlier, including the oxygen saturation, at 97 percent.

"All right," Michael said, lowering his voice and looking across at Lynn. "So far, so good." The busy nurses seemed indifferent to their presence. "Let's mosey over to the central desk. And try to relax, girl! You look like you are about to rob a bank."

Lynn didn't bother to answer. She tolerated his mildly disrespectful language just as she allowed her to call him "boy" on occasion. It was only when they were certain no one else was listening that they used such slang. It was another sign of their closeness and shared understanding of discrimination.

The circular central desk was usually dominated by the duo of the head nurse, Gwen Murphy, and the very capable long-term clerk, Peter Marshall, who had been around so long he felt proprietary. From their neurology rotation Michael and Lynn remembered both of them as efficient and professional and very helpful. At the moment only Peter was present. As usual, like all ward clerks, he was on the phone, but he raised his eyebrows questioningly as he gave them a once-over. At the moment Gwen was apparently occupied elsewhere.

Under the lip of the surrounding countertop were flat-screen monitors displaying the readouts of the vital signs of each patient. Lynn's eyes went directly to 8. Everything was normal. On top of the countertop was a rotating chart rack.

"Hey, dude," Michael said to Peter as a greeting, evoking a roll of the eyes on Peter's part. Not giving him a chance to respond, Michael turned his attention to the chart rack, which he gave a deliberate spin. He stopped it so the slot for cubicle 8 was facing him. Without the slightest hesitation Michael withdrew the chart, grabbed a couple of chairs, and pulled them off to the side. He motioned to Lynn to take one, and he sat in the other. He opened the chart and rapidly leafed through to the anesthesia record.

As Michael was doing this, Lynn watched Peter out of the corner of her eye. As Michael had anticipated, he seemed to ignore them, at least until he finished his current phone conversation. Then he said, "Hey, can I help you guys?"

"We were told to check out the anesthesia record on Vandermeer," Michael said. "And we got it right here. Thanks! Take a look, Lynn!"

Michael positioned the chart so that Lynn could see. There was a handwritten note by the anesthesiologist, Dr. Sandra Wykoff, as well as the three-page printed version done by the anesthesia machine. They read the handwritten note, which was thankfully easy to read in contrast to a lot of notes that they had had to read by doctors in hospital charts over the last couple of years:

Healthy 29 year old Caucasian male in excellent health
scheduled for anterior cruciate repair of right knee under general
anesthesia. Anesthesia machine function checked both manually
and automatically. Some pre-op anxiety. Pre-op medication
Midazolam 10mg IM at 7:17 am with good result. Patient
relaxed. Intravenous catheter placed without difficulty. Breathed
100% oxygen with face mask beginning at 7:22 am. Induction
with 125mg Propofol IV at 7:28 am. 100% oxygen given by face
mask before laryngeal mask airway LMA 4 placed and inflated
with no problems. Isoflurane, nitrous oxide, and oxygen began at
7:35 am. Eyes taped shut. Vital signs normal and stable. ECG
normal. Oxygen saturation stable at 99–100%. Spontaneous
respiration with normal volume and rate. Operation commenced
with placement of tourniquet on right leg. No changes in vital
signs, ECG, and oxygen saturation. Fifty minutes into the case at
8:28 am as requested surgeon communicates he is within forty
minutes of completion. At 8:38 am isoflurane shut off. Nitrous
oxide and oxygen continued. At 8:39 am low-oxygen alarm
sounds as oxygen saturation falls precipitously from 98% to 92%.
At same moment ECG shows tenting of T waves. Oxygen flow
increased. Oxygen saturation rapidly climbs back to 97% at 8:42
am. Low-oxygen alarm shuts off. ST waves on ECG return to
normal. Nitrous oxide flow reduced at 8:44 and ventilation
assist started. At 8:50 am decorticate leg hyperextension with
both lower extremities noted by the surgeon and pupils noted to
be dilated with sluggish reaction to light. Nitrous oxide stopped at
8:52 am and pure oxygen maintained. Ventilation assist turned
off at 8:58 am as patient's breathing returned to normal volume
and rate. Surgeon removes tourniquet and completes the case at
9:05 am. Patient fails to wake up. Chief of anesthesia, Dr.
Benton Rhodes, called in on the case. Under his direction
Flumazenil given in 0.2mg increments X 3 with no observable
result. At 9:33 am patient taken to PACU while continuing to

breathe 100% oxygen. Emergency neurology consult called. Vital
signs, ECG, and oxygen saturation remain normal and stable.
  Sandra Wykoff, MD.

Michael and Lynn finished at almost the same moment and looked up at each other. "I don't know much about anesthesia," Lynn said. "We only had that one lecture about the basics in our surgery rotation. I'm going to have to do some research to understand it all."

"But the important point is that there was some documented hypoxia," Michael said. "The O_2 level fell for a couple of minutes, and the ECG changed."

"But not much. The O_2 only fell to ninety-two percent briefly and then went back up to ninety-seven percent. That is not a huge fall and probably about what people experience getting off the plane in Aspen, Colorado. And it was only for three minutes." Lynn pointed to where it was noted in the handwritten summary.

"Then how come the ECG showed the T wave changes?"

Lynn shrugged. "I don't know enough to even guess."

"Let's check out the machine-generated record."

Michael turned to the relevant page of the three-page anesthesia record. What they were interested in was the intra-operative portion. Both knew that the modern anesthesia machine was computer driven and kept track of all the variables in real time, including what was portrayed on the monitor. At the end it printed it all out in graphic form. Everything that had happened was recorded, including gases, drugs, fluids used, and all the monitoring parameters.

"And what are you people doing?" a voice questioned. It was not antagonistic but definitely authoritative.

Both Lynn and Michael looked up. Looming over them was Gwen Murphy, the head nurse. She was a stout, ample woman with flame-red hair and rosy cheeks.

Without skipping a beat, Michael said, "We have been sent by anesthesia to check out this case of delayed emergence from anesthesia."

Gwen eyed Lynn for a moment, then nodded as if buying Michael's explanation. "The patient is scheduled for an MRI this afternoon." Without elaboration she turned around and went back to her post in front of all the monitors.

Lynn leaned over to Michael and whispered: "How did you come up with that?" She was impressed. Knowing that what they were doing was more than merely frowned upon by the authorities, Gwen's sudden appearance and challenge had scared her. She knew she would have tripped over her words had she tried to say anything. So she had been glad Michael had spoken up. She and all the other medical students had been warned they were not permitted to look at charts or electronic medical records, EMRs, unless specifically authorized, most specifically including those of friends or even family members. Patient confidentiality was taken quite seriously by the administration, and looking at records under false pretenses was a serious and punishable offense.

"Practice, I guess," Michael said. "Did you notice she didn't look at me?"

"Now that you mention it, I guess I do. I can tell you; she definitely stared at me. I thought it was because I was feeling so guilty that it showed."

"I don't think so," Michael said. "I believe her not looking at me is that unconscious discrimination at work that I've mentioned to you. Senior staff, both doctors and nurses, often don't look at me. But it is okay. I'm used to it. And sometimes it helps, like letting us get away with what we're doing right now."

"I'm sorry," Lynn said.

"Hey, it's not your fault. And it doesn't bother me anymore. Anyway, let's get back to why we're here."

Without another word, the two students turned their attention back to the printed anesthesia record. Both could plainly see where the oxygen saturation suddenly fell to 92 percent. Running their eyes down to the associated ECG recording of the heart, they could appreciate the changes that coincided.

"Is that a hypoxic change on the ECG?" Michael asked.

"I believe so," Lynn said. "I'll need to find out for sure. I certainly have my work cut out for me."

"What do you mean?"

"Just what I said. I'm going to figure out why this happened."

"I've seen a case just like this before."

Lynn looked up at Michael. She was surprised. "Really! When?"

Without answering, Michael looked over at Gwen and Peter. Both were occupied. Taking advantage of the situation, Michael pulled out his smartphone. After quickly turning off both the sound and the flash, he took a photo of the anesthesia record. In the next instant the phone disappeared.

"Jesus!" Lynn croaked in a forced whisper. "Why did you risk that?" Nervously she glanced back at Gwen and Peter. She was relieved to see that Gwen was involved in a conversation with another one of the ICU nurses, and Peter was on the phone busily taking dictation.

"We may need it," Michael said cryptically. "Are you finished with the chart?"

"I'd like to read the neurology consult, even though I already have a pretty good idea what it says."

"Let's do it and hightail it out of here. Then I'll tell you about the other case."

7.

A s soon as the heavy ICU door closed behind them, Lynn peppered Michael with questions about the supposedly similar case, wanting to know exactly how similar it had been.

"It was exactly the same," Michael said as they walked along the crowded sixth-floor hallway, skirting lunch carts.

"Was it a delayed emergence from anesthesia?"

"Absolutely. I'm telling you, it was just the same."

"When was it?"

"About three months back, when we were on pediatrics."

Lynn was about to ask how Michael had known about the case when she looked ahead. Coming toward them was Dr. Gordon Weaver and, most alarmingly, Markus and Leanne Vandermeer, Carl's parents.

Like a scared rabbit, Lynn froze. They had not yet seen her, as they were far enough away and there was enough commotion in the corridor between them to create a significant distraction. For a second Lynn thought about turning and running in the opposite direction. Having yet to come to terms with her own raw emotions by any stretch of the imagination, she didn't know how she would respond should there be any criticism or blame. There was little doubt in her mind that they would be as devastated as she was.

Sensing Lynn's reaction, and recognizing the parents, Michael firmly grabbed her arm. "Play it cool, sister," he whispered.

"I'm not sure I'm ready to deal with this," Lynn croaked. She tried to pull out of Michael's grasp, but he held on.

"Hang!" Michael said definitively. "You can handle it, and it's better to get it over with here in the hospital."

Her pulse racing, Lynn watched them approach. The first to recognize her was Leanne. She was a slight woman wearing a gray, conservative suit, looking like the elementary school teacher she was. When she caught sight of Lynn, her drawn face revived from grief to concerned sympathy. Without the slightest hesitation she came directly at Lynn and enveloped her in a sustained embrace. Lynn was pleasantly surprised. Previously Leanne had never given her more than a slight kiss on the cheek.

"How are you managing, my dear?" Leanne asked, still holding on to Lynn's arms after the lengthy hug. She was a good six inches shorter than Lynn and had to look up into her face. "Now, I want you to promise me you are going to take this bump in the road in stride. He'll be waking up soon. Trust me! Everything is going to work out just fine. I'm sure of it. I know how busy you are. Patients are depending on you. You have to take care of yourself and get back to your work."

Lynn glanced at Michael for support. Thanks to Carl's descriptions, she was aware Leanne was controlling, but this seemed beyond the pale. The woman was telling her how to respond to the disaster.

"I'm so sorry for you this mild complication had to occur," Leanne said. "But it will be over soon. I'm certain."

"I'm sorry, too," Lynn said. Leanne's apparent denial of the reality of Carl's condition was such a surprise that it made it easier for

Lynn to control her emotions. Lynn had feared censure and blame but was experiencing empathy. She was both relieved and thankful.

"You must be just devastated," Leanne continued. "Have you seen him?"

Lynn nodded, hesitant to admit she had in front of Dr. Weaver, who she thought might recognize her having done so as a violation of hospital rules, but Dr. Weaver, obviously having his own problems, didn't respond.

"How does he seem?" Leanne asked. Her expression of concern morphed back to grief.

"Very calm," Lynn said. "He looks like he's asleep."

Leanne let Lynn go, and Markus gave her a second hug. Carl's father was a sizable man like his son but heavier boned. His face was lined and always tan. He was an inveterate golfer who loved his bourbon. In contrast to his wife, he looked thoroughly shell-shocked and chose not to speak.

"Has there been any change?" Leanne asked when Markus let her go.

"I'm afraid not," Lynn said. She gestured to Michael. "You remember Michael Pender, of course."

"Yes, of course," Leanne said, briefly acknowledging Michael but immediately turning back to Lynn. "We are going to make sure that the best doctors are involved in Carl's care. I'm sure there will be a change for the better very soon."

"I hope so," Lynn said, nodding her head. She looked at Dr. Weaver, who was still dressed in scrubs. He didn't meet her gaze and encouraged the older Vandermeers to move on toward the neuro ICU, saying there was only a small window of opportunity for their visit.

After promises to get together, the Vandermeer parents continued down the hall. Lynn and Michael headed in the opposite direction toward the elevators.

"Now, that wasn't half-bad," Michael said.

"They were very generous," Lynn admitted. Quickly her mind reverted to what they had been talking about before catching sight of the Vandermeers. "What were the details of that similar case you mentioned, and how did you hear about it?"

"It was an African American female in her late twenties or early thirties, generally about the same age as Carl. She was operated on with general anesthesia after being shot in both knees. She didn't wake up. There was an episode of hypoxia just like with Carl, and that was it."

"She was operated on here at Mason-Dixon Medical Center?"

"Yes. I'm telling you, the case was a mirror image."

They arrived at the elevators. Lynn tugged on Michael's coat to get him to stop. She didn't want to talk about a case on a crowded elevator, but she wanted to hear more. "Well, how did you hear about it?"

"My mamma called me from Beaufort to tell me a distant rela-tion was having a major complication after surgery here. She asked me to look into it, so I did."

"What was the woman's name?"

"Ashanti Davis."

"What kind of relation was she to you?"

"Very distant and only by marriage. Cousin of the brother of an in-law on my mother's side of the family or something obscure like that. I knew her a little in high school because we went to the same regional school, but she was ahead of me and never finished, and we ran in different circles."

"Shot in the knees? Was that the result of some sort of gang war?"

"Someone had a serious beef with her—that much is clear."

"What's happened to her?"

"She permanently gorked out after the operation. Within days they moved her over to the Shapiro Institute."

"That's awful," Lynn said. "And is she still there?"

"As far as I know. I don't think anybody visits or asks. Nobody in her family wants to pay the kind of bread they get for room and board, if you know what I'm saying. She wasn't very popular in her family, to put it mildly, even in her surviving immediate family. In high school she was considered a slut with a penchant for dating all the aspiring gang members. I kept my distance. She even got one of my cousins shot dead, so her getting shot wasn't all that unexpected considering the people she ran with. She was a bad apple."

"What an awful story," Lynn said. "Before getting shot, was she generally healthy, like Carl?"

"As far as I know."

Lynn shook her head. The fact that there were two healthy people at Mason-Dixon who within months of each other did not wake up from anesthesia was more than disturbing; it was downright frightening. And it was terrifying to think of Carl being transferred over to the Shapiro. After the brief visit, she and her medical-student colleagues equated it to being shipped off to Hades.

"I would love to have a look at Ashanti's hospital record," Lynn said.

"Whoa!" Michael said, leaning away from Lynn as if she might be contagious. "That's the kind of thing that could get you kicked out of medical school. Carl's chart is different, as it is an active case, with all sorts of people having access. With Ashanti, it would be a totally different ball game. You'd have to use the EMR, and you would be caught right away."

"I wouldn't do it myself," Lynn said, thinking about who might be willing to get such a record for her. Earlier Dr. Scott had offered to help her, saying her office was always open. And Lynn thought about the anesthesiologist who had taken care of Carl. Maybe she would be interested, provided she wasn't the one who administered the anesthesia to Ashanti.

"I do have a photo of her intra-operative anesthesia record someplace," Michael said. "I took it in the neuro ICU the same way I just took Carl's."

"Really?" Lynn said with surprise. "Where is it? Could you find it?"

"I'll have to look. As I recall, it's either on my PC or on a flash drive that's got to be someplace in my room." As full-time scholarship students, both Michael and Lynn were expected to live in the dorm, a separate building on the medical center's expansive campus. Most of the other fourth-year students had moved out to private apartments. Lynn had not minded remaining since it was convenient when on call to sleep in her own bed rather than in the on-call room. Besides, she had been staying at Carl's most weekends.

"You'll look?"

"Of course I'll look. But not now, if that's what you're thinking." Michael glanced at his watch. "We're already late for the ophthalmology lecture. We better get our asses over to the clinic building."

"I'm not going to the lecture," Lynn said in a tone that did not brook argument. "There's no way I could sit still for an hour in my state of mind. I'm fried."

"What are you going to do?"

"I'm going to ride my bike down to Carl's house and try to chill." Lynn said. "I need to read up on anesthetic complications, particularly delayed emergence, and I can do it using his PC. I'll feel closer to him there. I might even pray a little. I'm that desperate."

Michael looked askance at Lynn. Religion had been a frequent topic of discussion for them, especially during their third year, when they were on pediatrics, and more recently during their advanced pediatric elective. Having to deal with suffering children with cancer had made them feel there could not be a God, at least not a loving, caring God that might be swayed by prayer.

"I know," Lynn said, anticipating what Michael was thinking. "It goes against what I said during all those late-night talks of ours, yet seeing Carl in the state he is in makes me want to cover all the bases."

Michael nodded. He thought he understood. This episode had cast his friend emotionally adrift.

8.

Lynn changed out of her scrubs and put on street clothes, anger bubbling up inside her. She was furious at the anesthesiologist, at the hospital, at medicine in general, and was reminded of how she had felt after her father died. She wanted to kick the locker where her clothes had been. She wanted to break something as she combed her hair with quick, angry strokes.

The trouble was in some respects that she knew too much. If she weren't a medical student she could have hoped he would just wake up and be fine, which was what the Vandermeers were apparently assuming. Lynn wished she could indulge in such optimism, but she couldn't. She knew that wasn't going to happen. The neurology resident expected the MRI to show in detail extensive laminar necrosis of the cortex, whatever the hell that was. Yet she was knowledgeable enough to know that it meant the death of a lot of cells in the part of the brain that made people human.

Translated, it meant that even if Carl were to wake up, he wasn't going to be the same Carl. There wasn't going to be a happy ending, no matter what. It was a lose-lose situation. For a brief second she thought that it would have been better had he died, but then she quickly amended the thought, embarrassed at its selfishness. At least now there was a glimmer of hope, no matter how unlikely. He was, after all, still alive. Maybe there could be a miracle.

Pulling on her white coat, Lynn looked back at her image in the mirror. Her lips, normally full, were compressed in a grim line. Her green eyes stared back with hostile intensity. She was now clearly in the anger stage of her grief reaction, having already abandoned the first stage of denial. She couldn't help but feel that the American medical system had failed her again. The first time had been in relation to her father, Ned, who had been unlucky enough to have had a rare genetic blood disease called by the acronym PNH. It was one of the so-called orphan diseases that affected fewer than ten thousand patients worldwide. After almost four years of medical school, Lynn knew a lot more about the disease than she did when she was in college. She understood now how the disease destroyed red blood cells during the night. She also knew she didn't have it and wasn't a carrier.

In 2008, when Lynn was a sophomore at college and the recession hit, Ned had lost his job and, with it, his health insurance. The health insurance had been paying the extraordinarily high cost of the medication that was keeping him alive. Although Ned had been able to pay the premiums himself for a year, the insurance company voided the policy as soon as they could, as it was before the Affordable Care Act. That meant no lifesaving drug, which ultimately meant Ned's death. At the time Lynn didn't know all of these details, just that the family was in difficult economic straits. When she did learn what had happened, it helped solidify her desire to go into medicine to try to change the system, especially after learning that the exorbitantly priced drug was so much cheaper in Europe and even in Canada. Now she felt the US health-care system had come back to bite her again.

To pull herself together, Lynn splashed cold water on her face.

Behind her she saw the tall figure of Dr. Scott come into the changing room and go to her locker. For a moment Lynn debated whether she should go over to talk with her and ask if she would help look into what had happened to Carl, but Lynn rapidly changed her mind. It was too soon. She recognized she didn't know enough even to ask intelligent questions, like how often something like Carl's case occurred around the country. At the moment all she knew was that it had happened twice at Mason-Dixon Medical Center, only a few months apart.

Instead of talking to the surgeon, Lynn concentrated on leaving before Dr. Scott happened to see her. She didn't want to talk to her or anyone. She knew she was on thin ice emotionally, especially now that her anger was trumping her denial.

Lynn used the stairs to avoid running into anyone she knew in the elevator. Once on the ground level, she ducked through the clinic building, which provided a shortcut to the dorm. She made it a point to steer well clear of the clinical amphitheater, where the ophthalmology lecture was being held.

Emerging from the hospital confines into the glorious Charleston mid-spring sunshine, Lynn felt a modicum of relief just to be outside. With the birds singing and the warm sunshine knifing down through the flowering trees in the landscaped quadrangle of the medical center, she tried not to think. But it was an effort to keep her thoughts at bay, and it didn't last. Off to her right was the immense hulk of the Shapiro Institute, loudly reminding her of the plight of the brain dead.

In sharp contrast to all the other buildings forming the Mason-Dixon Medical Center complex, the Shapiro Institute seemed to be only two or three stories tall. It was hard to determine, since it had almost no windows, making it appear as a monstrous rectangle of polished granite. Lots of flowering trees and shrubs were planted around its perimeter in an attempt to soften its stark lines. There was only a single, solid, blank entrance door set back under a stone arch along its facade. There had been times when Lynn and Michael were walking back from the hospital when shifts at the institute must have been changing, and they saw personnel emerge. There were never many people. Those they did see were always dressed in unique white uniforms, something akin to surgical scrubs but more stylish and form-fitting even though they were one-piece coveralls.

Stopping for a moment, Lynn stared at the building, wondering if Ashanti Davis was still there, and if she was, how she was doing. Lynn shuddered, wondering what it would be like for Carl if he were moved into the facility and whether she would be allowed to visit. She doubted she would, since she was not immediate family.

She thought back again to the single second-year official tour that she and Michael had had, along with their classmates. She clearly remembered the details of the story behind the name. It was in honor of Arnold Shapiro, a twenty-one-year-old college student from Texas, who ended up in a persistent vegetative state for fifteen years. The immediate cause of his condition was thought to have been hypoxia. His heart had stopped spontaneously and there had been a delay for an unknown period of time before he'd been resuscitated by EMTs. The case had ignited a fierce legal battle between Arnold's divorced parents whether to maintain him indefinitely or to discontinue the feeding tube and let him die. Ironically the case became a poster for both sides of the issue. Lynn and Michael had been told that the rationale for naming the facility after Arnold Shapiro was because throughout his ordeal Arnold had received excellent care from being in the spotlight. The goal of the Shapiro Institute was to give that same level of care to anyone who needed it, whether famous or not.

Thinking of Carl possibly getting shuttered away for years made Lynn shudder again and turn away from staring at the building. Quickly she recommenced walking toward the medical school dorm. She knew she had to get a grip on herself.

The dorm room she had occupied from the first day she had

arrived at medical school was on the fourth floor. It was small but pleasant, and most important it had an en suite bathroom. The window looked out across the Cooper River with a view of the graceful Arthur J. Ravenel Jr. Bridge arching over to Mount Pleasant. The river was wide at that point and looked more like a huge lake.

There was a framed photo of Carl on top of the bureau. Carl was laughing and holding up a pina colada, complete with a pineapple wedge, a maraschino cherry, and a miniature paper umbrella. The photo had been taken that past summer on his twenty-ninth birthday at Folly Beach, a popular nearby resort. They had rented a small but charming cottage for the weekend.

Lynn reached out and turned the photo over. It was painfully reminiscent of a different time and place. After tossing her white coat over the back of her desk chair, she changed into more appropriate biking clothes and grabbed her helmet, backpack, and sunglasses. In the backpack went her cell phone, a fresh legal tablet, and a couple of pencils. Other than her bike helmet, she didn't need anything else, since she had gradually stocked some basic clothing and toiletries at Carl's house.

Lynn biked due south until she could veer off onto Morrison Drive, which eventually turned into East Bay Street and finally into East Battery. It was a progressively scenic route the farther south she went, especially when she reached the historic downtown district. When she got below Broad Street, where most of the historic homes were located, she passed the area called Rainbow Row, a series of early-eighteenth-century row houses that had been built on the edge of the Cooper River. They were all painted in historically accurate pastel Caribbean colors, a legacy of the English settlers from Barbados. Lynn's mood cheered a smidgen. Charleston was a beguilingly beautiful city.

9.

Michael slipped his pen into the pocket of his white coat. He had tried taking notes to keep focused, but it wasn't working. The main problem was that the lecture wasn't about clinical ophthalmology, as he had expected. Rather it was a tedious review of the anatomy of the eyeball and its connections to the brain. It was material Michael and his classmates had studied extensively during their first year.

One of the secrets to Michael's academic success was that he could speed-read with remarkable retention. He had worked laboriously on the skill from early childhood, always careful to keep his developing proficiency a secret from his friends, particularly his male friends and particularly in high school. In the social circles he ran in, being a good student and the effort it took weren't assets. On the contrary, they were suspect.

As far back as Michael could remember, his hardworking mother, who cleaned houses and washed other people's clothes, had harped on the belief that education was the express train out of the ghetto poverty trap, and that speed-reading was the ticket. Michael had taken the advice to heart, and, thanks to good genetics inherited from his mother and the father he had never really known, he had had the ability to master it. Now, with his medical residency in the bag, suffering through a two-hour marathon review of material he had already been sufficiently exposed to was a ball-buster. The reality was that he could relearn what was being presented on his own in a fraction of the time and with better recall. It was also true that his mind was wandering. He couldn't stop thinking about Lynn, Carl, and, of all people, Ashanti Davis.

Michael glanced around at his classmates. It was obvious that just about the whole team was suffering. Those students who weren't sleeping had glazed eyes, suggesting to him that only a handful of neurons in their brains were functioning. "Fuck this," Michael said to himself. "I'm breaking out!"

Taking advantage of the dimming of the lights for yet another series of computer-generated images, Michael impulsively got to his feet and left. It took only a moment since he had taken an aisle seat in the rear, near the exit. Still, he knew he risked being noticed. As a black man entering into a profession where the percentages of black male physicians were low and falling, anonymity for him was rarely an option.

The clinic was in full swing. Every available chair was occupied by a patient. A number of them looked up hopefully when they glimpsed Michael and his white coat in hopes that their waiting was about to end. None of them had any idea their waiting was due to a lecture. Many of the white patients quickly averted their gaze. It was similar to the lack of eye contact with the attending physicians, the vast majority of whom were white, that had bothered Michael during his first year, when there was an introduction to patient contact. Now he took it in stride. He correctly realized it was their problem, not his.

Michael had good rapport with patients white and black once

they got over the initial hesitation his blackness occasionally engendered. In fact sometimes the white patients adjusted faster. Some
blacks would assume that Michael was an "Oreo," a black-vernacular
label for someone overly assimilated, or "black on the outside and
white on the inside." But that surely wasn't the case. Michael fully
identified with his roots and the black community, and intended to
serve it by bringing Harvard know-how back to Beaufort, South
Carolina.

Intending to head over to his dorm room to search for Ashanti's
anesthesia record, Michael left the clinic by the same exit that Lynn
had used earlier. As if further mimicking her, he stopped in the
landscaped courtyard at just about the same spot that she had and
gazed at the Shapiro Institute for the same exact reasons. He wondered if Ashanti Davis was still in there, being kept alive by the
wizardry of modern medicine. He also worried whether Carl was
destined to be transferred in there as well. He knew that would be
a major stumbling block for Lynn.

Michael was well aware, at least theoretically, that a patient in a
vegetative state could be kept alive almost indefinitely. He knew
there had been a patient who had been kept alive for thirty-seven
years. What it required was not rocket science but merely a careful
balance of the body's internal environment, meaning proper hydra-
tion and electrolyte balance, appropriate nutrition, and careful skin
care. For long-term nutritional needs, the best solution was a percutaneous gastrostomy tube, placed by surgery through the abdominal
wall directly into the stomach.

Of course, another major requirement was to keep all the various microorganisms at bay, such as bacteria, fungi, and viruses, since
it was often the case with such patients that their immune systems
weren't up to snuff. Appropriate drugs such as antibiotics and anti-
virals were used when needed, but the main defense was accomplished with reverse precautions, meaning to keep the bad bugs

away from the patients. Prevention of infectious disease was the reason visits to the institute were restricted to immediate family, and even these were discouraged for the patients' collective benefit. Immediate family had to view their stricken loved ones through a plate-glass window.

From his rotation in the ICU during third-year surgery, Michael was well aware that the biggest threats for long-term care of unconscious patients were pneumonia and the lowly bedsore. Patients had to be turned constantly to avoid being in one position for too long, because that was how infections and pneumonia were fostered. The more mobilization, the better, which was why such care was generally considered labor intensive, except in the Shapiro Institute. On Michael's one and only visit during the second year, he had learned that the Shapiro's secret was computerization and automation. What that really meant, he wasn't sure, because he and his classmates didn't get to see any real patients. The visit had been limited to a didactic lecture and a short stint in a family visitation area, where a dummy had been used for demonstration purposes.

Thinking about Ashanti Davis and her ignominious end reminded Michael of his own success at having defied the odds. Here he was, about to finish medical school and head up to a medical residency in the lofty Ivy League while most of his childhood acquaintances were either already dead or in prison, or with severely compromised futures, like Ashanti. About a week earlier, as a way to chill out after the anxiety of the residency matching program, he had hidden in his room and social-surfed himself to near brain death, looking up as many of his old friends as he could, using multiple sources. It had been a depressing pastime, and it made him really question how he had been so lucky.

Mostly Michael gave credit to his mother and the way she ragged on him about education and reading skills. But he also gave himself some credit for not falling prey to the culture in which he had found himself immersed. Things could have worked out very differently, and he very well could have ended up a hashtag in Beaufort, South Carolina's, homicide statistics. As a young, skinny teenager he had dealt drugs for a while, as it was an easy way to help support the family. He was also good in sports, and both activities pushed him to the head of the pack. But being at the head also meant trouble, and protecting his honor required quick response to threats. At first going to blows with fisticuffs was adequate, but by the eighth grade it meant having to pack.

For Michael, the meld of pistols and passion was what changed the game. He was judicious enough to understand that packing heat was a no-win situation, especially after his cousin had been shot dead by a supposed friend and fellow hoopster who had mistakenly become enamored with the flighty Ashanti. From that moment Michael had no more truck with drugs, would-be gangstas, guns, or hot spots. He was no longer interested in running wild. He avoided all situations that could lead to confrontation, like messing with any girls who dated gang members, or even trash-talking opponents on the b-ball court, or gloating over accomplishments of any sort.

As if waking up from the trance that his reverie had spawned, Michael found himself sprawled out on one of the many park benches that lined the quadrangle's walkways, still transfixed by the Shapiro Institute. He was taken aback by what his thinking about Ashanti had engendered. And as he reflected some more, he found himself wondering if it had been his mother's words or his own inclinations that had kept him from being killed or killing someone who he might have felt had somehow slighted him. He didn't know the answers. But it all certainly raised the question in his mind of how his life might have been different had he not learned to speed-read or if he had a father, and if he had, whether it would have helped or hindered. One way or the other, Michael felt he was one lucky dude.

10.

After applying her bike brakes, Lynn turned into the brick driveway that ran alongside Carl's house and led to the carriage house in the back. She had not come to the house directly as she had originally planned. As she had ridden south, she'd come to question whether going to Carl's was appropriate. So instead she had biked down to the base of East Battery Street and spent some time sitting on the seawall to try to come to terms with her roiling thoughts and emotions. From that vantage point, looking out over Charleston Harbor, she could just make out Fort Sumter in the distance at the easternmost end of James Island. It was a comforting place, as she'd gone there often with Carl. She knew it was his favorite place in the city.

Something had occurred to her that shocked her as she had cycled. She had tried to put it out of her mind but couldn't. Unwelcome, it kept coming back to torment her and demand her attention like the mental equivalent of a toothache. It was the idea of her sudden freedom stemming from the realization that if Carl ended up as she feared, being shut away in the Shapiro Institute, the whole reason she had decided to abandon an academic career and stay at the Mason-Dixon Medical Center for her residency training was moot. And even if he wasn't shut away but needed around-the-clock care, was she cut out for such a role? Hell, she thought, they weren't even engaged, and she truly didn't know if it had been in the cards. Whenever she'd brought up the issue of the future, Carl always changed the subject, which had made her plans for her residency extremely difficult.

These were disturbing thoughts and made her wonder if she was a selfish and bad person to be thinking such things, and so soon. Yet as she sat at the Battery, the peaceful scene and its association with Carl ultimately convinced her it would be good to be around all the things that helped define Carl as the person he was before that morning's events. It also convinced her that it would be far worse emotionally for her to return to her dorm room knowing that a comatose Carl was nearby, suffering from recent brain damage for which she felt she bore some responsibility. Had Carl gone to Roper Hospital, he'd probably be watching TV now and itching to be discharged.

Lynn had garage and house keys on a key ring along with her dorm key. She put her bike inside the garage next to Carl's red Jeep Cherokee. Then she headed for the house.

By far Carl's favorite arena of law was real estate, and the real estate scene in Charlestown was booming. A large number of the eighteenth- and nineteenth-century homes had been renovated, and those that had yet to be redone were in high demand. Carl had participated in many of the sales, and his intimate knowledge of the market and personal acquaintance with a number of the owners had given him the opportunity to buy one of the most coveted properties. The house was on Church Street, a particularly scenic lane. The style was called a single house. Because Charleston property taxes in the early days were determined by footage on the street, the original Charleston inhabitants built their houses with the long axis perpendicular to the street and only a single room wide. Along one side of the house, long verandas called piazzas were built on each floor. Before air-conditioning, Charlestonians lived as much out-doors as they did indoors during the long, muggy summers.

What made Carl's house so desirable were two things. Although it needed modern renovation, its period detail had not been lost over the years as its infrastructure had been slowly improved. And second, its original owners had acquired the neighboring lot and turned it into a large, formal garden, complete with a lily pond, a gazebo, shade trees, and various types of palms. Although the garden had not been tended for nearly a half century, it was an invaluable asset of which Carl had schemed to take full advantage.

After walking back around to the front of the house, Lynn keyed open what, for all intents and purposes, looked like the front door. Yet the only location the locked door led to was an open veranda, which, according to its design, a visitor could access as easily by climbing over the balustrade. It was another curious characteristic of a Charlestonian single house. She had to walk along the ground-floor piazza to the true front door located in the middle of the lengthwise porch. To her left was the tangled, overgrown garden, which sounded like an aviary, as it was a haven for a good portion of the local bird population.

Once inside, Lynn closed the second door and stood for a moment, listening to the silence of the house and smelling its familiar aroma. In contrast to herself, Carl was a meticulous housekeeper and had the place cleaned twice a week. Because of the tall shade trees, little sun managed to get inside, which was a distinct benefit during the hot months, but as a consequence it was quite dark. Lynn had to wait to allow her eyes to adjust from the bright sunlight out-side. Slowly the details of the interior emerged from the relative gloom of the high-ceilinged room. Suddenly she jumped and let out a small scream. Something had brushed up against her leg.

"Oh, my God," Lynn said in relief. Mildly embarrassed at her reaction, Lynn reached down to pet Pep and apologize to the cat for scaring it. "I forgot about you," she added. Pep pressed up against Lynn's hand as she stroked the animal. "I guess you're lonely. I'm afraid it's going to be just you and me tonight."

The first thing that Lynn did was go into the kitchen to check if there was dry food and water for the cat. There was, and there was a note addressed to Frank Giordano about how much food to put in the cat's bowl. She made a mental note to give Frank a call to let him know that he was off the hook as far as the cat was concerned. She was not looking forward to that conversation as she anticipated that Frank would undoubtedly be full of questions that she would be unable to answer.

With the cat issue taken care of, Lynn returned to the front hall and mounted the main stairs to the second floor. She was dreading going into the master bedroom.

As she stepped into the room, she marveled that Carl had taken the time to make the bed. It was so typical of him. It had been the one difference between them that Lynn had been mildly worried about, wondering whether her casualness about such details would wear on him or his compulsiveness on her. She was fastidious about her person and her work, but with mundane things such as making the bed, or folding and hanging her bath towel, or dealing with her soiled clothes she wasn't so exacting.

On the bureau was a picture of her that had been taken the same weekend at Folly Beach as her picture of him. She appeared to be as happy as he did in his, and she wondered whether she would ever feel that way again. Just as she had done back in her dorm room, she turned the photo over. Looking at it could only bring pain when she came back to the room later that night. She was going to sleep there to feel close to Carl and help convince herself she wasn't as selfish as she worried.

Next, Lynn made her way down the second-floor hallway to one of the smaller bedrooms that Carl had turned into a study. It was a large house with another three bedrooms up on the third floor, and two more in the dormered attic space. The bedroom Carl had turned into his work space had a door out onto the veranda, as most of the bedrooms did. The room had a very masculine feel. It was paneled in dark mahogany. One wall had floor-to-ceiling bookcases in which one shelf was filled with sports trophies he had won, starting with Pee Wee Football and Little League Baseball.

Lynn sat down at Carl's very neat, expansive desk and turned on his PC. She got her cell phone, legal tablet, and pencils out of her backpack. As the PC was warming up, she scrolled through her contacts in her phone until she got to Giordano and tapped his work number. Knowing herself and her tendency to put off unpleasant chores, she wanted to get it over with so that she could concentrate on immersing herself in Carl's medical situation.

The phone was answered by a secretary. Lynn gave her name and said that the call was personal. A moment later Frank was on the line.

"What's up?" Frank asked. Lynn sensed his concern. She knew he had taken Carl to the hospital that morning.

"I'm afraid there has been a complication . . . ," Lynn began.

"Don't tell me!" Frank interrupted. "Carl had a premonition things were not going to go right. What happened?"

"There was a problem with the anesthesia," Lynn said. "His oxygen level dropped during the surgery, and he hasn't woken up. He's in a coma."

"Oh, fuck!" Frank blurted out. "What's going to happen?"

"I spoke briefly with a neurology resident who was on the case. He's convinced there was brain damage. There's going to be an MRI this afternoon."

"Double fuck! Holy shit!"

"I'm sorry to lay this on you," Lynn continued. "I can't tell you any more. I'm in the dark myself. I didn't know enough to even ask the right questions, but I'm going to rectify that tonight. Maybe to-morrow I'll know more. I'll keep you posted."

"Please do! Jesus Christ! Do his parents know?" Frank and gone to elementary school and high school with Carl and knew the parents well.

"They know."

"Oh, my God! You must be devastated. I'm so sorry, Lynn. How are you doing?"

"I'm a basket case," Lynn admitted. "On top of everything else I feel responsible, since I recommended the surgeon." Her concern about her being selfish went through her mind, but she didn't mention it.

"That's crap!" Frank said without hesitation, mirroring Michael's reaction. "This is not your fault. No fucking way! I mean, I could just as much say it was my fault because I was the one who drove him to the hospital. That's bullshit! Give yourself a break!"

"I'll try, but I'm overwhelmed. The problem is I'm not fully in control of my feelings."

"Where are you now?" he asked.

"I'm here at Carl's. Which reminds me: you are off the hook about Pep. I'll see to her needs."

"Do you want me to come and pick you up? You could stay with Naomi and me." Frank had a single house similar to Carl's and not that far away. "You can stay as long as you want. We have plenty of room."

"I appreciate the offer, but I want to stay here."

"Are you sure?"

"As sure as I can be at the moment. I'm going to take it hour by hour, day by day. I'll call you if I need to talk. Meanwhile I'm going to occupy myself learning as much as I can about his medical situation."

"You have my cell. Call me anytime you want. Truly: anytime.

It doesn't matter. And if you don't mind, I'll check in with you later this evening."

"I don't mind," Lynn said.

"Okay, catch you later. And I'm sorry."

"Thank you," Lynn said before she clicked off.

Turning her attention back to the computer screen, Lynn first made sure of the Internet connection, then brought up Google Chrome. Before she could initiate the first of what was going to be many searches, she jumped in fright. Sudden movement off to her left caused her to leap to her feet, sending the desk chair skidding backward on its casters and crashing loudly into the bookcase. A few books that had been balanced upright to display their front covers fell to the floor. The cat who had initiated this chain reaction howled in equivalent fright and fled the room.

"Holy shit," Lynn voiced, pressing an open palm against her chest. Her heart was racing. For the second time the cat had innocently enough terrorized her, this time by leaping up onto the desk. The intensity of her reaction gave her an idea of the extent of her anxiety. She bent over and picked up the volumes that had fallen and returned them to the shelf. Next she pulled the chair back to the desk and sat down.

For a few moments she let herself recover before getting to work. She had three main areas of interest. The first was the incidence of complications involving anesthesia. The second was the specialty of anesthesia itself so that she could go over Carl's record with full understanding. She particularly wanted to know about problems related to hypoxia or low oxygen and what could cause them. Apparently that was the current explanation of Carl's delayed return to consciousness. And finally she wanted to read about the Glasgow Coma Scale.

A few minutes later Pep wandered back into the room. This time when she jumped up onto the desk to sprawl on its surface, Lynn didn't even notice. She was deep into a piece on hospital complications. The statistics floored her and even embarrassed her about the profession she had been working so hard to enter. She had known complications were a problem in some hospitals but nowhere near the extent that she now knew existed. It made her wonder why there had never been a formal lecture about it or even any discussions in her preceptor groups. The more she read, the more shocked she became.

Lynn had been furiously taking notes and suddenly needed an eraser. Assuming there would be one in the desk, she pulled out the drawer to look. Not unexpectedly there were several. She picked one up and was about to close the drawer when her eye caught something else. It was a small signature-blue Tiffany box.

Lynn froze, staring at the box. After a moment's hesitation and with a shaking hand, she reached into the drawer and lifted it out. Sliding off the white bow, she opened it. Inside, as she guessed, was a small, black, felt-covered box containing a diamond engagement ring. With a loud snap, Lynn closed it, put it back in its blue carton, and replaced it in the drawer.

For a moment she stared off into space. Now she knew for sure there was going to be an engagement that had been derailed by the events that morning. For a moment she struggled with a combination of overwhelming sadness and paralyzing anger, each trying to best the other. But instead of giving vent to either, she closed the desk drawer to return to her Internet search. She felt a renewed commitment to the task of finding out exactly what had happened to Carl and who was responsible as a way to avoid even thinking about lost opportunity and the disturbing freedom issue.

11.

For almost a half hour Michael stayed where he was on the park bench, staring at the Shapiro Institute and mulling over the realities of his childhood that had been awakened by thinking about Ashanti Davis. He was truly amazed at how lucky he'd been to escape the near hopeless, self-fulfilling web of poverty in which he and his friends had been enmeshed and the self-destructive methods that had evolved to deal with it.

Suddenly Michael sat bolt upright. In his direct line of vision, a man emerged from the single Shapiro Institute door. Considering the time of day, it was a rare sight and rarer still because the man was by himself and wasn't wearing the typical white outfit Michael had seen before. Instead of white scrublike clothes, this man was "flamed up," sporting a black leather suit jacket over expensive-looking jeans.

Surprising himself to a degree with his spontaneity, Michael called out, "Hey! Sir! Hold up!" Using his hands to restrain the collection of pens and other paraphernalia in his pockets, including his digital tablet, Michael ran toward the man, who was walking quickly, parallel to the building, apparently en route to the parking area on the other side. "Excuse me!" Michael added as he fell in alongside. "Can I speak to you for a moment?"

The man stopped and regarded Michael. He had on sunglasses and Michael could not see his eyes. He was a white, muscular fellow with heavy features and dark, lank hair. He had a goatee not dissimilar to the kind Michael had been tempted to grow on occasion. He was wearing earbuds with the wire looping down and disappearing inside his jacket, and carrying a laptop computer in his right hand and a soft leather briefcase in his left.

"I saw you came out of the Shapiro Institute," Michael said, slightly out of breath. "I'm a fourth-year medical student, Michael Lamar Pender. I have always been fascinated by the place."

The man took out one of his earbuds, and Michael could hear jazz at a not insignificant volume. The man cocked his head with a frown. Michael repeated his comment. He hoped a little friendly chitchat would open the man up as a potential source of information, but no luck. Not only did the man not say anything, he kept frowning.

"We medical students visited the institute during our second year. We learned a bit about the place but . . ."

Michael trailed off, hoping for some response. There wasn't any. "Do you work in the institute?" he added in desperation.

"No," the man said finally.

"Were you just visiting?" Michael persisted. "Do you have a relative who is a patient?"

"I don't understand question," the man said with a strong accent. "I am computer programmer. I fix problem."

"Cool," Michael said, and he meant it. Michael was suddenly more interested as he recognized the Russian accent. Over the years a number of Russians had been hired by the Mason-Dixon Medical Center to staff the Department of Clinical Engineering, which included IT. Michael had spoken with a couple of them on a number of occasions and found them generally friendly and very competent.

With the sizable computer servers associated with the hospital's electronic health records and all the other hospital equipment that were essentially computers, such as the anesthesia machines, MRI units, CT scans, and the like, the hospital needed a team of truly computer-savvy individuals. And Michael knew that Russians generally were talented with computer code. They had even become somewhat infamous of late with their involvement with high-frequency trading on Wall Street. Some of the hospital team had even been recruited from there.

"So you work here in the main hospital?" Michael said, speaking slowly and loudly, gesturing over his shoulder toward the main eight-story hospital tower behind them.

"No," the man said without elaboration.

"Cool," Michael repeated, nodding as if agreeing. It suddenly occurred to him that the man didn't speak nearly as much English as the Russians he had spoken with in the main hospital. Yet Michael didn't want to break off the conversation. Meeting this dude popping out of the Shapiro seemed so serendipitous, considering his sudden interest in finding out about Ashanti Davis. He thought that the chances were better than good that the man had administrator status with the Shapiro's computer system. He'd have to, if he was working on it.

"Is the computer fixed?" Michael asked to make conversation. If this guy was a computer admin guy, he could be very helpful if he was inclined. Michael was well aware that people, like himself, who had reasonable access to the main hospital system could not access the Shapiro Institute's. He knew it because he had tried several months back when he briefly attempted to find out about Ashanti.

"Computer not yet fixed," the man said. "But it work okay."

"Cool!" Michael repeated yet again, trying to figure out how he was going to get on this guy's good side. He was encouraged by something he had learned from hanging with the Russians in the hospital, namely that Russians generally admired black men and black culture. It had to do with the ambivalence Russians harbored about America, giving weight to the adage, the enemy of my enemy is my friend. It was common knowledge in Russia that the United States historically had not done right by its African American citizens. "I have met some Russians in the hospital," Michael added, again speaking slowly and loudly. "Who do you work for?"

The man quickly glanced around as if concerned someone might overhear. Michael took it as encouraging behavior, as if they were sharing a secret between them, but then the man did something Michael didn't expect. Instead of answering verbally the man put down his laptop and briefcase, then took out his smartphone. He opened an app and began typing. When he was done, he held the phone out toward Michael so that Michael could read what was on the screen. On the upper portion was a paragraph in Cyrillic. Below, presumably a translation: "I work for Sidereal Pharmaceuticals in North Charleston."

Michael nodded. It made sense. It was common knowledge that there was an ongoing relationship between Sidereal Pharmaceuticals and Middleton Healthcare. Not only had Sidereal funded a large portion of the Shapiro's construction, there was talk about Sidereal, with its deep pockets, gaining a controlling interest in the hospital chain.

Michael took the man's phone and quickly figured out how to type a message in English and have it appear below in Russian, and they began an electronic conversation:

> Michael: *My name is Michael Lamar Pender. I'm a fourth-year medical student. What's your name and where are you from?*
>
> Vladimir: *My name is Vladimir Malaklov. I am from Yekaterinburg, Sverdlovsk Oblast, Russia.*
>
> Michael: *How long have you been in the United States?*

Vladimir: *Short time. I came to New York and then here three months ago.*

Michael: *Were you brought over here for a specific reason?*

Vladimir: *I am a specialist in the MUMPS computer language. The system here is coded in MUMPS.*

Michael: *It must be hard for you being here to communicate.*

Vladimir: *English is a struggle. I studied some in Russia before I came, but it hasn't helped very much. I am trying to learn, but it is difficult.*

Michael: *Do you know any of the Russians who work in the hospital?*

Vladimir: *Yes. I know several from the same university where I trained. I am staying with one of them, which is difficult. He says that after all day he is tired of talking English, so I do not get to practice.*

Michael: *I'm about to finish medical school and have some free time. Maybe I can teach you some black-talk.*

Vladimir: *I do not understand. What is "black-talk"?*

Michael: *It is the way we African American sisters and brothers talk to each other. It's like the words in rap music. You like rap?*

Vladimir: *I love rap music. Here, listen!*

Vladimir changed the app, took out the second earbud, and handed both over to Michael. Michael held one of the buds close to his ear. He recognized the tune and the artist immediately. It was Jay-Z belting out "Hard Knock Life," a piece Michael knew well.

Michael took out his own phone with an attached Beats headset, brought up the same tune, and handed the earplugs to Vladimir. Vladimir's face quickly broke into a contented smile and his head bobbed to the beat. Michael wasn't surprised. He knew that the quality of his headset was far superior to the one the Russian was using. It was like night and day.

Michael motioned toward Vladimir's phone and pantomimed tapping the screen and then looking at it. At first Vladimir didn't understand, but then caught on when Michael said: "English to Russian."

Michael: *The music is better with my headset.*

Vladimir nodded and gave a thumbs-up, indicating he agreed. He was still bobbing to the percussive beat with a slight smile on his face. He was enjoying himself, and Michael was ready to reel him in.

Michael: *I give you the headset as a welcome present to the United States.*

Vladimir: *I cannot accept. You are too kind.*

Michael: *You have to take it. You dishonor me if you don't, and that would be a problem. In rap-talk we'd have a fucking beef, which means that I might have to shoot you, since everybody and his uncle packs a gun in this country.*

Michael watched Vladimir's face as he read the translation, wondering how the last sentence would be translated into Russian. He smiled inwardly, thinking that *beef* might be translated as *steak* or *hamburger*, neither of which would make any sense whatsoever. But a broad smile lit up Vladimir's face. The Russian then typed into his screen before holding the phone up for Michael to see.

Vladimir: *I accept with pleasure to avoid a fucking filet mignon, whatever that means, but you must accept a gift from me as well. I have some souvenirs I brought from Russia.*

Michael after a good laugh: *Whatever. Russian souvenir would be nice. How about a selfie with you and me?*

Vladimir: *I do not understand selfie.*

Michael alternately pointing to himself and to Vladimir: *A photo. The two of us.* To demonstrate, Michael quickly snapped a selfie picture of himself and showed it to Vladimir. Michael wanted a photo of this Russian fellow, thinking that Lynn was not going to believe his meeting this guy.

Vladimir: *Yes, photo, but with my camera as well.*

Michael first held his own smartphone at arm's distance, put his arm around Vladimir's shoulder, and took a photo. Then Vladimir did the same. Michael took Vladimir's phone back and typed into the translator app:

Michael: *I also have a collection of all of Jay-Z's albums on my PC that I can share, if you are interested.*

Vladimir: *Very interested.*

Michael: *How will I get in touch with you, say tomorrow or the next day?*

Vladimir: *I give you my mobile number and my e-mail address.*

Michael: *Perfect. And I will give you mine.*

For the next few minutes the two men concentrated on getting each other's information into their phone's contacts. Michael noted that the country code for Russia was 7, followed by ten digits. He wondered how much texting the man was going to cost. Although Michael bolstered his meager finances with various jobs around the medical center, like working at the blood bank, by the end of the month he was always a bit short.

When he and Vladimir finished exchanging their mobile numbers and e-mail addresses, Michael pantomimed he had more to say. Vladimir brought up the translating app once again on his phone.

Michael: *Pleasure to meet you. In black-talk we say good-bye as "catch you later!"*

Vladimir: *Okay! Catch later! And thank you for the headset.*

With a broad smile on his face, Vladimir stuck out his hand and vigorously pumped Michael's. When Vladimir let go, Michael balled the Russian's fingers, did the same with his own, and then proceeded to bump fists with him.

"That's how we black folks do it," Michael explained.

Vladimir kept it up, nodding and smiling. "Catch you later," he repeated in his accented, halting English.

"Cool," Michael said with a laugh. The guy was a piece of work.

Vladimir picked up his laptop and briefcase from the ground and insisted on bumping fists again, which necessitated tucking his laptop under his arm to free up a hand. As he managed this, he never stopped smiling, obviously enjoying himself. Then, with a final wave, he turned and headed off in his original direction.

Michael deliberately waited until the Russian was about thirty feet away. Then he called out the man's name and jogged toward him, struggling once more to keep his medical-student paraphernalia from flying out of his pockets. When he reached him, he motioned again that he wanted to use Vladimir's smartphone translation app. When he got it he typed in:

Michael: *I just thought of something. I have a distant relative who was taken into the Shapiro Institute a few months back. I haven't heard*

*anything about her and promised my mother I'd find out if she was
still there and doing okay, but I haven't been able to do it. When you
go back into the institute, would you mind just finding out if she is still
there so I can let my mother know.*

Vladimir: *I would need the name.*

Michael: *Ashanti Davis.*

Vladimir: *We could find out now if you would like.*

Michael: *I would be very grateful. Since I am not immediate family
I haven't been able to visit her. How could we check about her today?*

Vladimir: *We can go back into the institute, and I can quickly find out.*

Michael: *I can go in with you?*

Vladimir: *If you would like, but it is not necessary. It will only take a
few moments. You can wait here if it is better for you.*

Michael: *I would be interested to come with you. I didn't think I would
be allowed.*

Vladimir: *Who is to know? There is rarely anyone in the institute's NOC,
or network operations center, and I know there is no one there now.
The institute's servers are also monitored in the main hospital NOC.
I've been working in the Shapiro NOC for a month and haven't seen
anyone. The door that I came out leads directly to it.*

Michael: *I'm with you. Let's do it!*

Following a half step behind, Michael followed Vladimir back to the
blank door. Just to the right of the frame, at chest height, was a
small, hinged metal housing. Vladimir lifted the front. Beneath was
a touch screen. Vladimir pressed his right thumb against it, and almost instantaneously a click sounded as the door unlocked. Vladimir pushed it open and motioned for Michael to follow. Michael was

not impressed. He thought that the ultra-futuristic Shapiro Institute would have had something a bit more up to date than decade-old thumbprint security.

Beyond the door was a hallway. The walls were all white, and the hallway was illuminated by bright LED light behind translucent ceiling panels. As he walked, Michael's eyes roamed the ceiling for signs of video devices. He saw what he thought had to be one in the middle of the ceiling, about twenty feet from the door. If it was one, Vladimir was unconcerned, although as someone knowledgeable about the institute's IT system, he had to know about security. Michael shrugged. If Vladimir wasn't worried, he wouldn't be, either. Maybe over the years there had been no intrusions and they had become lax.

Pushing through the first door they came to, Michael found himself in a relatively small room housing four multiscreened computer terminals, each with a small work desk and an ergonomic chair. Like the hallway, the walls were all white and the illumination came from translucent ceiling panels. Opposite the door was a large window that looked into the server room, with its stacks of processors and storage devices. The room was air-conditioned to the point of feeling as cold as a walk-in refrigerator.

Without hesitation Vladimir sat down at one of the workstations, and Michael came up directly behind him. If Michael's proximity looking over Vladimir's shoulder bothered the Russian, he didn't let on. Quickly the Russian typed in his user name, which Michael could see was his e-mail address. Then, as he was about to type in his password, Michael stepped to the side so he could see the keyboard. The password started with a 7, and Michael tried to concentrate on the series of digits. With his speed-reading forte, this was an exercise he was relatively good at. By the time Vladimir got to the sixth digit, Michael realized it was the dude's mobile number. After eleven digits Vladimir switched to lowercase letters, the first one being M. Soon Michael recognized he didn't have to remember that, either. The Russian was merely spelling out his last name. So much for tight security.

"Okay, we good," Vladimir said as he navigated the task bar. When prompted, he typed in *Ashanti Davis*, which he had written out on a piece of scrap paper before logging in. A second later Ashanti's home page came up: Cluster 4-B 32. Beneath that was: DRO-ZITUMAB +4 ACTIVE. "She still here," the Russian said.

"Right on!" Michael said, looking at the screen, wondering what Cluster 4-B 32 meant as well as the meaning of drozitumab +4 active. Taking the initiative, Michael reached out for the mouse and moved the cursor to HEALTH STATUS on the menu bar and clicked. He then clicked on VITAL SIGNS in the drop-down. A second later he and Vladimir were looking at an active graph of the woman's vital signs, which were being followed in real time. Blood pressure, heart rate, breathing rate, oxygen saturation were all within normal range.

"Seems she is still in the game," Michael said. Without giving up the mouse, he went back to the drop-down menu under HEALTH STATUS and clicked on COMPLICATIONS. A moment later he and Vladimir were looking at a list of problems—some active, some solved. What jumped out at him among expected conditions like BACTERIAL PNEUMONIA/CURED, CYSTITIS/CURED, was the ominous diagnosis of multiple myeloma. Michael knew that it was a serious type of blood cancer seen more often in African Americans than among Caucasians, but more in males than females and very rarely in young people.

Michael pulled out his cell phone and made a motion as if to use it to take a screen shot. He treated Vladimir to a questioning expression with the explanation: "So I can tell my mamma how she is doing."

Vladimir seemed to understand the gesture. Responding with a shrug he said: "Okay."

Michael took the shot and checked to see if it came out adequately enough to read. It seemed to be fine. He would have liked to look at more of the record, but didn't want to push his luck. He had already accomplished far more than he could have dreamed of a half hour previously, and he surely did not want to alienate his new Russian buddy.

"We go?" Vladimir questioned.

Michael responded with a double thumbs-up. He couldn't believe his luck. Lynn was going to be shocked.

12.

As far as Darko Lebedev was concerned, the weather had totally cooperated. Although it had been a bright, clear spring day, early evening had witnessed a sudden change. The wind had shifted, blowing in moist, tropical air from the south that quickly turned into a dense fog. Now, as Darko looked out the windshield of the nondescript Ford van, he could see swirls of vapor enveloping the trees and scrubs around the target house, 1440 Bay View Drive. The moon was conveniently blotted out. The circumstances couldn't have been more perfect for what was about to happen.

Darko and his partner, Leonid Shubin, had driven about twenty miles north from Charleston earlier that evening to a town called Summerville, where they stole the van they were now using. It was dark blue with no markings whatsoever, which was the reason they had selected it. From Summerville they had driven to Mount Pleasant and had made a few drive-bys of the house they had targeted, to check it out. It was the last residence on a dead-end street, with only one way in and one way out, the single minor complication for what they were planning: a home invasion.

After their last drive-by a half hour earlier, they had pulled over to the side of the road in front of the closest neighboring house and killed the engine. They were waiting for signs that the family was in the process of turning in for the night. They didn't have long to wait.

"The lights just went out in what must be the master bedroom," Leonid said in Russian. Both men had become adept at English, as they had been living in the Charleston area for a bit more than five years, but when they were alone, they preferred Russian. They had known each other for almost fifteen years, having met as members of the Russian Spetsgruppa "B" Vega, in which they had served almost ten years in Chechnya, where they had done dozens of home invasions. They considered the process their specialty. In the north Caucasus, suspected terrorists were simply eliminated along with their families without any attempt at due process. It was the Russian way of dealing with what they labeled terrorism.

"Go!" Darko barked in Russian. Both men leaped from the van. They had been ready to move for almost an hour. They were dressed in black jumpsuits and black cross-trainer shoes. They carried everything they needed, including stun grenades and Russian-made AF-1 automatic pistols with noise suppressors. As they exited the vehicle, both pulled their black balaclavas down over their faces and activated their night-vision goggles. They were thrilled to be doing what they had been highly trained to do. In their minds they had been underutilized since their arrival in America.

Darko, the larger of the two, was in the lead as the men ran up the driveway, past the Mercedes sedan parked outside the garage, and up the walkway toward the front door. Both were in superb physical shape, working out and biking or running every day. As planned, Darko went to the right of the door and Leonid to the left.

With practiced efficiency Leonid placed a small C4 explosive charge in the angle between the door and the jamb just to the side of the doorknob.

After a nod from Darko, Leonid detonated the charge. The report seemed loud in the silence but was not much worse than the bursting of a birthday balloon. In the next instant, both men were inside the house. It was key to incapacitate the adults as soon as possible and then deal with an alarm if there was one. In Chechnya, alarms were few and far between, but they did go off every now and then. Even if an automatic phone call was made to security people, they weren't particularly bothered. They would be long gone before anybody came to the house to check. If there was no alarm system or if it was off, then they could take their time and enjoy themselves.

Having observed the house during their drive-bys, they had a reasonable idea of its layout. From their observation of the persistent light in one of the windows on the second floor, especially during the last half hour, they assumed that that was where the master bedroom was located. Accordingly they went directly up the stairs in a headlong rush with pistols at the ready. There had been no sound of an alarm as they breached the front door. A few seconds later they burst into the bedroom.

The king-size bed was directly across from the door to the hall. Kate and Robert Hurley were sitting up in bed, totally startled, with eyes thrown wide open and mouths agape.

Darko found a light switch and turned on a small crystal chandelier.

When Kate Hurley caught sight of the Russians, she gasped. Darko pushed up his night-vision goggles.

"What is this?" Robert Hurley shouted. "What the hell is going on?"

Darko didn't answer but rather nodded to Leonid. Everything was going according to plan. An instant later, Leonid was back out the door. It was his job to take care of the kids. The assassins had been told there were two boys.

"How dare you!" Robert snapped, trying to sound authoritative. Kate gripped his arm to get him to shut up, but it didn't work. "What the hell is a SWAT team doing in our house?" he demanded.

Darko still didn't answer. Instead he looked at the alarm system's keypad on the wall to the right of the door. It was in the off position. They could take their time.

Robert threw back the bedcovers and started to get out of bed.

Darko leveled his automatic at him and told him in a heavy accent, "Stay put!"

"Where are you from?" Robert demanded angrily, but he followed orders. He'd never had a gun pointed at him. It was unnerving, to say the very least. "Are you police or what?"

The next instant there were two loud thudding noises that sounded like someone hitting a couch with a baseball bat. Darko knew what the sounds meant, but the parents didn't. A moment later Leonid reappeared and merely nodded to Darko, meaning the job was done.

"Where is your computer?" Darko asked.

Robert glanced at his wife with a questioning expression as if to say "Can you believe these guys?"

"And do you have a laptop? What about a tablet? And your mobile phone: we want them all."

"Is that what this is about?" Robert demanded. He was incensed. "You people came in here to steal our computers? Fine! Take them!"

"Where are they?" Darko asked, keeping his voice calm. Things were going well and he didn't want to upset Robert unnecessarily. They needed his cooperation.

"Downstairs in the study," Robert said.

"Show me!" Darko said. He motioned toward the door with his pistol.

"I'll be right back," Robert said to Kate as he climbed out of bed, put on a bathrobe, and guided his feet into slippers. He gave Darko and Leonid a dirty look as he passed them, heading out into the hall.

"Have fun!" Darko said to Leonid in Russian as he turned and followed Robert. Before they had come into the house they had flipped a coin to decide who did what. The loser had to do the kids, but as compensation he also got to do the wife. The point was that they had to make it all look like a horrid home invasion and not an assassination. Akin to a number of infamous episodes, the last one being in Connecticut, violence was key, including rape and murder with robbery as an afterthought. It was important to convince the media.

"I intend to have fun," Leonid said also in Russian. "It's not going to be hard. She's not bad-looking."

Darko followed Robert down the stairs and into the study, where Robert switched on the light. He gestured to his PC on the desk.

"What about the laptop, the tablet, and the smartphone?" Darko said.

Without comment, Robert left the study and went into the kitchen. Darko followed, pistol in his hand but at his side. He didn't expect Robert to try anything, but he seemed less intimidated than the people Darko and Leonid had dealt with back in Chechnya. Of course in Chechnya people knew what was going to happen, and Robert didn't.

With all the electronic gear in his hand, Robert was forced to return to the study, where Darko made him sit down at his PC on the desk.

"I want you to access your files at your office," Darko said. He again used the pistol to gesture.

"You're joking," Robert said. His expression was of complete disbelief.

"No joke," Darko said. "Do it!"

Robert eyed the gun in Darko's grip. Hesitated for a moment then did as he had been told.

Darko watched the screen over Robert's shoulder. "Now," Darko said, his voice still calm, "I want you to find and delete all files and documents you have relating to Middleton Healthcare and the Mason-Dixon Medical Center, both in your office and on this machine."

"Okay," Robert said. He was flabbergasted and began wondering who could be behind this bizarre situation. There was a bit more than a week's worth of work involved on the class-action case, but he was confident he could put it all back together rather easily because he remembered all the sources. With that in mind, he did as he was told without hesitation. When he was finished he looked up at Darko. "All done," he said flippantly, as if he didn't care.

"Not all done," Darko said. He pointed with the barrel of his gun toward the other electronic devices. "All documents and all files off all devices."

"You and your bosses are too much," Robert said with a shake of his head. "Who exactly has put you up to this? Let me guess: Josh Feinberg, the CEO of the medical center? This is fucking crazy. Yet it's okay. I don't mind." Robert first turned his attention to his laptop. When that was done, he picked up his smartphone. "There!" he said when he was completely finished. He tossed the phone onto the desk. "Nothing's on the tablet. I hardly use it except to play games. That means all Middleton Healthcare and Mason-Dixon Medical Center documents and files have been deleted. I hope you are happy."

As someone reasonably competent with computers and other electronic devices, Darko was quite sure Robert was telling the truth, so he was "happy," although satisfied would have been a better description. He reached over in front of Robert and moved the laptop and smartphone to the side. Just as Darko did so, a scream came from upstairs, followed by a dull thud similar to the one Robert and Kate had heard before, when Leonid went to take care of the kids.

Robert's eyes shot up as if he thought he could see through the ceiling. "What the hell?" he demanded as he started to get to his feet.

Darko didn't answer but rather raised his pistol and pointed it at Robert's face. The sound it made was more of a hiss than a bang. Robert's head snapped back, and his body went limp in the chair, arms dangling to the side. A red dot the size of a marble appeared in the middle of his forehead, just between his eyes.

Quickly Darko went through the desk to find objects worth taking besides the laptop and the smartphone. It was important to make the event seem like a burglary. Leonid appeared a moment later, zipping up his jumpsuit.

"How was it?" Darko asked, reverting to Russian as he picked up the electronic gear to carry it out to the van.

"I like young Chechen girls better," Leonid said. "More fight. Maybe you want to run up and take a turn. She's still warm."

"Fuck you," Darko said. He flashed his partner a middle finger. "Did you remember to look for any jewelry?"

"Yes, and I found some. Not a lot, but I got what I could, including the lawyer's wallet and his Rolex."

"That should be enough. Let's get the hell out of here!"

13.

At first Michael tried to incorporate the thumping sound into a very enjoyable dream, but it didn't work. Reluctantly he acknowledged that someone was intermittently knocking on his door. "Shit," he said under his breath.

Assuming his tormentor was not going to go away, Michael swung his legs out from under the covers and glanced at the clock. It wasn't even six, and the dermatology lecture wasn't going to start until nine. "Shit," he repeated, hoisting himself to his feet. He couldn't imagine who could be disturbing him or why. Despite being clad only in skivvies, he threw the door wide open. To his surprise he was face-to-face with Lynn, who was sporting an exasperated expression that it had taken him so long to open the door. She was the last person Michael had expected to see.

The evening before, Michael had checked Lynn's room on several occasions to see if she had returned. Her room was only three doors down the hall from his. When she hadn't appeared by eleven P.M., he had thought about calling or texting to make sure she was okay. He was also eager to tell her about his serendipitous meeting up with Vladimir and getting into the Shapiro Institute. But by then he assumed she was going to spend the night at Carl's and worried that she might already have been asleep or at the least needed some private time. After all, she had Michael's mobile number if she had wanted contact.

"We need to talk!" Lynn said. She pushed past the surprised Michael and threw herself into Michael's desk chair, turning on his desktop gaming computer. She was sporting a fresh white medical student's coat.

"Why don't you come on in and make yourself at home," Michael said sarcastically.

"I want you to read an article, but first get your ass in the shower or whatever you do when you wake up. We need to check on Carl, and then go get some breakfast. I'm famished. I didn't have anything to eat last night."

"Nothing? Why not?"

"I was too busy. I learned a lot of shit that I want to throw at you. So get a move on!"

"Yes, sir!" Michael said, saluting. Michael's father, of whom he only had the dimmest recollection, had been in the Marines, and was stationed at Parris Island, about five miles away from Beaufort, where Michael had grown up. He had only been four when his parents parted ways, but he still remembered his father saluting him on occasion as if he too were a Marine.

Michael quickly showered, shaved, and dealt with his hair, which didn't need much attention. When he reemerged from the bathroom, Lynn was at the window, tapping her foot. It was apparent she was juiced and impatient and couldn't have cared less that Michael was butt naked, save for his shower towel. He went to his bureau, got out clean drawers and socks, and then went to the closet for the rest of his threads and kicks. When he was finished, he informed Lynn, who seemed mesmerized by the view across the harbor to Mount Pleasant, as if she had never seen the same panorama from her own room for almost four years.

"The article I want you to read is on your screen. Read it quickly and then let's jet over to the hospital."

Michael could tell that Lynn was in no mood to argue, so he took his seat and started reading. He was aware that Lynn had come up behind him, looking over his shoulder.

The article had the *Scientific American* logo at the top, which lent it strong credibility. Michael was well aware that the main trouble with the Internet was often not knowing the sources of material and hence its veracity. This article, however, was most likely legit. The title of the relatively short piece was "How Many Die from Medical Mistakes in U.S. Hospitals?" He was finished in less than a minute, and he looked up at Lynn.

"Oh, come on," Lynn said. "You can't be finished already."

"Slam dunk," Michael responded.

"Okay, smart-ass! What's the upper limit of estimated deaths for people going into U.S. hospitals each year and suffering a 'preventable adverse event,' a euphemism if ever I heard one? They should call it like they did in the title: a goddamn mistake!"

"Four hundred and forty thousand," Michael said without hesitation.

"Geez!" Lynn complained. "How the hell do you read so fast and still remember everything? That's discouraging for us mortals."

"Like I told you, my mamma taught me."

"Mammas don't teach that kind of skill. But regardless. Don't you find that statistic startling and embarrassing? Like the article says, that would make deaths from hospital errors the third leading cause of mortality in this country."

"So let me guess. You are now convinced that Carl suffered a mistake, or more accurately, a major screwup. Is that what I'm reading between the lines?"

"Of course!" Lynn said. "A strapping, athletic, healthy twenty-nine-year-old male has a simple knee operation and ends up in a coma. Somebody fucked up big-time, and if Carl doesn't wake up, he's going to change the statistic you just quoted to four hundred and forty thousand and one this year, and that's after a routine ACL repair!"

"Sweet Jesus, Lynn, you're jumping to conclusions. It's not even twenty-four hours, and Carl is sure as hell not dead. Maybe when we go back, he'll be sitting up in bed, taking nourishment, wondering how the hell Monday disappeared."

"Wouldn't that be nice," Lynn said sarcastically. "The neurology resident thinks there was extensive brain necrosis. I hate to say this to burst your bubble, but Carl's not going to be sitting up having breakfast this morning."

"Medicine is an imperfect science. If we've learned anything over the last four years, it's that. Everybody is unique according to their DNA. Maybe Carl reacted negatively in an unexpected way to the anesthesia and whatever else he was given. Maybe there was a mistake but maybe not. Maybe the anesthesia machine malfunctioned. Maybe a thousand things, but it wasn't necessarily a medical error."

"I think the anesthesiologist fucked up somehow," Lynn said. "My intuition tells me this is a 'people' problem just like the article suggests, not an idiosyncratic reaction or a technical problem. Mistakes are made by people."

"That's a possibility, too. But there are lots of possibilities. There are system mistakes as well as people mistakes. Even computers make mistakes."

"Well, I can tell you this," Lynn said with conviction bordering on anger, "we are going to find out what happened, meaning who screwed up, and we are going to see that they are held accountable so it doesn't happen again."

"Hold on a second!" Michael said with a wry smile. "What do

you mean *we*, white man?" It was the punch line for the only joke
Ronald Metzner had told during medical school that Michael had
found truly funny. It was about the Lone Ranger and his Native
American sidekick, Tonto, when the two of them found themselves
caught in a box canyon, surrounded by a slew of bloodthirsty Indi-
ans intent on doing them in. The punch line was Tonto's response to
the Lone Ranger saying: "It looks like we are in deep shit."

For a second Lynn was silent, hardly in the mood to respond to
being reminded of one of Ronald's stupid jokes. She was disbelieving
and crestfallen at Michael's attitude. "Aren't you as pissed off about
Carl's condition as I am?" she demanded.

"My point is that in many respects it is a little early in this
developing tragedy to go off the deep end, making all sorts of
assumptions."

"Well, I don't know about you," Lynn said, "but I can't sit around
on my butt, waiting for Carl to wake up, which I don't think he is
going to do, and let the trail go cold. I'm going to find out what happened, and I'm not going to rest until I do. I owe that to Carl. The
way I got to where I am today is by being a 'doer,' just like you, I
might add."

"Listen! I can understand your feelings," Michael said. "You
have every right to be pissed. But as your friend and probably your
closest friend, I have to try to rein you in. You could be jeopardizing
your medical career. No one is going to take kindly to your efforts.
Everybody is going to be touchy about this affair. And to make matters worse, let me remind you, violating HIPAA under false pretenses, which we have done, is a class-five felony. You're going to be
going for bad, girl. You know what I'm saying?"

"Are you finished?" Lynn asked, arms akimbo.

"For now," Michael said. "Let's get our asses over to the cafeteria. I think your blood sugar must be zero and it's affecting your
good sense."

For a few minutes, Lynn held her tongue, but in the dorm elevator she was back at it. "I find it extraordinary that we as medical students have been given so little information about hospital mistakes. And errors resulting in death are just the tip of the iceberg. Think of all the patients who go into the hospital for one thing and come out with another, totally different major health problem. That statistic is over a million. That's obscene."

"I don't find it so surprising that such statistics are not ballyhooed," Michael said. "A lot of hospitals, including this one, are owned by for-profit companies. Even the so-called nonprofit hospitals are money mills in disguise. That means there's a built-in conflict of interest situation to avoid publicizing such statistics, like so many things in health care. Hospitals don't want to talk about their shortcomings. We fledgling medical students are still under the delusion that medicine is a calling whereas, if truth be told, it is a business, a big business, and not a fair business from the public's perspective. Most everybody is mainly out to make a buck."

"I didn't realize you were such a fucking cynic," Lynn said.

"As a black man trying to break into an overwhelmingly white man's profession, I have had to be a realist!"

"That's fine, dude, but it's the kind of attitude that makes change impossible."

Michael smiled. "You outta control, girl."

"I'm angry," Lynn admitted. She took a deep breath. "I'm sorry if I sound like a bitch. I'm really having a problem with this and learning what I have learned. I knew there were problems with American health care but not this bad."

"That's cool, Blondie, but you have to chill, at least in the short run."

"I don't see it that way. I'm going to find out what happened."

"Let's get you some vittles. Your cerebrum isn't working much better than Carl's, and I've got some interesting shit to tell you about."

14.

The sun was threatening to rise within the hour as Lynn and Michael exited their dorm building. It was promising to be another gorgeous spring day, with not a cloud in the pastel inverted bowl of the gradually lightening sky. But the fabulous weather was lost on Lynn, as her mind was churning. She had already decided for sure that if Michael wouldn't help her find out the truth about Carl's disaster, then she would do it herself. It was an absolute must to keep her demons at bay.

"You know what else I learned last night?" Lynn said. She had to talk louder than normal to compete with the cacophony of the birds announcing the coming dawn.

"I'm afraid to ask," Michael responded.

"The usual major-complication rate for anesthesia for a healthy patient is one in two hundred thousand surgeries. If we take only your relative, Ashanti Davis, and Carl, that's two in about five thousand cases, considering that about one hundred surgeries are done here per day. Do you know what kind of multiple that means?"

"I guess a lot," Michael admitted. Doing math in his head was not one of his strong suits.

"It's eighty times the normal. Eighty times! And we don't even know if there weren't others, which would make it even worse."

"Speaking of Ashanti," Michael said, no longer able to keep his news to himself. He could tell Lynn was getting juiced all over again. "I found out she is still hanging out in the Shapiro Institute with normal vitals but a bad diagnosis of multiple myeloma."

"How the hell did you find out?"

"A strange way," Michael said. "Yesterday afternoon I ducked out of the ophthalmology lecture, which was shit, by the way. Just a neuro-anatomy review, so you didn't miss anything. On my way back to my room to look for the JPEG of Ashanti's anesthesia record, I ended up in the Shapiro Institute."

Lynn stopped in her tracks, looking at Michael as if he had just told her he had dined with the pope. "How in God's name did you manage that?"

Michael laughed. "I got into a little one-on-one with a Russian dude who's only been over here for a couple of months. He's a computer wonk brought here to fix a glitch or two in the Shapiro computer network. He came out the Shapiro door just as I was eye-balling the place." Michael pointed to the door in question.

"And you just started a conversation out of the blue?"

"It wasn't much of one. The dude can't speak English worth shit. We communicated with a Google translation app on his smartphone. But I knew you might not believe me, so I took a selfie." Michael got out his phone and pulled up the photo. "He's been working in the Shapiro network operations center."

Lynn took the phone and studied the photo. "Which one is the Russian?" she asked.

Michael grabbed his phone back and pocketed it. "Smart-ass!"

"Did you get to see Ashanti?"

"Hell no! I just saw the inside of the Shapiro network operations center and a couple of pages of her Shapiro electronic medical record."

"And you are warning *me* about HIPAA violations," Lynn said wryly.

"Hey, I didn't hack the system. The Russian dude logged in legit."

"You merely asked him, and he agreed."

"I buttered him up a bit," Michael admitted. "I gave him a Beats headset and told him I'd be willing to share my Jay-Z music file. I figured he had admin status with the network and could check out Ashanti sometime. I never expected him to invite me into the place on the spot."

"Did you get his name? God! He could be so useful."

"Vladimir Malaklov. I also got his e-mail and mobile number."

"Fabulous! But wasn't he concerned about security issues?"

"Didn't seem to be. My guess is that he knows that security inside the institute is lax. I mean, I saw a video cam in the ceiling outside the NOC, but it didn't bother him when we walked under it. Maybe he knows no one is watching the feed. And he said he has never seen another person in the network operations center the whole time he has been here."

"Strange," Lynn said. "I had the feeling that security was important for the Shapiro. That was what they implied during our tour, and the place is built like a bank vault." She glanced at the massive but squat granite structure with not a window in sight from where they were standing.

"Maybe security was big in the beginning, but since there haven't been any problems over the eight or so years it has been in operation, they've let things slide. Even security for the outside door isn't much. Thumbprint touchscreen access. That technology is really out of date."

"So how did you learn she has multiple myeloma?"

"Vladimir brought up her home page, and I got to click on her health status and then vital signs and complications. I would have liked to look further, but I knew I'd be pushing my luck. I did take a screen shot of her complications page."

"Let me see it!"

Michael pulled out his phone again and brought up the image. Lynn tried to examine it. "It's a bit hard to read out here."

"It's better indoors," Michael agreed.

"I can't believe you managed this," Lynn repeated.

"Her home page had Cluster 4-B 32."

"I see. What does it mean?"

"Not a clue. The home page also says drozitumab plus four active. I didn't know what the hell *drozitumab* was but looked it up last night. Drozitumab is a human monoclonal antibody used to treat cancer."

"Maybe that is what they are using to treat her multiple myeloma."

"I doubt it," Michael said. "In the articles I read, it was developed for a type of muscle cancer."

"Then I don't know what it refers to," Lynn said. She handed the phone back to Michael. "But tell me: didn't this Vladimir have any concerns about patient confidentiality?"

"No. My sense is that he knows zip about our HIPAA rules. They probably don't have anything like that in Russia. He doesn't even have a secure user name or password that anyone who knows a few details about him couldn't figure out. His user name is his e-mail address, and his password is his mobile number combined with his family name."

"You amaze me. You sure you weren't trained by the CIA?"

"You could have done the same thing. I'm telling you: he wasn't concerned about security. I was standing there in full view of what he was doing while he typed in his user name and password. He didn't give a shit."

"So Ashanti is still in a coma," Lynn said as she started walking again.

"Must be 'cuz she's still in the Shapiro," Michael said, falling in beside her.

"You didn't learn anything about her coma, looking at her EMR? What a missed opportunity."

"I'm telling you, I didn't want to push him or my luck on the first go-around."

"I'm not criticizing. It's amazing you learned what you did."

"I was surprised myself," Michael admitted. "And I'm planning on hitting him up again."

As they approached the door to the clinic building, Lynn asked, "What about the photo of Ashanti's anesthesia record? Did you find it?"

"I did," Michael said. "It was in my photo folder on my desktop. As I said, it looked a lot like Carl's, but I want to print them both out so that I can really compare."

"I'm eager to see it when you do."

"I'll think about it," Michael teased.

They walked through the mostly deserted clinic. The only people they saw were housekeeping, polishing the floor and wiping down the chairs with antiseptic.

When Lynn and Michael crossed the connecting pedestrian bridge and entered the hospital proper from the clinic building, they were immediately enveloped in a crowd. Although the clinic was still closed, the hospital itself was a different story. Another busy day was already in the making.

As Michael headed toward the cafeteria, Lynn went in the opposite direction, toward the elevators. Michael was the first to notice their cross-purposes, and he turned, caught up to Lynn, and pulled her to a stop. People jostled them as they stood in the middle of the main hospital corridor. "I thought we were going to the cafeteria," he said. He had to speak louder than usual over the general din.

"We need to check on Carl first," Lynn said. "This is the best time. The shift will be changing, and they will be less likely to question our presence."

"Good point," Michael conceded. "But your blood sugar? You sure you can hang in there?"

"I'll be fine," Lynn assured him. "Come on!"

They started toward the elevators. It was difficult to stay together. Lynn talked to him over her shoulder. "Even with the shift
changing in the ICU, someone might say something to us. If they do,
let's use the anesthesia explanation you came up with yesterday. I
thought it was brilliant. But to lend it more credibility, we should
put on scrubs and look the part."

"Now, that's slick," Michael agreed. Instead of joining the throng
waiting for an elevator, they went to the stairs. In the surgical lounge
they separated.

As Lynn entered the women's locker room, it was still well before seven, yet it was a busy place. Most of the women donning
scrubs were nurses just coming on duty. The surgeons scheduled for
seven-thirty cases wouldn't arrive until around seven-fifteen, after
making rounds on their post-op patients. Lynn found an empty visitors' locker, and as she began to unbutton her blouse, the intercom
crackled to life from a ceiling-mounted speaker. Since everyone had
mobile phones, it wasn't used much. The voice belonged to the head
nurse out at the main desk in the OR: "Dr. Sandra Wykoff! This is
Geraldine Montgomery. Are you in the changing area?"

"I am," Dr. Wykoff said, talking loudly and directing her voice
up toward the ceiling. As a courtesy, the buzz of voices coming from
the other women in the room quieted.

Lynn turned around. The name provided instant recognition.
Sandra Wykoff had been the anesthesiologist on Carl's case. Lynn
stared at the woman, who was no more than five or six feet away. She
was petite, a good six inches shorter than Lynn, with small, sharp
features and mousy hair, who nonetheless projected an intensity of
purpose. Her bare arms were thin but muscular, making Lynn think
she kept herself in shape, something that Lynn did as well. It was
Lynn's immediate impression that Sandra Wykoff was not someone
easily intimidated despite her short stature.

"Dr. Wykoff," Geraldine continued over the intercom, "you must have your mobile ringer turned off. I have Dorothy Wiggens from Same-Day Surgery Admitting on the other line. They have been trying to contact you."

Lynn watched Wykoff fish her phone from her pocket and check it, "You are so right," she said. "Apologize for me!"

"It isn't a problem, except they wanted to let you know your first case has been canceled. The patient forgot her pre-op instructions and had a full breakfast."

"Okay, I got it. I appreciate your letting me know."

"We'll let Dr. Barker, your second case, know as well. It is now scheduled for late morning. Maybe it can be moved up. We'll keep you informed."

"That would be terrific. Thank you."

As if on cue, the moment the intercom clicked off, the murmur of other conversations in the locker room recommenced.

Dr. Wykoff looked over at Lynn, who was regarding her with a wide-eyed gaze. "Better to find that out in admitting rather than up here in the OR," Dr. Wykoff said to make conversation.

"I suppose," Lynn answered. She looked away, suddenly realizing she had been staring. What to do, was the question. It seemed much too serendipitous not to take advantage of this fortuitous meeting. She had spent a number of hours during the night reading up on standard anesthesia procedure, so she felt confident she could hold up her end of a technical conversation about Carl's case. Yet was this the time and the place to bring up what would undoubtedly be a touchy subject, as Michael had reminded her? Lynn donned her white coat over her scrubs and closed the locker in which she had put her clothes. Impulsively she decided to give conversation a try. "Excuse me, Dr. Wykoff," she began, still unsure of what she was going to say, especially while struggling to keep her emotions in check.

After closing her own locker, Dr. Wykoff directed her strikingly bright blue eyes at Lynn.

"I understand you were the anesthesiologist attending Carl Vandermeer yesterday," Lynn said.

Instantly Dr. Wykoff's eyes narrowed and bore into Lynn's. She didn't respond immediately but proceeded to look Lynn up and down, as if appraising her. She then warily nodded and said: "I was the attending. Yes. Why do you mention it?"

"I read your note in the chart in the neurology ICU yesterday. I need to talk to you about the case."

"Really?" Dr. Wykoff questioned with a whiff of guarded incredulity. "And who are you?"

"My name is Lynn Peirce. I am a fourth-year medical student." She specifically avoided making any reference to why she had been in the neuro ICU and why she had been looking at the chart. She knew that the excuse of being on an anesthesia rotation wouldn't play with an anesthesia attending.

"Why exactly do you want to discuss this unfortunate case?" Dr. Wykoff asked warily.

"I've learned that a million people a year go into a hospital with one complaint and then end up with another serious medical issue they didn't have before being admitted. I think it is an important issue that we medical students aren't taught. The Vandermeer case might apply."

"I suppose we could talk," Dr. Wykoff said as she relaxed a degree. "But this is not the time or the place. You heard that my seven-thirty case has been canceled. If my next case is not moved up, I suppose I could speak with you this morning."

"I would appreciate it," Lynn said. "How will I get in touch with you?"

"Ask Geraldine at the OR desk. She'll know where I am." Then the anesthesiologist walked out.

15.

Michael pulled his medical student white coat over his scrubs. When he emerged from the men's locker room, he didn't want to hang out in the surgical lounge for fear of getting into a conversation with someone who might feel obligated to ask what the hell Michael, as a fourth-year medical student, was doing in scrubs. Instead he went out into the hall by the elevator to wait. He didn't have to wait long.

"Of all people, I bumped into infamous Dr. Sandra Wykoff," Lynn said in a forced whisper when she appeared. As usual, there were other people waiting for an elevator. "She was changing right next to me."

"And who might Dr. Wykoff be?" Michael asked, his voice rising for effect.

"Oh, come on!" Lynn complained irritably. "She was Carl's fucking anesthesiologist, who was responsible for what happened. How could you forget?"

"I'm trying to make a point, my dear. You don't know that she was responsible. That's the kind of comment that is going to get you in a whole shitload of trouble."

"Technically you're right," Lynn snapped. "But she was in charge when whatever happened happened. There's no denying that. If she didn't cause it, she could have stopped it or prevented it."

"You don't know that, girl. I'm telling you straight. You are going to crash and burn."

The elevator doors opened. The car was full. Lynn and Michael and several others had to squeeze on as people reluctantly made room. The two students didn't try to talk as the elevator rose, stopping on each floor. Once they got out on the sixth floor they walked slowly and let the other people who had gotten out pass by. Most were nurses and nursing assistants who were coming in for the morning shift.

"Wykoff's first case for today was canceled," Lynn said when she was sure no one would overhear. "She agreed to talk to me, provided her second case doesn't get moved up."

"I better come along just to keep you in line," Michael said. "You are on a self-destructive roll."

"Do you really want to come along?" Lynn said with a touch of disdain. "I thought you weren't going to help."

"Like I said. Somebody's got to protect you from yourself and make sure you cut this woman some slack, you know what I'm saying?"

As they got closer to the neuro ICU, Lynn's pulse began to rise and her anxiety ratcheted upward. If there had been a change in Carl's status, she would not have heard one way or the other, as she wasn't in the immediate family loop. Although she expected little change, she knew there was a slight chance that he could be better or worse. Unfortunately, with a provisional diagnosis of extensive brain necrosis, his chances of improvement were mighty slim, which left the downside much more probable.

Outside the double doors, Lynn hesitated out of worry about

what she was going to confront. Michael sensed her reluctance. "You want me to go in and see what's up?" he suggested. "Then I could fill you in."

"No," Lynn said. "I want to go in and see him. I'll be all right."

As Lynn and Michael had hoped, the nurses were busy at rounds. As the door closed behind the medical students, they could see that the nursing team going off-shift and the team coming on were all congregated in bay number 5, going over a new arrival. For the moment all the other patients, including Carl, were on their own.

At the central desk, the ward clerk, Peter Marshall, was already on duty, watching over the monitor feeds. His day had already begun, even though technically it wasn't supposed to begin until seven. Lynn remembered that had never bothered Peter. He always arrived early to get a jump on the day.

A female attending physician was also at the desk, busy at work with a number of charts stacked in front of her and one open. Lynn and Michael could tell from her long white professorial coat that she was an attending, and not a resident. They didn't recognize her.

The medical students went directly to cubicle 8, with Lynn lagging slightly behind, afraid of what she was going to see. Carl wasn't sitting up having breakfast, but he wasn't dead, either. He looked as serene as he had the day before, with his eyes closed, as if asleep. He was still in the exact same supine position, with the CPM flexing and extending his operated leg. His IV was running as it had been, but it had been repositioned as a central venous line and now went into his neck.

"Looks generally about the same as yesterday," Michael commented. Lynn nodded, restraining herself from reaching out to touch Carl's face. She noticed that his beard had darkened, and as her eyes traveled down his body, she observed that both arms were now relaxed. Apparently the decorticate posturing was gone. Whether that was a good sign or not, Lynn had no idea. The myoclonic jerks of his free leg had also stopped.

In order to look as if he were on a legitimate mission, Michael took out his penlight and tried Carl's pupillary reflexes. While he was busy, Lynn glanced up at the monitor. She didn't want to look into Carl's unseeing eyes again, as doing so had unnerved her the day before. She saw that the blood pressure was normal as was the oxygen saturation. The ECG looked normal to her as well. It was then that she spotted the temperature graph. Carl had a fever of 103 degrees, and it had been as high as 105! She knew that wasn't good news.

"Pupillary reflexes are better than yesterday," Michael said, straightening up. "I wonder if that is a good sign."

"His temperature is elevated," Lynn said with concern, pointing up to the monitor.

"So it is," Michael said after taking a look. "That can't be good."

"It's not," Lynn said. "Pneumonia is a big threat to people in a coma. I learned that last night."

"You got that right. Sounds like you learned a lot in one night."

"It is amazing what you can get done if you don't eat or sleep."

"Then let's get you down to the cafeteria before you flatline."

"Let's check the chart first. I want to see the results of the MRI he was supposed to have had."

Leaving Carl's cubicle, the duo walked directly toward the central desk. As they traversed the room, Lynn made momentary eye contact with Gwen Murphy, who had moved on to cubicle 6, along with all the other nurses. Fortunately Murphy's expression didn't change. For Lynn, being an interloper was a nerve-racking experience. She was impressed that Michael seemed to be taking it in stride.

At the circular desk, Michael smiled at Peter, who smiled back. The clerk was on the phone with Clinical Chemistry, trying to get the latest lab values before they were even in the computer. The attending physician didn't look up from her work. The stack of charts was still in front of her.

As he had done the previous day, Michael went directly to the circular chart rack and gave it a decisive spin. He stopped it at the slot for cubicle eight. There was no chart.

Tapping Peter's shoulder, Michael silently mouthed, "Vandermeer," and motioned toward the chart rack. Without interrupting his phone conversation, Peter pointed to the attending physician. Michael understood. The attending had Vandermeer's chart, a new, potentially problematic complication.

With a shrug, Michael started toward the attending, only to have Lynn grab the sleeve of his white coat and restrain him.

"What are you going to say?" Lynn questioned in a whisper.

Michael shrugged again. "I'm going to wing it, as usual."

"You can't use the anesthesia ruse because she might be from anesthesia."

"You are so right," Michael said with a nod.

"Hold on," Lynn said. She stepped over to Peter and scribbled on the notepad in front of the clerk: *Who's the attending, and what department is she from?*

Without interrupting his conversation, Peter scribbled: *Dr. Siri Erikson, hematology.*

Lynn mouthed a "Thank you" to Peter and then took the note back to Michael.

"Hematology?" Michael questioned, still in a whisper. "What does that mean? Carl's got a blood problem?"

"Who's to know?" Lynn said. "I hope not. Maybe there is some association with the fever."

"I would think a fever in a comatose patient would call for an infectious disease consult, not one from hematology."

"I agree. Anyway, let's see how friendly she is toward medical students."

Both Lynn and Michael were well aware that some medical attendings savored the teaching role whereas others saw it as a burden and acted accordingly.

"The good news is that she's not from anesthesia," Michael said, "so our cover is okay if it comes to that."

"You do the talking," Lynn said. "You're better at deception than I."

"I'm going to pretend I didn't hear that, girl."

"That's fine, boy!" Lynn responded.

Michael approached the hematologist. He cleared his throat to announce himself. "Excuse me, Dr. Erikson."

The woman looked up from her work. She was attractive, somewhat heavyset mature woman in her late forties or early fifties. Consistent with her family name, she looked Scandinavian, with blond hair and a pale complexion. Her eyes were a clear cerulean blue. "Yes," she said.

"My partner and I were wondering if we could take a quick look at Vandermeer's chart if you are not using it at the moment."

Dr. Erikson turned to the stack of charts in front of her and fished out Carl's. She handed it up to Michael but maintained a hold on it. "I'm not finished with it," she said. "So I need it back."

"Of course," Michael said. "We'll just be a moment."

"I assume you are medical students," Dr. Erikson said, glancing briefly at Lynn. She had yet to let go of the chart. "What is your association with the case?"

"My name is Michael Pender and this is Lynn Peirce. We've been asked by anesthesia to follow the case."

"I see," Dr. Erikson said. She finally released her hold on the chart. "Is it because it is a case of delayed return to consciousness?"

"You got it," Michael said. He smiled diplomatically, handed the chart to Lynn, and started to take a step away, hoping to end the conversation, but Dr. Erikson spoke up again: "Is it just Vandermeer you are interested in, or are you following Scarlett Morrison as well?"

"Should we be?" Michael asked.

"Not necessarily. But she is a similar case."

"You mean she is another case of delayed recovery from anesthesia?" Michael asked. He shot a glance at Lynn, whose eyes had opened wider, despite her fatigue. She was obviously taken aback.

"Yes, she is," Dr. Erikson said. "She was a Friday surgery. A very similar case, I'm afraid. I'm surprised someone in anesthesia didn't tell you."

"I'm surprised, too," Michael said. "We certainly should be following her." He glanced at Lynn, who looked as if someone had just slapped her.

"I'm using the Morrison chart at the moment," Dr. Erikson said. "When you finish with Vandermeer's, I'll give it to you."

"That's a deal," Michael said, grabbing Lynn by the arm and forcibly moving her away, over to a couple of empty chairs. The two of them sat down.

"If it is true there's another case, this is worse than I thought," Lynn said in an excited, horrified whisper. "If there was another case last week, then the incidence here at Mason-Dixon Medical Center is three in five thousand, meaning it is not eighty times the average, but one hundred twenty times!"

"Calm down!" Michael insisted, trying to keep his own voice low. He glanced over at Dr. Erikson in hopes she wasn't paying any attention. Luckily she was again totally absorbed in her work. "Let's take this one step at a time," Michael said. "We came here to look at Carl's chart. Let's do it and get the hell out!"

Making an effort to follow Michael's advice, Lynn opened the chart. The last entry was a short note by the neurology resident, Charles Stuart, who had been called during the night when Carl's fever had spiked. Stuart had ordered an emergency portable chest X-ray, which was read as clear, so no pneumonia. He wrote that the operative site was not red or swollen. He sent away a urine sample for bacteriologic studies and drew blood for a blood count and for blood cultures. He concluded his note with the statement "Fever of unknown origin. Will follow. Consult requested."

"Maybe Dr. Erikson is the consult," Lynn said.

"Could be," Michael said. "But hematology and not infectious disease? It doesn't compute."

Quickly Lynn flipped through the chart to get to the results of the studies, in particular the MRI, only to learn that a CT scan had been done as well. Laying the chart flat, she and Michael read the reports. Michael finished first and waited for Lynn to do the same.

"There are a lot of terms that I don't understand," Michael said.

"Likewise," Lynn said. "But it's pretty clear that it isn't good news, even if we don't understand all the details. The summary says the CT scan showed severe diffuse brain edema while the summary of the MRI says that the hyperintense cortical signal indicates extensive laminar necrosis. That's what Dr. Stuart expected. It all translates to extensive brain death . . ." Lynn trailed off, unable to finish her sentence.

"I'm sorry," Michael said as sincerely as he could.

"Thank you," Lynn said. Her voice caught. With such terrible news, she was trying not to cry. She was supposed to be a dispassionate medical student.

"Want to look at anything else in the chart?" Michael asked.

Lynn shook her head. As far as she was concerned, there wasn't any point. The verdict was in. Whether Carl would regain some level of consciousness or not was uncertain, but even if he did, he was never going to be the person she knew. Best-case scenario was probably his entering a persistent vegetative state, a horrid situation that she had read up on the evening before. He would have brain stem function without input from the higher or cortical areas. It would mean he might have sleep-wake cycles but still would be completely unaware of self and environment and need total care until death. In short, he would endure a dehumanized existence. Inwardly she shuddered, wondering if she could cope.

Michael stood up and gave Lynn's shoulder a reassuring squeeze. He took Carl's chart back over to Dr. Erikson, who gave him Scarlett Morrison's chart. He brought it back to where Lynn was sitting and placed it in front of her. She was in a trance, staring ahead. "You okay?" he asked.

"As good as can be expected," Lynn responded. Her voice quavered. Then, as if waking up, she shook her head, adjusted herself in her seat to be more upright, and opened the second chart.

16.

At first they didn't talk, but merely nodded to each other when they finished a page. The first question Lynn in particular wanted to know was why the neurology resident, Charles Stuart, hadn't mentioned that there had been a very recent, similar case. The answer turned out to be simple: a different neurology resident, by the name of Dr. Mercedes Santiago, was involved. With what they both knew about interdepartmental communication, the Neurology Department might not know that there had been two similar cases until they had their grand rounds.

As Lynn and Michael read on, significant similarities between the cases began to surface. First of all, Scarlett Morrison was nearly the same age as Carl, and unmarried. Second, she was a healthy individual whose only problem was gallstones. Her surgery, like Carl's, was elective, meaning it wasn't an emergency. Her procedure had been a laparoscopic cholecystectomy, or a small-incision removal of her gallbladder. It had been done without complications, according to the operative note, just as Carl's had been, and, like Carl's, it had been a seven-thirty A.M. case, so everyone had been fresh and rested.

As they continued to read they noticed there was no handwritten anesthesia note by the anesthesiologist, Dr. Mark Pearlman, only a terse mention of the problem of delayed return of consciousness, followed by a list of the medications that had been tried in vain to reverse the sedative and the paralytic agents in case there had been an overdosage of either. For information about the course of anesthesia during the operation, Lynn and Michael had to turn to the record created in real time by the anesthesia machine.

What they learned was that, as in Carl's case, the anesthesia had progressed normally until there was a sudden, unexplained decrease in the patient's blood oxygenation about three-quarters of the way through the operation. Looking at the graph, they could see that the oxygenation fell precipitously from near 100 percent to 90 percent for a couple of minutes before returning to 98 percent. Just as with Carl, there had been a brief episode of heart irregularity from hypoxia at precisely the moment the oxygen saturation fell.

As they examined the record further, some specific differences from Carl's case became apparent above and besides the fact that it had taken place in OR 18 instead of OR 12: First, the volatile anesthetic agent was desflurane instead of isoflurane; second, an endotracheal tube was used instead of a laryngeal mask; and third, a depolarizing muscle relaxant, succinylcholine, had been used to facilitate the intra-abdominal surgery. On the other hand, the preoperative medication, midazolam, and the induction agent, propofol, had been the same, with approximately the same doses administered according to weight.

When Lynn had finished studying the record, she looked up at Michael, who was holding his camera out of sight of Peter and Dr. Erikson. He motioned to Lynn to hold up Morrison's chart so that he could snap a picture of the anesthesia record without having to stand up. She did but in the process felt anxiously guilty. Michael took the picture and the camera disappeared in a flash.

Both Michael and Lynn glanced over at Peter and Dr. Erikson to ·

see if either had noticed. They hadn't. Lynn breathed a sigh of relief. Michael seemed immune.

"What do you make of the differences?" Michael asked.

"From my reading last night I know that recovery from desflurane is actually faster than from isoflurane, so that's not significant. And an endotracheal tube is more secure than a laryngeal mask, so there is no problem there. And the use of a paralyzing agent shouldn't be a problem as long as the patient is respired. I don't find the differences significant."

"Man, girl, you sure covered some ground with your reading last night."

"It was a lot of hours," Lynn said. At that point, she turned to the page in the chart that had the graph of Morrison's vital signs, recorded since she had been brought to the neuro ICU. Lynn pointed to the tracing of body temperature that showed that Scarlett Morrison had had a significant spike in temperature the night after her surgery, just like Carl, reaching the same high point of 105° F. Although the temperature stayed elevated over Sunday and Monday, it had gradually fallen and was now at 100° F, which most people would consider mildly elevated.

"I'm amazed," Lynn murmured. "So far the Morrison and Vandermeer cases seem clinically to be mirror images. Could that happen by chance?"

Michael shrugged. "And as far as I can remember, they are both similar to Ashanti's. I'm pretty sure she had a fever, too. Do you think it could be some kind of new, unknown reaction to anesthesia that also causes a fever?"

"Who's to know at this point," Lynn replied. She turned to the blood work section. "Seems there was an increase in her white count to go along with the fever. That suggests an infection."

Michael nodded. "But there isn't an increase in neutrophils or a shift to the left." Both medical students knew that in the face of an infection the body usually responded with an immediate increase of neutrophils, the body's cellular defense against bacteria infection. A shift to the left indicated newly mobilized cells responding to an acute microbial attack.

"But look," Lynn said, "the increase in the white count is with lymphocytes, not neutrophils. Doesn't an increase in lymphocytes usually happen later in an infection as a hormonal immune response?"

"That's the way it's supposed to work."

"And look, the lymphocyte count went up progressively with each passing day. What do you make of that?"

"I need to cheat," Michael said. He pulled out his tablet and Googled *meaning of increased lymphocytes*. Thanks to the Internet, he had multiple results in a fraction of a second. He read the conditions out loud: "Leukemia, mono, HIV, CMV, other viruses, TB, multiple myeloma, vasculitis, and whooping cough."

When Lynn didn't respond to his list, Michael glanced at her. She was busy reading the results of the infectious disease consult. "No source of infection was found," she said. "Chest was clear on X-ray, urine normal, no infection of the operative incisions, no nothing."

"Did you hear the list of what causes an increase in lymphocytes?" Michael asked.

Lynn shook her head. "Sorry. Come again!"

Michael repeated the list. Lynn listened and thought for a moment. "Well, we can ignore most. I suppose 'other viruses' and 'vasculitis' are the most probable."

"Yeah," Michael agreed, "but doesn't something jump out at you?"

"What do you mean?"

"Multiple myeloma causes an increase in lymphocytes. That caught my eye because of what I learned yesterday—that Ashanti has multiple myeloma. Maybe Morrison has it, too."

"Now, that would be too much of a coincidence," Lynn said.

"I've never seen a case of multiple myeloma and don't know much about it other than it involves too many plasma cells. Isn't it rather rare?"

"If I remember correctly, it's not that rare," Michael said. "Of course everything is relative. I remember the one lecture in pathology that included multiple myeloma."

"You remember the lecture we had in pathology about multiple myeloma?" Lynn questioned with a touch of dismay.

"I don't remember a lot, and not much more than that it involves plasma cells, like you said. But I do remember that among the brothers it is one of the top ten causes of cancer death. Maybe that's why I remember it. Anyway, of all the conditions that I just read that cause an increase in lymphocytes, I couldn't help but notice it."

"I wonder if it is because of the increase in lymphocytes that Dr. Erikson is seeing the patient," Lynn questioned.

"Makes sense," Michael agreed. "Do you think we should risk asking her?"

Lynn looked over at the attending, who was still bent over a chart, dictating a note most likely for the EMR. A few minutes earlier she had been writing a note. Until the hospital fully adopted the computerized record and gave up on the physical chart, consults had to do both and complained bitterly.

"I don't think we dare," Lynn said after a pause. "If we actually engage her in a conversation, she's bound to ask us more details of why we are here. As you said, people are going to be sensitive about these cases."

"Right on, girl!"

"Let's see if she wrote a note in this chart. That could answer the question."

Redirecting her attention to the chart in front of her, Lynn turned to the continuation notes, where progress reports were placed. The last note was from Dr. Erikson. The handwriting wasn't good.

*Thank you for asking me to see this patient again. As noted
on my previous [illegible word], the patient has had a persistently
elevated body temperature, although it has gradually subsided
and is today at 100° F. Her blood count continues to show a
moderate and [illegible word] lymphocytosis, currently at over
6,300 lymphocytes per mcl, representing 45 percent of the white
count. I am pleased to see that no source of infection has been
found. Total globulins are [illegible word] elevated. Protein
electrophoresis shows a small and narrow gamma globulin spike,
which suggests the [illegible word] of a developing monoclonal
gammopathy (MGUS). However, I do not see this possibility or
her persistent fever as contraindication for her scheduled transfer
to the Shapiro Institute. I believe such a transfer will be in her
best [illegible word], and I will continue to follow her. Dr. Siri
[illegible word but presumably Erikson]*

"What the fuck is a gammopathy or MGUS?" Michael asked with
frustration. "I hate it when consults throw around these shit-ass es-
oteric words and acronyms to make you feel incompetent."

"My turn to cheat," Lynn said as she pulled out her tablet and
Googled *gammopathy*. Although she didn't know the exact meaning,
she had a good idea. She selected the Wikipedia choice, and, placing
her tablet on the desk, they both read the article titled "Monoclonal
Gammopathy of Undetermined Significance."

When Lynn was finished Michael asked: "What's your take, besides knowing what MGUS stands for?"

"I'm so tired I'm having trouble thinking," she confessed.

"It's not surprising. You're exhausted and you're starving. Come
on! Let's go down and get you something to eat. You're running on
empty."

"In a minute," Lynn said, trying to rally herself. "At least I understood that MGUS involves a group of lymphocytes overproducing

the same antibody. What surprises me is reading how prevalent it is, and I barely remember it even being mentioned in pathology."

"But it is only prevalent in people over fifty. This patient is twenty-eight."

"True," Lynn said. "And I guess it's not that serious."

"It's not serious unless it develops into multiple myeloma. It makes me wonder if Ashanti started out with this MGUS, which then led to the multiple myeloma."

"I guess that is a possibility," Lynn said. "Let's look at the test Erikson mentions in her note: the protein electrophoresis. I know something about that from having used it to follow a patient with acute hepatitis last year in our medicine rotation."

Lynn flipped back to the section of the chart for laboratory tests. It didn't take her long to find the proper page with the results of the protein electrophoresis. The levels of the various plasma proteins were listed and also portrayed in a graphic schematic. She and Michael concentrated on the schematic. In the far right-hand portion where a smooth mound representing the gamma globulins was expected, there was a small, narrow peak at the mound's crest.

"That's easy to spot," Michael said. "So the woman's immune system is producing a specific antibody. What do you think is causing it?"

"Has to be an antigen of some kind. And maybe the antigen that stimulated the first lymphocyte to produce the specific immune globulin is still in Scarlett Morrison's body, continuing to stimulate more and more antibodies. What do you think of that?"

"It's definitely a possibility unless that first lymphocyte just went a little berserk, if you know what I am saying."

"You mean, sorta like a cancer cell."

"Something like that," Michael said. "The cellular machinery to produce an antibody got turned on, and someone forgot to turn it off."

"Going back to your question about whether the anesthesia

could have caused the fever. Now the question is if the anesthesia could have turned on this monoclonal antibody?"

Michael stared at Lynn, understanding perfectly where she was coming from. She desperately needed an explanation for Carl's sorry state and was willing to grasp at straws.

"I'm talking about some idiopathic reaction that has yet to be noticed."

"No!" Michael said finally but firmly. "There's nothing about anesthesia that could be antigenic. I'd like to say yes to get you off your collision course of thinking someone screwed up. But anesthesia agents have been used in too many people over too long a time for there to be an unrecognized immunological reaction that causes fever and monoclonal antibodies. Much less puts people into a coma. No way. Sorry, girl!"

"I knew you were going to say that."

"I say it because it's the truth. Now, let's get down to the cafeteria. We have a dermatology lecture at nine."

"I'm not finished," Lynn said. She turned off her tablet and pocketed it. Next she turned to Morrison's MRI. It was similar to Carl's, showing extensive laminar necrosis. Closing the chart, Lynn looked over at Dr. Erikson, who was still alternatively writing a chart and dictating with her phone.

"I want to look at Carl's chart again," Lynn said impulsively, getting to her feet and picking up Scarlett Morrison's chart in the process.

"But why?" Michael complained. He grabbed the arm of Lynn's coat to restrain her. "Why risk it? Nothing will have changed."

"We didn't look at his blood work," Lynn said, detaching her sleeve from Michael's grasp. "And maybe she wrote something in the chart. If she did, I'd like to see it."

17.

Excuse me," Lynn said as she came up to Dr. Erikson. She extended Morrison's chart. "Thank you for calling our attention to this case. It is very similar to Vandermeer's, and we should be following it for sure."

The hematologist glanced up briefly.

"Should I put Morrison's chart back in the rack or do you want it here with you?" Lynn asked.

Dr. Erikson pointed toward the desk next to her. "Here is fine," she said distractedly without looking back up at Lynn.

"I hate to trouble you," Lynn said, "but we would like to take another quick glance at Vandermeer's. There's something we missed."

Dr. Erikson's head popped up, and she regarded Lynn with icy blue eyes, and her nostrils flared. For a moment Lynn thought the woman was going to angrily deny her access to the chart. But then her expression softened.

"If it is a bother, we can come back later," Lynn added quickly. Although she had not noticed it before, now that her attention had been drawn to the woman's face, Lynn thought that the doctor did

not look well. The paleness of her skin was striking, almost translucent, and her cheeks looked hollow. Beneath her eyes were purplish,
dark circles. "I just thought you might be finished with it."

"It's not a bother," Dr. Erikson said. She separated Carl's chart
from those in front of her and extended it toward Lynn, asking:
"What year medical students are you two?"

"We're fourth-year," Lynn said. Her pulse quickened in anticipation of possible trouble. Now that she was close to the hematologist,
she could see that the woman wasn't exactly overweight, as she had
thought earlier. It was more that her abdomen was distended, as if
she might be four or five months pregnant, which seemed inappropriate, considering her age.

"And you are on a rotation in anesthesia?"

Lynn nodded. "The specialties are our final rotation before graduation." She hoped Dr. Erikson would assume anesthesia was considered a specialty at Mason-Dixon, even though it wasn't: just
ophthalmology, ENT, and dermatology.

"Have you come to any conclusions why these patients have suffered comas?" Dr. Erikson asked.

"No, we haven't," Lynn said. She was nonplussed, wishing she
had not gotten herself into conversation. "Have you any ideas?"

"Of course not," Dr. Erikson snapped. "I'm a hematologist, not
an anesthesiologist."

Lynn wanted to leave but felt caught as Dr. Erikson was still holding on to Carl's chart and staring at her with unblinking intensity.
After a moment of strained silence the hematologist asked another
question: "Do you have any hunches as to what might have happened?"

"Not so far," Lynn said.

"If you come up with any particular ideas, let me know!" Dr.
Erikson said. It was more of an order than a request. Finally she let
go of Carl's chart.

Relieved, Lynn said, "We'll be happy to let you know if something occurs to us."

"I'll be counting on it," Dr. Erikson said. Then she pulled a professional card from one of her pockets and handed it to Lynn. "Here are my contacts. Let me know right away if you come to any conclusion."

"Thank you," Lynn said, taking the card and glancing at it. She smiled uncomfortably and was about to flee back to Michael when Dr. Erikson added, "Do you have any questions for me?"

Despite her fatigue, Lynn tried to come up with a question. She desperately wanted to leave but thought it best to play the medical-student role and keep the conversation academic rather than take the risk of having it turn to what she and Michael were really doing: namely, violating rules and looking at unauthorized charts. "Well . . . ," she began, "in your consult note in Morrison's chart you mentioned a possible monoclonal gammopathy. Do you think that was caused by her having had anesthesia?"

"Absolutely not!" Dr. Erikson said with a dismissive chuckle, as if it were the most ridiculous idea she had heard in a long time. "There is no way anesthesia could cause a gammopathy. The patient had to have had the condition prior to her surgery. It just hadn't been recognized. With an asymptomatic gammopathy, the only way it can be discovered is by a serum electrophoresis, a test she never had had until I ordered one because of her unexplained fever."

"I see," Lynn said, trying to think up another question. "Are you doing a hematology consult on Carl Vandermeer?"

"Why do you ask?" Dr. Erikson said.

"Because you have his chart and you did a consult on Scarlett Morrison."

"The answer is no," Dr. Erikson said. "I am only seeing the patient as a courtesy since the nursing staff has told me the patient has had a temperature elevation, like Scarlett Morrison, with no apparent signs of infection."

"Do you think that her fever is due to her gammopathy?"

"Now, that is an excellent question," Dr. Erikson said.

Lynn breathed a sigh of relief. Now she knew she could break off the conversation without leaving behind an irritated attending who otherwise might be tempted to ask questions and blow their cover.

"An immune response can indeed cause a temperature elevation," Dr. Erikson said in a didactic monotone. "There is no way to know for sure, but since an infection has been ruled out, I think it is safe to say the elevated temperature is due to her gammopathy."

"Is something stimulating her immune system and keeping her temperature elevated?"

"I would have to assume there was. Perhaps it's the stress of what happened to her. But I really don't know."

"Is there any treatment for her gammopathy?"

"It is not necessary to treat it unless the elevated protein interrupts kidney function or if the gammopathy progresses to a blood cancer."

"You mean like multiple myeloma."

"Exactly. Multiple myeloma, lymphoma, or chronic lymphocytic leukemia."

"Since Vandermeer has an elevated temperature and no immediate signs of infection, do you think he has a gammopathy?"

Dr. Erikson didn't answer immediately, and Lynn feared the volatile woman was getting irritated all over again as her eyes had narrowed and her nostrils flared. Lynn berated herself for not leaving when she had the opportunity.

"Vandermeer's infectious disease workup has just begun," Dr. Erikson finally snapped. "We'll just have to see."

"Thank you for taking the time to talk with me," Lynn said, and quickly returned to her seat. As she put Carl's chart down on the desktop, she made eye contact with Michael, who was looking bored.

"Now, that was shooting some real shit," Michael said, keeping his voice low.

"I'm sorry," Lynn said with an equally low voice. "I couldn't get away."

"Yeah, sure."

"I'm serious. First she held on to the chart like she did with you and grilled me. She wanted to know what year we were. I thought for sure she was going to question our supposed anesthesia rotation. Luckily she didn't. One thing for sure, she's a bit weird."

"Really? Lay it on me!"

"It's hard to explain. For a moment it seemed to me she was acting pissed we were here, looking at these charts, which made me fear for the worst. But then her attitude changed. At least I think it changed. Actually my mind is not working at full power as tired as I am, so maybe I'm making all this up. But let me ask you: does she look healthy to you?"

"It didn't occur to me one way or the other," Michael said. He started to turn to look over at Dr. Erikson, who was only about a dozen feet away, but Lynn restrained him.

"Don't look!" Lynn ordered in a forced whisper. "Be cool! I'm telling you she's weird and could be trouble. Trust me! Let's not give her any more reason to question us. I really thought she was going to demand to know what we are doing here, looking at these charts. Luckily she didn't. And tell me this: did you notice her abdomen is distended, almost like she is pregnant?"

"Really?" Michael said, raising his eyebrows. He started to turn to look at the doctor again, but for the second time Lynn stopped him.

"I'm telling you, don't look!" Lynn snapped.

"I can't imagine she is pregnant," Michael said. "She's no spring chicken."

"I can't imagine she is, either," Lynn said. "Of course, with what's happening in IVF, it's not out of the question. My guess is that she has some kind of liver or kidney disease."

"I suppose it is possible," Michael said. He was growing bored with the whole situation. He was also starved.

"The strangest thing she said was that she wants to hear if you and I come to any conclusions to explain why Carl and Morrison didn't wake up from their anesthesia."

"I hope you didn't say that you think someone fucked up."

"I didn't."

"Thank the Lord."

"I said we didn't have any idea."

"That's God's truth. You're learning, girl."

"She made me promise that if we did come up with something, we'd let her know. She even gave me her card." Lynn showed the card to Michael, who merely shrugged. "You don't find all this a bit odd?" Lynn questioned. "Why would she be interested in what a couple of medical students might dream up? As an attending she could go to anybody in anesthesia, from the department head on down."

"Okay, it is strange," Michael admitted. "Are you happy now?"

Lynn closed her eyes for a moment, as if she needed to reboot. When she opened them again she said: "The last question I asked was if Carl might have a gammopathy like Morrison to explain his fever. Her response was to look mad."

"Now, that is odd. What did she say?"

"She said his infectious-disease workup had just begun, so we'd just have to wait and see. But she said it as if she was irritated I had asked."

"Okay, you've made your point. She's weird. Now, how about we make tracks for the cafeteria."

"Let me look at Carl's chart quickly." Lynn opened the chart to the progress note section. There was nothing from Erikson, although when she turned to the orders page, there was a request for a serum electrophoresis, on Dr. Erikson's order. Lynn looked off into the distance, as if thinking.

"Okay, are we finished?" Michael asked. "Come on! Let's get out of here."

"Just let me look at Carl's blood work," Lynn said, turning back to the lab section. "Okay," she said after a moment. "His white count is eleven thousand. Some people may not consider that elevated, but I think it is. The key fact is that his lymphocytes are also elevated, at almost five thousand, which argues against an infection."

"That's great. Now can we go to breakfast?"

"All right, but let me return this chart."

"Don't get in another conversation," Michael cautioned.

"Not on your life. I'm going to give the chart to Peter."

Their departure was just in time. As they were leaving the central circular desk, all the nurses had finished their rounds and were filing in. Gwen Murphy, the head nurse, eyed the students but didn't say anything, although she paused for a second to stare. Very little that happened in the neuro ICU went unnoticed during her shift.

Just before Lynn went through the heavy double doors leading out into the sixth-floor hallway, she stopped and hazarded another glance over at Carl. A nurse was at his side, adjusting something. Carl appeared as peaceful as he had earlier. The only discernible movement was from the flexing and extension of his operated leg.

Lynn shuddered. She knew all too well that his tranquillity was in sharp contrast to the mayhem that had occurred in his brain. The MRI and the CT scan had confirmed her worst fears, and the stark reality of his status gave her a new surge of energy and purpose. At the moment she didn't care that part of her motivation might have stemmed from guilt of possibly equating his bleak future with academic freedom for her. Her intuition, which had always served her well in the past, was sending alarms that something was amiss in this whole affair. She sensed that the hospital was going to be content to let the issue die a natural death, but she was not going to allow it. She would find out what had happened. She owed as much to Carl and future patients.

"Come on!" Michael urged. "Now I'm in as much need of calories as you, and the dermatology lecture isn't going to wait for us."

"I'm coming," Lynn said.

As they started down the hallway, the hospital PA system crackled to life, and like everyone else in the hospital, they stopped to listen. In the old days hospital PA systems provided a constant background of doctors being paged, but that was no longer the case, with smartphones and computer tablets. The Mason-Dixon Medical Center had a hospital-wide PA system, but it was only for disasters. So when the system came on, everyone in the hospital, even in the operating rooms, stopped to listen.

> *"All available medical personnel! There has been a serious head-on collision on the interstate near our campus involving a bus and a tractor-trailer. As the closest medical center, we will shortly be receiving the most seriously injured. Anyone who can, please proceed immediately to the ER! Operating room personnel, free up as many operating rooms as possible. Thank you!"*

Lynn and Michael exchanged a hurried glance. "What do you think?" Michael asked. "Does that include us medical students?"

"We're almost doctors," Lynn shot back. "Let's go!"

They ran down the hallway, effectively dodging nurses, orderlies, ambulatory patients, and food carts to the elevators, but instead of waiting for one, they ducked into the stairwell. As they thundered down the metal steps, they found themselves in a swelling bevy of stampeding doctors and nurses, with more joining at each floor.

18.

The ER was a madhouse. A continuous stream of injured patients was being frantically wheeled in and distributed to various exam rooms. The trauma rooms had already been filled. Several of the senior ER physicians were doing quick triage out on the receiving dock, as patients were unloaded from ambulances. The more seriously injured were immediately handed off to waiting groups of doctors and nurses who started assessment and treatment even before the gurney got into an exam room. Those patients with relatively minor injuries were rolled off to the side to wait their turn.

Neither Lynn nor Michael had much experience with emergency medicine other than a brief didactic exposure in lectures and a short tour of the department during third-year surgery, and they didn't know any of the emergency room personnel. Although the house officers they arrived with had a general idea of what to do, Lynn and Michael had no clue. Lacking any specific destination, they ran up to the front desk. At first no one paid them any attention. What they didn't realize was with white coats over scrubs, the nursing staff took them for residents, not medical students.

"Can we help?" Lynn asked one of the harried nurses who seemed in charge, as she was directing traffic more than anyone else, hollering orders to various people. She was standing just behind the chest-high counter of the ER check-in desk along with a roiling crowd of almost twenty people. Everyone was busy with phones and paperwork, some abruptly racing off to one of the rooms while others arrived. Over the babel of voices the sounds of sirens could be heard, as more ambulances pulled up outside.

At first the nurse whom Lynn had addressed just looked at her but didn't respond. Her eyes were distantly focused, suggesting her mind was processing too many things at once. As Lynn repeated her question, the woman recovered from her mini-trance. She reached out and snapped up a clipboard from a pile in front of her. She handed it to Lynn, saying, "Take care of this case! Exam room twenty-two. Male with a mild breathing difficulty. Blunt-force chest trauma."

Before Lynn could respond, the charge nurse yelled to a colleague across the room to bring down several more portable X-ray machines from X-ray and to get them into the trauma rooms. Then she turned to another nurse behind her and told her to check on what was happening in Trauma Room 1 to see if the patient was ready to be sent up to surgery.

Lynn read the patient's name: Clark Weston. It was scrawled in longhand on the ER admission form, along with a chief complaint: breathing difficulty, blunt trauma. Lynn noticed the blood pressure was normal although the heart rate was a bit high, at 100 beats a minute. A scribbled note said: *mild dyspnea but good color. Sternal contusion but no point tenderness over individual ribs. No lacerations. Extremities normal. No broken bones.* That was it. There was nothing else. After a quick glance to see if she could again get the head nurse's attention—which she decided was unlikely, as she had momentarily disappeared—Lynn looked at Michael, who she knew had read what was on the clipboard over her shoulder. "What do you think?" she asked. "Can we handle it?"

"Let's do it," Michael said. Both realized that the head nurse had no idea they were medical students. Both were wearing lanyards with their ID cards around their necks, but one had to look at them closely to see that there was no *MD* after their names.

Despite the chaos and no one to ask for directions, they found Exam Room 22 without much difficulty. The door was closed. Lynn went in first, and Michael followed right behind her, pulling the door closed behind him. The room was an island of tranquillity in the middle of a storm.

Alone in the room, Clark Weston was supine on a gurney but propped up on both elbows, struggling to breathe with shallow, rapid respirations. He was a middle-aged blond man, mildly overweight, and fully dressed in a suit jacket, white shirt, tie, and dark slacks. The tie was loosened. The shirt was open and pushed to the side, revealing a pale, expanded chest with obvious central bruising. Both medical students immediately noticed the man's color was not good, contrary to what was noted on the admission form. His skin had a bluish cast, as did his lips. His expression was one of desperation. Concentrating on trying to breathe, he couldn't talk. It was obvious he thought he was about to die.

Lynn ran to one side of the gurney while Michael went to the other. Both felt an instantaneous rush of terror with that sudden realization that this was no mere difficulty breathing, and as neophytes, they were in totally over their heads, facing a patient in extremis.

"I hope you have some idea of what to do," Michael croaked.

"I was counting on you," Lynn said.

The patient, hearing this exchange, rolled his eyes before closing them to concentrate on trying to breathe.

"I better get a resident," Michael blurted, and before Lynn could respond, he bolted from the room, leaving the door ajar.

Left on her own, Lynn dashed over to an oxygen source, turned on the cylinder, and then rushed back to put a nasal cannula around the patient's head. Placing the bell of her stethoscope on the right side of his chest, she listened. The man was breathing so shallowly and rapidly, she could barely hear any sounds. The competing noise from the ruckus coming in through the open door didn't help.

At that point Lynn realized how overly expanded the man's chest was. It was as if he was blown up like a balloon. What did that mean? She tried to think and access her memory banks about what she had been taught in physical diagnosis, but her exhaustion combined with the terror engendered by her feelings of incompetence made it difficult. She vaguely remembered that an expanded chest meant something important, but what? She didn't know.

Moving the bell of the stethoscope to the left side of the man's chest, Lynn was surprised to hear almost nothing. At first she thought it was her problem, meaning she was doing something wrong, but then she compared the two sides. It was apparent that she could hear breathing sounds on the right, even if they were bearly discernible, and nothing, or close to nothing, on the left. Suddenly an idea of what was going on began to form in her mind. Taking the stethoscope out of her ears, she tried percussion: placing her left middle finger on the patient's chest and taping it with the middle finger of her right hand. The resultant sounds between one side and the other were different. The left side was hyper-tympanic, like a drum, compared with what she heard on the right side.

Michael flew back into the room, panting from exertion. "I couldn't find anyone free. The only person I found was an ER doc two doors down struggling with a dislocated shoulder. He promised he'd be here as soon as he got the arm back in the joint. How is the patient doing?"

"He's getting oxygen, which should help some," Lynn shot back. "But he is in trouble. But I think I know what is going on."

"Clue me in!" Michael demanded.

"Listen to his chest! See what you think. But do it quickly."

Michael struggled to get his stethoscope in his ears. While he listened first to the left side, then to the right, and then back to the left, he kept his eyes on Lynn, who was taking the man's pulse. "There's no breath sounds in the left side," Michael said.

"Try percussion!" Lynn said. "But do it fast. His heart rate is up to one hundred twenty. That can't be good." Lynn could feel her own pulse in her temples beating almost as rapidly.

Michael quickly did as Lynn suggested. The hyper-resonance on the left was immediately apparent, and he said as much.

"Does that ring any bells to you?" Lynn said. "Especially since he has dilated neck veins." She pointed.

"Tension pneumothorax!" Michael blurted.

"My thoughts exactly," Lynn cried. "If so, it is a real emergency. His left lung must be collapsed, and with every breath, the right is being compressed. He needs an X-ray, but there's no time."

"He needs a needle thoracotomy on the left!" Michael shouted. "And he needs it now!"

In a panic, the two students regarded each other across the body of the patient. For a second they hesitated, even though they were frantic. Neither had ever seen a needle thoracotomy performed, much less done one. They'd read about it, but to go from book learning to actual performance was a giant step.

"How soon do you think the ER doctor might get in here?" Lynn demanded anxiously.

"I don't know," Michael said. Perspiration appeared on his forehead.

"Mr. Weston," Lynn yelled as she gave the man's shoulder a shake. The patient didn't respond. Instead he collapsed supine onto the gurney, no longer supporting himself on his elbows. "Mr. Weston," she called louder, with a more significant shake to his shoulder. Nothing. The patient was no longer responding.

"We can't wait," Lynn said.

"I agree," Michael replied. The two of them rushed over to a crash cart that had all sorts of emergency equipment. They grabbed a large syringe, a sixteen-gauge intravenous cannula, and a handful of antiseptic pledgets. Then they rushed back to the patient.

"My memory is that it is supposed to be done in the second intercostal space between the second and third rib."

"You do it!" Lynn yelled, thrusting the cannula into Michael's hands. "How the hell do you remember such details?"

"I don't know," Michael retorted as he quickly snapped on a pair of sterile gloves. He then tore open the sterile wrapping on the cannula. It had a needle stylus to facilitate insertion.

"What if it is hemothorax and there is blood in there instead of air?" Lynn questioned anxiously. "Would we be making it worse?"

"I don't know," Michael admitted. "We're in uncharted territory here. But we got to do something or he's going to check out."

Lynn tore open several alcohol pledgets and rapidly swabbed a wide area below the patient's left collarbone. Michael positioned the tip of the cannula with its needle stylus over what he thought was the correct position. He'd located it by palpating the area and feeling the bony landmarks. Still he hesitated. It was a daunting task to blindly plunge a needle into someone's chest, especially the left side, where the heart was.

"Do it!" Lynn snapped. She knew that she and Michael were an example of the blind leading the blind, but the needle thoracotomy had to be done, and it had to be done immediately. The patient's color had deteriorated despite the oxygen.

Gritting his teeth, Michael pushed the catheter through the skin and advanced it until he felt the needle tip hit the rib. He then angled it upward slightly, and pushed again. He could actually feel a pop after advancing the needle another centimeter or so.

"I think I'm in," Michael said.

"Great," Lynn said. "Take out the stylus!"

Michael pulled out the stylus. Nothing!

"I guess I have to advance it a bit more," Michael said. "I must not be in the pleural space yet."

"That, or we have made the wrong diagnosis," Lynn said.

"Now, that's a happy thought," Michael added sarcastically. He reinserted the stylus and then pushed deeper into the patient's chest. He felt a second pop. This time when he removed the needle, both he and Lynn could hear a rush of air come out through the needle like a balloon being deflated.

Lynn and Michael's eyes met. Both allowed a tentative smile. Over the next few minutes their smiles broadened as the patient's breathing and heart rate improved, as did his color. He also slowly returned to consciousness. Lynn and Michael had to hold his hands to keep him from reaching up and touching the cannula sticking out of his chest while they waited.

"Maybe we should do a residency as a single person," Michael said. "I think we make a good team."

Lynn smiled weakly. "Maybe so," she agreed, pushing away the thought that she wished she were heading up to Boston with Michael.

Just then a blood-spattered ER doctor by the name of Hank Cotter and a nurse rushed in. They went directly to the patient, crowding Lynn and Michael to the side. While the nurse took Clark's blood pressure, Hank listened to the man's chest. He saw the needle thoracotomy.

"Did you guys do this?" he questioned.

"We did," both Lynn and Michael said in unison.

"Collectively we decided it was a tension pneumothorax," Lynn explained.

"We thought we had to do something, as the patient was going downhill fast," Michael added. "We didn't think it could wait."

"And you guys are medical students?" Hank asked. "I'm impressed. Have either of you rotated through the ER?"

Both Lynn and Michael shook their heads.

"I'm even more impressed," Hank said. "Good pickup." Then, turning to a nurse who had just entered, he said: "Let's get a portable chest film stat and bring in a pack for inserting a chest tube."

Hank turned back to Lynn and Michael. "Now, I'm going to have you guys insert a chest tube. Are you up for it?"

BOOK 2

BOOK-2

19.

Lynn had been the one to insert the chest tube using local anesthetic. Michael had watched. It was far easier than when they had inserted the needle thoracotomy, because Hank, a third-year emergency medicine resident, had been the instructor and stayed with them through the procedure. It went without a hitch and both Lynn and Michael felt reasonably confident they were much better equipped to handle the emergency care of chest trauma cases in the future.

After Clark Weston had been stabilized, Lynn and Michael went back out into the ER proper to see if they could lend a hand with any other patients. To their surprise, what they found was that the emergency situation was essentially over. While they had been seeing to Clark Weston's needs, the rest of the patients from the accident had been taken to the MUSC Medical Center while the ones that had arrived at Mason-Dixon had all been seen and were in the process of being treated.

While they were still at the ER desk, checking if there was anything else they could do to help, Lynn caught sight of Dr. Sandra

Wykoff, who had also responded to the call to come to the ER. Impulsively running over, Lynn caught up with the woman as she was about to leave. Controlling her emotions, Lynn quickly reintroduced herself and again asked about getting together. Graciously the doctor agreed but said, "It has to be now since I'm about to begin a case. Will that work for you?"

"Absolutely," Lynn said.

"Then come up to the anesthesia office on the second floor, next to surgical pathology. I'll meet you there but don't dawdle."

"I'll come right away," Lynn assured her.

Rejoining Michael, Lynn snapped under her breath: "See the woman I was just talking with? That's Wykoff, the anesthesiologist who screwed up with Carl." She motioned with her head in the woman's direction.

Michael watched Wykoff disappear before turning to Lynn. "Come on, sis, we've been over this. Be cool! For the tenth time, you don't know there was any screwup."

Lynn gave a short, mirthless laugh. "We'll see," she said. "The important thing is that she's willing to see me now. Are you interested?"

"Since we missed the derm lecture, I guess I don't have any excuse, and somebody has to keep you in line. But we're going to go via the cafeteria so you and I get a few calories. I'm about out of gas and you've been on empty for hours."

"All right, but it's got to be takeout and fast," Lynn said. "There is a narrow window of opportunity. She's about to start a case. She even warned me 'not to dawdle.' Can you believe it? I don't think I have ever heard anybody use the word *dawdle*."

"You are certainly looking for ways to fault her," Michael said. "*Dawdle* is a perfectly fine word. You catch my meaning, right?"

"I suppose," Lynn agreed reluctantly.

Lynn was willing to take the risk of going via the cafeteria because she knew what food meant to Michael. She teased him on occasion that he was a growing boy. Taking the time now to get him

some food was a way of showing her appreciation that he was willing to come with her to talk to Wykoff. As a realist, she knew she
probably needed some protection from herself, and he was the one
to provide it. She couldn't help but feel anger toward the woman
and knew that expressing it would certainly be counterproductive.

The visit to the cafeteria was appropriately short. They grabbed
a couple of bread rolls and some fruit at the register to eat on the
run. As far as Lynn was concerned, there was another reason it was
good that they did not stay. In her fragile emotional state, she didn't
want to take the chance of running into anyone who might ask about
Carl's surgery.

Five minutes later when they arrived outside the anesthesia office door, Michael pulled Lynn aside. "Wait a second," he said. "We
have to think what to say if Wykoff asks why we are interested in
Carl's case and how it was we read her note. She's bound to ask us,
and we can't use the anesthesia story."

"Obviously," Lynn said. Because of the detour to the cafeteria,
even though it was short, she was particularly impatient to get inside the office. She was afraid of Wykoff being called out at any
moment and cutting the meeting short.

"The only thing that comes to mind," Michael continued, "is to say
we are on a neurology rotation, which I suppose is a laugh. It means
we use anesthesia for neurology and neurology for anesthesia."

"I don't know," Lynn said hesitantly. She didn't like the idea and
struggled to find another. "I agree she might ask, just like she might
be touchy about Carl's disaster. The problem is that it's too easy for
an attending like Wykoff to find out we're lying. All it would take is
one phone call, and we'd be in deep shit, and all doors for finding
out about Carl would slam shut. No, we have to come up with
something else so we're not lying. Why don't we say we are researching hospital-acquired morbidity? At least it's true."

"I'm not sure saying we're studying hospital-acquired morbidity
would be much better," Michael said. "With the administration, the

idea of its own medical students researching something like that will go over like one of Ronald's bad jokes."

"Well, I can't think of anything else," Lynn said. "I think we're stuck with the morbidity angle. That is, if she brings it up. Maybe she won't. Come on! We have to get in there!"

"All right," Michael said, throwing up his hands. "You're the boss."

"Hardly," Lynn said. Facing the door, she hesitated. Not knowing if they should just go in or not, Lynn knocked, thinking it best to err on the conservative side. The sign on the door just said ANESTHESIA. A voice from inside called for them to come in.

It was a relatively small office without windows. There was no secretary. The space had four modern desks supporting computer terminals to be shared by all the anesthesiologists to handle their paperwork. A large bookshelf ran along the right wall and was filled with anesthesia texts and journals. Dr. Sandra Wykoff was sitting alone at one of the desks. As the students approached, she motioned for them to bring over a couple of the other chairs.

"So . . . ," Dr. Wykoff said once they were seated, "who, may I ask, are you?" She was looking directly at Michael, and unlike many of the other attendings, she maintained eye contact.

"Another fourth-year medical student," Michael said. He was impressed that she continued to stare at him.

"And you are researching the Vandermeer case along with Miss Peirce?" Dr. Wykoff's tone was surprisingly matter-of-fact, neither friendly nor unfriendly.

"Yes," Michael said. He didn't elaborate. He wanted this to be Lynn's ball game. All he was there for was hopefully to keep Lynn out of trouble.

"Why are you two interested in this case in particular?"

Michael noticed that the woman's gaze had now appropriately shifted to Lynn.

The students exchanged a quick, nervous glance. It was Lynn who spoke up: "We have become aware of the huge problem about hospital-acquired morbidity. We think this case fits that category all too well."

Dr. Wykoff nodded and paused, as if thinking. Then she said, "Have you read my note in the Vandermeer chart?"

Both Lynn and Michael nodded, afraid of what was coming, namely a question as to why they were looking at the chart and under whose authority. But to their relief it didn't happen. Instead the doctor asked, "What is it about this case that you want to discuss?"

"What the hell happened?" Lynn blurted out, causing Michael to wince inwardly. "I mean, how could a healthy twenty-nine-year-old man having routine elective knee surgery end up suffering brain death?"

"If you read my note, then you already know that nothing out of the ordinary occurred," Dr. Wykoff said, seemingly not taking offense. Michael was both surprised and relieved. "The case was entirely normal. I thoroughly checked the anesthesia machine before the case and after. It functioned perfectly in all regards. The sources for all the gases and the gases themselves have all been checked and rechecked. All the drugs and dosages have been checked. I have gone over the case with a fine-tooth comb. So have several other anesthesiologists. Nothing happened that would have contributed to the unfortunate outcome. It had to have been some sort of idiosyncratic reaction."

"There had to have been a screwup," Lynn snapped.

Lynn's tone and words made Michael now visibly wince. Before the doctor had a chance to respond, he said, "We did see in your note and in the anesthesia record that the blood-oxygen saturation suddenly went down." He deliberately spoke in a measured tone as a counterpoint to Lynn's outburst. "Do you or anyone else have idea of what made that happen?"

"The oxygen level did go down," Dr. Wykoff said. "But it only dropped to ninety-two percent, which isn't that low, and, just as important, it immediately began to rise. Within minutes it was back to near one hundred percent. But to answer your question, I have no idea why it went down. The inspired oxygen concentration and the patient's tidal volume had not changed."

Lynn started to speak again but Michael gripped her arm to keep her quiet, saying, "We imagine it must have been a very disturbing case for you."

"You have no idea!" Dr. Wykoff said, and paused before adding, "I had never had a serious complication before this case. It is my first."

"In retrospect, would you have done anything differently?" Michael asked, wanting to keep the conversation going but without being accusatory.

Dr. Wykoff took another moment to continue. "I asked myself the same question. But, no, I wouldn't have done anything differently. I handled the case the same way that I have handled thousands of others. There were no screwups! I can assure you of that."

"There had to have been something," Lynn interjected, despite Michael still gripping her arm. Although her voice wasn't quite as strident, it was still harsher than Michael thought appropriate. "There had to have been something out of the ordinary that you did even if you didn't think it could have made any difference."

Dr. Wykoff silently stared at Lynn long enough to make Michael think Lynn had finally done it. He girded himself for an outburst from the doctor, but it didn't happen. Instead, to his surprise and relief, Dr. Wykoff said, "There was something, but it was very minor and can't have been significant. It is not something I did, but something I noticed. It did bother me when it happened."

"Like what?" Lynn demanded, again with a bit too much emotion.

Michael desperately tried to think of something to say to cover up Lynn's insensitivity, believing her carping tone was asking for trouble, not only for her but for him, too. The reality was that they had already seriously violated HIPAA by looking at Carl's and Scarlett's charts and photographing the anesthesia records, and here Lynn was doing her best to alienate a woman who was being unexpectedly cooperative with a couple of medical students even though struggling emotionally herself. Michael sensed that the woman was deeply troubled by what had happened, which along the lines of "misery loves company" was probably the reason she was willing to talk with them at all.

"It involved the technical equipment," Dr. Wykoff said. She spoke calmly, to Michael's relief, and then paused to stare off into the middle distance.

"You mean with the anesthesia machine?" Michael said. He tightened his grip on Lynn's arm to keep her quiet. From the sounds of her breathing he sensed she was about to say something.

"Not the machine per se," Dr. Wykoff said. "But with the monitor. I happened to see it only because I was concentrating on looking at the monitor at the moment it occurred. It was when the surgeon began drilling into the tibia. I wanted to make sure that the depth of analgesia was adequate. Since the periosteum has a lot of pain fibers, I was watching the vitals closely."

"And what happened?" Michael asked.

"Let me show you," Dr. Wykoff said. "It is actually part of the anesthesia record." Dr. Wykoff directed her attention to the screen of the computer terminal and began punching in commands.

While she was busy, Michael gave Lynn's arm an extra squeeze to get her attention. "Cool it, girl!" he mouthed along with a harsh expression when she looked at him. He was serious. Lynn responded by trying to get her arm back, but Michael would not let go. Under his breath he said, "Let me do the talking! You're going to get us thrown in jail if you keep up! Seriously!"

"All right, here it is," Dr. Wykoff said, interrupting. The doctor angled the monitor's screen more toward the students. It was the image of the anesthesia machine–generated record in graphic form of what had been on the monitor during the case, including blood pressure, pulse, ECG, blood oxygenation, end tidal CO_2, expired tidal volume, and body temperature. Michael and Lynn stood up to get a better view, even though it was what they had already seen in Carl's chart.

"Look closely," Dr. Wykoff said. She enlarged the image and used a pen as a pointer. "Here is when the oxygenation fell from close to one hundred percent down to ninety-two. It's at eight-thirty-nine, or sixty-one minutes into the operation. That was when the alarm sounded. And you can see the ECG simultaneously shows tenting of the T waves, suggesting the heart isn't getting adequate oxygen. Now, that doesn't make sense. An oxygenation saturation of ninety-two percent shouldn't cause the immediate appearance of T waves in a normal, healthy heart. Also there's no change in any of the other parameters, which would certainly happen if there was low enough oxygen to cause brain damage."

"We saw that when we looked at the chart," Michael said.

"It's hard not to see it," Dr. Wykoff said. "It jumps out at you, since the oxygenation tracing was essentially a straight-line until that instant. But the fall is not what I want to show you." She used the cursor to move back along the oxygenation tracing to fifty-two minutes into the operation, where there was a slight vertical blip upward. "Do you see this?"

"I do," Michael said. "It is a sudden notch upward, whereas the O_2 tracing otherwise is like a flat, smooth sine wave, varying between ninety-seven and one hundred percent. What does it mean?"

"Probably nothing," Dr. Wykoff admitted. "But notice the notch upward occurred with all the tracings on the monitor: blood pressure, oxygen saturation, everything. It scared me when it happened because I was actually closely watching the pulse rate. If a patient feels any pain when the surgeon drills into the periosteum, the pulse rate goes up, meaning the anesthesia is light. Well, the pulse rate didn't go up. Instead, while I was watching, the whole monitor blinked at the precise moment the slight vertical jump appeared."

"Blinked?" Michael repeated. "Does that happen often?"

"Not in my experience," Dr. Wykoff said. "But then again we anesthesiologists don't spend a lot of time staring at the monitor. None of us does unless there is a specific reason. When it happened, it scared me, which is why I remember it."

"Why did it scare you?" Michael asked. It seemed inconsequential to him.

"What scared me was the worry of losing the feed from all my sensors, meaning I would be without electronic monitoring. I was relieved when it didn't blink again."

"You had never seen anything like that before?" Michael asked. He bent close to look at the image as the anesthesiologist magnified the section. To him it still looked trivial.

"No, I haven't," Dr. Wykoff said. "But that doesn't mean it doesn't happen. Maybe it happens often. I don't know. It is such a small change. Electronics are not my thing. But it can't have any significance since all the vital signs, as you can plainly see, stayed completely normal right up to the moment the oxygenation alarm sounded. As I said, the reason I remember it is that we anesthesiologists are accustomed to continuous electronic monitoring. Giving anesthesia without it would be like flying an airplane blind."

"Do you see it?" Michael asked Lynn.

"Of course I see it," Lynn snapped.

Michael rolled his eyes and again tightened the grip he had on Lynn's arm as he made her step back from the monitor. He regretted trying to bring her back into the conversation for fear she would ruin the rapport that had been established with Dr. Wykoff and maybe get them in trouble after all. He knew it was time to leave. "We want to thank you, Dr. Wykoff, for—" He didn't get to finish. The door to the corridor burst open, and a man charged into the room.

Yanking off a surgical face mask, the newcomer headed for a computer terminal, but, catching sight of the others, he stopped short. It was apparent he had assumed the room to be empty. He was a powerful-looking, golf-tanned Caucasian man dressed in scrubs. Adding to his physical stature were big hands and muscular forearms. At first his expression was one of perplexity, but it quickly changed to aggravation. He looked back and forth between Michael and Lynn. Both knew who he was from their third-year surgery rotation. He was Dr. Benton Rhodes, the volatile, New Zealand–born chief of anesthesia who was renowned for having little love for medical students.

"We were just leaving," Michael said quickly. He turned back to Dr. Wykoff. "Thanks for your time and willingness to talk to us about such a disturbing case. We appreciate it."

"What case?" Dr. Rhodes demanded with his Anzac accent.

"Carl Vandermeer," Lynn said defiantly.

"Vandermeer?" Dr. Rhodes repeated as if shocked. "Who are you two?"

"We're fourth-year medical students," Michael said quickly, urging Lynn toward the door. She resisted, fanning his fear that this unexpected encounter might not end well.

"What are your names?" Dr. Rhodes demanded.

"I'm Lynn Peirce and this is Michael Pender."

Dr. Benton turned to Dr. Wykoff and shouted angrily in apparent disbelief: "You were discussing the Vandermeer case with these medical students? I don't understand. Yesterday afternoon we were warned by the hospital counsel not to discuss the case with anyone."

"They are interested in hospital-acquired morbidity," Dr. Wykoff explained. "It is an important and legitimate issue, and they are our medical students."

"I couldn't care less who they are," Dr. Rhodes continued to shout. "The case is not to be discussed with anyone, period!" Then, turning to the students, he snapped, "And I want you two out of here. But be warned! I am going to be giving your names to the hospital counsel. The order not to discuss the case with anyone now includes you. Don't talk about it with anyone: friends, family, fellow students, whatever. Doing so will jeopardize your status as medical students. Do you understand? It is hugely important that I am very clear about this."

"We understand," Michael said, dragging Lynn toward the door. He wanted to get her out of the room before she said anything else.

20.

As the door to the anesthesia office closed behind them, Michael and Lynn heard Dr. Rhodes's tirade continue. The man was clearly beside himself with rage at Wykoff.

"Talk about burning bridges and making enemies," Michael said as they headed down the central corridor. "That turned out to be a big-time fuckup."

"It wasn't our fault," Lynn said, keeping her voice down as they passed people. "It was just bad luck that Rhodes showed up. Everything had been going fine until then."

"One way or another, we're not going to be able to go back to Dr. Wykoff. Of course it might have happened anyway, considering the way you were talking to her."

"What is that supposed to mean?" Lynn said, taking offense.

"You were accusing her of screwing up, just like I told you not to do. That ain't the way to keep your options open, girl. Take it from me. The reason that I never got shot or that I'm not in prison is that I learned early not to piss people off. The way you were acting, I'm surprised we got as much out of Dr. Wykoff as we did."

"I'm the one who is pissed. I didn't feel like giving her any slack."

"And you certainly didn't."

"I still think she is hiding something. She has to have done something wrong. I'm sorry, but that's the way I see it."

"Well, I don't," Michael said. "My take is that she is hurting over the case and has no idea what happened. She wouldn't have gone on about that blip. Electronic equipment has little burps like that, particularly video and sensory feed. It's called a frame offset. My take is that she's almost as desperate as you are to find out what the hell happened."

"We are going to have to agree to disagree," Lynn said. "And I'm bummed out we weren't able to bring up either of the other cases, as similar as they seem to be. I also wanted to ask her what she thought of the idea of an anesthetic causing the protein abnormality Morrison has. And the fever she and Carl have. Hell, I've got a lot of questions that need answering. I think we should try to meet with the other anesthesiologists. Do you remember who did Ashanti's case?"

Michael hated and pulled Lynn to a stop in the process. They were just abreast of the Surgical Pathology Department. He looked at her with disbelief. "You're joking, of course. Tell me you're joking!"

"No, I'm not joking. I think we should talk with the other anesthesiologists. Maybe they all made the same mistake. It could be the only way to find out. I'm not convinced they talk to each other when something like this happens. In that sense you are right: they are all defensive."

"First of all, I don't remember who the anesthesiologist was for Ashanti. But if I did, I wouldn't tell you. You heard how pissed Dr. Rhodes was that we were discussing Carl with Wykoff. If he finds out you're even thinking about talking with the other anesthesiologists, he'll go berserk. He could get our asses kicked out of school. Wouldn't that be nice now that we are within sight of graduating?

I'm sure that a big reason he was so pissed is because Carl represents the third case."

"Are you finished?"

"Yes, I'm finished. Let's get changed and get out of here."

They started walking again.

"I think we were lucky to get away pretty much unscathed," Michael said.

"That's not a given," Lynn said. "What do you think the chances are that either Wykoff or Rhodes might say something to the nurses in the neuro ICU? It might occur to them to ask how it was we were able to look at Carl's chart. If they do, it would be bad. We wouldn't be able to go back, and I wouldn't be able to follow Carl much less find out how this happened."

"I think it's hard to say what they might do. If they think about informing the nurses, they might. I believe it will come down to that, but in our favor, they have a lot on their minds. I'm sure they are running scared about a possibility of a serious lawsuit."

"I don't think Carl's parents will sue," Lynn said.

"I don't think you can say that. With the dad being a lawyer—a litigator, no less—I personally think the chances are good. One of the malpractice guys will talk them into doing it supposedly as a way of keeping other people from falling victim to the same fate. I'm sure fear of a big lawsuit is why the hospital counsel is so concerned."

They reached the main elevators and paused before going into the surgical lounge. Michael checked his watch. "We're going to have to make tracks to get to the derm clinic. They are not going to be happy we missed the lecture. Thank God we can use the ER as an excuse. Listen, I'll meet you out here after we change back into our street clothes."

"I'm not going to any clinic," Lynn said. "Particularly a derm clinic. In my state of mind there's no way I could concentrate on looking at pimples and rashes."

"What are you going to do? You're not thinking of going back to talk to any anesthesiologists, are you?"

"No! I've got to make myself sleep, at least a few hours. I know I'm not thinking right, and I have a shitload of studying I want to get done. I need to learn more about those monoclonal gammopathies and multiple myeloma."

"Suit yourself, but I'm going to the clinic. I don't want to risk pissing off the admin at this point so close to graduation, especially with Rhodes possibly on our case."

"Be real! You really think they might deny graduation from missing a few crummy specialty lectures and clinics?"

"Who knows? What I do know is that it ain't worth the risk. If there is a sign-in for attendance, I'll add your name."

"Thanks, bro. One other thing! Can I look at that photo of Ashanti's anesthesia record on your desktop computer?"

Michael eyed Lynn and hesitated, as if debating. "I'd have to give you my room key. You might copy it and come in and molest me."

"As tempting as that may be, I'll give you my word to hold myself back. And I promise not to disturb your stash of smack."

"You better not! All right, then, I'll meet you out here at the elevators in five."

While Michael was changing back into his street clothes, he found himself wondering what would have happened had he not accompanied Lynn to meet Wykoff. As bad as it had turned out, he was certain it would have been much worse if she had been on her own. As he saw it, no matter what he had said, she needed close monitoring, as she'd copped an attitude Michael was certain was destined to get her in real trouble and possibly him, too. Yet he could understand and sympathize. If what happened to Carl had happened to his girlfriend, Kianna Young, he'd be a basket case, too.

When Michael got back out to the elevator lobby, he was moderately surprised that Lynn was already there. He thought he had changed quickly and had expected to have to wait. He handed her his room key and said: "Would you mind making the bed and cleaning the bathroom while you are in there?"

"Fat chance, you male chauvinist," Lynn said as she snatched the key. "I'm going to e-mail the photo of Ashanti's record to myself and that's it. Another request! Would you e-mail me the photos you took of Carl's and Morrison's records? Then I'll have all three. By comparing them, maybe I'll be able to find something unexpected."

"I think the first thing you need to do is get some sleep."

"Thank you, Doctor. Meanwhile do the e-mails."

"Yes, ma'am," Michael said, saluting.

21.

Benton Rhodes slammed the door to his private office with such force that some of his framed diplomas on the walls tilted, requiring him to walk around and straighten them. He imagined that the concussive sound had probably jolted the Anesthesia Department secretary sitting at her desk just outside. She had been listening to dictation and typing on her monitor when he had walked by, and hadn't seen him. Yet if he'd startled her, he didn't feel the slightest bit guilty. When he was enraged, he often took it out on anybody and anything. The idea that he'd scared the secretary actually calmed him to a degree.

He was still dressed in scrubs, even though he had left the OR and descended to the admin area, where most of the department heads had their formal offices. But before he had left the floor, he'd ducked into the locker room to get his phone. Sitting down at his desk, he pulled it out of his pocket and went into his contacts. Then he paused. He didn't know whom to call first about this latest stupid screwup.

For the life of him, Benton couldn't understand how people

could be so smart in some things and so stupid in others, which was why he had yelled at Sandra Wykoff. As dedicated an anesthesiologist as she was, he couldn't comprehend how she could have misinterpreted the instructions from Bob Hartley, the hospital counsel, about not discussing the Vandermeer case with anyone. The lawyer couldn't have been any clearer. Not discussing it with anyone meant no one, period. Especially not a couple of medical students rummaging around for a cause to make a name for themselves. "Hospital-acquired morbidity," my ass, he thought glumly. The next thing they might do is put on Twitter or Facebook what they believed to be sage observations about the case. God, it would be a disaster!

Drumming his fingers on his desk, Benton thought that running the Mason-Dixon Medical Center's Anesthesia Department was turning out to be more of a bother than he had bargained for. When he'd been recruited five years previously at the age of sixty-four, he had been in charge of the anesthesia department of a much larger, Ivy League center that did twice the surgical volume and had an anesthesiology residency program to boot. Yet it had somehow seemed easier in New England and without the anxiety he was dealing with here in Charleston. It was the South, for God's sake, where he'd heard people were supposed to laze around and sip mint juleps. His goal had been a semi-retirement to enjoy life. Unfortunately it was not working out that way.

Making a decision, Benton pulled up Robert Hartley's office number on his mobile but didn't use it to make the call. Instead he dialed the number on his hospital landline, knowing he'd get better service from the law firm's office help. The Mason-Dixon Medical Center was an important client.

As the call went through, Benton calmed down further. There had been some problems running the Anesthesia Department before, maybe not as big as the current fiasco, but problems nonetheless. Yet the perks he'd received from taking the job had been sweet, particularly the stock options. Their value had escalated, especially now that there was talk of a takeover of Middleton Health-care by Sidereal Pharmaceuticals, owned by the billionaire Russian expatiate Boris Rusnak. If that happened, Benton could really retire in style.

As he expected, he was put through to Bob Hartley directly, and the lawyer picked up the phone almost before it had a chance to ring.

"What can I do for you, Benton?" Bob said. His voice was deep and reassuring. Over the years they had gotten to know each other well enough to be on a first-name basis.

"I'm afraid there's been a breach in your directives to Dr. Wykoff. I thought you should know immediately."

"That's not good. What exactly happened?"

"I walked in on Dr. Wykoff having a chat about the case with a couple of fourth-year medical students. I couldn't fucking believe it after what you said yesterday."

"Did these medical students seek her out?"

"Yes. One of them bumped into Wykoff in the women's locker room and asked out of the blue if she could talk about the Vander-meer case. And for some reason Wykoff agreed."

"Do you have any idea why she agreed?"

"She says she is really upset about what happened and needed to talk about it as a kind of therapy. And get this: she said she thought of the medical students as family. Jesus Christ! Medical students. Can you fucking believe it?"

"How did the medical students hear about it? Do you know?"

"I have no idea."

"Do you know why they are interested in the case?"

"Wykoff said they were concerned about the issue of hospital-acquired morbidity: people going into the hospital for one thing and getting something worse in the process. In that regard, I'm afraid Vandermeer is a prime example. Actually, it is a real issue."

"Did the students mention the other two cases?"

"No, they did not."

"Did you get their names?"

"I did. Michael Pender and Lynn Peirce. I briefly checked them out. Both are really good students in the very top of their class."

"So they could be leaders, which might make it more of a problem. Do they have a history of being activists?"

"I have no idea, but nothing like that was suggested in either academic record."

"Whom have you told about this?"

"You are the first."

"I think you should tell Dr. Feinberg. The hospital president has to be aware, because if the media gets ahold of this, it could scuttle the takeover negotiations, and we certainly don't want that to happen."

"Of course not!"

"I assume you told the students that they are not to talk about the case with anyone, friends or family. I mean really told them."

"I made it very clear."

"Why is Dr. Wykoff being more of a problem than Dr. Pearlman or Dr. Roux? Those two have been extremely cooperative."

"It is really hard to say. Believe me. It could be because it is her first major complication. Some doctors take it very personally. The one thing I can say is that she is not worried about a malpractice case. She is that confident she did nothing wrong."

"She's being naive. Malpractice cases can go either way, no matter what the particulars."

"She's also a workaholic who doesn't socialize much and lives alone. Professionally she's very reliable and conscientious, but something of an odd duck, at least in my estimation."

"The other two anesthesiologists live alone, too."

"What can I say? I don't know why she is being uncooperative."

"Do you think she should be terminated as a precaution after this violation of my directive?"

"I think we should wait and see how she responds from this point on," Benton said. "She's a damn good anesthesiologist and usually a team player. A lot depends on whether a lawsuit gets filed. But I'll leave that decision up to Josh Feinberg. He's being paid a fortune to deal with issues like this."

"Sounds like a plan," Bob said. "Thanks for letting me know. I'll give it some thought. Something might have to be done with all these people if they don't toe the line. I'll talk with Josh after you clue him in. We'll be in touch."

With a sigh of relief, Benton replaced the receiver. He felt a lot better now that he had pushed the issue into Bob Hartley's capable lap. Intuitively Benton knew he would feel even better after speaking with Josh, who would have no trouble making decisions about Wykoff. He also knew that Josh could talk to the dean about the students and nip that problem in the bud.

Getting up from his desk, Benton went out to his secretary and asked her to check to see if Dr. Josh Feinberg could spare a few minutes to see him right away. Benton wanted to do it before he went back up to the OR. With as many surgical cases going on as there were, he needed to be up there to put out sparks before they became fires.

A minute later Benton's secretary leaned into his office. "Dr. Feinberg can't see you until three P.M."

"Okay, thanks," he said. After getting all riled up he now felt let down. Yet what could he do? So he'd see the president at three. Until then he had other issues to deal with.

22.

Despite her exhaustion, Lynn had taken a short detour to the cafeteria. After leaving Michael she reluctantly decided that hunger had trumped her lack of sleep. The calories from the banana and bread roll she had eaten en route to the meeting with Wykoff had quickly disappeared. She felt weak, a little dizzy, and even a bit nauseous.

With little fear of running into any of her close friends, because of the derm clinic, she opted to sit down at a table. Sensing she needed some protein, she ordered scrambled eggs and wolfed them down with a cup of herbal tea. The food helped enormously, and made her believe she could think much more rationally and less emotionally. It also made her dizziness and nausea go away, something she noticed particularly as she headed over to the dorm, passing literally and figuratively in the shadow of the hulking Shapiro Institute.

Just as she had done the previous day, she paused for a few moments, eyeing the structure. She thought about Scarlett Morrison being transferred into the institute, and the idea brought up the issue of Carl being sent over as well. She questioned what she would do if that happened, as she wasn't family. It would mean she'd be reduced to getting updates from his parents. They had been gracious when she ran into them the day before, but that could change when they remembered that she had been the one to recommend he have his surgery at the Mason-Dixon rather than the Roper Hospital at MUSC. She might be left out in the cold. Lynn shrugged. She knew she was getting way ahead of herself. With a sense of resignation, she continued toward the dorm.

It felt weird going into Michael's room without him. After closing the door behind her, she stood for a moment, taking in the familiar sights and aroma. Michael was far neater than she, and everything was in its place. Even the books were shelved according to subject matter. Over the years she had teased him about the fastidiousness in his lifestyle, just as he had given her grief about her lack of it.

Although it was a bit strange to be in the room without Michael, just being there also felt comforting. She had spent considerable time in his room, as he had in hers. Especially during the first two years, they had studied a lot together in one or the other's room. Many of the other students had preferred the library or the student center for communal learning. Not Lynn and Michael. What made studying together so rewarding was that they silently pushed each other to make greater efforts than what they would have had they studied on their own.

She sat down at Michael's computer. He had cobbled it together from various components to maximize the gaming experience. She had gone through a gaming period herself but had grown out of it. Not so with Michael. She knew that he still used it to relieve anxiety and difficult emotions that medical school was capable of engendering, especially for a black man in a southern, mostly white professionally staffed medical center. He had admitted to her that he often gamed for fifteen minutes or so late at night, explaining that when he was a teenager, gaming had been a much-needed escape from the pressures of the 'hood, and a way of dealing with aggression.

After turning on the system, Lynn pulled up pictures. Expecting to find a well-organized and well-thought-out photo filing system as further evidence of his compulsiveness, she found something quite different. The photos were organized merely by date, meaning the chronological order in which the photos were taken.

Remembering that Ashanti had had her surgery several months earlier, Lynn started looking at photos taken in January. To her surprise, she came across a series of pictures that had been taken on a Saturday-afternoon excursion to the gorgeous Middleton Place, the apparent namesake of Middleton Healthcare, a sixty-acre landscaped garden begun as a rice plantation in the seventeenth century and now listed as a National Historic Landmark. Michael, his girlfriend, Kianna, Carl, and she had gone.

Lynn's breath caught as she found herself looking at a photo of herself and Carl and Kianna in a horse-drawn carriage. Michael was not in the photo because he was the photographer. It was a happier time: a sublime time.

For a second Lynn closed her eyes and let the reality of Carl's coma flood her thoughts. She had been getting by on a ton of denial and intellectualization, but now the realization that his mind and memories were gone descended on her like an avalanche. For the first time since the tragedy had begun, she let herself be enveloped by raw emotion. She began to cry. And cry she did, with shuddering intensity like a summer thunderstorm.

After what seemed like an eternity, the tears slowed. Eventually Lynn managed to get up and get some toilet paper to dry her cheeks and blot her eyelids. The small amount of makeup she used came off in a dark, dirty smudge.

Regaining a semblance of control, she went back to shuffling through Michael's extensive photo collection, avoiding pictures of Carl and herself as much as possible. It was difficult because there were a lot. She had forgotten they had double-dated with Michael and Kianna quite so often. There were photos of all sorts of things, including hundreds of shots of Charleston historic houses.

Eventually Lynn found the image she'd been searching for and brought it up onto the screen. It was entirely readable, especially since its compression had been slight, and she was able to enlarge sections. Satisfied, she e-mailed the image to herself in a large format. She wanted to preserve her ability to look at the details, particularly his vital signs. A moment later she heard the phone in her pocket announce she'd gotten the e-mail.

Lynn was back in her room a few minutes later. She took off her white coat and draped it over the reading chair, which also contained a ball of recently washed clothes. It always took her time to sort through the bundle when she brought it up from the laundry room in the basement. Sometimes she didn't bother. On those occasions she just used the clothes as they were needed.

For a moment Lynn eyed her bed, which she made only when she washed her sheets, which wasn't often. She had always thought she had better use for her time. Briefly Lynn considered lying down for just a few moments. Then she changed her mind. She knew that once she was horizontal, it might be difficult to get up.

Instead she sat down at her laptop and went into her e-mail inbox. There at the top was the JPEG she'd just sent to herself. Immediately below were two other e-mails from Michael. As promised, they were Scarlett Morrison's and Carl's anesthesia records. Lynn checked to be sure. Then she loaded all three into a flash drive, which she would take down to the student common room on the first floor to utilize the communal printer. But before doing so, she Googled *gammopathy* as she had done in the neuro ICU and immediately found the same article: "Monoclonal Gammopathy of Undetermined Significance." She downloaded a PDF version into the same USB device. Then she downloaded Wikipedia articles on multiple myeloma and serum protein electrophoresis. The last article she knew she wanted was on monoclonal antibodies, but when she rapidly read through it before downloading it, she realized there was one more she needed. It was on hybridoma technology. From an immunology lecture in her second year she remembered that monoclonal antibodies were made by hybridomas.

So armed, Lynn went down to use the printer. She had to swipe the magnetic tape on her student ID to get the machine to operate. While the machine did its thing, she sat in one of the leather club chairs and practically fell asleep.

With her printouts in hand, she went back to her room and lay down on her bed. For a few minutes she debated which of the printed pages she should read first. She thought about looking at the anesthesia records but decided she needed a completely clear head for those. Instead she turned to the articles. She settled on the gammopathy article, since it would be a review, as she had already read it once before in the neuro ICU. After that, she planned to read the one on multiple myeloma. But the reality was that she managed only four or five sentences of the first article before falling into a deep, dreamless sleep.

23.

With a sense of relief Sandra Wykoff left the PACU after making sure her second and final case was fully awake and functioning normally. It had been a hip replacement, and she was confident the patient would be going back to the fifth floor in short order. During both cases, when it came time for her to wake them up, she'd had a degree of anxiety, but both had awakened as expected, just as all the other cases she had done in her career, except for Carl Vandermeer's.

Once out in the main hallway, Sandra walked down to check the whiteboard to make sure she had not been scheduled for another case since her first case had been canceled. Although she was confident Geraldine Montgomery, the OR supervisor, would have let her know, she wanted to be certain. After the tongue-lashing she'd suffered from Benton Rhodes that morning, she wanted to be absolutely certain she didn't do anything to provoke the man further. She had known about his reputation for having a short fuse but until that morning had never experienced it personally.

The more Sandra thought about the Vandermeer case, the less

harsh she became on herself. She was absolutely confident that she hadn't done anything wrong during the procedure. She had not even taken so much as a shortcut, which she knew other people in the department did on occasion, particularly neglecting to manually check the anesthesia machine before each use. Most relied completely on the automatic check, which she thought was a mistake.

It had taken only a little more than an hour after Rhodes had stormed out of the communal OR anesthesia office for Sandra to be again totally convinced that whatever had happened during the Vandermeer operation was not her fault. She was absolutely sure of this, since she had, as she had told the students, gone back over the case in minute detail, questioning every step and consulting with several other anesthesiologists whose opinion she admired and trusted.

Sandra had even tried to have a conversation with Mark Pearlman, who had had a strikingly similar case the previous Friday, but he had refused to talk with her about his case or hers. He had chosen to follow Rhodes and Hartley's orders to the letter, even to the extent of not talking to a fellow anesthesiologist. Sandra thought that was a mistake despite what the hospital counsel felt. She knew that complications often led to advances in medicine.

The long and short of it was that if there was a lawsuit, Sandra was confident that no one would find the hospital or herself culpable. And, contrary to what Benton Rhodes had said, she was sure that the two students were Mason-Dixon family and could be trusted. She had made the effort to call the dean of students to ask about Lynn Peirce prior to seeing her and had learned that Miss Peirce was going to graduate number one in her class, just as Sandra had done over at MUSC almost seven years before. There had been no reason not to talk to her and her classmate and perhaps salvage something from the disaster. Students had to learn that medicine was not all-powerful or completely predictable.

And there had been a positive aspect to the conversation with the students. For Sandra, talking about the case in detail had helped ameliorate the guilt that had been haunting her since the tragedy had struck and boost her confidence in her professional abilities. Confidence was important if she was to continue being an anesthesiologist.

The other thing the conversation with the students had done was remind her of the blip that had occurred on the monitor. It had been so insignificant, but considering it was the only thing about the case that was at all unusual, she now thought it was worth checking. The problem was that doing so necessitated calling Clinical Engineering, something she was reluctant to do, since it meant risking having to deal with Misha Zotov.

Steeling herself against such a possibility, Sandra walked back down the main OR corridor whence she had come and headed for the room where the extra anesthesia machines were stored. Her hope was to corral one of the Clinical Engineering technicians and ask a few questions about the blip she'd seen on the monitor. She wasn't looking forward to going all the way down to the Clinical Engineering Department, located in the hospital basement, where she had first encountered the irritating Russian.

The good news was that Misha Zotov wasn't in the room. The bad news was that no one else was, either. Turning around, Sandra retraced her steps to the main desk. It seemed that if she was going to ask about the blip, she would have to go to the Clinical Engineering office, after all.

At the busy main desk, Sandra got Geraldine's attention and told her she was leaving the floor and that if she was needed for anything, she could be texted. Geraldine gave her a thumbs-up to indicate she got the message.

After retrieving a long white lab coat from her locker in the women's lounge, Sandra was able to put off going down to the basement, at least for the time being. Thinking about Carl Vandermeer made her want to check on the man's status. She had gone into the neuro ICU for a quick visit the previous afternoon before leaving the hospital and also early that morning on her way in to work. Although she was aware of the MRI and CT scan results and had read the neurology residents' notes, she couldn't help but harbor a bit of hope that there might be a change for the better, knowing how little hypoxia he had suffered.

Once in the neuro ICU, she went directly to cubicle 8. Seeing Carl, Sandra could immediately tell there had been no change in his condition. A nurse had rolled him onto his left side so that she could wash and powder his back. Sandra shuddered at the enormity of the situation for which she, on some level, was responsible for causing. She knew that dealing with a comatose patient required almost constant care and attention. She also knew that Carl would probably need a percutaneous gastric tube. Doing so required an operation. Sandra shuddered again, wondering how she would feel if it fell to her to do the anesthesia.

"Any improvement?" Sandra asked, even though she already knew the answer.

"Oh, yeah," the nurse said optimistically. "He's doing okay. A few minutes ago he sneezed."

Good grief, Sandra thought but didn't say. The patient's having a sneeze was such a pathetic indication that Carl was doing okay. At the same time she understood that a sneeze was a positive sign, as it meant that at least the brain stem was functioning. She glanced up at the monitor. The temperature was elevated, as it had been that morning, but everything else was normal. She then left the cubicle and headed over to the central desk. En route she noticed that Scarlett Morrison, Mark's coma case, was gone, as her cubicle was occupied by a man named Charles Humphries.

The previous afternoon she had had a short conversation with the head nurse, Gwen Murphy, about Carl, and again Sandra sought her out. "Any change with Vandermeer?" she asked, a bit of hope against hope.

"Nope," Gwen said. "But on the bright side he is very stable. And the infectious disease consult hasn't found any infection to explain his elevated temperature. And the fever has come down a bit."

Sandra looked over at the cubicle where Mark Pearlman's case had been. "I see Scarlett Morrison is gone. Did she go out to the neuro floor?"

"Nope!" Gwen repeated. "They took her directly to the Shapiro Institute. To be honest, they don't really have the equipment or the manpower out on the neuro floor to handle a long-term comatose patient. At the Shapiro they are specifically set up to do it."

"Seems awfully quick," Sandra said. "She was here only three days."

"As stable as she was, she didn't need to be here in the ICU," Gwen said. "And it's better for everyone, the patient included, and the hospital bean counters also like it. Keeping someone here in the neuro ICU is ten times more expensive than it is over there."

"Ten times! Wow! I knew there was a difference but not that much. That's quite a stimulus."

"It sure is. We're hoping Vandermeer goes, too."

"Really?" Sandra said with dismay. "But he just got here. Maybe he is going to improve." In her mind, sending a patient over to the Shapiro Institute meant "pulling the plug" on hope, even if hope was unrealistic.

Gwen shrugged. "Not according to the neuro residents. It's their feeling that getting him over to the Shapiro sooner rather than later is indicated, and we surely could use the bed."

Feeling more depressed leaving the neuro ICU than she had when she had arrived, Sandra went back to the main elevators. She squeezed into the next down car as she had run out of excuses for postponing a visit to Clinical Engineering. Although the elevator was jammed when she boarded, descending from the first floor to the basement she was the only person left. When the elevator doors opened, she paused for a moment. Then she shook her head, feeling embarrassed at her timidity. If she ran into Zotov, she would just ignore him. She thought she was acting like a teenager.

Sandra first passed the Pathology Department and the morgue, and then the Informational Technology Department, where the hospital's servers could be seen in their air-conditioned isolation. Next to IT was the central security office, and Sandra caught a glimpse of the banks of monitors fed by cameras sprinkled all over the medical center.

As she walked, Sandra reflected on why Misha Zotov bothered her so much. He reminded her of her ex-husband, Adam Radic, in both looks and mannerisms. Both were darkly complected, tall, muscular but slender with intense, lidded eyes and heavy beards. Both were also fawning to the point of overdoing it. With Adam, time had proved it had been an elaborate act. Somehow she was certain it would be the same with Misha.

Initially, when Sandra had first met Adam at the very beginning of her residency, she had been quite taken by his flattery and attention. She also had found him exotically attractive and much more sophisticated than she, having traveled and studied around Europe. He had come to America from Serbia to do a surgical fellowship. Believing his declarations of love were sincere, Sandra had fallen in love with him. For a highly motivated doctor like herself, it helped that he was a recognized and talented surgeon.

Within less than a year after they had started dating, she and Adam were married. But after the marriage things quickly changed, especially once Adam got his green card. He became a tyrant and had beaten her severely several times. Thanks to her father's intercession, Sandra got divorced, but not without suffering considerable trauma. For her, the issue of domestic violence had become a distinct reality.

Sandra pushed through the door into Clinical Engineering. It was a large room with service benches piled with a mixture of all manner of hospital apparatuses, from anesthesia machines to respirators. It was all neat and orderly, with tools on Peg-Boards. The noise level was moderate, with various power tools competing with a background of classical music. At a table against the back wall two men played chess.

As Sandra's eyes swept the room she estimated that there were about fifteen people at work, all dressed in white coveralls. Most continued doing what they were doing. A few looked up. Most of them resembled Misha Zotov. There were a few blond men, but they were a distinct minority. There were no women.

To Sandra's mild dismay, Misha Zotov was one of those who looked up, as he was at the closest service bench, working on an anesthesia machine. She caught an expression of recognition on his face, and to her chagrin he immediately put down the tool he was using, stood, and started toward her.

Sandra's eyes quickly scanned the room again, this time looking for Fyodor Rozovsky, the department supervisor. She had met him on her previous visit. It had been he who had answered her service-related question. Unfortunately he was nowhere to be seen.

"Ah, Dr. Wykoff," Misha said, crowding her space. It sounded as if his English had improved, but he still spoke with a distinctive Russian accent. "You look beautiful. How can I help you?"

"Where is Fyodor Rozovsky?" Sandra asked. She took a step back, avoiding eye contact with the man. By inappropriately and presumably insincerely referring to her appearance, she could tell he had not mended his ways. She wanted nothing to do with the man. She glanced around the room yet again.

"He is in his office," Misha said. "Please! I could get him for you. No trouble at all."

"Thank you, but I'll find him myself," Sandra said curtly, and headed off. The office was in the back. Unfortunately Misha did not get the message and tagged along, continuing to try to engage her in conversation. Whether she answered or not didn't make a difference. He was carrying on about the weather and how beautiful it was in

Charleston with all the flowers and how bad it was in his hometown in Russia this time of the year. His English vocabulary had definitely expanded.

Sandra didn't respond. It was amazing how much the man reminded her of Adam Radic, and the memory made her skin crawl. When she got to the door to the office, Misha was still behind her. The fact that she was ignoring him had no effect on him whatsoever. He was again suggesting they have a drink together at his favorite bar on the rooftop of the Vendue Inn, saying it was a great place to watch the sunset over the Charleston skyline. Sandra knew of the bar. It had been one of Adam's favorite hangouts, but without her.

Sandra went into Rozovsky's office. Without breaking a step, Misha accompanied her. Inside the office were a small service bench and several desks. One was occupied by the Clinical Engineering supervisor, and the others were empty.

Before Sandra could say anything, Misha pushed past her and engaged Fyodor in an animated conversation in Russian. Fyodor peered around Misha as Misha spoke. Sandra wondered what in God's name Misha was talking about since she'd said next to nothing to him. Finally Misha finished and stepped to the side. Fyodor stood up and gestured to the straight-back chair Misha proceeded to pull over. "Please, Dr. Wykoff, sit down." In contrast to Misha, he spoke with very little accent, and his English was very good. "I remember you. You came down to ask how often we did routine service on the anesthesia machines."

Sandra sat and glanced over at Misha, hoping he would leave, but he didn't. He was content to just stand there with a kind of smirk on his face, as if he expected some favor from her for having accompanied her into Fyodor's office. As pushy as he was, she was glad she had not run into him alone upstairs.

"I have another question," Sandra said, directing her attention to Fyodor.

"We are at your service, Doctor," Fyodor said. As far as Sandra was concerned, even he exuded a suggestion of insincerity that made her uncomfortable.

"There was a very unfortunate anesthesia incident yesterday . . . ," Sandra began, but then hesitated. She felt she needed to give some background, although Rhodes's orders about not talking about the case made her reluctant to say very much. Yet she was talking to the people responsible for the performance of the anesthesia machine she had used, and she needed to be reassured.

As if sensing her quandary, Fyodor said, "We have heard about the event from Dr. Rhodes. First, we want to reassure you that the machine you were using had been serviced appropriately and in a timely manner. All its paperwork was in order. And as soon as we heard about the event, and following Dr. Rhodes's orders, we brought the machine back here to our service center. We went over it extensively. I can assure you that it checked out perfectly, and it is back in service. There was no problem with the machine or its monitors, and Dr. Rhodes has been informed of this."

Sandra nodded. Fyodor's little spiel was more than she had expected. She didn't know that Rhodes had asked to have the machine checked by Clinical Engineering, but it made sense. Perhaps she should have asked herself, but it didn't matter, as it had been done.

"Do you have any additional questions?" Fyodor said.

"I think that covers it," Sandra said, and started to rise. But then she hesitated. Settling back onto her chair, she said, "There is one other thing."

"Please," Fyodor said agreeably. He even managed an unctuous smile.

Similar to what she had said to the two medical students, Sandra then went on to describe the jump, or blink, or blip—she really didn't know how best to describe it to these professionals—that she had seen on the monitor when the surgeon had begun drilling into the tibia. As she spoke, she sensed from his expression that Fyodor was disbelieving that such a thing could occur. In response, Sandra said that it could actually be seen on the machine-generated anesthesia record. "It is a very small change, but it is visible. If you bring up the Vandermeer anesthesia record on your terminal, I'll show you."

After a quick glance between Fyodor and Misha, which included a nod from Fyodor, Misha went to the computer monitor on Fyodor's desk, brought up the record, and then stepped aside. Sandra then took over. As she had done when she'd been with the medical students, she zoomed in on the tracing of the vital signs. She pointed to the place fifty-two minutes into the case, where all the tracings notched upward. "There," she said, pointing. "See the vertical jump? And when it happened, the monitor blinked, which caught my attention. It made me worry I was about to lose my feeds."

"Interesting," Fyodor said, leaning closer to the monitor. "I see what you mean. What do you think it is?"

"You are asking me?" Sandra questioned. "I don't know. You people are the experts. To be truthful, I'm not all that knowledgeable about electronics. I came down here to ask you."

Fyodor sat back and looked up at Misha for a beat. "I don't know what it could be, but it can't be anything significant." Then his attention went back to the monitor. "The tracings all look totally normal before and after. What do you think, Misha?" Fyodor leaned back and caught Sandra's surprised expression and explained, "I might be the department supervisor, but Misha is our key anesthesia machine technician. We brought him from Russia specifically to work on the anesthesia machines. He did a lot of the original coding for the model that we have here at the Mason-Dixon. He is what you say in English the go-to guy."

Sandra was impressed by this news since she thought so highly of the anesthesia machine, although it still didn't influence her negative visceral reaction to the man.

Misha made it a point to bend over and study the image on the monitor.

"I know it is small change," she went on to explain, "but I had never seen it before, and since the case turned out to have such a terrible outcome, I just want to make sure it has no significance. I mean, if the patient had awakened after the case, I might not even have remembered it happened. Well, maybe that's not totally true, since it did scare me about the possibility of losing my electronic monitoring."

"It's not important," Misha said. He stood back up.

"But what was it?" Sandra persisted.

"It's just a frame offset," Misha said. "It's nothing. It could happen from a number of things, like . . ." He gestured with his hands in the air, struggling to express himself with his English.

"Like what?" Sandra asked.

"What you have to remember is that the machine's computer is constantly compressing data," Fyodor said, coming to Misha's aid. "You have no idea how much data is being constantly generated. So seeing little changes on a monitor is not surprising. There can be blips from hardware malfunction, like one of the hundreds of capacitors prematurely discharging, or from a software problem confronting momentary input overload or even from just too many applications running at the same time."

Sandra nodded as if she understood. She didn't, but it was clear they did not think a frame offset had any real significance. She was about to thank them and leave when the two men suddenly launched into an animated and spirited conversation in Russian. For Sandra it was like momentarily watching a Ping-Pong game up close, her eyes darting from one man to the other. Then, as suddenly as the heated discussion had started, it stopped.

Fyodor smiled. "Sorry, it is rude for us to speak Russian. We disagree on a small issue. No matter. The important point is that whatever caused this small frame offset you noticed certainly didn't affect the anesthesia machine's function." He smiled again. "Is there anything else we can help you with, Doctor?"

"That's it for the moment," Sandra said. She stood up. "Thank you for your time."

"We are here to serve," Fyodor said. "Anytime you have a question, please come down or call. As you know, we have technicians available twenty-four hours, seven days a week."

As she left the supervisor's office, Sandra fully expected Misha to follow her. She had been mildly concerned about getting away from him, the way he had glommed onto her when she had first arrived. To her surprise and relief, he stayed inside the office with Fyodor.

Heading back to the elevators, Sandra thought she would go back up to the OR and see what she had been assigned for the following morning. If any of them were inpatients, she would go check them out. She would review the nascent electronic medical record for the ones having same-day surgery to get an idea of what the day would be like. The episode with Carl was making her more compulsive than ever. When she finished all that, she would head for home.

24.

For a few minutes after Dr. Sandra Wykoff had left, silence reigned in the Clinical Engineering supervisor's office. The only noise came from out in the service area and was the muted whine of various electric tools combined with a hint of classical symphonic music. The two Russian expats regarded each other while immersed in their own thoughts. Both were not happy, but for slightly different reasons.

Fyodor Rozovsky had been in Charleston for several years before he had recruited Misha Zotov. The men had known each other since childhood, having both grown up in Saint Petersburg. Also, both of them had attended the Moscow Institute of Physics and Technology. Fyodor had been brought to America almost a decade earlier, when Sidereal Pharmaceuticals had agreed to fund the Shapiro Institute. With Fyodor's knowledge of computer coding and robotics, he had been clearly essential to the project's success. His contributions had been such that after the Shapiro was successfully up and running, Middleton Healthcare happily offered him the opportunity to run Clinical Engineering for the entire medical center. The company felt that progressive automation was key for hospital-based medicine.

"I don't like this," Fyodor said. He was now speaking Russian, and his irritation was apparent. "Sergei Polushin is going to be as angry as a bear if this blip becomes a subject of general discussion in the Anesthesia Department."

Sergei Polushin, a financial genius, was reputed to be the closest confidant to Boris Rusnak, the billionaire Russian oligarch who had created Sidereal Pharmaceuticals. Living in Geneva, Rusnak, with Sergei's help, had aggressively merged a number of small drug firms by a series of rapid, hostile takeovers to build one of the world's largest. More important, the company was poised to become the dominant player in the newest pharmaceutical gold mine: making and marketing biologics, or drugs made by living systems, not by chemistry. Sergei Polushin had been the force behind the Shapiro Institute, and continued to treat it as his personal fiefdom.

"I need to have a frank discussion with my team of programmers," Misha said. Gone was any hint of the fawning facade he presented to Sandra. He was clearly as angry as Fyodor. "A frame offset like that is just sloppy programming. The trouble is I didn't see it myself."

"I don't need to tell you, but Sergei will undoubtedly hold you responsible if this thing causes trouble."

"You don't need to tell me," Misha said. "I will see that it is eliminated immediately. When is the next case scheduled?"

"Not until next week, so you have plenty of time. But it is important to get it fixed. The schedule is to do a case a week in all the Middleton Healthcare hospitals. There cannot be any bugs. Is it possible this same phenomena occurred with either of the two previous test cases?"

"I don't know," Misha said. "Let's check the pilot case!" He grabbed a chair, sat, and used the terminal on Fyodor's desk to pull up Ashanti Davis's anesthesia record. When it was on the monitor, he magnified the central portion just as Sandra had done with Vandermeer's.

"There it is," Fyodor said. "That's not good. Let's check Morrison."

Misha quickly did the same with Morrison's anesthesia record as he had done with Davis's. "Shit! There it is with Morrison as well. Sorry about that!"

"Fix it!" Fyodor said gruffly.

Misha exited the screen. "Luckily, no one has noticed the offset on either of the previous test cases."

"Are you suggesting that it not be fixed?"

"I will see that it is fixed today. My point is questioning whether we should go back and try to eliminate the offset in all three documents."

"Can you do that?"

Misha shrugged. "Actually, I don't know. Probably, but then again we could make it worse, meaning leaving a fingerprint that it had been altered after the fact. I could have someone try before actually executing and show you in an hour or so what it would look like."

"All right. But, most important, fix the bug itself."

"Certainly. But that leaves the issue about Dr. Wykoff and whether she is likely to enlist the help of anyone else in explaining the frame offset."

"That question has occurred to me, too. We know that both the chief of anesthesia and the hospital lawyer have urged the parties involved against loose talk. Talking about even a minor blip in the vital sign tracings would certainly qualify as loose talk."

"That is true, but is it worth the risk? I'm afraid she has become a major liability. It seems to me that this is a circumstance where the services of Darko and Leonid are called for and sooner rather than later."

Both Fyodor and Misha had met Darko Lebedev and Leonid Shubin. They knew the two had been members of the Soviet Special Forces and had served a number of years in Chechnya, tracking down and eliminating people Moscow deemed terrorists. They knew that Boris Rusnak had hired the two men away from the army early in Boris's meteoric rise in the rough-and-tumble business world of post-Soviet Russia, where people of Darko and Leonid's abilities and mind-set were a necessity. Fyodor and Misha were well aware that both killers had seen a lot of action. They also knew that Sergei Polushin had sent them to Charleston as a potential resource to support Sidereal's considerable US investment.

Easing back in his chair, Fyodor let his eyes roam up to the ceiling and allowed his mind to wander. Misha had a point, and a good one. Dr. Sandra Wykoff represented a very weak link in what was otherwise a strong chain. She could set the program back, maybe even stop it for a time. It would be irresponsible for Fyodor to let such a risk continue, especially when it could easily be eliminated. Wykoff had been selected as one of the test cases specifically because she was a loner, as were the two other anesthesiologists that had been chosen before her. Misha had been tasked to try to get close to her, although that tactic had fallen flat. They had used Russian call girls with the other two male anesthesiologists to keep tabs on them, and that had worked well. But Sandra Wykoff had been different and now presented a real problem. There was no way to find out what she was thinking.

Fyodor tipped forward in his chair. He'd made up his mind. "I don't like this woman," he said.

"She is a high-and-mighty bitch," Misha agreed. "I tried to be nice to her. Trust me! She thinks she is something special. She is going to be trouble."

"All right," Fyodor said. "She's got to be taken care of. Do you want to talk with Darko and Leonid, or should I? I know they have been eager to be useful."

"It will be my pleasure," Misha said, getting to his feet. "I'll call Darko as soon as I get my team of programmers busy."

"Keep me informed," Fyodor said.

"I will," Misha promised.

25.

Benton was ushered into Josh's posh digs by one of the president's aides. It was a corner office looking out onto the manicured hospital grounds. It was as large and as well appointed as any Fortune 500 CEO's and befitting Josh's role as both president of the Mason-Dixon Medical Center and chairman of the board of Middleton Healthcare. Benton couldn't help but be jealous. Josh was a new kind of doctor. He had gotten an MBA at the same time he'd gotten his MD to take advantage of health care's being the biggest business in the United States, at $4 trillion a year and counting.

Benton also knew that Josh was holding down an annual salary of over $4 million, with hefty stock options to boot. Under his tenure, Middleton Healthcare had grown from twenty-four hospitals in the Southeast to thirty-two spread throughout the country. Equally as impressive, he had forged the lucrative alliance with Sidereal Pharmaceuticals. As a department head, Benton was aware that significant cash infusions from Sidereal were coming into Middleton's coffers every month to bolster infrastructure.

From Benton's perspective, Josh Feinberg didn't look the part of an accomplished CEO or even a doctor. He was a slight man with an intense, gaunt face and shifty eyes more suggestive of a crooked used-car salesman than an accomplished hospital administrator. Although his suits were probably expensive, they hung on his bony frame like clothes on a wire hanger. But despite having less than a commanding appearance, Benton knew that Josh was a superb businessman, with his MBA from Benton's Ivy League alma mater.

Before being recruited to take over Middleton Healthcare, Josh Feinberg had a stellar record of founding and managing a highly successful health-care consulting company called Feinberg Associates. Although functioning behind the scenes, this company had been responsible for a slew of medical products and procedures ranging from medical software to teeth-whitening strips. The source of its success was that it employed many hundreds of Russian PhD scientists who'd found themselves out of work after the dissolution of the Soviet Union.

Once at Middleton Healthcare, Benton was well aware that Feinberg had not only expanded the company but had also spearheaded the lucrative Sidereal Pharmaceutical connection. In the process, Feinberg had fostered a personal relationship with the otherwise reclusive billionaire Boris Rusnak. From the Russian's reputation, Josh's connection with the man might have been his biggest coup of all.

Josh offered Benton one of the chairs facing his massive desk, but Benton declined, saying he'd rather stand because he had to get back up to the OR and what he had to say wasn't going to take much of Josh's time.

"Have you spoken with Bob Hartley?" Benton asked, as a way to begin.

"No. Should I have?"

"No matter," Benton said. "Let me clue you in." He then had the same conversation he'd had with Hartley. Like Hartley, Josh took the story seriously, writing down the names of the medical students as Benton talked. The longest part of the conversation concerned Dr. Sandra Wykoff and what to do about her. Rhodes said she was a good anesthesiologist and committed to her work but somewhat of a loner and not always a team player. He admitted he didn't have a full understanding of her.

"And you say Hartley will be getting in touch with me?" Josh asked.

"That's what he said."

"Good. About the two medical students looking into hospital-acquired morbidity: I'm sure that can be nipped in the bud. I'll talk with the dean to make sure they toe the line. But on the off chance one or both don't and persist with their inquiries, I want you to personally let me know immediately."

"You mean if they contact Dr. Wykoff again?"

"Precisely. Whether they contact Dr. Wykoff or one of the other involved anesthesiologists, give me a heads-up. They could be a big problem, especially in the context of investigating hospital-acquired morbidity. We don't want to stimulate any kind of unanticipated inspection by the Joint Commission with the way they are already busting our balls about access to the Shapiro Institute."

"How will I get in touch with you if it's off hours?"

"Text me!" Josh said. "I'll have one of my aides give you my personal mobile number."

"You got it," Benton said. He felt flattered that Josh would be willing to give him his mobile number, but he wasn't totally surprised. Josh had specifically and heavily recruited him five years earlier, and they had a somewhat social relationship.

"I certainly will take it from here. Thank you, Doctor." As if by magic, the door to Josh's office swung open. Standing on the threshold was Josh's closest aide, Fletcher Jefferson. Josh gestured toward the man to let Benton know the meeting was over.

"You're welcome," Benton said, a bit surprised at being dismissed so summarily. If he hadn't been flattered by the course of the meeting, he would have felt slighted. As he passed out of the room, Mr. Jefferson gave Benton a piece of paper. On it was Josh's mobile number.

For several minutes after Dr. Rhodes had left, Feinberg played absentmindedly with his computer mouse, moving it in small circles to watch the cursor dance on his monitor. He hated picayune annoyances requiring his attention in the middle of big, momentous events. This current issue involving a spinster woman anesthesiologist and a couple of greenhorn medical students was a prime example.

Josh and Boris Rusnak currently were orchestrating a complete revolution in the pharmaceutical industry by modernizing and significantly improving the manufacture of biologics, and he needed to be on the top of his game. Biologics were where the industry was heading, thanks to the prices they were commanding and thanks to Middleton Healthcare's alliance with Sidereal Pharmaceuticals. Since he and his team had forged this marriage, he was positioned at the very vortex of the change and stood to be rewarded beyond his wildest dreams. Within the hour he expected a conference call from Boris arranged by his chief aide, Sergei Polushin, and Josh already knew what was going to be discussed. They were going to propose that Sidereal double its projected antibody production by utilizing all thirty-plus Middleton Healthcare hospitals rather than the five that had been originally proposed. Such a situation would be huge and would essentially guarantee a merger between Sidereal and Middleton. With that kind of dependence, there was no way that Sidereal would allow Middleton Healthcare to go off on its own, as it would undoubtedly be courted by other multinational drug firms.

Pressing a button under the lip of his desk, the same button he'd pressed to end the meeting with Benton Rhodes, Josh waited for

Fletcher to reappear. Seconds later he handed Fletcher the paper on which he had written the names of the two medical students.

"I want a rapid rundown on these kids," Josh said. "I want to know where they live, where they are from, their family situations, and their significant others. Later I want details, but for now, the basics. Go!"

While he waited, Josh went back to fidgeting with his cursor. He knew that the upcoming call from Geneva might be the defining event in his life. Yet he wasn't nervous, because he was prepared. Although he thought he knew what the agenda was going to be, he was ready to field a wide variety of curveballs. What he counted on was that Sidereal needed Middleton, and not vice versa.

After only five minutes, a muffled knock preceded Fletcher's reappearance. He came directly to the front of Josh's desk and put down a single sheet of paper. On it each student had a paragraph. Josh snapped up the paper and read it rapidly.

"Good," Josh said, looking it over. "Perfect. They are both living in the dorm: that's good. Both accomplished students: that's good, since both have a lot to lose. Both on full scholarships: that's helpful, too, as they probably are grateful. And they are good friends, which makes dealing with them easier: convince one, and that one would surely convince the other."

Josh looked up. "Well done. Now, get the details!"

As Fletcher turned to leave, Josh reached for his phone. He knew that the best administrators knew how to delegate, and that was exactly what he was going to do. Thanks to Sergei Polushin, there was a resource to handle problems raised by the likes of Robert Hurley and now Sandra Wykoff and a couple of medical students. With a touch of a button Josh was on a direct line with Fyodor Rozovsky.

"There are a couple of other problems," Josh said with no pre-amble, not even identifying himself. Names were not needed, as they knew each other's voice, as the "project" required frequent contact, and they talked rather than e-mailed or texted to eliminate any potential paper trail. "The anesthesiologist, Sandra Wykoff, has become a true threat."

"We are already aware," Fyodor said. "She just visited us here in the service center to ask probing questions. It has already been decided, and an appropriate call has already been made. The problem will be solved tonight."

Josh was taken aback that they were a step ahead but pleased. "I commend your efficiency."

"We have only the best and most experienced personnel," Fyodor said with pride.

"I guess commendation is in order for the solution to the previous Hurley threat."

"Thank you. There were no problems."

"One other thing while I have you on the phone. There is another minor problem that might be best handled by your experienced personnel. I'm sorry that all this is happening at the same time."

"We are here to deal with problems. No need for an apology. What minor problem are you referring to?"

"There are now a couple of medical students, a male and a female, who are close friends. They have made a nuisance of themselves talking with Sandra Wykoff about the Vandermeer case. The motivation is because of a misplaced interest in the issue of hospital-acquired morbidity. This has to stop! I'll try to address it through the dean of the school, but I thought you should be aware. Maybe a warning to one of them might be in order, although I will leave that up to you. I'll send down the names and the particulars."

"We will be looking for it. In the meantime, rest assured that the anesthesiologist will be taken care of. As for the students, we'll have someone talk convincingly to the female. In Russia we found that was the best course of action with couples."

"I'll trust your judgment," Josh said simply before disconnecting the line. He was pleased and relieved to have the issue about the rogue anesthesiologist already behind him. It was easy to delegate when one had the right people. With the most important part of this new problem already solved, he placed a call to the dean of the medical school, Dr. Janet English, about the rogue students. This conversation was even shorter and to the point. "Talk to them as soon as you can," Josh said at the end. His mind was already back to anticipating the imminent conference call from Geneva.

"I will contact them immediately," Dr. English said. "Consider it done."

26.

T he text tone wasn't loud, but in the total silence of her room, it startled Lynn. At the moment it sounded she was in deep concentration, and had been for several hours. She had started out scanning the articles she had printed from the Internet and then had moved on to studying the printouts of the anesthesia records for Carl, Scarlett, and Ashanti. After finding something rather startling on the printouts, she had gone back to the images themselves on her computer screen, because it afforded magnification. What she had discovered and corroborated was that all three records had the little frame offset that had bothered Dr. Wykoff in Carl's case, and, more surprising still, the frame offset had occurred at the exact same time: precisely fifty-two minutes into each operation!

As far as Lynn was concerned, she couldn't imagine that the timing, being so exact, could be by chance. It was too Newtonian in a quantum world. Turning her attention back to the printouts, which she had placed side-by-side, she discovered something else that she had not noticed earlier when comparing the cases. This new finding was another similarity, but one that she might not have appreciated had she not been looking at all three cases together, and it was equally as startling and disturbing as the corresponding time of the frame offsets. Again, she didn't know the significance, but was certain it too had to be important, and she couldn't wait to tell Michael and get his take on both. It was at the moment of the second discovery that the text tone had sounded.

After recovering from the initial shock of the tone, Lynn snatched up her smartphone. With her heart thumping in her chest from being startled, she looked at the screen. What she expected to see was a text from Michael, maybe telling her she better get her ass over to the clinic. On any given day, he was the one who most often texted her. But the message wasn't from Michael. Instead it was from Dr. Janet English, the medical school dean! With trepidation, Lynn read the text. It wasn't long.

> Miss Lynn Peirce, I want to see you in my office at 5:00 p.m., immediately after ophthalmology clinic. Respectfully yours, Dr. Janet English, Dean, Mason-Dixon School of Medicine.

Slowly Lynn put the phone back down. A feeling of dread crept over her. She leaned forward and read the text again. Her heart rate, which had begun to slow from the initial start, now speeded up again. The question was, why would the dean of the school want to see her? Her initial thought was that it might be about her missing a few ophthalmology and dermatology lectures, but then she realized it couldn't be something so benign. The message said she should come after the ophthalmology clinic, meaning the dean thought that Lynn was there, as she was supposed to be.

Lynn had never actually met the dean of the school face-to-face, despite her having been at the school for almost four years. She had seen her only from a distance at various medical school functions, as she had on her first day, when Lynn was a freshman and Dr. English gave the welcoming address at what was touted as the "white coat" ceremony. The dean was not known to be a particularly sociable individual. It was common knowledge that she preferred her admin functions and research interests over direct student contact, which she delegated to the dean of students.

Rather quickly Lynn began to worry that Rhodes and/or Wykoff had gone ahead and checked whether she and Michael were authorized to look at Carl's chart in the neuro ICU. If the dean had been informed, she would be livid and was now summoning them to accuse them of a major HIPAA violation. Lynn could hear Michael's reminding her it was a class 5 felony. Would the school prosecute them? Lynn had no idea. In a way she doubted it, as it would be a first offense, but who was to know. And if they did prosecute them, would it be the end of their careers in medicine? Lynn had no idea about that, either, but recognized there was a chance. She shuddered, having a major guilt trip about involving Michael.

Thinking of him, she wondered if he had gotten a similar text. Quickly she texted him and posed the question. She knew he was most likely in the ophthalmology clinic but guessed that he could probably manage to text her back. She was right. His text popped up on her screen within minutes:

Michael: *That's affirmative. What's the deal?*

Lynn quickly texted back.

Lynn: *Wish I knew. Afraid Rhodes and Wykoff might have blown our cover re/Carl's chart.*

Michael: *Possible but doubt it. More likely pissed we spoke with Wykoff.*

Lynn: *hope ur right. I'll meet you in clinic just before 5. We can go together.*

Michael: *ur on, girl* ☺!

Replacing her phone on her desk, Lynn was amazed Michael was taking this text from the dean in stride enough to use an emoticon. Under the circumstances, it seemed inappropriate and out of character. He had never used an emoticon before in any text he had sent her. Yet it did make her feel better. It certainly suggested he was relaxed about the dean's demand that they appear in her office, and if that were the case, maybe she should be, too.

Yet even in the best-case scenario, that Dr. English wanted to meet with them merely to chastise them about talking with Wykoff, Lynn was enough of a realist to understand that afterward there was a good chance that Carl's chart and even visiting him would be off limits. The staff in the neuro ICU might very well be forewarned, and that would be a major problem for Lynn.

Of course she wasn't sure about anything. Was such paranoid thinking a form of denial her mind was using to avoid dealing with the reality of Carl's coma and gloomy prognosis, and her own guilt? Was she jumping to unwarranted conclusions? Lynn didn't know. And another thought occurred to her. Maybe she should do her investigating more on her own. She now recognized more than she had before that there might be a personal cost. If someone was going to take a fall, it should be her, and her alone, not Michael.

Lynn looked at the time. It was almost three-thirty. That meant that the neuro ICU day shift would have changed to the evening shift. There would be new people. Also there wouldn't be a problem getting to the dean's office by five. If she wanted to look at Carl's chart again, which she did, now was the time to give it a try. All she could do was hope that the reason the dean wanted to see her and Michael didn't have anything to do with their overt HIPAA violations.

27.

Forgoing the shower and change of clothes she had planned on, Lynn hustled over to the hospital. In her paranoia, she found herself worrying that the dean might have forewarned the neuro ICU staff about her activities even prior to the scheduled meeting in the dean's office. Unfortunately there would be no way to know before walking in and giving it a try.

Deciding to continue with the anesthesia rotation ruse if she was asked what she was doing in the neuro ICU, she made another stop in the women's surgical locker room to put on scrubs. Dressed as such, she didn't stand out as a medical student.

Reaching the neuro ICU, she paused outside, just as she had done on previous visits, only this time it wasn't because she feared what she was going to see vis-à-vis Carl but rather that she worried about her reception. Gathering her courage, she pushed in.

As the door closed behind her, she hesitated as her eyes quickly scanned the room. Ostensibly the ICU was the same as it had been that morning, with the same sounds and smells. As usual, the patients were for the most part stationary. The only activity in the room came from the nurses and aides going about their business. A few looked in Lynn's direction, but no one registered any untoward response or recognition, and no one approached her. She felt encouraged and was able to relax a degree.

She glanced over to Carl's cubicle from where she was standing. Except for his leg in the CPM, he was as immobile as he had been that morning. A nurse was adjusting his IV. Lynn considered going over to his bedside but decided against it, as it would accomplish little more than to possibly upset her, which she didn't need. Looking over into Scarlett Morrison's cubicle, she could see that the woman had been transferred. There was a new patient in her place, attended to by a neurology resident. Thankfully the resident wasn't Charles Stuart, as that might have been potential trouble.

Turning her attention to the central desk, Lynn picked out the woman who was most likely Gwen Murphy's equivalent on the evening shift. She was sitting in the charge nurse's command seat. She didn't look up as Lynn approached. Peter Marshall, the ward clerk, had left for the day. An attending physician was sitting with her back to Lynn, bent over a chart, dictating. Lynn did a double take. As chance would have it, it was Dr. Siri Erikson!

For a moment Lynn thought of hightailing it and returning later when the hematologist was gone. After having a mildly disturbing encounter with the woman that morning, Lynn wasn't sure she wanted to risk another conversation. But, not knowing what was going to happen in the dean's office in less than an hour, this might be her only opportunity. She had to take the chance.

After a reassuring breath, Lynn entered the circular desk area. She smiled pleasantly at the charge nurse, who looked up with a questioning, wrinkled brow. Lynn hoped her disguise would carry the day, as medical students were not a common sight in the neuro ICU late in the day and without a preceptor. Lynn could see her name. It was Charlotte Hinson. She was a heavyset blonde in her late thirties but with a sprinkle of freckles across her nose that made her look particularly youthful. "Can I help you?" she asked. Thankfully her tone was pleasant and not confrontational.

"I've come to check in on Dr. Stuart's patient, Carl Vandermeer," Lynn said, keeping her voice low. "I wanted to see the result of the serum electrophoresis."

"You could have checked the EMR," Charlotte said cheerfully. "It's in there. It was mentioned at report. It would have saved you a trip."

"I was in the neighborhood," Lynn said, forcing another smile. If she could have looked at the electronic record, she certainly would have. Right from the beginning of this nightmare, she knew enough not to try to access Carl's EMR. She might have gotten to see it once, but then her doing so would have been flagged immediately, and she would have heard from the security people in the Medical Records Department. The EMR were protected more diligently than the physical charts.

To be helpful, Charlotte gave the chart rack a spin, as it was within her reach, but both she and Lynn noticed the 8 slot was empty.

"I've got the Vandermeer chart," Dr. Erikson said, overhearing the conversation. She had turned to face Lynn. "Miss Peirce, nice to see you again."

"Thank you," Lynn said. It seemed conversation was inevitable. "Sorry to be a bother yet again."

"No bother! Please, sit down! I enjoyed our chat this morning. We can talk about the case together. I've been asked to do a formal consult on Mr. Vandermeer."

To Lynn's surprise, the woman seemed friendly, not at all like she had been that morning. After a brief hesitation, Lynn pulled a chair over and sat down. She felt she didn't have a lot of choice if she wanted to avoid offending the mercurial hematologist. Dr. Erikson immediately pushed Carl's chart over. It was open to the page with the results of the serum electrophoresis, just what Lynn wanted to see.

Lynn glanced at the graph of the serum proteins, separated by size and electric charge, which she now knew considerably more about, having just read the Wikipedia article within the hour. To her it looked like a squiggly range of mountains drawn by a child. A definite narrow spike in the gamma globulin range interrupted the otherwise smooth contour. The spike wasn't nearly as tall as Morrison's, but otherwise it was in a similar location.

"What do you think?" Dr. Erikson said.

"I guess I think that is not normal," Lynn said. Medical students learned to hedge their bets. "What I don't know is if it qualifies to be called a gammopathy." She had also reread the gammopathy article and felt reasonably capable of holding up her side of a conversation.

"Does it surprise you?"

"I suppose so," Lynn said. "If it is a gammopathy, he seems too young for it. I've read that gammopathies are not common until after age fifty, and he is only twenty-nine, the same age as Scarlett Morrison."

"But this is not a gammopathy, merely a possible warning he might develop one. He will need to be followed. If the spike enlarges, we'll have to do a bone marrow exam to access the plasma cell population."

"What does it mean if it increases?"

"It depends on how high it goes. A spike like that means that he is producing a particular protein. In someone as young as this it would be called a 'paraprotein abnormality of undetermined significance.' But then again, the spike could be the precursor of something more serious, like multiple myeloma or a lymphoma."

"Interesting," Lynn said, to say something. She was tempted to mention Ashanti Davis and her diagnosis of multiple myeloma, but she held back for fear that Dr. Erikson would ask how she knew about the woman. Instead she said, "I'm afraid this is all a little over my head. But why do you think he has developed this paraprotein? This morning you said it didn't have anything to do with anesthesia."

"Absolutely not!" Dr. Erikson said with a touch of the same irritation she'd exhibited that morning, making Lynn inwardly cringe. "I am one hundred percent certain it had nothing to do with anesthesia." Then, catching herself, she said more calmly: "I'm sure he had this serum protein abnormality, or at least a tendency for it, prior to his operation. No one knew because there hadn't been any reason to do a serum electrophoresis. A low-level abnormal paraprotein like this would be entirely asymptomatic. I'm just surprised you bring up the anesthesia issue again. Has someone raised this idea in the Anesthesia Department?"

"Not that I have heard of," Lynn said. She tensed. She certainly didn't want to talk about the Anesthesia Department and possibly reveal she wasn't taking an anesthesia elective.

"It's an absurd association," Dr. Erikson added. "But if you hear of any reference to gammopathy in any context in the Anesthesia Department, I would like to hear about it, just as I'd like to hear if you or anyone else comes up with any conclusions about how these two patients suffered comas."

"Of course," Lynn said to be agreeable, again tempted to mention that there had been a third case, not two, but she held back for the same reason she had earlier.

"In return, I'll keep you abreast of any changes with this case. Now that there has been a formal consult, I will be following Mr. Vandermeer, even when he gets transferred over to the Shapiro."

"What?" Lynn said explosively enough to cause Dr. Erikson to jump. Although Lynn's voice hadn't been that loud, it was magnified by the subdued environment in the ICU. It was a place where everyone was tense. When things went wrong, and they occasionally did, they went really wrong.

Although Lynn had understood there was a chance that Carl might be sent to the Shapiro Institute at some point, the fact that it might be imminent dismayed her. Even though she knew his prognosis for recovery was gloomy, she also knew that his being transferred to the Shapiro meant that the neurology team was giving up, and she would have to relinquish the modicum of hope she had been vainly trying to hold on to. With an attempt to modulate her voice, she asked: "When is this supposed to happen?"

"You seem upset?" Dr. Erikson questioned. She stared at Lynn.

"I had no idea a transfer was being considered," Lynn said, trying to recover her composure and suppress her emotions. "Dr. Stuart, the resident, didn't mention it."

"I can't imagine why," Dr. Erikson said. "The neurology team suggested the move, and they're in charge. Since the infectious disease consult has come up with nothing, it might be soon. If I had to guess, I'd say he might be transferred as early as this afternoon or this evening. Certainly by tomorrow morning at the latest. He hasn't had a gastrostomy for nutrition yet, but Shapiro patients are routinely brought over here if surgery is indicated."

"It seems so soon," Lynn said despite herself.

"He'll get better care over there for his condition," Dr. Erikson said. "That's the point."

"Have his parents been informed?"

"Of course!" Dr. Erikson said. She looked at Lynn askance, questioningly. Then she added, "The parents are very much involved. I've have seen them in here on several occasions. I mean, everyone knows that admission to the Shapiro Institute is voluntary. The family has to agree. Most do when they learn how much it is for the patient's benefit."

"What about his blood count?" Lynn asked quickly to change the subject. "Have the lymphocytes continued to go up? What if this paraprotein problem continues?"

The hematologist didn't answer immediately. She stared at Lynn with such intensity that Lynn thought the worst. She worried she had given herself away and that the very next question would be a demand to know exactly what Lynn's relationship was with the patient. But to her relief, when Dr. Erikson spoke it was just to answer her question. "The white count has gone up to fourteen thousand, with most of it lymphocytes."

"Interesting," Lynn said insincerely. Suddenly all she wanted to do was get away. As upset as she was about Carl's possibly being sent to the Shapiro, she truly feared that if the conversation continued, she'd end up exposing herself as hardly a disinterested party. But she stayed where she was. They talked for a short time about bone marrow function and the origin of the various blood proteins, but Lynn wasn't concentrating. As soon as she could, she said she had to get back to the OR and excused herself.

"Remember to get in touch with me if you come to any conclusions," Dr. Erikson called after her. "And I can keep you up-to-date about Vandermeer and Morrison. I'll be following both patients at the Shapiro."

Lynn nodded to indicate that she had heard and then quickly left the ICU. As she hustled down the central corridor, she tried to calm herself. She felt a sense of panic now that Carl might be physically taken away from her. It meant that she wouldn't be able to check on how he was doing or the kind of care he was getting. First it had been his mind and memories that had been stolen, and now it was to be his body.

Lynn knew all too well from her brief student introduction to the Shapiro Institute that only immediate family were allowed to visit a patient, and only for brief periods scheduled in advance. And the visits weren't much. The family members could only observe their loved one through a plate-glass window in order to protect the inmate from outside contamination. Some families complained but ultimately they understood it was for the patients' collective benefit.

Lynn shuddered to think of Carl locked away in such a dehumanized place, remembering her student visit two years before as if it were yesterday. The tour that she and her classmates had been given had been restricted to a conference room and then to one of three visitation rooms where family member visits took place, both located in the institute immediately beyond the connector to the main hospital. The area beyond the plate-glass window in the visitation room was like a stage set where the unconscious patient was placed on what looked to be a regular hospital bed but wasn't, with its unique structure camouflaged by the bed linens. The patient transport was fully automated, reminiscent to Lynn of an assembly line in an automobile plant.

Lynn remembered a mannequin had been used, not a real patient. Lynn and her classmates had been duly impressed at the demonstration. There hadn't been any real people involved. The whole back wall of the set had opened and the mannequin had arrived automatically by the use of robotic equipment, placed in the ersatz bed in a matter of seconds, and covered up to the neck with a sheet. At that point all the machinery folded back into the wall and disappeared. The students were told that the immediate family members didn't see the comings and goings; they were brought in only after the patient was already positioned.

Lynn and her friends had speculated about what the rest of the Shapiro Institute must have been like to enable them to take care of a thousand or so vegetative patients, which is what they had been told was projected to be the average occupancy. They were never given specifics above and beyond told only that automation and computerization made it all possible.

After the mannequin demonstration, there had been a short question-and-answer session run by the individual responsible for the medical student tour. Lynn had asked why families chose to have their loved ones at the Shapiro in the face of such limited visitation. The answer had been simple. It was because the Shapiro's record of keeping such patients alive was far superior to any other hospital or clinic. The tour guide had gone on to say that in most institutions, up to 40 percent of patients who were comatose from a variety of causes were dead in the first year, whereas the Shapiro had lost no patients in the first year of operation and had lost only twenty-two patients total after six years.

Lynn remembered that Michael had also posed a question, because the mannequin used in the demonstration was outfitted with what looked very much like a football helmet. As a college player himself, Michael was curious. The answer had been that the helmet was a breakthrough technology developed specifically for the Shapiro Institute and that all their patients were equipped with them. It was described as a wireless unit that monitored brain activity in real time and, more important, was also capable of stimulating portions of the brain.

Now, as Lynn approached the hospital elevators, her panic peaked with all these thoughts swirling in her head. She had to do something. She could not allow Carl to be stashed away in such a callous place with contact with her denied. All at once she impulsively decided, no matter what, she would visit him, and not in the restricted-visitation room, staring at him through a plate-glass window. If Carl was to be transferred, she would figure out a way to see him up close and personal. She would need to know exactly what was happening to him and exactly how he was being cared for. She didn't know how she would manage it, but she would do it.

28.

eez!" Michael complained. "You scared the hell out of me." Lynn had come up behind him out of his line of sight in the waiting area of the ophthalmology clinic and without warning roughly yanked him out of earshot of the waiting patients. At the time he had been standing off to the side, busily texting her to find out exactly where she wanted to meet up.

"Carl is going to be transferred to the Shapiro," Lynn blurted out in a forced whisper. The possibility had devolved to a reality in her mind.

"Okay, okay," Michael soothed. He could immediately appreciate her panic.

"You know what kind of place that is," Lynn pleaded. Now that she was talking with Michael, the emotion that she had held in check with Erikson threatened to take over.

A quick glance told Michael that a number of patients, who were still waiting to be seen, were taking notice of a young black man talking to a young, distressed white woman. Southern eyebrows of both whites and blacks rose.

"Come with me!" Michael said in a voice that did not brook dissent. He took Lynn by the arm and quickly led her back to an empty exam room and away from prying eyes. Since the clinic was almost over, there were lots of such rooms available. He shut the door.

"You gotta be easy, girl," he urged. He put his hands on Lynn's shoulders and looked her in the eye. "You know what I'm saying? You can't jump the couch now. We got a meeting to go to where we need to be on our game. I don't know why the dean wants to see us but it sure ain't to pat us on the back."

"But . . . ," Lynn started.

"No buts! Pull yourself together. After the meeting we'll hash out this Shapiro business. But now we gotta get our shit together and be cool."

"You're right," Lynn said, wiping her eyes with a knuckle. "You're always right, you bastard."

"Now, that sounds like the Lynn I know. Listen! We gotta have some sort of a plan."

"What do you think she is going to say to us?"

"Your guess is as good as mine. Chances are she heard from our new buddy, Benton Rhodes, and knows that we talked to Sandra Wykoff about the Vandermeer case. That's at a minimum. It stands to reason, considering the time frame."

"Do you think she is going to accuse us of a HIPAA violation?"

"I hope not, at least not yet. That's why we need a way to explain how we heard the details about Carl's anesthesia disaster."

Lynn nodded. She knew Michael was right and was thankful he was being levelheaded, even if she wasn't. There had to be a way for them to have heard of the details without violating HIPAA. Obviously the anesthesia ruse wouldn't hold water with the dean. From the text both of them had received, it was obvious she knew they were on the fourth-year specialties rotation and not taking an anesthesia elective.

"Does the dean know you and Carl were an item?"

"I haven't the faintest idea," Lynn said. "I suppose it's possible, since the dean of students certainly knew."

"Yeah, but they are such different people. The dean of students is so personable and the dean of the school is so aloof and detached. It's like they're from different planets."

"I have an idea," Lynn said suddenly. "I could just say that one of the neurology residents told me about the case to show me the doll's eye reflex. It's not a lie, just not the whole story. But it rings true. I mean, this is a teaching hospital."

"That's a little weak," Michael said. "Especially if she knows you and Carl were tight. It also begs the question of why you were talking to a neurology resident. But no matter. At least it's a plan the dean might buy." He looked at his watch. "The reality is we're running out of time. This is not the kind of a meeting we should be late to. You got your act together?"

"I think so," Lynn said. She took a tissue from a dispenser on the exam room countertop and blew her nose. "Let's get it over with."

The two students quickly used the connector to get into the main hospital building. The administration offices, including the dean's offices, were on the first floor. As quickly as they could navigate the crowded main hallway, they entered the administration area through a door with a cut-glass insert. The atmosphere changed abruptly. It was serene, with a carpeted floor and framed original oil paintings on the walls. They passed the hospital administration offices and arrived in the academic area. Here the furnishings were not quite so opulent.

After giving their names to a staid secretary, they took seats. It was three minutes before five.

"We made it," Lynn said in a whisper.

They ended up having to wait for a quarter of an hour. They didn't talk after sitting down. The atmosphere was appropriately funereal to fan their fears. Both Lynn and Michael knew the dean of students well but not the dean of the medical school, whom neither had even met.

Lynn tried to relax as Michael appeared to be, but couldn't for a variety of reasons, mostly centered around the disturbing idea of Carl's being transferred to the Shapiro and the uncertainty of what they were facing with Dr. English.

"The dean will see you now," the secretary finally said, gesturing toward the closed door that led into the office beyond. The two students approached the door, with Lynn slightly in the lead. They shared a glance. Both shrugged. Michael made a fist and pretended to knock in the air. Lynn actually did it. They heard a voice tell them to come in.

In keeping with the general decor in the immediate outer area, Dr. Janet English's office was attractive but not as over the top as everyone knew the hospital president's was. There was no mahogany paneling and the artwork was framed prints, not oil paintings. There was a desk and a sitting area for informal meetings. The students approached the desk. There were several chairs, but without being advised otherwise Lynn and Michael remained standing. The dean was finishing signing a stack of papers. After a moment, she looked up. It was obvious from her expression she was annoyed. She didn't suggest they sit down.

Lynn guessed the dean was somewhere between fifty and sixty. Her complexion was dark. Likewise, her hair was the color of anthracite coal. Through her rimless spectacles, her eyes were like black marbles. If Lynn had been forced to guess, she would have said India was part of the dean's genealogy.

"I got a major complaint about you," Dr. English snapped. "You can understand how disappointed I was to learn that two of our best students are causing trouble—students on full scholarship, I might add. And to make matters worse, the trouble was bad enough to involve Dr. Feinberg, the president of the hospital and chairman of

Middleton Healthcare. He was upset enough to call me personally to complain."

There was a pause. Lynn felt an almost overwhelming urge to apologize. She was well aware that the financial support the school had extended to her had been key to her being able to attend medical school. But Michael was as financially dependent as she, and he wasn't saying anything.

"I was told that you had taken it upon yourselves to question one of our attending anesthesiologists about a recent, very sensitive case. Is this true?"

Both Lynn and Michael started to speak at the same moment, then stopped. Lynn gestured for Michael to talk. She knew he was far better at diplomacy than she, even when she wasn't as emotionally strung out and sleep deprived as she was now.

"We did talk with Dr. Sandra Wykoff," Michael said. "But we weren't, as you say, questioning her. We went to ask her about a case of delayed return of consciousness. As tragic as the case was, we thought that there had to be something for us students to learn."

"Did you not think of the legal aspects?" Dr. English asked.

Lynn felt herself relax a degree. The dean did not seem to know that Lynn and Carl were romantically involved, which was probably good. Also her voice had moderated. The edge was already gone. It was another reminder for Lynn that Michael was clever at this kind of confrontation. She also noted he was using the King's English, without the slightest hint of the 'hood.

"As doctors to be, we were thinking more about it from the patient's perspective," Michael added.

"I suppose that is commendable from a student's point of view," Dr. English said. "But unfortunately there is another aspect. The potential malpractice implications are horrendous when a healthy young man becomes comatose after a simple operation, even when there is no malpractice involved. Such a lawsuit could damage this hospital and affect its ability to take care of thousands of patients. In today's litigious world, avoiding a lawsuit or controlling it if it does happen in a case like this has to be a prime consideration."

"We certainly understand that," Michael said.

"There had been a strict directive from our legal department that no one was to discuss this case."

"We hadn't heard that," Michael said. "But now that we have, we certainly understand and will be cooperative."

"How exactly had you heard the particulars about this case to begin with?" Dr. English asked.

Michael and Lynn exchanged a quick glance. So far the discussion had been going better than they had anticipated, especially with HIPAA not even being mentioned. But here was the question they feared. Michael nodded to Lynn to take over and try her idea.

"I was talking with the neurology resident on the case," Lynn began. "He had offered to show me a doll's eye reflex, which I had never seen before. That was when I had learned the details."

Dr. English didn't respond but nodded almost imperceptibly. After a pause she asked, "Did you see the reflex at least? Was it apparent?"

"Yes, I did see it. It was very dramatic."

"Okay. This is all making more sense to me now. But tell me this: have you two talked about this case with anyone else, like with classmates or anyone besides Dr. Wykoff?"

Lynn and Michael looked at each other and both shook their heads and said no simultaneously.

"Good," Dr. English said. "As I said, this case is extraordinarily sensitive from a legal perspective. Do not discuss it with anyone!" Dr. English poked a finger at each student in turn to hammer home her point. "If you fail to heed my warning and do discuss it with anyone, anyone at all, I will see to it that you are expelled. Needless to say, being expelled would be a tragedy for both of you, especially this close to graduation. I don't know how to make it any clearer. I trust you understand the gravity of this?"

"Absolutely," Lynn and Michael said in unison as if they had practiced the response.

"All right," Dr. English said. "Let's move on to another issue."

Both Lynn and Michael tensed. They thought they were in the clear. Now they weren't sure. Neither had any idea what was coming.

"When I spoke with the president he said one other thing. As a matter of explanation of your behavior he told me that you two were researching the issue of hospital-acquired morbidity. Is that true, and if it is, why, and why now?"

Lynn and Michael exchanged another glance. A slight nod from Michael encouraged Lynn to answer. "I came across an article recently from *Scientific American*, which presented some disturbing statistics. It estimated that four hundred forty thousand people die each year in hospitals from mistakes, and that a million leave the hospital with a significant medical problem they didn't have before they were admitted.

"We were honestly flabbergasted. I mean, we'd heard about the problem during third-year medicine, but we had no idea of the numbers. When we heard about this current case, we thought it was another glaring example and wanted to try to understand how it could have happened."

Again the dean didn't respond immediately. She took off her glasses and rubbed her eyes. Then she put her glasses back on and said, "The statistics you quote are sobering. Hospital-acquired infections, or HAI, are the major problem. Did the article point that out?"

"Not specifically," Lynn said. "It didn't break the statistics down to specific causes."

"Well, let me assure you that hospital-acquired infections are the crux of the matter. On a national scale, HAI rates are anywhere from five to ten percent of admissions in the best institutions. In the offending institutions, the rate can go much higher. Do you know what the HAI rate is for Middleton Healthcare hospitals, including this medical center?"

Lynn and Michael shook their heads.

"Let me tell you," Dr. English said proudly. "Our combined rate is less than two percent."

"That's impressive," Lynn said, and she meant it. Both she and Michael knew that the medical center made a big effort at infection control in many ways, including an active campaign encouraging hand washing and hand sanitizer use in addition to strict control of intravenous lines, respiratory machines, and catheters. Neither was aware of the true extent of the success.

"If you students are interested in hospital morbidity, you should look into nosocomial infection control. That is where you and your classmates could make a difference, not with an isolated case of delayed return to consciousness. Am I making myself clear?"

"Absolutely," Lynn and Michael again said simultaneously. Their relief was palpable.

"In fact, I will make it easy for you," Dr. English said. "I will contact IT and arrange for you both to have access to the hospital's discharge statistics in our medical center system, provided that you adhere to one major condition: If you are going to talk with anyone outside of our community, particularly the media, I want you to run whatever it is by me first. Is that clear?"

"Absolutely," the two students reiterated.

"We are justly proud of our success with infection control," Dr. English continued. "But some of the statistics are not for general consumption. I hope you understand."

This time both students nodded agreement without verbalizing.

"Good!" Dr. English said. "I will let the president know that you understand now about this unfortunate anesthesia case and the need not to discuss it. I can assure you that it is already being carefully investigated by the Anesthesia Department. If you are interested in hearing about the investigation and what is learned, I imagine I will be able to get the chief of surgery to invite you to the morbidity and mortality session when it will be discussed. Would that be of interest?"

"Absolutely," Lynn said. Michael nodded.

"Okay," Dr. English said, looking down at her desk and moving the stack of papers she had signed to the side. "That is all." Without even looking up again, she reached for her phone and started speaking with her secretary about putting a call through to Dr. Feinberg.

Mildly surprised by the suddenness of the meeting's end, but without needing any further encouragement, the two students quickly left. It wasn't until they got back into the hustle and bustle of the hospital that they slowed enough to speak to each other. First they fist bumped. They had to talk loudly to be heard.

"That was a piece of cake," Lynn said.

"Right on!" Michael said. "But it could have gone either way. It was a good thing we thought about what to say if she asked how we knew about Carl. That tipped the balance. It was like putting in a three-pointer at the buzzer from downtown to win the b-ball game. You did good, girl!"

"It's weird she never mentioned Carl's name." The slight euphoria she'd felt from surviving the meeting with the dean was already beginning to evaporate.

"I noticed that, too. But what I found weirder is that we went in there expecting to get busted, and we come out with increased access to the hospital data bank. We might take advantage of that. Hospital-acquired infection is serious shit."

"It might be," Lynn said. She sighed. "But right now I'm not interested. Now I want to talk about Carl being sent to the Shapiro." There was a sudden catch in her voice.

"Hold off, woman. Wait until we get back to the dorm. If there's a chance you might bust out bawling, I don't want people gaping at us. You know what I'm saying?"

Lynn got the message loud and clear and appreciated how he

worded it. The fact that someone with his intelligence and academic record could so easily flip back and forth from Oxford English to the language of the 'hood amazed her. It always did, and he knew it, which is why he did it, and only with her. For her it emphasized their closeness. With everyone else, including patients, he always spoke with the diction of a college English professor.

And she knew he was right about her possibly losing control. For the moment she had her act together, but she knew that might change when she started talking about what was in Carl's limited and dismal future.

They cut through the nearly deserted clinic as they normally did. Only a few stragglers were still waiting to be seen. Outside it was a beautiful Charleston early evening. The sun was still reasonably strong, with another two hours of early-spring daylight left. After they had walked for several hundred feet through the landscaped inner courtyard with flowers busting out of their beds, Lynn slowed. Like she had the day before, she couldn't help gazing at the hulking granite silhouette of the Shapiro Institute. The mere sight of it brought on the rush of emotion that she had been holding back.

"I cannot believe that Carl might be shut away in there," Lynn said, losing the battle of fighting off tears. "He might even be going this evening."

Hearing her voice tremble, Michael guided her off the main walkway and over to an empty park bench, half-hidden by shrubbery from the considerable pedestrian traffic. They sat down. They were far enough out of the way that the other students trekking back to the dorm didn't see them, or if they happened to look in their direction, didn't pay them any heed, which was good, because Lynn quickly lost it and suffered through an extended bout of tears. Michael didn't say anything, thinking it best for her to let it out.

When Lynn finally had herself under control and could talk, he asked how she had found out that Carl might be going to the Shapiro.

"From Dr. Erikson," Lynn managed. There were still catches in her voice, but she was succeeding in calming herself down.

"She called you?"

"No. I ran into her," Lynn said. She found a tissue in one of her jacket pockets and carefully dried her eyes. "I went back to the neuro ICU before we met with the dean because I was worried that afterward I might not be allowed. I thought it might be the last time I got to see him for a long time. I also wanted to see what the serum electrophoresis test showed."

"Was it abnormal?"

"It was, which is why Erikson was there doing a formal consult."

"How abnormal?"

"Only mildly so far. Just a small spike in the gamma globulin curve, but my sense is that Dr. Erikson expects it to get worse. She was quite friendly to me this time, but I have to say, I find her strange and unpredictable."

"How did she happen to tell you Carl might be transferred?"

"It just came out in the conversation. She is one weird lady. I can't read her at all. One minute she seems friendly, the next pissed. Maybe she doesn't feel well because, frankly, she doesn't look well. Anyway, remember I told you she asked me to let her know if we came to any conclusions about how Carl or Morrison became comatose. Well, today she added to the list. She wants me to tell her if I hear anyone in Anesthesia talking about gammopathy. Now, I find that strange. I mean, why is she asking me, a medical student? As an attending she could ask anybody she wanted to in the Anesthesia Department, including Rhodes."

"It sure as hell means she bought into our ruse about anesthesia," Michael said. "But she has to know that no one in Anesthesia is going to be talking about gammopathy. There is no way anesthesia and serum protein abnormalities can be related."

"I'm not so sure," Lynn said as finished drying her eyes. "There is something about all this that smells bad."

"Oh, come on, girl! There's nothing about anesthesia that is antigenic. It has been used in millions upon millions of cases without pumping up anybody's immune system. There is no association."

"Let's put it this way," Lynn said. "I'm just not sure. We have three cases in which it seems to have played some role."

"Only one that we know for sure: Morrison."

"Carl could be developing a gammopathy and Ashanti must have had one, too, if she has multiple myeloma. This can't be by chance. Something is not right in all this. And I'll tell you something else: If and when Carl goes into that place, come hell or high water, I'm going to go in there and visit him."

"They are not going to let you visit," Michael said. "They were very clear about that. Only immediate family is allowed, and you, my friend, are not immediate family."

"I wouldn't be satisfied with that kind of visit even if they let me," Lynn said with a wave of dismissal. "I want to go into the place and actually see how Carl is being treated, not look at him through a plate-glass window."

"Come on, girl! You can't be serious. They are not going to let you do that."

"I'm talking about breaking in. You told me you went through that door over there, which led into the network operation center." Lynn pointed to the single entrance. "I'll do the same and start from there."

"You're not serious, are you? Tell me you are not!"

"If Carl gets transferred, I'm going in there. I've made up my mind. I think I could do it. My sense, from what you told me of your visit yesterday, is that their security is pretty lax. I mean, you said so yourself. They probably haven't had a security episode for the whole eight years they have been in operation. I mean, who would want to sneak into a holding facility for brain-dead people, for God's sake?"

"It might be true that they have become lax but . . ."

"It stands to reason."

"The trouble is, it's a big huge risk. To be honest, I don't think we should do this," Michael said, becoming serious.

"What do you me 'we,' white man?" Lynn said with cynical laugh, referring to the Ron Metzner joke involving the Lone Ranger that Michael had reminded her of yesterday. "I'm going to do it myself. When we got those texts today from the dean, I realized that you shouldn't take a fall, if that is what happens. This is my battle because Carl was my squeeze. If there is a consequence, it should be mine."

"As your twin, it's my job to keep you out of trouble. Let me decide how much risk I want to take. But you know something? The more I think about it, the more I might be exaggerating the fallout of going in there. Maybe the worst-case scenario might only be a slap on the wrist for trespassing. I mean, it is part of this institution, and we are legit medical students. Hell, the way we have been violating HIPAA is worse than our going into an area of the hospital that's supposed to be off limits."

"If Carl gets sent in there, I'm going in. I've made up my mind."

"All right, you made up your mind. But tell me how you think you are going to pull it off."

"I will need your help," Lynn admitted. "Because the key is going to be your newfound friend, Vladimir whatever his name is."

"Vladimir Malaklov, my Russian programmer buddy! What can he do?"

"Get me one of the scrub suits like we've seen on the people that work there. I don't want to stand out if I bump into anyone, which is probably a given. Since he works in there, like you said, he probably has one, just chooses not to wear it. There must be a source for them, like there is for regular scrubs in the main hospital."

"How the fuck am I going to explain why I need a Shapiro suit?" Michael shook his head in disbelief.

"Be creative! Say you want it for a costume party. I don't care. But tell him you need it in my size."

"Shit, girl!" Michael complained. "Is that all?"

"No," Lynn said. "I want you to give me Vladimir's user name and password."

Michael groaned out loud and then laughed sarcastically. "If I do that I think my friendship with my Russian buddy is going to be short-lived. Why do you need it?"

"Remember when we made our visit to the Shapiro, and they bragged that they had had only twenty-two deaths over six years? I'd like to find out what the causes of those deaths were. And how many people have died since our tour. And while I'm at it, I'd like to find out how many people woke up from their vegetative state and were discharged. In one of the articles I read last night, it says as many as ten percent of patients in a vegetative state from head trauma eventually achieve enough return to consciousness to go home. A few even completely recover. I wonder what that figure is for the Shapiro. They didn't tell us that."

"Please don't tell me you are planning on trying to hack the Shapiro system from your laptop with Vladimir's log-in! If you do that, they'd be onto you in a matter of hours, and you'll be doing hard time in Bennettsville."

"Don't worry. I'm not that stupid. I'll use a hospital terminal, preferably one in the IT Department. If Vladimir really has admin status, which he has to have to do what he's doing, there wouldn't be a red flag. And I also want to find out more about Ashanti Davis and how close her case matches Morrison's and Carl's."

"Maybe we can find all this out using the access Dr. English said she would provide us."

"Oh, please!" Lynn said mockingly. "She's not going to give us access to Shapiro data. In fact, she probably will only be allowing us to look at data about infections and only in the main hospital. If I'm going to find out the kind of things I want to learn, I'll need Vladimir's log-in. I need carte blanche access."

"You're on a roll, girl. And I understand. You need to keep yourself busy, so I'm not going to say much. But tell me this: even if you're sporting one of those Shapiro suits, how are you thinking of getting in?"

"You are going to help with that, too," Lynn said.

Michael rolled his eyes. "Why did I bother asking?"

"You told me that the security of the door you went in has only a low-level, decade-old thumbprint touchscreen. That shouldn't be much of a hurdle. You are going to get me Vladimir's thumbprint. Do it when you invite him over to share your Jay-Z collection. I researched how to foil a generic fingerprint scanner with a bit of latex and wood glue. It's amazing what you can get off the Internet. I already got the stuff I need."

"My goodness!" Michael marveled with a shake of his head. He sat back against the bench, and, following Lynn's line of sight, stared over at the Shapiro. "Okay! For the sake of argument, say this works. What's the plan once you're inside, just to wander around blindly and get fucking lost? The place is huge!"

"I'm working on that angle," Lynn said.

"Lay it on me, girl!"

"Later," Lynn said. "Right now I want to show you some other stuff that I discovered today when I was comparing the anesthesia records for all three cases. There are several disturbing points of similarity, and they are motivating me to up my efforts."

"Like what?"

"I prefer to show you. The printouts are in my room. Come on!" Lynn grabbed Michael's arm and pulled him to his feet.

29.

Despite suffering an emotionally exhausting bout of tears on top of her basic fatigue from having had only four hours of sleep over the last thirty-four, Lynn was now, according to Michael, "juiced." Although she knew enough about psychology to guess that it represented another form of denial, she didn't care. It gave her the feeling she was actively doing something rather than just passively being emotionally tortured.

Prior to her discussion with Michael about breaking into the Shapiro, the plan had been somewhat vague in her mind. Now she had a good idea of what she needed to do and what she needed Michael to do, and she was eager to get started. But before she did, she wanted to show Michael what had ignited her mounting unease about the whole situation. She thought it might motivate him to help her get what she needed from Vladimir. It had certainly motivated her.

Lynn keyed her door and pushed it open. Michael followed her inside but paused on the threshold. "Maybe I should get a hazmat suit," he said, surveying the disarray. He was accustomed to her casual attitude toward domestic order, but this seemed beyond the pale. Computer printouts scattered on the floor, along with a number of textbooks, made it impossible to walk without stepping on them. More printouts cluttered most horizontal surfaces along with a mixture of soiled clothes and clean clothes with no readily apparent distinction. The bed was free of debris, although unmade.

"Very funny," Lynn said. She pulled him into the room and kicked the door closed. "I know the place is a god-awful mess, but ignore it for the moment!" She guided him over to the desk chair, which was clear, like the bed, and made him sit. Pushing aside papers to create an open space on the desk in front of him, she put down all three anesthesia record printouts in a row so that they were visible at the same time.

"Okay," Michael said. "What am I supposed to be looking at?"

"Remember this blip that Wykoff pointed out on Carl's record?" Lynn asked, pointing it out.

"I call it a frame offset," Michael said. "What about it?"

Using her index finger, Lynn pointed to the same upward jump in the vital signs on the other two printouts. "All three cases have the same distortion or whatever it is, and all at exactly the same time: fifty-two minutes into the case."

"Yo!" Michael exclaimed, looking from one printout to the other. "Now, that's a righteous pickup." He glanced up at Lynn. "That's big-time weird. What's your take?"

"I haven't the slightest idea," Lynn admitted. "But it has to be significant. I wish I could ask Dr. Wykoff what she thinks."

"That's not going to happen."

"Agreed," Lynn said. "We can't go to anybody in Anesthesia, at least not for the moment. We're on our own to figure out what it might mean. But that's not all. There's one more surprise."

"What? Was the timing of the low-oxygenation alarm the same, too?"

"No. It was close but slightly different in each case."

For a moment Lynn didn't move, just stared at Michael.

"Well?" Michael said impatiently. "You going to lay it on me or what?"

"You don't see it?"

"You got the ball, twin. Either dribble, pass, or shoot!"

Again, with her index finger, Lynn pointed to a very small box in the right-hand corner of each record. It was labeled MACHINE, and in each case it had the same number: 37.

Michael again raised his eyes to Lynn's. For a moment they regarded each other. It was Michael who broke the silence: "All three cases involved the same freaking anesthesia machine!" he exclaimed. "That's also got to mean something."

"The same anesthesia machine having the same blip at the exact same time in all three cases. Statistically that happening by chance is nil. With two cases, maybe, but with three, no way."

Michael looked back down at the anesthesia records. "I agree. But what do we do about it? Should we tell someone, and if we should, who?"

"It's got to be significant, which means something weird is going on, but I can't come up with a single, even potentially plausible explanation. And there is nobody we can go to with this without incriminating ourselves big time. The only thing I can think of doing is getting more info out of Shapiro."

"This timing thing is what amazes me," Michael said, looking back at the records.

"It more than amazes me," Lynn said with sudden ferocity. "My intuition is ringing alarm bells, especially when I combine this timing issue with what I have learned from all these other printouts." Lynn wildly gestured toward all the articles littering the floor. "And then with Carl going there . . ."

"Whoa, girl!" Michael cautioned. "Get a grip! You have to slow down. Remember, Carl's not been sent to the Shapiro yet."

"Morrison has, and Carl's case is just like hers."

"True, but you're jumping the gun, my friend. Listen, I don't mean to sound patronizing, but you are under a lot of stress! I think you need some food and a good night's sleep and then you can reboot. Let's go back over to the hospital and get dinner."

"Of course I'm stressed," Lynn snapped. "And I know I'm exhausted. But I'm not sure I could sleep even if I tried. I mean, why are they rushing to transfer Carl and Morrison? It's way too quick in my estimation. Maybe the same thing happened with Ashanti. But why? What's the rush? It can't just be economics. Maybe it's for better care, but I just don't know." Lynn again gestured toward all the printouts scattered about her room. "These articles point out there are always a few patients who defy the odds and wake up. Carl's problem is less than thirty-six hours old. Why transfer him so soon? What if he wakes up in the Shapiro? With all the automation that is involved over there, would someone even notice? Whether my getting in the Shapiro can answer such questions, I don't know, but somehow I think there's a chance. I have to do it!"

Michael nodded. The last thing he wanted to do was make Lynn more upset than she already was. Instead of arguing with her, he glanced down at the floor and picked up the nearest article. It was the article that he and Lynn had read in the neuro ICU after seeing the Morrison chart, the one titled "Monoclonal Gammopathy of Undetermined Significance."

"So let me guess," Michael said finally, as he quickly flipped through the printout for a second quick read. "You're thinking that this paraprotein stuff has some significance."

"I do!" Lynn said. "I have no idea how or why or anything. But it seems that a paraprotein was or is involved with all three patients. Well, we don't know for sure if a paraprotein was involved with Ashanti, but the fact that she has multiple myeloma is at least suggestive. It's the worst-case scenario for a paraprotein gammopathy."

"Seems to me you are heading out into the stratosphere on all this, if you don't mind my saying so," Michael said. He shook his head as he reached down for another article. This one was titled "Monoclonal Antibodies." He began to speed-read it.

"You might be right," Lynn said. "But remember what you said was on the home page of Ashanti's Shapiro EMR: drozitumab. Remember?"

"Of course I remember," Michael said.

"Do you remember what drozitumab is?"

"Of course," Michael repeated. He glanced irritably at Lynn. He was losing patience. She needed food, and she needed sleep. And he needed food, too. "What is this, a test?"

"Drozitumab is a monoclonal antibody, like you said this morning," Lynn added, ignoring Michael's mild peevishness. "It is used to treat a kind of muscle cancer, not multiple myeloma."

"I said I remember," Michael repeated.

"If Ashanti is given drozitumab and had a serum plasma protein test, it would show up as a paraprotein."

"I suppose you are right. What's your point?"

"I don't know. I'm thinking out loud and asking you to do the same."

Michael shook his head. "It's a mystery. There are too many loose pieces." He went back to reading the article on monoclonal antibodies.

"Why was drozitumab put on the front of Ashanti's record?" Lynn asked.

"Like I said this morning, I have no idea. Do you?" Michael didn't look up from his reading.

"No, I don't," Lynn admitted. "But if I had to guess, I'd say that maybe they are trying it as a treatment for multiple myeloma."

Michael raised his eyes and looked at Lynn. "You mean like just trying it to see if it might work without any specific scientific rationale, sorta shotgun style? That's questionable, my friend."

"I know that doesn't make any sense," Lynn agreed. "Okay, scrap that idea! Maybe it is simpler. From reading these articles about monoclonal antibodies forming the basis of biologic drugs, I know they have been having some problems. Maybe they are giving Ashanti various forms of drozitumab to see which ones cause less of a reaction."

"That sounds a lot more probable than the shotgun treatment idea. Of course it means they would be using her as a guinea pig. Do you really think that might be happening?"

"I'm suddenly thinking it is a possibility," Lynn said.

"But it doesn't explain the paraprotein problem."

"I know. But maybe they want their immune systems stimulated for some reason. And Carl's and Morrison's immune systems are acting up, producing the paraprotein and their fevers. Their immune systems are acting as if they are being stimulated."

"That's all very hypertheoretical."

"I know, but I'm convinced that something weird is going on. Maybe Sidereal Pharmaceuticals built Shapiro to use the patients for illicit clinical drug testing. It's certainly a captive audience who wouldn't complain. I mean, you have to admit, it makes diabolical sense. And if that's what's happening, it's another reason I sure as hell don't want Carl transferred there. Certainly not to be experimented on. No way!"

"God! That's a creepy idea," Michael said. The thought and implications raised a few hairs on his neck. "Do you really think that might be going on?"

Lynn shrugged. "I don't know, but it's an idea," she said. "It would save time and money in drug development. Drozitumab is definitely a biologic, meaning made from living cells, and biologics are the newest and biggest thing in the pharmaceutical industry. And there is a race to perfect them and test them. And, in point of fact, biologics are Sidereal's main product line!"

"No shit?" Michael said.

"Here, read this!" Lynn said as she picked an article off the bureau and handed it to Michael. It was titled "Biopharmaceutical."

Michael took the article and began to speed-read it.

While Michael read, Lynn asked: "Do you remember exactly how monoclonal antibodies or biologics that drug companies sell are made?"

"Yeah! They're made from mouse hybridomas. I just read it in the previous article. Also we had a lecture about it in second year. Why do you ask?"

"Because it's the biggest reason that a lot of testing is needed," Lynn said. "Since biologics are made from mouse cells, the drug companies have to humanize them to make them less allergenic for humans. That requires a lot of testing, particularly testing in humans. People in a vegetative state would be perfect subjects, especially if their immune systems were hyped up."

"Wow!" Michael said, finishing the latest article. "I had no idea biologics are already a fifty-billion-dollar-a-year industry and climbing. I really had no idea."

"It's going to become really huge," Lynn said. "It will top a hundred billion before long."

"You really think so?"

"I do, and for two reasons. First, because biologics have a lot of promise to provide cures, as these articles say. Second, because drug companies here in the United States get to charge whatever the hell they please. It's not like in the rest of the industrialized world, or should I say 'civilized' world."

Michael nodded. "Which they are already doing with traditional drugs." He picked up another article specifically about hybridomas.

"Exactly! And unfortunately it is not going to change with biologics, not with the money they throw around with their lobbyists."

"You're right about that," Michael agreed. "By controlling Congress, drug companies in general are enjoying legalized robbery of the American public."

"If Sidereal gets a jump in the biologics field by solving the allergy problem, they could dominate it and make an absolute fortune."

Michael finished the fourth article and tossed it aside. "Okay, I suppose now I have an idea where you're going with all this. Maybe a quick, undercover visit to the Shapiro might be just what the doctor ordered to see if they are using the patients as guinea pigs for biologics, not that I'm advocating it, mind you. I still think it is a crazy, risky idea. In the meantime, we got a more pressing problem. What to do about anesthesia machine thirty-seven? The Anesthesia Department should know about it if they don't already. Actually, the more I think about it, the more I'm sure they already know. It's too obvious to miss."

"I agree," Lynn said. "They have to know. Nor can there be anything wrong with the machine." Lynn pointed back at the anesthesia records on her desk. "Look how the patients' vital signs stayed completely normal in all three cases after the frame offset right up until the oxygen level fell! Same with all the other variables the machine was monitoring. Obviously the patients' depth of anesthesia didn't change. And remember: Wykoff specifically said she checked the anesthesia machine before Carl's case and after."

For a few minutes the two friends looked at the records and didn't speak. Each tried to decide what it all meant.

"If we go to Rhodes with any of this he's going to see red all over again," Lynn said. "And he'll want to know how we discovered it. What could we say without implicating ourselves in having violated HIPAA? After his reaction to our just talking with Dr. Wykoff, I think he'd go apeshit if he knew we had these anesthesia records. We can't go to him until we know a lot more."

"I hear you," Michael said.

"Listen," Lynn said. "How about texting your buddy Vladimir to see if you can get him to come over this evening. I want to move forward."

"You're serious about all this?"

"Very serious," Lynn said. "Thinking about Carl possibly going in there without knowing what might happen to him is driving me crazy. I need a Shapiro outfit and his thumbprint."

"I hope I don't regret this," Michael said as he got out his phone. Quickly he texted an invite for Vladimir to come over to his room for an impromptu Jay-Z party and a beer. With a flourish, he sent the message.

"Now, let's see his user name and password," Lynn said, getting out her own phone and preparing to add Vladimir to her contacts. Michael saluted before dutifully handing his phone over to Lynn with the information displayed. While she was busy adding the data into her phone, Michael's phone chimed. A text came back from Vladimir accepting the invite and saying he would be bringing the Russian souvenir he had promised for Michael.

"Satisfied?" Michael asked.

"No," Lynn said. "Text him back about the Shapiro scrubs."

"Shit, girl!" Michael complained but did as she said. As an explanation for the request he used Lynn's earlier suggestion, saying he and his girlfriend were going to a costume party. He pushed the SEND button, and then held the phone so Lynn could see it.

A minute stretched into another. Then a second text popped onto Michael's screen: *I stop and get outfits. Maybe I a little late. No problem.*

"Seems that my Russian buddy is going to come through," Michael said. "Now let's go get some dinner."

"Sounds like a plan," Lynn said. "But I need to take a quick shower." Without waiting for a response she went into her bathroom and closed the door.

"While we are over there, let's go up to the OR and see if we can find number thirty-seven," Michael shouted through the door.

"Finding it might not be so easy. With twenty-four ORs, there must be fifty or more machines."

"Probably more, but no matter. We know number thirty-seven

was used on Monday in OR Twelve. It could be still in there. Usually this time of day the OR is quiet. If it is not in twelve, we could check the storage room they use to keep the extra machines."

"If we do find it, what would we do with it?"

"That's a good question." Michael shrugged. "I guess I'd like to find out if it has been used since Carl's case. If so, and there hasn't been any problem, I'll sleep better."

"I hear you," Lynn yelled. "I'll go with you up to the OR if you come with me to the neuro ICU and IT."

"You got a deal," Michael said. "But first I'm going to my pad and clean up, too."

"Good idea. I'll meet you downstairs."

30.

Sandra Wykoff logged out. She'd been on one of the computer terminals in the OR anesthesia office for over an hour. She was perplexed. She had no idea what to make of what she had just learned, but she felt it had to mean something—but what?

After she had left Clinical Engineering she'd been paged by Geraldine Montgomery and asked if she could do an emergency case: an open reduction of a compound fracture in a teenage boy's forearm. She had welcomed the diversion, and the case had gone well.

During the middle of the short case, when she had been on cruise control, she'd thought more about Vandermeer, Morrison, and Davis. After the surgery, she'd gone into the Anesthesia office and logged onto the computer to go over Morrison's and Davis's anesthesia records with the same attention to detail that she had given to Vandermeer's in hopes of finding any similarities above and beyond the same anesthesia machine. For more than an hour nothing had caught her attention. Then suddenly she'd seen it: all three cases had the blip, or frame offset, and, more disturbing, all had it at exactly the same time after induction!

Staring off into the middle distance, Sandra wondered if such a finding could be significant. She couldn't help but believe it had to be on some level. Why was the anesthesia machine doing it despite the machine's being checked after each episode? Could it be a program error despite what she had been told down in Clinical Engineering? She doubted it, as it wasn't happening with any of the other machines. She had already checked by examining the printouts of other cases she had done using different machines. There hadn't been any frame offsets on any of the cases she'd looked at. She'd even found a few records from machine 37. They were all clean. The frame offsets had occurred with only the three cases of delayed return of consciousness.

With sudden resolve, Sandra stood up from the desk. She hurried back to the changing room to get out of her scrubs. Once she had her clothes on, she went down to the administrative area of the hospital. What she had in mind was to see if Benton Rhodes had left for the day. If he hadn't, she wanted to show him this new finding. But his office was empty.

For a moment Sandra debated having the hospital operator contact Dr. Rhodes. But then she had second thoughts, considering the harangue she'd endured earlier. What she didn't know was whether her boss was aware of this time similarity. It was entirely possible, and if he was, her bothering him after hours was probably not the best idea. It was common knowledge the chief didn't like to be disturbed at home unless absolutely necessary.

"Tomorrow is time enough," Sandra said under her breath.

Retracing her steps back into the hospital proper, she headed for the garage. She was looking forward to getting home to unwind with a glass of wine. She still felt unnerved, guilty to a degree, and generally out of sorts from yesterday's disaster. Would she ever completely get over it? The run-in with Dr. Rhodes hadn't helped. Nor had Vandermeer's continuing coma. She'd always thought that conscientiousness, meaning close attention to detail and no shortcuts, would shield her from such an experience. Obviously she had been wrong.

From the bustling first floor of the medical center, Sandra exited out into the quiet parking facility. During the hospital shift change around three in the afternoon the garage was a beehive of activity. Then between five and six there was another burst of activity, although not as intense. By six o'clock, activity fell off precipitously, only to recommence around eight, when visiting hours ended and then again around eleven, when the night staff came to replace the evening shift.

As Sandra walked to her car in the silence of the deserted garage, she was aware of the sharp clicking sound her heels made as they echoed off the concrete. It was an unsettling reminder that she was alone. She glanced around as she walked in hopes of seeing someone, but she didn't. She had always found garages after hours to be intimidating. To rein in her imagination she forced herself to think about getting home and taking a hot bath. As she pressed her comfort access key to open her BMW's doors, she wondered about the best way to tell Rhodes of her new finding without aggravating him. As the department head whose job it was to review all three cases, it was probably something he should have seen. If he hadn't, she vaguely worried with his irascibility whether he might take the possible oversight personally and blame the messenger.

Sandra climbed into the driver's seat, pulled the door closed, and reached over her shoulder for her seat belt. At the same time her right foot depressed the brake pedal in anticipation of starting the engine. It was all by reflex. She'd done it a million times. But she didn't get the seat belt. Instead her heart leaped into her throat, as the passenger-side front door and driver's-side rear door were both suddenly yanked open. A fraction of a second later two large men in dark business suits leaped into the car in a flurry of activity.

Sandra started to scream in shocked terror, but it never got out. A gloved hand had come around from behind and clasped itself over the lower part of her face, suppressing what would have been a piercing cry. What came out was a muffled gurgle. At the same time and by the same hand her head was roughly compressed back against the headrest. Simultaneously the man in the front passenger seat thrust a needle into her thigh and injected its contents. It was over in a second.

Unable to breathe, Sandra reached up and desperately tried to pull the hand away from her face. She couldn't. The man was too strong. The next instant, the man beside her snatched the electronic key from her hand and started the car. A moment later the image of the parking garage through the windshield blurred and dimmed. Then her body went limp.

To Darko Lebedev's delight he had gotten the call from Misha Zotov just before three P.M. giving him and Leonid Shubin their orders. After such a long down period with no action whatsoever, there were two new jobs to be done, and one was to be the second hit in so many days. The second was to be merely a strong warning for a female medical student to mend her ways, or at least those had been Misha's words. Darko understood, and he couldn't have been more pleased with both assignments. He knew Leonid would feel the same.

For the hit, the orders had been simple. The woman was to just disappear, and her car was to be taken by a driver Misha would provide out to a hospital in Colorado, where the target's ex-husband worked. There the car was to be abandoned. As it had been explained to Darko, the idea was to focus suspicion concerning the woman's disappearance on the former spouse and center the investigation out of state. The only other stipulation was that Misha wanted the woman to be brought drugged but alive and left with him for a few hours. He'd said he had a score to settle with the uppity bitch.

Along with the orders had come the information that Darko needed to plan both jobs. That included where Sandra Wykoff lived, the make and model of her car, and the number and location of her parking slot in the garage. He'd also been informed that she lived alone, rarely entertained, and seldom went out at night. Misha had explained that there was a lot of information available about the woman because she had been carefully vetted by security before she had been selected as one of the initial anesthesiologists in the program.

To Darko it had all sounded as if the hit would be a relatively easy task, even though, like the intimidation assignment, it had to happen immediately, that very day. It meant they had to work quickly and without the benefit of prolonged research and observation, which was the way he liked to do things. It also meant that the hit had priority.

For the second job, intimidating Lynn Peirce, Darko had arranged for help from one of the Russians who worked for the hospital security, named Timur Kortev. He'd sent the man to the medical dorm with Lynn's photo to keep tabs on her so that when Darko was finished with Wykoff, he'd know where to find the student. He counted on her being in her room at the dorm, but he wanted to be sure. He didn't want to waste time and risk going into her room if she wasn't there.

For the hit, the first thing that Darko and Leonid had done was check out Wykoff's home. Accordingly they had driven out to her condo development in North Charleston. What they discovered was that it was less than opportune for their purposes. She lived in a rather narrow row house, sharing common walls with two other units. This situation magnified the chance that there would be witnesses. For her to disappear, supposedly of her own accord, no one could see them take her. The only good thing was that there was a sliding glass door onto a lanai in the back. In their experience, such doors were easy to breach. The men had decided that if they were to be forced to go into her house, that was how they would enter, but they weren't happy about it.

Returning to the hospital, they checked out Sandra's vehicle. Their thought was that if she came out in a press of people, they would follow her, hoping she would make a stop or two on the way home so that they could improvise. As it turned out, they had been in luck. She'd come out after the rush and by herself.

Speaking in Russian, Darko said: "Let's get her in the backseat. Do you see anybody?" Sandra had collapsed against him.

"No one," Leonid said, checking out the rear window.

"Let's do it!"

Both men exited the car and quickly pulled Sandra's limp form from the front seat and got it into the back. Darko spread a small blanket over her that had been in the car. Both men climbed back into the vehicle. With Darko behind the wheel, they pulled out of the garage after the automatic gate opened for them. A moment later they stopped behind a nondescript white van. Leonid got out.

"See you at Misha's," Leonid said, before running ahead and climbing into the van. A moment later he drove out into the street heading north. Darko followed in Sandra's car, with her unconscious on the backseat.

Misha and many of the other Russians working in Clinical Engineering, IT, and the security staff of the Mason-Dixon Medical Center lived in a residential development bought by Sidereal Pharmaceuticals. It was located in a secluded area to the east of a small town called Goose Creek. A few, like Misha and Fyodor, had standalone houses. The others, like Darko and Leonid, were in a condominium complex. Except for Fyodor, all had been ordered to leave wives and girlfriends back in Russia, at least for the time being.

31.

ait a second," Michael said, pulling Lynn to a stop. Coming up from the cafeteria, following a quick dinner, they had just emerged from the stairwell on the second floor of the hospital. Their mission was to find anesthesia machine 37, mostly for Michael's benefit. Ahead was the open door to the surgical lounge occupied by what appeared to be a sizable portion of the evening OR staff. From where they were standing they could see that the TV was tuned to a game show. "I hate to have to constantly bring this up, but we need an excuse of what we're doing up here if anybody asks. It's hardly a med-student hangout. Any ideas?"

Lynn thought for a moment. "You're right. And no need to excuse yourself. I'm glad you think of these details. Let's say that we just spoke with the dean about hospital-based infections, which is true, and now we are looking into the issue. We don't have to be specific."

"Smooth!" Michael said with admiration. "It's amazing how you can bend the truth."

"I've been learning from a master."

Michael laughed at the backhanded compliment.

Armed with an idea of what to say if confronted, the two students entered the surgical lounge. Only one orderly out of the half dozen people even looked up. No one made a move to speak with them. Everyone in the room was glued to a news brief that had suddenly interrupted the regular programming. Instead of the game show, a couple of the local news anchors had come on the air to report that the Mount Pleasant police were investigating a horrific home invasion that had occurred sometime the previous night in Mount Pleasant but had just been reported.

Lynn and Michael paused. Their attention was immediately drawn to the lurid details. Like everyone else, they listened with rapt attention.

The scene on the television shifted from the evening-news set to a young women correspondent holding a microphone and standing outside a suburban house on a wooded lot. In the background, multiple police cars and other emergency vehicles were parked at odd angles, with their emergency lights flashing. "I am standing outside of 1440 Bay View Drive, Mount Pleasant," the correspondent said. "Behind me you can see this home where the Hurley family resided. All we know now is that sometime last night this family experienced a devastating home invasion involving burglary, assault, rape, and murder. The entire family, including two children, was killed. At this time we do not know the details of this tragedy and have been told that the Mount Pleasant chief of police will be making a statement shortly. The killings were discovered by Mr. Hurley's assistant, who came to investigate when his boss failed to show up for work. Mr. Hurley is a successful lawyer here in Mount Pleasant. Mrs. Hurley, a third-grade teacher at the Charles Pinckney Elementary School, had also been missed, but everyone at the school thought her absence was due to a recent illness. Mrs. Hurley had been hospitalized for a few days at the Mason-Dixon Medical

Center for food poisoning a little more than a week ago. School officials knew that during her hospitalization she had been diagnosed with some kind of blood disorder and that after discharge she had not been feeling one hundred percent. When she failed to show up for work, it was assumed it was because of this new illness. Back to you, Gail and Ron."

As the two news anchors picked up the story and began talking about the possible similarities to the case involved in Truman Capote's *In Cold Blood* and a more recent case in Connecticut, the surgical lounge erupted in multiple shocked conversations.

"Good God!" Lynn said to Michael. "What is this world coming to?"

"If it can happen in Kansas and Connecticut, it can happen here," Michael said. "At least it's a good time for us to look for number thirty-seven with everyone hung up watching the tube."

"I suppose," Lynn said. "But what do you make of the woman having been diagnosed with a blood disorder here at our hospital? Do you think it's possible she had a gammopathy like Morrison and possibly Carl?"

"I suppose it is possible. Infectious gammopathy! That would be a new one!"

"I'm trying to be serious," Lynn said.

"And I'm trying to lighten you up," Michael said. "Let's change our clothes and get this over with. I'll meet you in five."

"You got it!"

Lynn got out of her clothes and quickly pulled on scrubs. She couldn't stop thinking about the tragedy in Mount Pleasant. It unnerved her to be reminded that human beings harbored the capacity for such terrible things. In the middle of these disturbing thoughts, she wondered exactly what kind of blood disorder the murdered mother might have had. Could it involve a paraprotein? When she got back out to the surgical lounge, Michael was already there, watching the TV news alert like everyone else.

"The irony is that the guy was a personal-injury lawyer," Michael whispered when Lynn joined him.

"What else did you learn?"

"Not much. I've only been out here for a minute or two."

"Anything more about the protein abnormality the wife had?"

"Nothing."

"Come on! Let's get this little errand over with."

After donning booties, the two students pushed into the OR proper. All the lights were blazing, but the place was deserted, even the main desk. Everyone seemed to be back in the surgical lounge. There were no cases going on. As Lynn and Michael passed the PACU they did hear some music drift out into the hallway, but they avoided looking into the room. Although they had a story to offer for what they were doing, they still preferred not to bump into anyone.

"How should we go about this?" Lynn asked. "Should we just check every room, maybe you on the right and me on the left?"

"Let's check twelve first and go from there."

"I wonder how many patients leave this hospital with a diagnosis of a blood protein abnormality," Lynn said as they walked.

"I'm wondering the same thing," Michael said.

They got to twelve and had to put on the lights. The anesthesia machine was off to the side. Lynn struggled with an emotional reaction she didn't expect, wondering if she was looking at the machine responsible to some degree for Carl's tragedy. Michael walked directly over to it.

"It's number thirty-seven," Michael said, having bent over to read the service record.

For a few beats the two students stared at the machine with its profusion of dials, gauges, flow meters, vaporizers, and monitors. Three cylinders of compressed gas were hanging off the back.

"Okay," Lynn said. "Now that we found it, what do you want to do?"

Michael shrugged. "I suppose I'd just like to make sure it has actually been used."

"That's easy. We can just go back to the main desk and see if there were any cases in this OR today. I'm sure there were, but come on!"

With no one at the main desk to tell them otherwise, the two students checked the surgical log. OR 12 had been busy. There had been a hernia, a lumbar fusion, and a mastectomy. Apparently there had been no problems. All the patients had gone back to their respective rooms after short stays in the PACU.

"Satisfied?" Lynn asked.

"I guess I'll have to be. What do you want to do now?"

"Let's head up to the neuro ICU while we're still in scrubs," Lynn said. "I have to find out about Carl's possible transfer, but if you don't want to come, I understand."

"I'm with you for the long haul, girl!"

As they waited for the elevator they could see that the TV in the surgical lounge was back to its original game show. They rode up to six in a mostly empty car. When they got off, the only other person still in the elevator was a uniformed member of hospital security.

Like the rest of the hospital, the neuro floor was comparatively tranquil. Visiting hours were about to end at eight, so good-byes were being exchanged by the visitors who were staying until the last moment. A few patients were wandering about for exercise, pushing IV poles in front of them.

Lynn and Michael didn't speak until they got to the doors leading into the ICU.

"Maybe I should make it easier for you," Michael said. "I could go in and see if he is there."

"Maybe that's a good idea," Lynn said. The closer they had come, the more nervous and emotional she felt. Michael sensed it.

"Okay, I'll be right back," Michael said. "Try to chill."

All Lynn could do was roll her eyes, as there was no way she was going to relax. After the doors closed behind Michael, she did try to take her mind off Carl's status by thinking about what she was going to do for the rest of the evening. Having told Frank Giordano that he needn't worry about Carl's cat, she was obligated to go back to Carl's house. It wouldn't be difficult to get there because she had driven Carl's Cherokee to the hospital that morning.

Lynn checked the time. She also wanted to call her architect friend up in Washington, DC, to see if he had any bright ideas about navigating around inside the Shapiro Institute, since his firm did commercial building design, including health-care facilities. She figured it best that it was not too late when she called as he was married with two young kids. Lynn had known him in college, when they'd had a brief affair that ended pleasantly. Over the years they'd stayed in touch. His name was Tim Cooper.

Lynn had anticipated that Michael would come back out from the ICU immediately. She didn't know how to interpret that he didn't. Either Carl was still there or he wasn't. Lynn guessed that Michael had gotten himself involved in a conversation. Was that good news or bad? She didn't know. To keep from thinking the worst, she pulled out her mobile phone. She had Tim's number in her contacts and as a diversion decided it was a good time to make a call, as she could make it quick. It turned out to be a good time for Tim, too, and he answered on the first ring.

As soon as they got through the pleasantries, she turned the conversation over to why she was calling. She started by asking him if he had ever heard of the Shapiro Institute.

"I certainly have," Tim said. "It was quite a project. It was done by a design firm from Chicago called McCalister, Weiss, and Peabody, which specializes in automation. They generally design automotive assembly plants, although they have done a number of medical labs. It was a coup for them to do a health care facility."

"Do you know anybody at that firm?"

"I do. Why do you ask?"

Lynn explained that she was going to be visiting the Shapiro Institute and wanted to have an advance idea of its layout. She asked if Tim would be willing to call his acquaintance and see if he could possibly get her a floor plan.

"I'd be happy to," Tim said without hesitation. "But I have a better idea. As I recall, the Shapiro is within the Charleston City Limits. Am I right?"

"It is," Lynn said.

"If you want plans, go down to the Charleston Building Commission. They'll have a full set available. All public buildings like hospitals have to have blueprints on file, including an as-built set. They have to be submitted to get an occupancy permit, and it's public information."

"I never knew that," Lynn admitted.

"Most people don't," Tim said.

Pleased to have learned what she had, and certain that Michael would soon be appearing, Lynn wrapped up her conversation with Tim. It wasn't difficult. She told him she was in the hospital at that very moment, about to go into the intensive care unit. Both agreed they would talk soon.

Replacing her phone in her jacket pocket, Lynn looked at the ICU door. She shook her head. Her patience was exhausted. She stepped forward with the intent of going in when the door opened. It was Michael on his way out.

32.

B y merely seeing Michael's expression, Lynn could tell instantly that Carl was gone. She felt a wave of emotion bubble up inside her.

"I'm sorry," Michael said. "My bad!"

"It's not your fault," Lynn managed, fighting back tears.

"It's my bad for taking so long and having to give you bad news on top. Carl was transferred about an hour ago. What kept me was that I ran into our third-year neurology preceptor. He was all excited about my residency plans. Seems that he did his neurology at Mass General in Boston and insisted on giving me all sorts of tips. I couldn't get away. Sorry!"

Lynn nodded multiple times, as if agreeing with what Michael was saying. Actually she wasn't listening. Now that she knew for sure Carl had been sent to the Shapiro, she wasn't at all surprised. Although she had tried to think more positively before she'd gotten the news, deep down she knew it was going to happen. There had been a disturbing inevitability about it. And thinking in this vein changed her emotional response from sadness to angry determination.

"Let's go!" Lynn said with sudden resolve, interrupting Michael in midsentence as he talked about what he had been told concerning housing in Boston. Without warning, she turned and strode off. Michael had to make an effort to catch up with her.

"What's the program?" Michael asked. Having to dodge patients in the hallway made it difficult to stay alongside her.

"I'm going down to IT and see if I can log on to one of their computers," Lynn said. "This is war! I have to find out more about the Shapiro and what's going on over there. If it is some kind of unethical drug-testing facility, I'm going to get Carl out of there ASAP. I don't know how I'll do it, but hell will freeze over before I let him be a human guinea pig."

A number of hospital visitors and even a member of hospital security were waiting at the elevators, as the end of visiting hours had arrived. Michael would have liked to keep Lynn talking, to get her to calm down and keep her out of trouble, but he couldn't without people overhearing. Lynn was ignoring him and staring into the middle distance, her mind obviously in overdrive.

Michael thought Lynn would get off on two to change out of the scrubs and give him a chance to talk to her. But she didn't. It wasn't until everybody got off on the main floor that he had the chance.

"I think we should go back to the dorm and chill," Michael said as soon as the elevator doors closed and they were alone. "You got to cut the system a little slack here before you do something that gets us in real trouble. We've already got the medical school dean and the chief of anesthesia bent out of shape. Listen! We can always come back and visit IT later if you insist. I really think you should calm down first."

"You can go back to the dorm," Lynn snapped. The elevator bottomed out and the doors opened. Lynn got out with Michael on her heels.

"I'm not going back to the dorm until you do," Michael said defiantly.

"Suit yourself," Lynn said as they passed the Pathology Department and the morgue. Suddenly she stopped. "Why are you so intent on helping me now? You've told me that, growing up, you were always risk avoidant. We both know what I am planning on doing down here is a risk. It's another serious violation of HIPAA, made even worse by fraudulently using someone else's access. This is much worse than looking at Carl's chart, which you reminded us is a class-five felony. This is way more serious. Why are you doing this?"

"I'm helping you because we've been helping each other for almost four years."

"That doesn't cut it, dude," Lynn said. "Neither one of us has ever broken the law for the other. That's never been asked. Legally, a class-five felony has mandatory jail time."

"Okay, my friend. I'm doing it because I really feel for you. I feel your pain losing Carl. I'm doing it because I believe that if the roles were reversed and Kianna was involved, you'd do it for me."

For a few minutes the two students looked at each other, their minds churning.

"I don't know whether I'd do it or not for you," Lynn said, trying to be honest.

"As my mamma used to say, 'That don't make no never mind for me.' I wouldn't have known I'd do it, either, but I'm doing it. And I'm convinced, no matter what you say, you'd do it for me. It's called trust. We have that kind of a relationship."

There was another short period of silence as the two continued to stare at each other.

"Okay," Lynn said finally. "Maybe you are right. Maybe I would do it. Who's to know? In the meantime, let's get on with it!"

Just then a security guard appeared from behind them. Lynn and Michael held their collective breath, but the man ignored them and disappeared into the security office fifty feet ahead. Only then did they recommence walking.

Just beyond the security office they came to the Informational Technology door. They knew that the department was staffed 24/7, although it was common knowledge that there was only a skeleton crew after hours. Lynn tried the door. As she expected, it was unlocked.

Even though no one was in the large office, all the lights were on, just like in the OR. The room had a half dozen workstations with terminals, presumably for programmers. At one terminal was a coffee mug and some open manuals. In contrast to all the other monitors, which sported the usual hospital screen saver, this monitor had what looked like a spreadsheet. From where they were standing a bit of vapor could be seen rising out of the mug.

"Someone's working here," Lynn said.

"Very observant, Sherlock," Michael said with a touch of sarcasm.

Along one wall were fixed windows looking into the room beyond, filled with large upright computer servers. Against the back wall was a row of private offices. Lynn made a beeline for the last office. A small plaque at eye level on the door said ALEXANDER TUPOLEV, DEPARTMENT HEAD. Without hesitation, Lynn opened the door and stepped in, holding it ajar for Michael. Then she closed the door and locked it.

"Hell, girl, what the fuck are you doing?" Michael said nervously. Shell-shocked, as if he had been duped into robbing a bank, he gazed around the modern office, with its minimalist decor. There was a large, freestanding desk totally devoid of clutter. There was also a desk-height countertop along one wall. On it were several computer terminals, each with a printer, and each fronted with Herman Miller Aeron chairs. "We can't be caught in here."

"This is the safest place for us to be for what we are doing," Lynn said as she went directly to one of the computers and quickly made herself at home. She took out her cell phone and brought up Vladimir's ID and password that Michael had given her. She placed the phone on the counter so that she could see the screen. "Considering

it is eight o'clock at night, I was ninety-nine-point-ninety-nine percent sure Mr. Tupolev would not be in here. I sincerely doubt anyone will come knocking, provided we are quiet as mice. But if you
want to bag it, I imagine the coast is still clear. I'll meet you back at
the dorm."

"I'll stick," Michael said. He grabbed a chair and pulled it over
as Lynn typed the user name, vm123@zmail.ru. And the password,
74952632237malaklov.

"The moment of truth," Lynn said just before hitting ENTER. To
her satisfaction, the log-in went flawlessly. She was in the hospital
system with admin status.

"Slam dunk," Michael said. "Okay, whatever you're going to
search for, do it fast! It would be sweet to get out of here before
whoever is working in the outer office comes back."

Lynn nodded. She knew what she wanted in general but in her
rush hadn't thought of specifics. "Let's see: for starters, we should
find out how many patients in the Shapiro have a gammopathy like
Morrison."

"We should also find out more about Ashanti Davis," Michael
suggested. "Like, why she is being given the drozitumab antibody.
That should tell us if they are using her as a human guinea pig."

"Right!" Lynn said. As per usual Michael's insight was to the
point.

"We should also get Shapiro death stats," Michael said.

"For sure," Lynn said. "It will be very interesting if we can learn
the cause of death for each patient who passed away over the eight
years they have been in operation. It's also going to be interesting to
find out how many patients have been discharged. No one thought
to ask that when we had our tour."

"Start with Ashanti," Michael said. "It will give us an idea of what
we are up against. Maybe we won't even have to go into the Shapiro
if we can somehow prove they are doing unethical drug testing."

Lynn nodded and quickly typed in *Ashanti Davis* in the search window and hit ENTER. Both students were optimistic and both were disappointed when a message popped up saying there was no file for Ashanti Davis.

Undeterred, Lynn retyped the name and added Shapiro Institute. Immediately a window appeared but not the file they'd hoped for. Within the window it said: ACCESS DENIED! SEE IT ADMINISTRATION.

"Shit!" Lynn said. "I guess Shapiro records can only be accessed on Shapiro terminals."

"Mothafuckas!" Michael said.

"I was so psyched," Lynn said, making fists with both hands.

"Well, that's that," Michael said. He rolled his chair back and went to the door. Carefully he cracked it, peered out, then opened it farther to get a better view. "The coast is still clear," he called back to Lynn. "Let's jet our asses out of here while we still can."

"Okay," Lynn said. "But just a second." She was busy typing. A moment later the printer next to her sprang to life and kicked out several pages. Lynn logged out, grabbed the papers, and joined Michael at the door.

"Let's run," Michael said.

A few minutes later, as they were abreast of the Pathology Department, they passed a rather large man who'd come out of the elevator, carrying a take-out bag from the cafeteria. When they got onto the elevator Michael said: "That guy looked like Vladimir's twin. Must be the guy holding down the IT fort. Damn Russians are taking over."

"That reminds me," Lynn said, checking her watch. "You have company coming."

"No problem," Michael said. "I've been watching the time. What did you print out?"

"I didn't want our visit to be a complete wash. I looked up the percentage of patients being discharged from the Mason-Dixon Medical Center with a diagnosis of a gammopathy that was discovered while they were in the hospital."

"That's all?"

"No! I also queried about the incidence of multiple myeloma."

"What did you learn?"

"One percent of people being discharged have a paraprotein abnormality that was discovered during their stay."

"That seems way high," Michael said.

"Seems high to me, too, but I'm going to have to find out what the incidence is in the United States in general. I think it's in that article we read about gammopathy, but I don't remember what it was."

"What about multiple myeloma? What percentage of patients being discharged have multiple myeloma?"

"That's point one percent."

"Point one percent of people being discharged have multiple myeloma?" Michael asked with surprise. "That seems way high, too."

"I know. It can't be right," Lynn said. "Like with gammopathy, I'm going to have to look up the incidence in this country. It's not a common cancer; at least I don't think it is."

They took the stairs to get up to the first floor, then crossed over the pedestrian bridge to the deserted clinic building.

"I found out something interesting while you were in the neuro ICU," Lynn said. She told Michael about the call to Tim Cooper and that she could probably get detailed plans for the institute from the Charleston Building Commission.

"Cool," Michael said. He was impressed with her resourcefulness but didn't want to encourage her. He was still hoping she'd change her mind.

"I'm going to stop in tomorrow morning on my way here to the hospital," Lynn said as they exited into the courtyard gardens. It was a balmy spring night.

"You're going back to Carl's tonight?" Michael asked. He was a bit surprised, as it was now going on nine. He could imagine how tired she was.

"I don't have a choice," Lynn said. "I promised to feed Carl's cat. I had told Frank Giordano I'd take care of the poor thing."

"As late as it is, why not call Frank and renege? He lives down there, South of Broad. I'm sure he wouldn't mind. This is no time for you to be out riding your bike."

"I'm not riding my bike. It's not even here. I left it at Carl's and drove his Cherokee this morning."

"So I have to party with our Russian buddy by myself?"

"I could stay if you want," Lynn said. "And then go."

"No need," Michael said. "If you are going to Carl's, you should do it sooner rather than later. Are you sure you want to stay again in that big house by yourself?"

"It will make me feel closer to him," Lynn said. She stopped walking and looked over at the Shapiro Institute. "God! It pains me no end to think of Carl in there." Once again her voice caught.

Michael put his arm around her and pulled her toward him to give her a reassuring hug. "Try not to think about it now. We'll figure it out. We'll make sure that he is being cared for appropriately and not being used as a test object. I promise!"

"Thank you, bro," Lynn managed.

33.

Darko and Leonid tossed the shovels into the back of the van. Leonid added the pickax they had shared. Both pulled off their gloves and coveralls and tossed them in, on top of the tools. They were in a deeply wooded area with Spanish moss hanging like festoons from all the trees. Both the men were fatigued and perspiring profusely from the rapid, nonstop work. There had been no conversation between them to slow them down. Nearby was a dismal swamp, and the creatures of the night were making a racket. Mosquitoes had made their job all the more difficult.

They had scouted the location six months earlier for just this kind of job. They wanted an unpopulated place so as not to attract any attention and with earth firm yet soft enough to dig a grave. It also had to be accessible by a passable dirt road. They had found it about twenty-five miles due west from the Charleston International Airport, on the grounds of an abandoned farm, partially surrounded by extensive wetlands. Although it was only an hour out of Charleston, it could have been on the dark side of the moon.

They had worked with planned dispatch, using the headlights of the vehicle to do it all properly. When they had finished, the plot appeared untouched. They even added some local plant seed. Considering the way things grew at that time of year, they were confident that all traces of their activity would quickly disappear. Satisfied, they had gotten into the van and headed back toward Misha's, where Wykoff's car was waiting in the garage to embark on its westward journey.

After a quarter hour, with the van's air conditioner on at full blast and with several Marlboros smoked, the men started to feel normal enough to begin a conversation. As usual, they spoke in Russian.

"The grave digging went well," Darko said. He was at the wheel.

"Hardly a challenge," Leonid said in agreement. "Except for the humidity and the mosquitoes."

"You remember I have another job tonight," Darko said.

"I remember, but you didn't elaborate."

"I have to threaten a female medical student to get her to mind her own business. She and a friend have been asking too many questions about anesthesia. It's going to be a pleasure. From the photo Misha got for me from hospital security, she's a piece of ass."

Leonid chuckled. "Sounds like a choice assignment. Why not share the wealth?"

"You need to finish up with this Wykoff job. When we get back to Misha's, you have to drive her car back to her town house and pack a bag and make it look like it was done in haste."

"I know the routine," Leonid said.

"When you return to Misha's with the luggage, the driver will be there to take the car to Denver."

"Where will you be?"

"I don't know for sure," Darko said with a shrug, "but I presume at the medical student's dorm. Or I might be finished. If so, we could meet at the Rooftop for a vodka. Check and see if your phone has a mobile signal yet!"

Leonid got out his cell phone and turned it on. "There's a signal.

It's not great—one bar. Wait! Now there's two bars. Who do you want me to call?"

"Timur Kortnev. Put him on speakerphone."

As the call went through, neither man talked. The sound of the distant ringing could be heard. Four rings, then five. Leonid was about to disconnect when Timur answered. He sounded mildly out of breath. He, too, spoke in Russian.

"Sorry," Timur said. "I needed to change location before I answered."

"Did you make visual contact with the girl?"

"Yes. I've been following her and her friend all evening. It hasn't been easy."

"Why? Where has she gone?"

"First the two of them went over to the hospital cafeteria. But then they went up to the OR. I have no idea what they did there. Following that, they went to the neuro ICU. She didn't go in. but her friend did."

"And then she went back to the dorm?"

"No. They stopped at the computer center."

Darko had the distinct feeling that the warning he was to deliver to Lynn Peirce was becoming more critical.

"Do you know what they did in the office?"

"I don't. There was no one there. The person on duty was up in the cafeteria at the time."

"Did they then go back to the dorm?"

"Yes, but only briefly."

"So she's not there now?"

"No. About eight-thirty she left again. She went into the garage and then drove off in a Jeep. I had to scramble to commandeer a security vehicle so I could follow."

"Was she with her friend at this point?"

"No, she was alone."

"Where did she go?" Darko glanced over at Leonid. Darko didn't like surprises, and all this was a surprise.

"She went into a single-family house on 591 Church Street down here in the very south of Charleston. I was trying to look in the front windows when you called."

"Is she is alone?"

"I think so. The house was dark when she arrived and no one has come to visit. She turned on many lights initially, but now they are mostly off."

"Okay," Darko said with a smile. When he heard Lynn Peirce was, strangely, moving around the medical center, he'd become concerned. Now, alone in a private house, it seemed as if she wanted to make his job easier. "Any idea of whose house it is?"

"Yes. It belongs to Carl Vandermeer, one of the program's test cases."

Darko recoiled. Like a few people close to Sergei Polushin, he knew a bit about the program. He also stood to profit immensely from the Sidereal stock he'd been given over the years. He knew why he had been tasked to kill Sandra Wykoff. She was asking too many questions about her patient, Carl Vandermeer. And now this Lynn Peirce was staying in the man's house!

Without realizing he was doing it, Darko pressed down on the van's accelerator. Intuitively, he sensed his second job of the evening might be as important as the first. He was also counting on its being significantly more fun than being eaten by mosquitoes at the edge of a swamp.

34.

Lynn could not believe what she had just discovered. In shocked wonderment she tipped back in Carl's desk chair to stare at the ceiling and think about the implications. It seemed that every time she studied the anesthesia records, she came across something new. On this occasion she was even more flabbergasted than she'd been that afternoon and immediately the question arose in her mind whether the phenomena she'd just found could be the result of an intermittent software glitch inside the anesthesia machine. But almost as soon as the idea occurred to her, she shook her head. The anesthesia machine had been used on innumerable cases, including a few that very day. Why would it happen only on three if it was a software problem? She couldn't imagine it could be a glitch. Instead, if anything, she told herself it might be a hack. Was that possible? She didn't know and would have to ask Michael, as he might know. But one way or the other, what she had stumbled on was yet another horrifying hint that what had happened to Carl, Scarlett Morrison, and Ashanti Davis might not have been an accident or a screwup. This finding was in the same unsettling category as the coincidental unexplained frame offset that had occurred at exactly the same time in all three cases. In fact, it was more disturbing, suggesting the unthinkable: This whole nightmare might be deliberate!

Lynn had gotten to Carl's house at about a quarter to nine. Pep had been ecstatic to see her and had purred with such ferocity, Lynn had dropped everything and fed her right away. Once the cat had been taken care of, Lynn wandered around the house, going from room to room, thinking about Carl.

In retrospect, such reminiscing was probably not a good idea. Same with her coming back to Carl's house at all. As Michael had suggested, she should have called Frank to take care of the cat because being there made her sense of bereavement overwhelming. Everything in the house reminded her of her stricken lover and his unique personality, his keen intelligence, his love of life, and even his compulsive neatness, which was a step beyond Michael's. With a bit of embarrassment she remembered some of the petty quarrels they had had about how she hung up her bath towel and sometimes left her underwear on the bathroom floor.

With these thoughts in mind, the extent of her loss had weighed on her, and Lynn became depressed. It had gotten to the point of wondering who was worse off, she or Carl. What saved the day from such negative self-fulfilling reminiscence was the sudden realization that she couldn't just wander around feeling sorry for herself. Instead she had to make a concerted effort to occupy her mind as she had done the evening before. To that end she had gone into Carl's bathroom first and taken a long, hot shower. She'd stayed under the hot torrent long enough to dilute the day's emotions. Following the shower, she'd donned one of Carl's oversize bathrobes and gone into his study. At his desk she'd turned on the PC and went online.

What she had done first was find out how many people in the general population had blood serum protein abnormalities or gammopathies. The issue had been gnawing at her ever since she'd read

Morrison's chart and since she found out that Carl was seemingly developing it. Adding to her curiosity was finding out, from the otherwise disappointing visit to the IT Department, how many people discharged from the Mason-Dixon Medical Center had been diagnosed with that condition while they had been an inpatient.

What she had learned surprised her. Although the Mason-Dixon had far fewer episodes of hospital-based infections, as Dean English had pointed out, the hospital was off the charts when it came to the incidence of blood serum abnormalities. When Lynn looked into multiple myeloma, she'd found the same situation. Patients coming from the Mason-Dixon had five times the national rate for both problems. Lynn had no explanation for such discrepancies. Could it have something to do with the hospital or the lab? She had no idea, but she had definitely decided she had to bring up the subject with Michael to get his take.

At that point, to continue to keep herself from falling back to obsessing over Carl and feeling sorry for herself in the process, she'd turned her attention back to the anesthesia records she had brought from her room. Studying the printouts from a new and unique perspective had led to her shocking new discovery.

Lynn tipped forward again, taking her eyes away from staring blankly at the ceiling. The mere thought that Carl's disastrous condition might not have been an accident made Lynn's blood run cold. It was such an unnerving idea that she wondered if she was becoming delusional. Was her fragile emotional state turning her into a conspiracy theorist?

Intent on proving herself wrong, she went back to what she had been doing. Spread out in front of her on Carl's desk were sections of vital-sign tracings from each of the three cases. With a pair of scissors she'd found in Carl's top desk drawer—after briefly looking again at the engagement ring—she had cut them out of the anesthesia record graphs. The segments she had chosen showed the blood pressure, pulse, oxygen saturation, and ECG of each patient from the moment of the frame offset to the sudden fall in blood oxygen. Her idea was to look for slight alterations in the vital signs in all three cases to see if there were any similarities. What she hadn't anticipated was that by isolating these portions and just looking at one of them before comparing all three, she was able to see something that apparently everyone else had missed, including herself.

To confirm what she thought she had noticed, Lynn took the cut-out segment of Carl's record and proceeded to cut it up into smaller pieces, each representing one minute of anesthesia time. Once she was done, she took all the pieces and arranged them in a vertical column so that she could compare one to the other. Once she did this, what she thought she had seen earlier became even more apparent. There was definite periodicity, meaning the tracing repeated itself. Every minute the recording of the vital signs had been looped, meaning the same one-minute segment was playing over and over, from the moment of the frame offset until the oxygen saturation suddenly dropped.

Printing another copy of Carl's anesthesia record and taking one of the minute segments she'd cut out, Lynn was able to match the repeating segment. It had come from the minute time period just prior to the frame offset.

Lynn was stunned. For a moment she didn't move or even breathe as her mind churned. What she had discovered was definitely real, and the implications were more than disturbing. One thing she understood: from the moment of the frame offset until the fall in the blood oxygen, the anesthesia machine wasn't monitoring Carl's vital signs. Instead it was constantly replaying the same, normal segment and masking what was really happening to her lover while the monitors suggested everything was normal. "My God!" she said out loud. With copies of Scarlett Morrison's and Ashanti Davis's records, she quickly determined it was the same.

Grabbing her mobile phone, Lynn speed-dialed Michael's number. Her pulse was racing as the call took its time going through. She looked at the clock. It was almost eleven-thirty. It was late, but Michael usually stayed up until midnight. The distant phone rang four times. On the fifth Michael picked up.

"Yo!" Michael said with no preamble, knowing it was Lynn. "Vlad here is just about to bag it. Can I catch you in a moment?"

"I need to talk," Lynn said with unmistakable urgency.

"You all right?"

"I'm not sure."

"Are you in mortal danger this very second?" There was a touch of sarcasm in his tone, which wasn't all that unusual.

"Not literally, but I just discovered something that has me totally unglued and will blow your mind."

"Okay, I got you covered, but I need five. I'll be right back to you." He then disconnected.

Feeling moderately panicky after her metaphoric lifeline was summarily terminated, Lynn put her phone down. She did it slowly. Her mind was going a mile a minute. As bad as the implications were about Carl's, Morrison's, and Davis's anesthesia disasters not being accidents or even episodes of malpractice, the added issue of the serum protein abnormality popped back into her head.

Could the gammopathy and the looping of the anesthesia record be related? It didn't seem possible, but if there was one thing that Lynn had learned about medical diagnostics during her four years of medical school, it was that even when you were faced with a patient with disparate and seemingly unrelated symptoms, more often than not the underlying problem was one disease.

A sudden noise, not necessarily loud but somehow foreign, registered in Lynn's ears. It came from the floor below, either from the living room or the foyer. It was more like a vibration of the whole structure of the house than just a sound carried in the air. Trying to figure out its origin, Lynn held her breath, listening intently. Her first thought was that it was a book falling and landing flat. Her second thought was perhaps Pep had jumped from a piece of furniture onto the floor. But Lynn quickly ruled out Pep as the culprit when she caught sight of the cat fast asleep in the club chair by the fireplace. Seeing that the animal's keen senses had not been disturbed gave her a bit of encouragement, but it didn't last.

Alone in the large, aging house, Lynn had been careful to make sure she had completely closed and securely locked the front door when she had arrived. Although she had turned on a number of lights during her despondent wanderings, she had turned them all off. As far as she knew, the only lights on in the whole house were the two library-style brass lamps on Carl's desk in front of her. Even the corners of the study were lost in shadow.

Then there was another noise, a faint creak. Was it her imagination from her heightened sensitivity from not having identified the first noise? Then, almost instantly, came a rapid series of creaks from the ancient wood flooring in the foyer below, followed by another rapid series of noises from the stair treads. With a shudder of fear, Lynn sensed she was not alone. Someone was coming up the stairs!

In a panic Lynn snatched up her mobile phone. Quickly she tapped in 911. But then she hesitated to place the call. It suddenly had occurred to her that she was the trespasser, and the people coming might be Carl's parents or a neighbor with a key who knew what had happened to Carl and were responding to the light in the study.

Unfortunately for Lynn these thoughts came more from hope than reality, and her hesitation cost her the chance to call for help. In the next instant a large figure dressed in black with a black balaclava silently flashed into sight from the dark hallway. Worse yet, clutched in the individual's hand was an automatic pistol with a silencer. Lynn's heart leaped into her chest.

BOOK 3

BUOK 3

35.

Darko had arrived at the southern end of the Charleston peninsula twenty minutes earlier. He'd parked the van on South Battery. Wearing a long Burberry coat and carrying a small satchel, he'd met up with Timur, who had been standing vigil beneath a large shade tree on Church Street, across from Vandermeer's house.

Both expatriate Russians spoke fluent English, as the two had been living in Charleston for five years, like Leonid, and had made an effort to learn the language. Still, when they were together, they much preferred the mother tongue.

"Was the house dark when you got here?" Darko asked Timur while eyeing the structure. He liked that on the side of the house with the veranda there was an empty lot, the remains of what had once been a formal garden. That meant there was a close neighbor on only one side, instead of both.

"Yes," Timur said. "But I was in the car at that point and couldn't see all the windows."

"Has anyone come by?"

"No. She is alone. Initially she moved around a lot, as lights went on and off in various rooms, but for the last hour the only light has been in one window on the second floor." Timur pointed to be sure Darko could see the light through the heavy drapes.

"Good job," Darko said. "Sorry it has been a bit of an effort. I'll take it from here. You can head back."

"You don't want me to help?" Timur asked, his voice reflecting his disappointment that his role was over. Darko was a legend among a number of the security and enforcement personnel of Sidereal Pharmaceuticals. Working with him on a job beyond mere surveillance would have afforded Timur bragging rights.

"No need for help," Darko said. "I want to do this alone. I intend to enjoy myself."

Timur laughed and nodded. "Got it! And she's a looker."

After taking what he needed from the satchel, he left it and the Burberry coat in a safe and convenient location to pick up later. With the proximity of neighbors, since the houses were built close to one another, Darko eschewed the normal explosive entry technique, which he generally favored, but instead used a Halligan bar, a tool he had become acquainted with only after coming to America. It was generally used by US fire departments for gaining access through locked doors. He knew that, handled appropriately, it was nearly silent in comparison to an explosive charge.

Once he breached the front door, Darko knew that timing was of the essence. Moving quietly but quickly, he ascended the main stairway and dashed toward the lighted room. Lynn was sitting at the desk, holding a mobile phone.

Darko reacted by pure reflex. He covered the distance between the hallway and the desk in the blink of an eye, snatching the phone from Lynn's grasp with his free hand before she had a chance to react to his presence. Carelessly, he tossed it aside to bounce off the carpet and skid across the bare floor into the far corner of the room.

Lynn started a scream of terror, but it barely got out. Darko vi-

ciously backhanded her as part of the follow-through of getting rid
of the phone. The blow caught her squarely on the side of the face,
crushing capillaries in her upper lip and in her nose and sending her
sprawling facedown to the floor. The sudden action and noise propelled the cat into a headlong retreat to safer areas of the dark house.

Lynn tried to get up to follow the cat and save herself from this
whirlwind assault that had materialized out of the night, but her
legs temporarily wouldn't cooperate. The next thing she knew was
being pressed against the floor with a foot in the small of her back.
She struggled to free herself to be able to breathe.

"Stay still!" Darko hissed. "Or you will be shot!"

Lynn let her body go limp. The foot eased up the pressure
against her.

"Roll over!" Darko commanded.

Lynn did as she was told, looking up at her attacker. The only
details she could see were his dark eyes and yellowed teeth. After
her initial panic that the attack had caused, she now began to think
in a survival mode. Would the neighbors hear if she suddenly
screamed bloody murder?

"I will shoot you if you yell," Darko snarled, as if reading her
mind. Then, without warning, he reached down and yanked the
cinch around her waist to loosen the knot of the bathrobe. The robe
fell partially open, exposing one of her breasts.

With a quick flick of her wrist, Lynn covered herself. At the
same time she brought her other hand up to her face and touched
her lip, which was swelling and tender. Taking her hand away, she
could see that she was bleeding. She knew she was also bleeding
from her nose.

As if taunting her, Darko reached down with the gun and used
the end of the silencer to re-expose the breast. Lynn didn't try to
re-cover herself. She had the impression the man was smiling behind his mask, possibly leering at her. Was this a rape? Her first
thought was that perhaps the man standing over her had somehow

heard about Carl's condition and had come to rob the house and that she was a surprise. Except for Michael, no one knew she was there.

Reining in her terror as much as she could, Lynn had the presence of mind to understand that her survival might depend on cunning. Perhaps she should try to get the man to talk. Maybe she should pretend to cooperate, as it might help. It had registered in her mind that he had an accent, which her panicked mind had yet to identify other than thinking it was familiar.

"Take off your robe!" Darko commanded. He took a step back and lowered the pistol to his side.

Assuming a false smile, Lynn sat up and then re-covered herself. "Why so fast?" she asked. She eyed the gun. Her goal was to get the man to put the gun down. If he did, maybe she could flee. With a little lead, she might be able to get away, as she knew the house intimately and assumed the intruder did not.

"Don't play with me!" Darko snapped.

"And why not?" Lynn asked with raised eyebrows. She shakily got to her feet and recinched the robe, berating herself for not having gotten dressed after her shower. Her nakedness was a handicap on many levels, magnifying her vulnerability.

Steeling herself against what the man might do, she started toward the door. She moved slowly but deliberately, becoming more stable with each step. Her ear was still ringing from the blow she had taken.

"Stop!" Darko ordered.

"I'm just going to get a cold washcloth for my face," Lynn explained, making a supreme effort to speak normally. "My lip is bleeding, which isn't very pleasant for either one of us. Come with me if you'd like!"

When Darko didn't answer, Lynn continued and stepped out of the study into the dark hallway. Her vague idea was to get him off stride and off balance. As she expected, Darko followed right behind her.

"Where are the lights?" Darko said.

"There's no need," Lynn said. "The bathroom is right here." As Lynn entered, she switched on the sconces on either side of the mirror. Moving to the sink, she regarded her reflection. To project a casualness that she didn't feel, she purposefully avoided even looking back at Darko. She sensed he had paused at the threshold. With her index finger she carefully examined her split lip. The laceration was mostly on the inside, having been made by one of her own teeth. Her nose had spontaneously stopped bleeding.

"Not as bad as I thought," Lynn said while running the cold water. "Need to use the facilities?" Lynn couldn't believe she was asking such a question. Darko didn't bother to respond, but she had the sense she was confusing him.

With a wash rag soaked in the cold water pressed against her mouth, Lynn pushed past Darko back out into the hall, turning off the light as she did. All the while she maintained a nonchalance she didn't feel. The man had a feral smell of perspiration and tobacco that she found particularly repulsive. Darko didn't try to stop her and seemed flustered that she went back into the study. They faced each other in the middle of the room.

"Where would you like to sit?" Lynn asked, as if Darko had come by on a social visit.

With a suddenness that took Lynn's breath away, Darko grabbed the lapels of her bathrobe and yanked her face within inches of his, practically lifting her off her feet. She now could smell his heated cigarette breath as well as his body odor.

"Enough of this shit," Darko snapped with uncamouflaged anger. Then with an impressive shove, he propelled her backward onto the couch facing the fireplace. Her head hit hard against the back of the sofa. Had it not, she would have experienced whiplash.

"That's it!" Darko snarled. "No more games."

"Whatever you say," Lynn said, cowering. She'd been shocked at how strong the man was, strong and vicious. Her nascent confidence of somehow controlling the situation and possibly being able to flee vanished in a new sense of helpless terror.

"Now, listen, bitch!" Darko snapped. He was still holding the gun and was now using it to gesture in the air in a way that Lynn found particularly unnerving, since she could see that his finger was on the trigger. He leaned forward, crowding her space. Again she could smell and feel his hot, fetid cigarette breath.

In a vain attempt to protect herself, Lynn pushed back into the couch and pulled the bathrobe tighter. Then she wrapped her arms around her torso, hugging herself.

"You and your friend have pissed off a lot of people in high places," Darko snarled. "It has to stop, completely stop, otherwise we will kill both of you."

There was a pause, although Darko did not lean back. He remained with his masked face inches from hers. He continued to stare at Lynn with his dark eyes as if daring her to either contradict him or move and give him a reason to shoot her on the spot. Lynn held her breath. She was frozen in place.

"You understand what I am saying?" Darko questioned with somewhat less intensity. Then, after a short pause, he added with renewed venom, "Talk to me!" He slapped her again, causing her ears to ring all over.

Lynn righted herself and nodded but couldn't speak. She couldn't take her eyes off the man's yellow teeth, which were bunched together at all angles in his lower jaw. She was terrified he would hit her again, maybe even pistol-whip her with the gun he was still brandishing.

"Not so cocky now," Darko snarled. "Talk or I'll shoot you!" He leaned back and slowly raised the gun to the point where Lynn could look directly into the barrel at the tip of the silencer.

"What do you want me to say?" Lynn squeaked.

"I want you to tell me you understand."

"Yes," Lynn managed. "I understand."

"What are you doing in this house?"

"Mr. Vandermeer and I were friends," Lynn said in a shaky voice. "He gave me a key. Some of my things are here."

At that moment Pep reappeared, causing Darko to jump and briefly aim the gun at the animal. The cat nonchalantly made her way over to the club chair where she had been earlier and jumped onto it.

"So you and Mr. Vandermeer were lovers?" Darko said, turning his attention back to Lynn. He lowered the gun.

"Yes." Lynn was relieved not to be staring into the gun barrel.

"Okay," Darko said. "Lovers or not, I don't give a fuck, but from now on, you leave the investigation of his anesthesia problem to the hospital authorities. Let it drop. Understand?"

"Yes."

Darko straightened up. He then walked over to the desk, giving Lynn a moment of relative respite. He used the index finger of his free right hand to move some of the anesthesia segments around. "What is this?" Darko demanded. "Was this part of Vandermeer's anesthesia record you cut up?"

Lynn nodded again. A new fear gripped her, sending a shiver down her spine. What if this intruder found out what she had so recently discovered? As significant as she thought it was, especially now that she was being told to stop her investigations by this hoodlum, would he then kill her rather than just warn her?

"Get over here!" Darko demanded.

Reluctantly Lynn got to her feet. She momentarily felt dizzy but made it over to the desk.

"What the hell were you doing cutting it up into pieces?"

Lynn hesitated, her mind in high gear. She knew she had to talk or the man might strike her again. But she didn't want to tell the truth. Instead she started to describe how the anesthesia machine monitored the patient's vital signs, going into details that she either knew or made up on the spot. For more than five minutes she produced a word salad that would have made a true schizophrenic proud, never getting around to why she had resorted to scissors.

"All right, all right!" Darko yelled. "Shut the fuck up!" He gave her a forceful shove that sent her stumbling back to the couch. She sat down and again hugged herself and crossed her legs in a vain attempt to feel protected. She saw him look at his watch. Wondering why, she glanced up at the clock on the mantel. It was past midnight. Was he expecting someone else to come?

"All right, let's review," Darko said. "You and your friend are going to go back to being full-time medical students, am I right?"

Lynn nodded, though she didn't know how Michael was going to respond to threats of violence by this lowlife.

"I warn you that if you don't, we will kill both of you. You tell that to your friend."

Lynn nodded. She would tell him, all right.

"Say it!"

"Yes!"

"Now let me add to the consequence of noncompliance."

All of a sudden Lynn recognized the man's accent. It was Russian. Now that she had identified it, she didn't know why she hadn't earlier but assumed it was because of her terror. The accent wasn't heavy, and the man was very fluent in English.

"I know about your family. I know where your mother, Naomi, lives, and I know where your two sisters, Brynn and Jill, are going to college. I also know all about your friend's family. If you don't follow my orders, we will kill them all. I have killed many people in my life and a few more means nothing to me. Do we have an understanding?"

The blood drained from Lynn's face. She believed this blackguard implicitly. Up until that moment the idea that her family and Michael's could be at risk from her actions had not even occurred to her. Now, suddenly, she knew differently, and saw the whole affair in a much more dangerous context.

"Needless to say, the same consequence will result if you say anything to the police. In fact, if you tell anyone about our meeting other than your involved friend, you and everyone I named will be killed. Is that perfectly clear?"

Lynn nodded. She wasn't sure she could speak.

"And one more thing," Darko said. "After we are finished, I want you to leave this house and not come back."

"Why?" Lynn asked, finding her voice.

"You are not in a position to ask questions," Darko said. "Just do it."

"But I need to feed the cat," Lynn said. She pointed to the sleeping pet.

With a sidelong glance, Darko raised the pistol in his hand, aimed, and fired. There was a concussive hiss, and Pep's body jolted. The cat raised her head briefly before collapsing.

"Feeding the cat is no longer a requirement," Darko said.

Lynn's lower jaw had dropped open. She couldn't believe that this goon had just shot the cat.

"Enough!" Darko said. "Time for fun." He confidently laid the pistol on the desk before walking back toward the sofa. About three feet away he stopped. "Now I want you to take off that bathrobe."

A jolt went through Lynn's body. This awful episode was not over. Afraid he would hit her again if she didn't comply, she slowly untied the belt and then slipped her arms out of the robe, letting it puddle around her waist so that it still covered the lower half of her body. As she did this, she kept her eyes glued to the leering eyes of the intruder, fearing the worst. The man was disturbingly unpredictable, with lightning-fast reflexes and overwhelming strength, and she worried he would explode at any second if he sensed any resistance whatsoever. As a consequence she felt totally helpless, which was a new feeling for her. In the past, when she had pondered what she would do in a circumstance of potential sexual assault like she was now facing, she had thought that her own strength, athleticism, and years of kickboxing lessons would help. Now she no longer entertained the delusion. The man had her completely cowed, and it was apparent he knew, as he was secure enough to have to put the gun down.

"All the way!" Darko commanded, arms akimbo.

Lynn reluctantly opened the robe across her lap and pulled it aside. She was now completely naked. Despite the ski mask, she could tell the despicable man was smiling.

"Now," Darko said. "I want you to give me head!"

36.

With a feeling of overwhelming disgust, Lynn tensed her muscles to move forward off the couch with the intent of getting to her knees. All sorts of things were flashing through her mind, such as making a mad dash for the gun or butting the man in the groin with her head or even biting off the tip of his penis, but she knew she would do nothing, out of pure fear for her life.

Suddenly a high, piercing scream shattered the silence, making Lynn think she was about to jump out of her skin. She blinked by reflex and raised her arms to fend off a blow, but she wasn't hit. Instead the intruder shot forward and plowed into her, crushing her against the back of the couch. The man's arms had shot out on either side of Lynn to break his fall. A grunt of air escaped from his mouth.

For a few seconds Lynn couldn't move or even breathe for the sheer weight of the writhing mass bearing down on her. In the next instant she realized she was being pressed against the back of the couch by two men, not one, and there was a mad scramble for dominance. Someone had rushed into the room and tackled the intruder.

Darko, too, had been caught from behind totally by surprise. With his extensive training and combat experience he knew that he was dealing with someone his own size or even larger. Using his honed martial arts skills, he was able to break the hold the attacker had around his chest as he and his attacker rolled off the couch and fell onto the floor. In the next second he was on his feet, but so was the attacker, who came at him again. This time the attacker had him face-to-face in a bear hug, and with his legs pumping, he drove Darko back against the wall of the room. Darko could now see that he was right. The man was bigger and more muscular. And he was black. But there was a good side: it was apparent the man was untrained in martial arts, as he was relying only on his body mass and strength.

To Lynn's shock, it was Michael! Oblivious to her nakedness, Lynn leaped from the couch and rushed for the desk. She had never handled a gun, but didn't care. Reaching the desk, she snapped up the pistol with both hands, slipping her right index finger into the trigger guard. Spinning around, she pointed the gun at the two struggling men and ran over to a point several paces away.

"Stop!" Lynn shouted.

The men ignored her. They were momentarily locked in an embrace and strained against each other. Michael had Darko's arms pinned to his sides.

"Stop!" Lynn shouted yet again. To get their attention she fired the gun, unprepared and surprised by its recoil. She had aimed at a framed print hanging on the wall and had scored a direct hit. The combination of the suppressed sound of the gun and the tinkle of the shattered glass made the men pause. Michael let go of his hold on Darko.

Darko responded like the professional he was. He delivered a sharp karate blow to Michael and in the next instant disarmed Lynn with a fearsome kick. His foot hit the pistol with such force that the gun shot up and glanced off the ceiling. It ended up near the fireplace with a clatter, snapping off the silencer. In the next instant Darko was gone.

It had all happened so fast that for a second both Lynn and Michael were too stunned to move or even talk. They merely stared at each other. Michael was the first to recover, and he flew out of the room in pursuit. Lynn was momentarily frozen in place, holding her numbed hand with the other.

Within seconds Michael was back. "He's gone," he said breathlessly. Lynn threw herself at him, sobbing in relief. The fact that she was naked didn't even occur to her.

"Hold off, girl!" Michael said. He pulled Lynn's arms from around his neck and immediately went for the gun. As he did so, Lynn went for the bathrobe that was crumbled in a heap on the couch.

Michael snatched up the gun and checked the magazine. There were still plenty of rounds available. He unscrewed the broken portion of the silencer and tossed it aside. He could tell the gun was operable.

Lynn rushed over and again enveloped him in an embrace. For a full minute she just held on to him and again cried. After what she had been through, she thought Michael was heaven sent. A miracle.

"It's okay," Michael soothed. His heart was pounding in his chest. His breathing was returning to a semblance of normal.

Finally Lynn leaned back so that she could look Michael in the eye. "Thank you! Thank you! Thank you," she repeated. "How did you know I was in trouble?"

"I didn't," Michael admitted. "But I wasn't willing to take the risk to let you stay here alone. You were really stressed out on the phone. I called you right back as soon as I got rid of Vlad, but your phone immediately went to voice mail. Considering how stressed out you sounded, I suppose I thought the worst, like maybe you'd do something to yourself. I don't know. I didn't agonize. I ran over to the hospital and jumped in a cab."

"Thank God you did. But how did you know to come storming in here?"

"That was easy. When I got to the front door, I could see someone busted in."

"That asshole was about to rape me!" Lynn said angrily, fighting back more tears. "You were in the nick of time."

"Do you have any idea who he is?"

"I don't! I couldn't see his face under that mask. But I can tell you one thing that might not be a surprise. He had a goddamned Russian accent."

"Why would that not surprise me?" Michael asked. He was confused.

"Wait till I tell you why he came in here and scared the hell out of me. But first let's get the fuck out of here in case he or any of his buddies come back. I imagine he is pretty pissed at you for interrupting his fantasy, the prick. He was going to make me give him a blow job."

"We are not going to call the police?"

"Hell no!" Lynn said. "This is all a lot bigger than a breaking-and-entering or even rape. I have a lot to tell you, but first, let me get my clothes. Come with me! I don't want to be alone. And bring the gun."

Lynn rushed back to the master bath, where she'd left her things, and dressed rapidly.

Michael followed close behind. He kept hold of the gun dangling at his side. "If we don't report this, we might be considered accessories after the fact," he said. "I just want you to know. And this gun might be hot."

"At this point I couldn't care less," Lynn said. Then, as she slipped on her shoes, she added: "Did you see Carl's poor cat in the club chair?"

"No, why?"

"The bastard shot the cat for no reason," Lynn said. "He killed the poor thing!"

"Probably to intimidate you."

"Well, it worked. The guy's a narcissistic sociopath, loud and clear, that much I can tell you. He bragged about how many people he has killed."

"Should I call a taxi?"

"No! I don't want to wait around for a cab. We'll take Carl's Cherokee. I'll get it back here in a day or so. But before we leave I want to put the study back together and get the poor cat out of the house. There shouldn't be any evidence of a struggle. And what about the front door?"

"What do you mean?"

"How bad is it? Will it close?"

"It's off one of its hinges and the jamb is split near the striker plate," Michael said, "but I think we can get it to close."

"It just has to look okay," Lynn said.

"Wait a sec," Michael added. For the first time he noticed Lynn's lip laceration and the welt on her cheek. "He hurt you, the bastard. Let me see!"

Lynn waved him off. "It's nothing. Let's clean up the place and get the hell out of here!"

37.

Michael and Lynn lost little time getting out of the house. Dealing with the study had been easy. They picked up the broken glass, doctored the bullet hole in the print so that it wasn't visible except up close, and righted the frame on the wall. After a short discussion, they put Pep in a double trash bag with the idea of finding a garbage can or a Dumpster to get rid of it. Lynn was squeamish about the choice but couldn't think of anything else in the press of time. The front door had been more of a challenge, but with Lynn pulling from the inside and Michael pushing from the outside, they got it back into its jamb and secure. It was literally wedged into place. Lynn had to use the back door to get out. They met up at the garage.

With Lynn feeling shaky from her ordeal, she was happy to take Michael up on his offer to drive. Several blocks away at a construction site, they found a convenient Dumpster. At the last minute the gun and the broken silencer went into the trash bag with the cat. They were relieved to have gotten rid of it all.

As soon as they started north, Lynn filled him in on what had happened. "The goon threatened to kill me," she said to begin, trying to keep herself calm. Merely thinking about the episode got her heart racing all over again. She twisted in her seat to be able to look directly at Michael. The headlights of the oncoming traffic shining through the windshield played across his face. "Actually, he threatened to kill us both."

Michael shot her a surprised look. "He said my name?"

"He didn't say your name. To be exact he said, 'You and your friend have pissed off a lot of people in high places.'"

"He actually said 'people in high places'?"

"Those were his exact words. He said we, 'will kill you and your friend if you don't leave the investigation of Carl's case to the hospital authorities and go back to being full-time medical students.' Well, maybe those weren't his exact words, but pretty damn close."

"And he said 'we,' not 'I,' when he was talking about killing us?"

"Absolutely."

"Terms like 'people in high places' and the pronoun 'we' make this sound more and more like a fucking major conspiracy."

"I couldn't agree more," Lynn said. "We've stumbled onto a hornets' nest. And my tête-à-tête with the goon got worse. He threatened killing my mother and my sisters if we went to the police. He even knew their names and where they were. That takes resources and connections."

"Did he include me at that point?"

"Yes! Your family, too!" Lynn shook her head in disbelief that this was all happening. She turned around and faced forward in her seat. They were nearing the commercial center of historic Charleston. Lynn looked at the revelers, surprised at how many there were despite the hour. She wished her life were so simple.

"So that's why you didn't want to call the police?"

"Partially. The other reason is that uncovering whatever this conspiracy is all about certainly is a hell of a lot more important than nabbing this single shit-ass psychopath. The idea of 'people in high places' being involved blows me away. Something major is in the works, and I think it concerns Sidereal Pharmaceuticals with its Russian connection, and you know how I feel about pharmaceutical companies."

"I know you are not a fan," Michael said.

"That's putting it mildly, whereas I actually hate them," Lynn said with enough venom to cause Michael to glance over at her.

"Brang it on, woman! Wow! You're big-time wound up about the drug business. What's the beef?"

"Where to start?" Lynn said. She sighed and looked back at Michael. "I know we agree on the basics from conversations we've had in the past, like the pharmaceutical industry's hypocrisy. They want people to think their motivation is for the public good when they are, in fact, poster boys for capitalism run amok."

"You mean how they justify their out-of-the-ballpark prices supposedly because of how much money they have to spend on research."

"You got it!" Lynn said with disgust. "The reality is that they spend more money on advertising prescription drugs directly to the public than they spend on research. And that doesn't even include the money they spend on lobbyists and politicians."

"We agree on all that," Michael said. "But I'm sensing a lot more emotion here on your part."

"Did I ever tell you that my father died because he couldn't afford the medication that would have kept him alive?"

"No, you haven't," Michael said, taken aback. Michael knew that Lynn, like him, was never completely open about her childhood, but, considering all their discussions about medical care, he was surprised she had never shared this information about her father's death.

"That's right!" Lynn snapped, staring out through the windshield. "To stay alive he had to take the drug for the rest of his life, and it costs almost a half million dollars a year. It's obscene."

"Really?" Michael asked. "There's a drug that costs five hundred thousand dollars a year?"

"It's a monoclonal antibody, or biologic, like the drozitumab you saw on the front of Ashanti's record. My father lost his job in the 2008 subprime catastrophe and ultimately his health insurance. He died because we couldn't afford to pay for the drug."

"That sucks," Michael said. "Big-time!"

"Tell me about it! Anyway, I'm thinking Sidereal is doing something damning, maybe using people in the Shapiro for clinical trials, like we said. Yet somehow it seems overkill to me for us to get death threats for that unless they are somehow behind these anesthesia disasters."

"You mean to create more subjects?" Michael asked, aghast at the idea.

"I know, it sounds too dastardly to even think about, but who's to know? The only way I can think of possibly finding out is going into the Shapiro. If nothing else, once we are in there, I can use one of the terminals in the network operations center where you visited and look at their data. Of course that brings up the question of how you did tonight with your buddy Vladimir."

Michael chuckled. "It was a slammin' good time. Really, the guy's got a good vibe and a good heart. He even brought me a souvenir, like he promised. I got to show it to you. It's called a *matryoshka* doll. There's one inside the other for about fifteen dolls, the last being a tiny thing."

"Did you get the Shapiro scrubs?" Lynn asked, totally uninterested in the doll.

"No problem. We have two, just like you wanted, including hats and masks."

"One set will be enough," Lynn said. "I'm thinking I should go in by myself. This whole affair is getting more and more serious and risky. I think it is my battle, because of Carl."

"We've been over this," Michael said. "Case closed! We both go or neither of us goes."

"We'll see," Lynn said. "How about the thumbprint?"

"I'm sure I got that, too. He had a couple of beers, and I was careful with the bottles. There should be plenty of prints."

"Excellent," Lynn said. They passed the ramp that led up to the Ravenel Bridge to Mount Pleasant. It was marked by a large over-head traffic sign. The name of the town reminded her of the horrific home invasion that they had learned about from the TV in the surgical lounge. The mother had been a patient at the Mason-Dixon Medical Center and had been diagnosed with a blood protein abnormality. All at once, the confusing gammopathy issue came back into her overstressed mind.

"There's another aspect of all this that troubles me," Lynn said, trying to organize her thoughts. She still felt shaky and discombobulated from what she had been through with the Russian goon. "It's this gammopathy stuff. It keeps popping up. Before that bastard broke in, I learned something curious that I can't explain. Remember those stats I got down in the IT office about the discharge diagnosis of gammopathy and multiple myeloma from the Mason-Dixon Med Center?"

"I remember," Michael said. "But not the actual numbers."

"The actual numbers don't matter," Lynn said. "The significant issue is that the number of people on discharge with these two diagnoses is five times the national average. Five times!"

Michael nodded as he considered what Lynn had just told him, but he didn't say anything.

"Doesn't that surprise you?" Lynn asked. She couldn't believe he was seemingly taking it in stride.

"It surprises me," Michael said. "Let me get this straight. You're saying that the number of people coming into our hospital with an unrelated illness and leaving with a diagnosis of a blood serum abnormality is five times the national average?"

"That's exactly what I am saying. And to make it more confusing, most of these patients are relatively young, in their thirties and forties, whereas gammopathy usually appears in an older population, like people in their sixties."

"And patients with a discharge diagnosis of multiple myeloma is five times more common in our hospital."

"That's what I'm telling you."

"Okay, how do you explain it?"

"I don't," Lynn snapped. "That's why I'm bringing it up, for Chrissake."

"Okay, keep it cool, girl," Michael said calmly. "We're on the same team here."

"Sorry," Lynn said. She took a deep breath to calm down.

"Is discovering this gammopathy and multiple myeloma info what had you 'totally unglued' and upset when you called me earlier?"

"Oh my gosh, no!" Lynn blurted. She swung back around to face Michael, thumping her forehead with her knuckles in mock punishment. "I can't believe I forgot to tell you my most important discovery. The anesthesia records show that in all three cases the tracing had been looped."

Michael shot a quick glance at Lynn to make sure she wasn't jerking him around. "Looped, as in being played over and over?"

"Exactly," Lynn said, with her voice reflecting her sudden excitement. "From the moment of the frame offset in each record, the records were looped with the minute prior to that point, when everything was normal. It means that from the frame offset until the low-oxygen alarm sounded, the anesthesia machine wasn't recording the patient's real-time vital signs. Those signals were interrupted, and the looping was giving the false impression that everything was normal."

"That's serious shit," Michael said.

"The question is, could it be a software glitch?"

"I can't imagine," Michael said. "It has to be a hack job, and if it is, who's doing it and why? Holy shit!"

"It has to be all tied together," Lynn said.

"What do you mean?" Michael asked. He turned into the hospital grounds and headed for the multilevel garage.

"What's going on in Anesthesia has to be connected somehow with the protein abnormalities."

"That seems far-fetched," Michael said.

"I thought so at first. But remember what we learned last year in diagnostics: even when symptoms seem entirely unrelated, they are almost invariably part of the same underlying disease. My intuition tells me we are going to find the same here with the abnormal proteins and the anesthesia disasters."

"If they are associated, I can't think how," Michael said.

"Nor can I," Lynn admitted. "I might be delusional, but I can't stop thinking that I have to get into the Shapiro, even if just to get access to their records."

"We, white man," Michael said, again making reference to Ron Metzner's Lone Ranger joke. "We're a team, girl. There's no way I'm going to let you go into Shapiro by yourself. If this is some major conspiracy, the risks go up."

"It will be your decision if we get to that point," Lynn said. "There's still that thumbprint access that has to be overcome."

They left Carl's Cherokee in a visitor parking spot and walked across the hospital campus toward the medical dorm, a bit overwhelmed by what they had experienced and what they had been talking about. Neither one spoke, particularly as they passed the dark, nearly windowless Shapiro Institute. Both were now thinking about Carl being locked away in its bowels. It made it personal.

Such thinking was the hardest for Lynn, as it immediately evoked a combination of guilt, benumbing anger, and crushing loss, threatening her life on so many levels. She had to look away from the massive, sinister-looking building and force herself to think of something else. "I guess I'm going to have to make an effort to look like I'm back to being a medical student."

"Hallelujah, woman!" Michael exclaimed. "If we are dealing with a major conspiracy that's uptight about us asking questions about Carl, then we gotta believe somebody is going to be keeping tabs on us."

"Sounds so Orwellian," Lynn said.

"I hope this means you're planning on coming to the ophthalmology lecture in the morning?"

"I guess I have no choice."

As they rode up in the elevator they leaned against opposite sides, regarding each other.

"Are you okay?" Michael asked.

"I'm a basket case," Lynn admitted. "I'm wasted and I'm still shaky. I don't think I've ever been so tired and drained. I feel like I've been run over by a truck."

"Will you be able to sleep?"

"I hope so."

"I might be able to find an errant sleeping pill if you'd like."

"I'd like," Lynn said. "And I do have yet another request."

"Hit me!"

"Would you mind if I dragged my mattress down to your room? I don't want to be alone tonight."

"Not a problem, as long as you don't take advantage of me."

"Under the circumstances, I don't find that at all funny."

"Sorry!"

38.

Lynn put her pen down on top of her spiral notebook. She had been trying to take lecture notes but wasn't able to concentrate. She was distracted by the previous night's horrific experience and what she had learned from the anesthesia records. To make matters worse, the lecturer spoke in an all too typical medical-school monotone. On top of that, the subject matter seemed to her to be truly stultifying. As beautiful as the eye was in its overall structure, this minutiae of the retinal circulation was overkill in relation to what she would need to know once she was a practicing orthopedic surgeon. Even if eye surgery had the benefit of being short and bloodless, she couldn't understand why her friend Karen Washington wanted to study ophthalmology as a specialty. After spending four years learning about the whole body, it seemed much too narrow in scope from her perspective.

Adding to her inability to focus, Lynn felt groggy, despite having slept for more than six hours. Six hours was about normal for her, but what she had experienced last night had not been entirely normal sleep. She had taken the Ambien tablet Michael had found for her. As she rarely took sleep meds, she was sensitive to them, and when she did use one, she invariably felt a residual hangover.

When she had awakened that morning just before eight on her mattress on the floor of Michael's room, Michael was already in the shower. It had been the sound of the shower turning on that had aroused her from her drugged slumber. She didn't get up immediately as it had taken her a few minutes to unscramble her brain and try to put in perspective what had happened the previous evening.

There had been a few times during her first year in college when she'd found herself in mildly problematic situations involving the potential of sexual assault, thanks mostly to alcohol, but she'd never suffered an actual episode. Actually, it had never even come close until last night. The mere thought of how close made her feel almost nauseous. Never had she felt quite so thankful and appreciative of Michael's friendship, size, and strength. If he hadn't thrown caution to the wind the night before when he couldn't get ahold of her on her mobile and when he attacked the intruder, she knew she'd be feeling very differently at that moment.

After sticking her head into Michael's steamy bathroom to yell at him that she'd be ready to head over to the hospital in a half hour, she carefully collected the beer bottles Vladimir had handled and went back to her own room. Making sure not to touch the bottles, to avoid messing up any of the Russian's fingerprints, she put them on her desk before getting into the shower herself.

On the way from the dorm to the hospital, Lynn and Michael talked about the paranoia that came with the worry that they were possibly being watched. To both of them, everyone who eyed them looked suspicious, even a couple of the gardeners working in the flower beds who happened to glance up as they passed.

For the first twenty minutes of the ophthalmology lecture, Lynn had tried her best to pay attention, but it wasn't working. When the lecturer turned off the lights once again to go through another series of slides, this time showing fluorescence angiography studies of the back of the eye, she leaned over to Michael, who was sitting next to her as both had taken seats near the door: "I'm outta here," she whispered.

"I thought the deal was that you were going to make it look like you were back to being a full-time medical student."

"My mind's going a mile a minute. I can't sit still and can't concentrate worth a damn. I've got a couple of errands to run."

"What I'm worried about is what you might do. Don't try to get yourself into the Shapiro without me or you and I will be having one hell of a beef!"

"I wouldn't think of it. Take good notes for me!"

"Screw you! You gotta stay and take your own goddamn notes. It's not like I'm enjoying myself. This guy is trying to put us to sleep."

Lynn had to smile. After a quick glance at the lecturer, who had his back to the audience while using a laser pointer to indicate a subtle detail, she stood up and headed for the nearest exit. To make it look like she would be returning, she left her spiral notebook on the arm of her chair. She knew Michael would bring it back without having to be told.

Once outside the lecture room, Lynn went directly to the restroom. Her thinking was that if anybody was watching her, going to the bathroom wouldn't raise any suspicions. As she walked, she tried to see if anyone in particular took note. No one did.

As long as she was in the restroom, Lynn decided to use the toilet. Afterward she looked at herself in the mirror, thinking she looked like death warmed over. There were dark circles under her eyes and her split lip was crusted with a small scab. There were also a few broken capillaries over her cheekbone that she had tried to cover up with a bit of makeup. She used a damp paper towel to get rid of the crust on her lip.

After combing out her hair and putting it back into her barrette in an attempt to look as presentable as possible, Lynn walked out of the restroom. At first she headed in the general direction of the lecture hall, all the while scanning the busy clinic area for anyone paying even the slightest bit of attention to her. Except for a few waiting patients who responded to her white coat in hopes it meant the ophthalmology clinic was about to begin seeing patients, no one seemed to give her a second look.

Deciding she was in the clear, Lynn headed over to the hospital. Since she'd awakened that morning she had given a lot of thought to the "looping" she'd discovered in the anesthesia records. She knew it had to be seriously significant and that someone had to be told, and the sooner the better. Initially she'd thought of Dr. Rhodes, but had quickly nixed the idea after remembering his ranting the day before. It also occurred to her that if there was a major conspiracy there was a chance that Rhodes, as head of Anesthesia, might possibly be involved on some level. She thought the chances small, but not nonexistent. Ultimately she settled on letting Dr. Wykoff know. After a lot of thought, she'd come to agree with Michael that the woman was shaken by what had happened to Carl, and if that were the case, the chances of her being involved in some grand conspiracy seemed nil.

Once in the crush of the hospital, Lynn wasn't as worried about being observed. There were just too many people. Going to the information booth near the front door, she got a piece of hospital stationery and wrote a short explanation of the looping she'd found in the three cases. There was nothing else in the short note, not even a signature. She folded the paper and slipped it into a hospital envelope and sealed it. On the outside she wrote simply: Dr. Wykoff.

With the envelope in hand she went back to the main elevators. In the packed car, she felt a touch of paranoia and wondered why in hell she hadn't taken the stairs. One of the passengers was a uniformed security guard who seemed to be staring at her. She wasn't certain, but it made her uneasy. She had always found the strained

silence of packed elevators mildly unsettling. On this particular day
it was even more so. She was glad that the man didn't get off with
her on two.

Lynn's plan had been simple. She would find out which room
Dr. Wykoff was in and then find a circulating nurse to take the message to the doctor. Lynn even went so far as to take her name tag off
her white coat to remain anonymous.

Gazing at the monitor in the surgical lounge that listed all the
morning cases, Lynn searched for Dr. Wykoff's name. When she
didn't see it, she started at the top again. Only then did she decide
it wasn't there. Apparently Dr. Wykoff was not scheduled that
morning.

Lynn cursed her luck under her breath. It had been her understanding that all the more junior anesthesiologists, like Dr. Wykoff,
were scheduled every day. She couldn't understand why it wasn't to
be today. Instead Lynn walked down to the anesthesia office, where
she and Michael had met Dr. Wykoff the previous day. When no one
responded to her knocking, Lynn opened the door and looked in.
The room was empty. What she did find was a bank of cubbyholes
with one for Dr. Wykoff.

For a moment Lynn debated what to do. She wanted to make
sure that someone actually put her note in Dr. Wykoff's hand rather
than just leaving it, in hopes she might get it. Finally accepting the
inevitable, Lynn went back to the woman's locker room and changed
into scrubs.

Although most people didn't put masks on until they were in an
operating room with a case under way, Lynn put one on in the locker
room to mask her identity just as she had done Monday, looking for
Carl. She didn't know if she was being excessively paranoid, but she
didn't care. With her note in hand, she pushed into the OR proper
and went to the hectically busy main desk. At that time in the
morning, a number of the ORs were in the process of moving from
their first cases to their second. Everybody was busy.

Lynn had to wait several minutes. She knew that Geraldine Montgomery, the OR head nurse, would be the best person to ask about Dr. Wykoff, but she was already being besieged by several other people. In the meantime, Lynn checked the white board in case there had been a change. Dr. Wykoff still was not listed. When Lynn finally had an opportunity, she said she was looking for Dr. Wykoff.

"You and everyone else," Geraldine said with a laugh. "She's AWOL!"

"What do you mean?" Lynn said, but she didn't get an answer right away. She had to wait for Geraldine to shout to someone across the hall to stop dillydallying and get the patient down to four, pronto.

"I'm sorry, honey," Geraldine said, glancing back at Lynn. "What did you say?"

Lynn had to repeat her question.

"For the first time in I don't know how many years, Dr. Wykoff didn't show up this morning. It was so unusual that Dr. Rhodes called the police. Apparently Dr. Wykoff had some sort of family emergency. She packed a bag and is gone to parts unknown. At least that is what we've been told."

Stunned, Lynn crumpled the envelope, thanked Geraldine, who didn't respond because she had already been drawn into another issue, and went back the locker room to get out of her scrubs. This story about Dr. Wykoff was totally unexpected and unsettling. Getting the note about the "looping" to the woman was to ease her guilt about not communicating her extraordinary discovery to anyone, but now, being unable to do it because of the anesthesiologist's uncharacteristic disappearance, only made her that much more upset, especially since she couldn't think of anyone else to tell.

39.

Having to deal with this new conundrum of Dr. Wykoff's unexpected disappearance, Lynn knew that she would find trying to suffer through the ophthalmology clinic as bad as the lecture. Instead, she had decided to use the time to solve the problem of getting a floor plan for the Shapiro. To that end, she'd gotten Carl's Jeep out of the parking garage and headed downtown.

It seemed particularly auspicious to her to find a parking spot on Calhoun Street directly in front of the Charleston County Public Library with time still on the meter. What made it so convenient was that the library was just across the street from 75 Calhoun, the impressive and relatively new municipal building that housed the Charleston Building Commission.

Lynn hurried inside. She wanted to find the right office well before the lunch hour. From her experience with city bureaucracy in Atlanta, where she had grown up, she knew that midday was a time to avoid, as civil servants became progressively distracted and unhelpful. But she soon learned she needn't have worried. Not only was the building commission easy to find but the people behind the counter immediately gave her the impression they were there to help, particularly a balding, jovial, and colorful fellow named George Murray. The man wore bright-red suspenders to keep his pants up despite a particularly protuberant abdomen. When he saw Lynn's white coat and correctly guessed she was a medical student, he laughed and told her to go ahead and give him the standard lecture on potential evil consequences of his beer belly. "I like my suds," he confessed. "Anyway, what can I do to help you?"

"An architect friend has told me that you would have plans available for public buildings, like hospitals."

"Provided the hospital is in Charleston," George said with a laugh. "Plans have to be submitted and approved to get a building permit. It's all in the public domain. What hospital are you curious about?"

Lynn paused, trying to think of how much she wanted to reveal. The last thing she wanted was for it to get back to the dean or anyone at the school or the hospital that she was in the building commission asking for plans for the Shapiro. But she didn't see any way around the issue. "The Shapiro Institute," she said, hoping she wouldn't regret admitting it. The trouble was that, without plans, she worried that she might not get much benefit from making the effort to break into the Shapiro other than possibly accessing the institute's electronic medical records. She wanted to maximize the chances of finding Carl, which she knew might not be easy among a thousand or so patients unless she had a pretty good idea how the place was laid out.

"That's part of the Mason-Dixon Medical Center," George said without hesitation. "What kind of plans are you interested in?"

"I don't really know," Lynn admitted. "What kind of plans do you have?"

"There's floor plans, electrical plans, HVAC plans, plumbing plans. You name it, we have it."

"I guess I'm mainly interested in floor plans."

"Let's see what's available in the file," George said agreeably. He was gone for only a few minutes before returning with a very large burgundy-colored folder tied with string.

George heaved the folder onto the countertop and opened it. He slid out the contents. "We are gradually going digital, but we've got a long way to go." He pawed through the material, eventually locating the floor plans. They were bound on one side with staples. "Here you go. Knock yourself out!"

Lynn flipped through some of the pages. She'd seen architectural floor plans before and knew something about how to read them. What surprised her right off was that although the building had a relatively low silhouette in real life, suggesting it was about two to three stories tall when compared with the attached hospital building, it was actually six stories, with four being below grade. "Which is ground level?" she asked.

George turned the plans around so that he could read all the small print. "Apparently it is the one labeled the fifth floor," he said, comparing the floor plans with their accompanying elevations. He turned the pages of the floor plans until he was on five. "Doesn't look like it has many external doors leading outside. Strange, but I'm sure it was cleared by the fire department. Must have a damn good sprinkler system. What kind of hospital is this?"

"It's for people in a vegetative state," Lynn said. She turned the plans back around and, by looking at the fifth floor, was able to locate the connection with the hospital proper and see the conference room she had been in for her tour during second year. She could also see the three patient visiting rooms. She was also able to locate the door Michael had used when he entered the building with Vladimir. Down a short hall from the door was a room labeled NETWORK OPERATIONS CENTER. She guessed that was what Michael had called the NOC. Immediately adjacent to it was a room for computer servers, and across the hall was a room labeled LOCKER ROOM. So far, so good.

"What's a vegetative state? You mean people in a coma?"

"Yes, but they are not all in a coma. Some of them have sleep-wake cycles, which unfortunately often gives families unjustified hope they are going to wake up completely. Anyway, the hospital is for people with brain damage who cannot take care of themselves in even the most basic ways. They all need a lot of attention. It takes a lot of effort on the part of the nursing staff."

"Sounds terrible."

"It is," Lynn agreed. She noticed that beyond the NOC was a hallway off of which was a profusion of rooms. Some were labeled as SUPPLY ROOM. Many were labeled AUTOMATION ROOM, whatever that meant. One was labeled AUTOMATION CONTROL. A few weren't labeled at all. Two of the largest rooms were named CLUSTER A and CLUSTER B and also could be reached from the same hallway. Lynn remembered that Michael had said that on the first page of Ashanti's record it had Cluster 4-B 32. Lynn now guessed that these were the spaces where patients were housed. Apparently Ashanti was on the fourth floor, or the first subterranean floor in the B cluster room.

"What do you think Cluster A and B refer to?" Lynn asked, just to see what George might say.

"No idea," George said. "But I can tell you one thing: they are good-sized rooms and look like they need a lot of electrical power."

"They are narrow in comparison to this open space in the middle," Lynn said. The area she was pointing to was a large rectangle, and it occupied the center of the building. Around its entire periphery was a hallway that could be reached from the cluster rooms.

George looked at the space on the floor plan but appeared confused. He turned the plans around again, but there was nothing to read. It was just a blank space. He then shook his head and said: "I don't know for sure what it is. Maybe it is a space open above and below. Let's check the fourth floor." George flipped the page over.

"I was right. On the fourth floor it is definitely a room, which is open above, apparently all the way to the roof. That is a hell of a room. It's got a three-story ceiling."

Lynn studied the space that now was labeled RECREATION, and a door at each end. Otherwise, the fourth floor looked like the fifth. "What do you think it is?"

George scratched his bald pate, appearing as confused as ever. "If I had to guess, I'd say a gym! If I had to be more specific, I'd say a basketball gym. I know that sounds ridiculous, but the dimensions are about right. But I don't know what all the wiring is in the floor."

"There can't be a gym in a hospital for comatose people," Lynn said.

"Maybe it's for the staff. You know, to let off a little steam. You said it is hard to take care of these vegetative patients."

"I suppose it is possible," Lynn said. "Let's see what's on the other floors." She flipped a page back to see the third floor. It was just like the fifth floor, with the center space a bank. Same with the second floor. Then the first floor was a mirror image of the fourth, with the center space labeled RECREATION, and with the same wiring in the floor. "Two gyms?" Lynn said in disbelief.

"One for the men and one for the women," George said with a laugh that suggested he wasn't serious. "Why are you looking at plans? Are you going to visit?"

"I already have," Lynn said. She told George of the limited visit given to her and her class. "Unfortunately all we saw was a tiny bit of the fifth floor. Needless to say, we have been curious ever since. That's why I wanted to look at the plans."

"Do you want to see anything more in this file?" George said, motioning to the stack.

"Do you think any of the other plans might give us a hint as to what the gym area really might be?"

"Don't know!" George said. He pulled out the electrical plans and quickly flipped through them. "I don't have any better idea about the gym, but I can tell you that the whole place must be highly automated. Seems to me there is enough power to run a manufacturing plant." He tossed aside the electrical plans and pulled out plumbing. After he scanned them he remarked, "Wow! The place also uses a lot of water. The specified intake pipes are huge. Maybe those big rooms aren't gyms but swimming pools. Just kidding!" Next he looked at the HVAC details. He was again impressed. "This is one interesting hospital, young lady. Look at this!"

George spun around the plans so that Lynn could read the labels.

"What am I looking at?" The plans looked superficially like the floor plans but were overlaid with all sorts of dotted lines, symbols, and labels similar to those on the electrical plans. She had to lean over to read some of the labels, which said things like FLOOR LEVEL RETURN or MAIN INDUCTION.

"This is an impressive HVAC system, which stands for heating, ventilation, and air conditioning," George said. "Look at the size of these ducts, particularly from the gyms." He pointed with a stubby index finger. Lynn wasn't sure what he was pointing to and didn't really care, but she didn't want to appear disinterested since he was being so helpful. She was appreciative that he didn't just hand her the file folder and leave her to her own devices.

"They can probably change the air in those gyms at will," George said. "I worked for an air-conditioning company before I snared this city job. Much better benefits. You have no idea."

"Why would they want to change the air in the gyms so quickly?" Lynn asked.

George shrugged his shoulders. "It's pretty typical for well-designed gyms."

"So you are saying that by looking at these HVAC plans you think these large rooms really are gyms."

"I don't know what I'm saying," George confessed. "But I do see that the HVAC system is actually tied in with the system in the hospital proper. That's where the cooling towers are and all the elaborate filter systems hospitals have to have. I bet that saved a bundle."

"Well, thank you very much," Lynn said. She felt that she had gotten the basics of what she needed. "You have really been very helpful."

"It's not every day that I get to help a good-looking medical student," George said with a wink.

Good grief, Lynn thought but didn't say. George was now ruining it by being patronizing. She hoped to hell he wasn't going to ask her out for a drink.

"Would you like any copies of these plans?" George added, totally unaware of his faux pas.

"Is that possible?" Lynn asked. The idea had not occurred to her.

"Of course it is possible," George said. "There is a small charge for the copier, but I could run it off for you right away, before lunch."

"That would be terrific," Lynn said.

"What plans would you like besides the floor plans?"

Quickly Lynn took another quick glance at the electrical, plumbing, and HVAC plans. She pulled the HVAC ones free of the others. "Maybe these," she said. All at once a contingency plan sprang into her mind. She didn't know if she was going to be able to get into the Shapiro, or exactly what she would find, but she was enough of a realist to know the risks, and the idea of having some sort of backup appealed to her.

"I'll be right back," George said with another wink.

This time Lynn didn't mind.

40.

The door to the Clinical Engineering Department opened, and Misha Zotov looked up. He always insisted on occupying the workbench closest to the entrance. It gave him an opportunity to monitor who and what came in and out. Although Fyodor Rozovsky was nominally the department head, Misha was responsible for its day-to-day operations, making sure all the computer-driven hospital equipment was running smoothly. Misha knew that Fyodor's attention was often elsewhere, since he also was the behind-the-scenes coordinator of hospital security.

Misha put down his soldering iron when he saw who had entered. It was Darko Lebededev, who appeared mildly indisposed, with red-rimmed eyes. He was dressed as usual in a hospital security uniform, as he had been advised to wear on the rare occasions he came calling. Misha made a point of staring at his watch for a beat before speaking in Russian: "Where the hell have you been? I've been trying to contact you all fucking morning."

Darko lowered himself onto a workbench stool next to Misha, wincing, as if he had a headache or a sore back. Like Misha, he spoke in Russian. "It was a late night and a lot of vodka at the Vendue. Leonid and I met up with those Russian babes you people brought over to keep tabs on the two male anesthesiologists. They have been complaining about their charges, claiming they are boring boneheads. Leonid and I felt it was our patriotic duty to show them a proper good time, and a good time it was."

"According to Sergei Polushin you and Leonid are supposed to be available twenty-four/seven. It is not that we have been overworking you two."

"I'm here now," Darko said sardonically. Confident of his reputation and of the demand for his services, he was not about to be intimidated by the likes of Misha. Darko considered the guy a mere apparatchik programmer who sucked up to Fyodor.

"How did it go last night?" Misha demanded. "Needless to say, we need to know."

"Taking out the anesthesiologist went like a dream. No problems whatsoever."

"I know about the anesthesiogist," Misha snapped. "I'm referring to the damn medical students. I talked with Timur Kortnev, and he filled me in about their strange activities last night and that she ended up in Vandermeer's house. I need to know if you think what you did was adequate so I can tell Fyodor, who wants to brief the hospital CEO."

"I suppose I'd have to say it went reasonably," Darko said.

"*Reasonably* doesn't sound adequate, my friend, especially coming from you. Did she get the message?"

"I warned her. I even slapped her around a bit, but I never got to scare her as much as I planned."

"Why the hell not?"

"Her friend showed up in the middle of things and got the jump on me. To make matters worse, she got ahold of the gun, and I had to get the hell out of there before I had the chance to do her."

Misha stared at Darko with his mouth agape.

"I didn't have any choice. If I had stayed, I would have had to kill at least one of them, if not both. I left for the good of the program."

"Maybe it would have been better if you had killed them."

"I wasn't going to do that unless I knew that was what Sergei or Fyodor would have wanted. Anyway, we know she got the message."

"How do we know?"

"Because they didn't call the police. I told her we'd do her sisters and mother if she did, and obviously she didn't. We would have heard."

"Do you have any idea why she was at Vandermeer's house?"

"She and Vandermeer were lovers."

"Shit!" Misha snapped. "Security should have found that out before we chose him as a test subject. Getting one of our goddamned medical students involved is a fucking big-ass mistake. Now she and her friend may have to be eliminated like Wykoff to clean this up."

"No problem, if that's what you and Fyodor want."

"The trouble is that eliminating a couple of socially connected medical students will ignite a hell of an investigation, something we don't want or need."

"That's why I didn't kill them last night," Darko said.

"I'll talk it over with Fyodor," Misha said irritably. "But for now we will just need to keep a close eye on them. I'll leave it up to you and Timur. She will not recognize you, will she?"

"What do you think I am, a fucking amateur?"

41.

There's a bunch of free tables back against the far wall," Michael said, nodding his head in the general direction. He and Lynn had just met up in the cafeteria after she had texted him to meet there. She had just come from parking Carl's Cherokee in the garage. He had come from the ophthalmology clinic. Once again he could tell she was juiced about something.

"I see it," Lynn said. "Let's take it! We'll have some privacy." She was carrying a large manila folder under her arm while holding on to her cafeteria tray with both hands. The cafeteria was in full swing with the usual lunchtime crowd. Just getting through the cafeteria line had taken almost a quarter of an hour. Surrounded by people, some of whom they knew, they hadn't talked about anything serious. Lynn had had to bite her tongue to keep from telling him what she had done.

Just as Michael and Lynn were sitting down, Ronald Metzner appeared out of nowhere, having spied them from the checkout. "Hey, guys," he said, sliding his tray onto the table. It was a four-top.

"You are both in luck. Wait until you hear the joke of the day. Did you ever hear the one about . . . ?"

"Ronald," Lynn said, interrupting. "I know this is going to come as a surprise to you, but maybe later for the joke. Michael and I have something private to discuss. Would you mind?"

"It's a quickie," Ronald said, almost pleading. "It's really funny."

"Please," Lynn persisted.

"Okay, okay," Ronald said. He hoisted his tray back up and scanned the room for a more receptive audience. "Catch you later," he added, and walked off.

"I hated doing that," Lynn confessed, watching Ronald head to the sitting area outside. "There is something forlorn about Ron."

"I know what you're saying," Michael offered.

"Anyway, I want to show you what I got." Lynn slipped the copies of the building plans out of the folder. They had been reduced to standard paper size, eight and a half by eleven inches. "I went down to the Charleston Building Commission to see if I could find plans of the Shapiro. I hit pay dirt."

Michael took the sheaf of printouts, which was stapled in the upper left-hand corner. He glanced at the first page. "My God, you need a damn magnifying glass."

"It's small but legible," Lynn said. "You have to hold it close. They couldn't copy them without reducing them."

Michael did as Lynn suggested. "Okay, what am I looking at?"

"The first six pages are the floor plans of the Shapiro. From the outside the building looks like it's a bit more than two stories tall, but actually it is six, with four floors under grade. The floor you went in on and the one connected to the hospital is actually the fifth floor."

"That's odd. I wonder why."

"I guess the designers felt the inmates wouldn't be interested in a view," Lynn said, making a stab at humor. "I suppose from the standpoint of heating and cooling, it is a lot more efficient. Maybe they also didn't want the institute to stand out too much. I mean, it looks big enough the way it is, especially with so few windows, but no one can imagine how big it really is."

"There's more than six pages here," Michael said, leafing through the entire collection before going back to the first page for a closer look.

"There are twelve pages," Lynn explained. "The last six are the HVAC plans."

"HVAC plans?" Michael asked with a crooked smile and an exaggerated quizzical expression. "Now, that's going to come in handy."

"Don't be a wiseass," Lynn snapped. She snatched the plans out of Michael's grasp and put them down on the table. "You can be as sarcastic as you like, but mark my words: this little treasure trove is going to be a big help when we get in there."

"*If* we get in there," Michael corrected. "There's still the hurdle of the thumbprint touchscreen."

"I'm going to work on it right after lunch."

"The hell you will!" Michael said. "You were assigned patients today in the ophthalmology clinic. I had to see mine and yours this morning. I'm not going to cover for you this afternoon in dermatology. I hate dermatology. We're lucky you weren't missed this morning."

"Okay," Lynn said soothingly. "We can talk about it."

"Bullshit!" Michael said. "We decided you're going back to being a medical student. That means coming to the lectures and the clinic. You know what I'm saying?"

"Okay! All right," Lynn said. She put her hand on Michael's forearm to calm him down. "Don't get so bent out of shape."

"I won't get so bent out of shape if you hold up your end of the bargain. We have a lot of powerful people who are on our case."

"Okay, okay, enough already," Lynn said. She motioned back at the floor plans and pointed out the two relatively large rooms labeled

CLUSTER A and CLUSTER B. "That's where I think the patients are kept on each floor."

"How do you figure?"

"You told me that on Ashanti's Shapiro electronic medical record it said Cluster 4-B 32. I think it's her in-house address, seeing the size of those rooms. I think she's on the fourth floor, in Cluster B, bed thirty-two."

"Maybe so," Michael said. He picked up the plans again, holding them up almost against his nose. He was studying the first floor plan.

"Do you notice the huge room in the center that is labeled *recreation*?"

"It's hard to miss, even at this scale. What the hell is it? There's nobody getting recreation in the Shapiro Institute."

"The clerk in the building department and I were trying to figure that out."

"Is it on every floor?"

"No, only on two floors, one and four, but the ceilings are three stories tall. The clerk thought they might be gyms for the staff. He said that they were about the right size for a men's and a women's basketball court." Lynn gave a short, glum laugh. "He wasn't being serious. Whatever they are, we're going to have to check them out."

Michael nodded in agreement. "Can we eat now? I'm famished."

For a few minutes they ate in silence. Lynn was hungry, too, but after wolfing down her sandwich she said, "When I came out of the Charleston Building Commission I realized I was in the neighborhood of Carl's father's law firm. I decided to drop in and see if he was available."

Michael put down his sandwich and stared at Lynn in disbelief. "Did you see him?"

"For a few minutes. He was off to a business lunch, which was good, so there was no trouble breaking it off."

"What the fuck did you say? You do know we could be in a shit-load of trouble for not reporting the break-in at Carl's house and messing with the evidence."

"I know, I know," Lynn repeated. "I'm not an idiot. I told him that you and I had gone down to Carl's house around midnight to feed the cat, and we found the cat was nowhere to be found and the front door was worse for wear but that nothing else was missing except the cat. That's all I said. Well, I also let him know I have been using Carl's car. I thought he should know about the door so he can have it fixed."

"That's hardly justification for taking the risk of talking with him and telling him we were there. What if he reports the front door to the police, and the police want to question us? That could be trouble. It could be more than trouble, because we are going to have to lie."

"I played down the damage to the door, and even suggested it was probably one of Carl's friends who was worried about the cat and didn't know I was feeding it. I seriously doubt he's going to be calling the police. There is too much on his mind, considering Carl's medical situation."

"Why take the risk at all?"

"Because there were two other things I seriously wanted to talk to him about. First was about Carl. I wanted to know if anything was said about Carl having an early serum blood protein abnormality."

"Had they been told?"

"No, it had not been mentioned, which I find strange, since there had been a formal consult by a hematologist to look into it. Obviously it is now part of his EMR. I also wanted to ask if he and his wife were going to visit. I said that if there was any way I could be included, I would like to be."

"What was the second reason you wanted to talk to him?"

"I wanted to ask him what we should do if we find out that Sidereal Pharmaceuticals is doing unethical drug testing on patients without their knowledge. I didn't mention anything about the Shapiro Institute, for obvious reasons, or about the anesthesia looping and all that. But I thought he would be the best person to ask this general question since he had been a district attorney in his early career and is well connected with law enforcement above and beyond the local police. I thought he would know what we would need to do. If we find out something significant by going into the Shapiro, we might not have a lot of time to sit around on our asses deciding what to do. If this is the kind of conspiracy we think it might be, they probably have a lot of contingency plans in place if a couple of gadflies like us get in the way."

"I wish you had asked me first what I thought about talking to him. I think it was premature and taking a risk, especially after last night."

"Okay, sorry. I was in the area, and I thought we should be prepared."

"I believe you," Michael said. "But we're in this together. Keep that in mind. So what did he say?"

"He said if we found something serious to come to him! Since Sidereal is a multinational company based in Geneva and doing business in all fifty states, he'd feel comfortable going to both the FBI and the CIA."

42.

hat's your take?" Lynn asked Michael. They were sitting on the same, semi-secluded park bench in the inner court-yard garden where they'd sat the previous afternoon, when Lynn bawled her eyes out after learning that Carl was going to be transferred. On this occasion, it was in deep shadows, thanks to being boxed in by trees and shrubbery. There were Victorian-style street lamps placed at wide intervals along the walkway from the hospital to the dorm, but none close enough to shed much light on the bench. From where they were sitting, they could see the door into the Shapiro Institute that Vladimir had used when he had taken Michael on his brief visit.

Michael checked the time, using his phone. Its illumination briefly lighted his face before he quickly turned it off. "We've been here now for more than forty-five minutes," he said. "I think that's it. I don't think we are going to see any more people coming out or going in."

"That wasn't much of a shift change," Lynn said. Just before eleven P.M. they had seen six people go in. A quarter of an hour later six people came out. All were wearing the Shapiro coveralls. They could hear conversation, but not individual words. They couldn't even tell if they were speaking English.

"I'm shocked there weren't more people," Michael agreed.

"I wonder if some of the Shapiro staff come and go via the connection to the main hospital," Lynn said. "It's hard to believe that there are only six people working during the evening and the night shifts. That would mean only one person per floor."

"Some must use the hospital," Michael said. "There's no way six people could take care of all the vegetative patients, even with automation. That's absurd."

"Absurd or not, it can't be good care. It is all the more reason I hate the idea of Carl being put in there, above and beyond the possibility he's being used as a guinea pig for clinical drug trials."

"The only good aspect is that if there are only six people on the night shift, we might actually get away with going in there. If I had to guess, with only one person per floor, that one person is probably minding the automation and not concerned about possible intruders. So if you are still committed to giving it a try, this is the time."

"You're not getting cold feet, are you?" Lynn asked.

"No more than I've had from day one. Let's go get our stuff and get it over with."

They stood up and stretched. They had been sitting there now for almost an hour. Both briefly eyed the Shapiro as they joined the main paved pathway. The dark, massive building was, if anything, more intimidating at night. It could have been a tomb or mausoleum. What they didn't see was that another figure had emerged from the shadows and followed them at a significant distance as they headed back to the dorm.

The afternoon had been difficult, almost painful, for Lynn. If she thought the ophthalmology lecture was humdrum, then the dermatology talk was worse. Yet she persevered. At one point she thought seriously about bagging it, but Michael had somehow sensed it and whispered, "Don't even think about it!" So she had stuck it out. Same with the clinic after the lecture.

Later that evening, at dinner, Lynn and Michael had made it a point to eat with a group of friends as a way of pretending they were acting normally. At the table Lynn had voiced her negative reaction to both ophthalmology and dermatology. A few people, Michael included, felt as she did. Others had different ideas. Two of their dinner partners mentioned they were soon heading off to dermatology residencies, so Lynn didn't belabor the point.

After dinner, Lynn and Michael had excused themselves and headed back to the dorm. There they had spent more than three hours following the instructions Lynn had downloaded from the Internet for fooling fingerprint scanners in general, and thumbprint scanners in particular. Lynn had already gotten the necessary gear, which included a high-resolution digital camera, which she had borrowed, super glue, wood glue, a good laser printer, and transparency film.

They had experimented by making mock-ups of their own prints and using Michael's HP laptop, which had a fingerprint lock, to see if they would work. It had taken several attempts, but eventually they did work. The step that they had found the most difficult was going from the negative toner print on the transparency sheet to the positive made from the wood glue. But they had kept at it until they thought they had perfected the step. Finally, feeling relatively confident, they had tackled Vladimir's prints and made a number of copies.

When they had finished, they debated whether to walk over right away and see if the fake thumbprints would open the Shapiro door, but they decided against it, as the chances of being seen were too great. Instead, they would try to go into the Shapiro after the shift change at eleven o'clock, when they reasoned there would be fewer people out and about in the medical center quadrangle.

Now, as midnight was approaching, both Lynn and Michael were feeling progressively keyed up as they boarded the dorm elevator to go up to Lynn's room to get the paraphernalia they needed for the break-in. Unfortunately, just as the elevator door was about to close, several fellow students who'd come back from studying in the library got on. Reluctant to talk in the presence of others, Lynn and Michael bit their tongues and stayed silent. Once they got to their floor and found themselves alone again, the floodgates opened, and they excitedly went over the general plan they had agreed on if and when they got into the institute.

The first order of business was to go directly to the NOC and try to access the Shapiro data bank and learn what they could, including finding out Carl's location. Then they would visit the appropriate cluster room. After that, they planned to check out the supposed recreation space on either the first floor or the fourth, whichever was more convenient, since those floors had the only access.

"My sense is that we should make this visit as short as possible," Michael said as they approached Lynn's room, where they had left their gear. "We have to be fast. No foot-dragging! The longer we're in there, the greater the risk. You know what I am saying?"

"Of course," Lynn said. "It stands to reason, but I am determined to get what we need from the Shapiro computer with Vladimir's log-in. It might take a few minutes, and I don't want you to be ragging on me. We need to find out how many deaths the Shapiro has had, and the cause, since it opened. We also want to know how many people have recovered enough to be discharged. It's important, since I know from my reading what the stats should be."

"And we want to find out Carl's location," Michael added.

"Obviously," Lynn said. "That's going to determine which cluster room we go to. Will you want to try to visit Ashanti?"

"Not necessarily," Michael said.

Lynn keyed open her door and entered. Michael followed, closing the door behind.

"Okay, I think it's time we dressed for the occasion," Lynn said, adding a touch of humor to temper her growing anxiety. Her intuition told her they were going to find something disturbing if they managed to get in, but it also reminded her that if they were caught, there was going to be hell to pay. She didn't agree with Michael's hope that they might only get a slap on the wrist because of their medical-student status.

Without further discussion they quickly changed out of their clothes and got into the white one-piece Shapiro coveralls Vladimir had provided. When they were finished, they looked at each other. Lynn was the first to laugh but Michael quickly joined in.

"Yours is way too small," Lynn said. "Sorry to laugh."

"Yours is way too big," Michael said. "Rest assured: no one is going to accuse us of being dipped."

"Surely not," Lynn said. She knew that in Michael's vernacular "dipped" meant "dressed up." Both pocketed their mobile phones, each with a flashlight app and fully charged. Lynn checked the time. It was just after midnight. "It's just about the time we thought appropriate."

"Okay," Michael said. "Let's go kick butt!"

Over their distinctive scrubs they both pulled on long raincoats. They didn't want any fellow students who might see them asking any questions about their outfits. Both picked up an envelope containing one of the fake thumbprints. Lynn put the stapled floor plans into a pocket—the one-piece Shapiro coveralls had an abundance of them.

They were almost out the door when Lynn remembered something else. "Hang on a second!" she said. A moment later she was back, brandishing a screwdriver.

"Why a screwdriver?" Michael questioned.

"You'll probably make fun of me if I tell you," Lynn said. She pulled her door closed and made sure it was locked. Usually she didn't care, but with someone else's high-resolution digital camera on her desk, she didn't want anyone going in.

They headed toward the elevators. "You're not going to clue me in about the screwdriver?"

"No," Lynn said. "I know you too well. I'll tell you later when we come back here to the dorm."

"Suit yourself," Michael said.

They rode down by themselves.

"I'm getting a bit nervous, bro," Lynn admitted.

"You're not alone, sis," Michael said.

A few students were on the first floor, patronizing the vending machines and conversing in small groups. Lynn and Michael ignored them and went outside. It was not uncommon for third- and fourth-year medical students to leave the dorm at that hour, often being called over to the hospital, and no one questioned them. In the relative darkness they headed into the medical center quadrangle, following the serpentine walkway leading to the clinic building and the main hospital beyond. Very few stars were visible because of the light issuing mostly from the medical center windows. To the left, the Shapiro Institute loomed out of the darkness.

Walking quickly in and out of puddles of light cast downward by the Victorian street lamps, they approached the turnoff for the Shapiro about midway between the dorm and the clinic building. It was on their left. Opposite it, to the right, a short stretch of walkway branched off toward the bench where they had recently been sitting to watch the shift change. They couldn't see the bench itself as it was completely lost in shadow.

The students stopped and paused, first looking ahead and then behind. Both were disappointed to see a figure coming in their direction, seemingly from the dorm. A moment later the individual entered the cone of light from one of the lamps. They could tell it was a uniformed member of the security staff.

"What should we do?" Lynn asked with moderate alarm. They didn't want to draw attention, which they might by standing there.

Michael pointed to the right. "Let's return to our bench. We'll let him pass. Maybe he'll think we've come here to make out!"

Lynn had to smile in spite of herself.

It took them only twenty seconds to get to the bench. They sat down. Surrounded on both sides with shrubbery, they couldn't see the security man initially, but in less than a minute he appeared and stopped for a moment, looking in their direction.

"He might be able to see us," Lynn whispered. "Kiss me! Make it look real!"

Michael obliged, wrapping his big arms around Lynn's relatively narrow shoulders. It was a sustained kiss. Both closed their eyes.

After almost a full minute, they hazarded a look back toward the main pathway. The security man was gone. They detached themselves from their embrace.

"It worked," Michael whispered.

"Such sacrifice!" Lynn teased.

"Let's promise never to do that again," Michael teased back, "but it must have been convincing, since he decided not to mess with us."

Lynn nodded but didn't respond audibly. Her attention had been absorbed by the Shapiro building silhouetted against the black sky. Its intimidating appearance was causing her to struggle with her intuition, which was now telling her a different story than it had back in the safety of her room. Now it was saying they shouldn't go in. But that was not the only inner voice clamoring for attention. At the very same time another part of her brain was screaming at her that she had to check on Carl; she had to find out once and for all how he was being treated and if he was being used as an experimental subject. It was an ambivalence-fueled mental tug-of-war.

"All right!" Michael said excitedly, unaware of Lynn's sudden indecision. "Let's do this quick, fast, and in a hurry." He leaped to his feet but noticed Lynn wasn't moving. "What's up, girl? You ready to step up or what?"

Lynn stood. Her hesitancy eased in the face of Michael's eagerness. "I'm ready, I think."

"Let's do it!" Michael said. He moved quickly. Lynn had to almost run to catch up. When they got to the door, Michael popped up the protective cover for the thumbprint security pad with the Russian's fake fingerprint already positioned on his thumb. He pressed it against the touchscreen, but nothing happened. "Fuck," he said. "It's not working."

"Let me try mine," Lynn said. She and Michael rapidly changed places. She put her fake fingerprint on her finger and pressed it against the pad. Again nothing!

"Mothafucka!" Michael blurted. Anxiously he glanced back along the walkway, fearing they might be observed while hesitating at the door. From the walkway they were in plain sight.

"Wait!" Lynn said. "I remember reading that sometimes you have to heat it up." She opened her mouth widely and thrust her thumb in, being careful not to touch the layer of pliable, almost rubbery wood glue to her teeth or tongue. She exhaled through her mouth, taking several breaths. Then she tried pressing it against the touch pad again.

There was an audible click. She pushed on the heavy, solid door with her shoulder, and it opened.

"Hallelujah!" Michael exclaimed.

A moment later both students were inside, blinking against the brightness of the whiter-than-white hallway, evenly illuminated by LED light coming through the translucent ceiling. Lynn lost no time pulling the door closed. There was another audible click as the release lever fell into place. At that moment both pulled on Shapiro hats and masks.

Looking up, Michael saw, attached to the ceiling about twenty feet down the hall, what he had thought was a video device when he had visited the Shapiro Institute the first time. He pointed it out to Lynn, then whispered, "Best if we ditch the raincoats!"

After he and Lynn got their overcoats off, he balled them up into the tightest bundle possible and stashed them in the far corner by the door.

Lynn was already looking at the floor plan for fifth level.

"No need for a map," Michael said. "The NOC is straight ahead on the right. Let's move it!"

"There's a locker room on the left," Lynn said, still studying the floor plan as they started forward. "Maybe we should leave the raincoats in there, instead of out here in the hall."

"My vote is we leave them be. There's too big a risk of running into staff in the locker room, where we'd probably end up having to have a conversation, which would mean we'd get exposed as party crashers before we started. We can only expect to get so many miles out of these Shapiro suits."

"Maybe you're right," Lynn said. She looked up at the video device as they passed under it, wondering if they were already under observation. She hoped not, as it would mean their visit would be a short one.

Walking quickly, they approached the pocket door leading into the NOC.

43.

Misha Zotov was notorious for being a deep sleeper, especially after getting very little sleep the night before, and his cell phone's selected ring tone was almost too melodious to pull him out of Morpheus's grasp. To make things worse, he had passed the evening imbibing considerably more vodka than usual. Overdrinking was his method of dealing with stress, which he was experiencing more than usual thanks to the series of threats to the biologics program. Up until a few weeks ago, there had been nary a blip. Unfortunately that had changed dramatically, particularly over the last week or so. The last, and possibly worst, was due to Darko's screwup with the two medical students.

After the fourth ring, Misha was conscious enough to recognize the sound. With great effort he reached for the phone on his bedside table. As he did so, he looked at the clock and cursed loudly. Blinking madly to focus, he checked to see who was calling. When he saw it was Darko Lebedev, he started cursing anew.

Misha slapped the phone to his ear and flopped back onto his pillow. "This better be good," he growled in Russian.

"It's good," Darko said, sounding strangely upbeat. "Very unexpected but good: the medical students have taken care of themselves."

"What the hell are you talking about?"

"Timur and I have been keeping them under observation since
you and I talked this afternoon. At first they seemed to be acting
normally and apparently did not tell anyone about my visit last
night. But then this evening they went out into the hospital garden
around ten-thirty and sat for an hour in the dark on a secluded
bench that had a view of the door to Shapiro Institute."

"You think they were observing it?"

"That was our impression, because it was during the shift
change."

"So how is this taking care of themselves?"

"It gets better. After they left their observation spot, we thought
we were done for the night. Then, to our surprise, Timur called me
to come back because they reappeared a bit later, dressed in raincoats. They then went back outside to the same bench and after
making out for a while, they went over to the Shapiro door. We had
no idea what they were planning. To our shock, they opened the
door and went inside!"

Misha sat up suddenly, pulling the covers off his companion for
the night. "How the fuck did they open the door?"

"We don't know. Apparently they fooled the thumbprint scanner, which isn't all that difficult."

"This is terrific," Misha said. "It's like having fish jump into the
boat."

"I thought you would be pleased."

"Listen! Call whoever is heading up security tonight. Tell them
that I have authorized a lockdown for the Shapiro until further notice. Have them electronically seal the external door and even the
door through the visiting area to the hospital."

"I already did," Darko said. "The Shapiro is in total lockdown, which includes all communication with the outside world except for the hotline from control center. Do you want Leonid and me to go in and take care of them?"

"No!" Misha said. He bounded out of bed. "I'll get in touch with Fyodor. We'll consult with Dr. Rhodes and Dr. Erikson. We should figure out a way to add these pests to the inventory."

"Let me know if you change your mind after talking with Fyodor," Darko said. "Leonid and I will be happy to do whatever is necessary."

"Will do," Misha said. "Good job!"

Misha disconnected from Darko and pulled up Fyodor's number in his contacts. A few seconds later, he could hear the phone ringing. He knew Fyodor was going to be a bear upon awakening, but he also knew he would be pleased with what he had to tell him.

44.

Lynn glanced up at Michael, who was looking at the monitor screen over her shoulder. They were in the Shapiro NOC, which they had found empty, as they had expected, going by Vladimir's comments. Lynn was sitting at one of the terminals. She had quickly logged in to the Shapiro network without difficulty, using Vladimir's user name and password, and, once connected, had first typed in Carl's name. What had popped up was his home page, which Michael said looked the same as Ashanti's, even with the same apparent location: Cluster 4-B, but with a different number. Carl's was 64, whereas Ashanti's was 32. What also was different was that it didn't say DROZITUMAB +4 ACTIVE but rather ASELIZUMAB PRELIMINARY.

"What do you think?" Lynn asked.

"I think it is convenient they are both in Cluster 4-B and the number must be their bed like you suggested. We can check them both."

"I'm asking about the 'aselizumab' reference."

"I guess he is going to be given aselizumab, whatever the hell that is."

"We'll have to look it up later," Lynn said hurriedly. "At least we know from the 'ab' at its end that it is a biologic drug." Exiting the window, she then queried how many deaths the Shapiro Institute had logged since its doors opened in 2007. The answer flashed on the screen: 31.

"That's incredible," Lynn said. "Do you believe that's true?"

"The system has serious restricted access. Why wouldn't it be true?"

"Hell, if it is a true stat, they must be doing something right," Lynn said. She was impressed, even a bit relieved. "Two years ago, when we visited there had already been twenty-two deaths in six years, but they had a low census, a fraction of the potential capacity. They must be full now and have had only nine deaths in two years. That's phenomenal."

"Find out the current census!" Michael suggested.

Lynn turned back to the screen and typed in the question. The answer came back instantly: 931 patients out of possible 1200. "There you go," she said. "They have almost a thousand patients! And if they lose less than five patients a year, that is an incredible statistic. In my research Monday night, I found out that the mortality for people in a vegetative state is ten percent up to as much as forty percent per year. Here they are managing less than one percent, if I'm doing the math right."

"You're doing the math right," Michael assured her. "In fact it is less than half of one percent. I'd say it's a damn good advertisement for automation, which is what they had told us was key."

"Like I said, they have to be doing something right. It's even more impressive if they are using their patients for drug testing."

"What did you say you found was the major cause of death in coma patients?"

"Pneumonia and other infections often stemming from bedsores. It is because the patients are so immobile."

"Maybe keeping visitation to a minimum really works. It's like reverse precautions for immune-compromised people."

Lynn nodded. Michael had a good point, even though the visitation policy bothered her from a personal perspective because of Carl. "Let's look at the other side of the coin," she said, "and check how many people recovered enough to be discharged. Remember, trauma is a major cause of coma and around ten percent of them recover enough to go home."

Suddenly Michael straightened up. He looked back toward the hallway.

"What's the matter?" Lynn asked nervously. As focused as she was on what she was doing, she had forgotten where they were.

"I thought I heard something," Michael said.

For a few moments both students listened intently, holding their breaths. All they could hear was the hum of the powerful ventilation system.

"I don't hear anything suspicious," Lynn said.

"Nor do I," Michael agreed. "Okay, my mind must be playing tricks." Nervously he glanced at his watch. "I'm thinking it's best if we get our asses out of here. Someone someplace is going to be aware that these stats are being accessed by someone in the middle of the fucking night. What we are doing here is legally more serious than our coming into this place."

"I'm with you," Lynn said. "I know! But this is important. Just a few minutes more." She went back to the keypad and quickly asked for the number of people discharged since the Shapiro had been in operation. The answer was as surprising as the death rate: none!

Lynn looked back up at Michael. She was taken aback. "I'm not sure which is more incredible: the low death rate or the lack of any discharges."

"Well, maybe they don't take trauma patients."

"I can't believe that. As I said, trauma is a major cause of per-sistent vegetative state and coma." Lynn laughed even though she didn't find anything funny. "They are doing a bang-up job with sur-vival but have a piss-poor cure rate."

"Okay, let's go," Michael said. He tried to pull Lynn's chair back from the terminal.

Lynn resisted. "Just one more thing," she said. "Let's see what the cause of death was for the thirty-one patients. I'd guess pneu-monia will top the list." Quickly Lynn typed in the query, and when the answer came back, she was as shocked as she had been when she found out there had been no discharges. Almost half the deaths were from multiple myeloma!

Throwing up her hands, Lynn said, "This can't be true. No way!"

"It's big-time weird," Michael agreed, but at the moment he had other things on his mind even if she didn't. With a bit more force he succeeded in pulling her chair back. "Enough data surfing if you want to try to visit Cluster 4-B and the recreation space, like we planned!" Without waiting for a response, he went to the door and opened it. When he was sure the coast was clear he said, "All right, let's go, girl! Get your ass in gear!"

Lynn followed him out into the hallway. She looked stunned. "Those numbers are crazy! How can the Shapiro have a death rate from multiple myeloma that is one hundred times what's seen in the general population?"

"Let's hold off this conversation until we get out of here," Mi-chael snapped as he got the NOC door to close. It was a pocket door operated by a touch pad in the wall at chest height. "Come on! Let's get to the stairway."

For the rest of the way down to the stairwell door, Lynn held her tongue, but her mind was roiling. As soon as the stairwell door closed behind them, she stopped and said, "I'm sorry, but there is something truly weird about multiple myeloma and this institute."

"Listen!" Michael said with exasperation. "Let's get this visit over with before we launch into a lengthy discussion about what it all means. You seem to be forgetting we're on borrowed time in hostile territory." He undid his mask for a moment to wipe the perspiration off his face. It was warm and humid in the stairwell.

"Okay, you're right," Lynn said. "But I wish I'd had tried to see if there is any data on the incidence of gammopathy in here. Maybe on our way out, we can stop back in the NOC. It would only take a couple of minutes."

"We'll keep it in mind," Michael said, replacing his mask. "Provided, of course, we are not being chased."

"Don't joke about such a thing," Lynn said.

"I'm not joking," Michael said.

As they descended the stairs down to level four, Lynn consulted the floor plan. When they reached the landing, they paused outside the door and she showed him that there were several ways for them to get to Cluster 4-B.

"Let's stay as far away as we can from the room labeled 'automation control.' My sense is that is where the staff will be holed up."

"Good point," Lynn said. "That means we should go left out of the stairwell and follow the hallway to the end and then turn right. I hope the doors are labeled. If they are not, it will be the fourth door on the right after the turn."

Michael cracked the door onto the fourth floor and listened. Except for the omnipresent sound of the HVAC, silence reigned. He opened the door just enough to look up and down the hallway. It was a mirror image of the hallway above on five and just as white and brightly illuminated. Most important, it was similarly without a soul in sight. The only difference was that, at its far end, it lacked a door to the exterior. "Let's not make this our life's work, you know what I'm saying?"

Lynn knew exactly what Michael meant. "I'll be right behind you," she said.

It wasn't a mad dash, but they moved as quickly and silently as they could, passing under a number of what they guessed were ceiling-mounted video cameras. The doors that they passed were labeled, for the most part. They turned the corner and resumed their speed. They hadn't needed to count. Cluster 4-B was clearly labeled on the door in black sans serif letters and numerals.

"You ready?" Michael questioned.

"As ready as I ever will be," Lynn responded, bracing herself. Seeing Carl in this sterile, deserted place was going to be an emotional challenge.

45.

The door to Cluster 4-B was a pocket door, like the one to the NOC, only stouter. And like the door to the NOC, it was operated electronically, with a lever to the right of the frame. Michael pressed it and the door started to slide open.

Before they could see inside the room, they heard the intermittent whining of electrical motors and the clanking of heavy machinery. The noise had been completely muffled by the sound-insulated door and the walls. As the door opened all the way, Lynn and Michael were treated to a view of what looked like a completely mechanized, highly complex assembly line in an automobile plant, with robotic arms, and a forklift-like apparatus with oversize rubber tires connected to a constantly moving conveyor system. No staff was in attendance.

With some trepidation they entered, and the door automatically closed behind them. It was a large rectangular room about the size of a small theater, with a very high ceiling. The level of sound was so loud that they practically had to yell to hear each other. The air was warm and humid.

"Can you fucking believe this?" Michael half shouted.

"It's like a futuristic horror movie," Lynn yelled. She was taken aback, unsure if she truly wanted to see what was in front of her. "This is automated patient care taken to the nth degree."

"And there are eleven other rooms just like it," Michael said in awe.

The entire right side of the room was composed of a hundred angled but mostly horizontal Plexiglas cylinders in twenty-five vertical stacks of four. Each cylinder in each stack was about four feet in diameter and seven feet deep, separated from other ones on either side by a three-foot-wide metal grate. These grates formed a scaffold as a means of access for service, and could be reached by metal ladders that were attached. The opening to the lowest cylinder was waist high and the highest was near the ceiling. Each cylinder was numbered and had a computer monitor on an adjustable arm.

As Lynn and Michael stared in horror, they could now appreciate that about half the cylinders contained a patient, each naked save for the headgear resembling a football helmet that they remembered the mannequin wearing during their second-year introductory visit.

Suddenly, through an opening high up, on the left side of the room, a supine, naked, comatose patient entered the room moving quickly on the conveyor system. He, too, had a helmet. In a manner that reminded Lynn and Michael of a modern baggage-handling system at a major airport, the patient was rapidly transported to a specific area of the room not too far away from where they were standing. With some additional clanking and grinding noises the entire conveyor system adjusted to bring the patient just outside the proper cylinder, which was the top container in the sixth row. There, the robotic arms went to work to make all the appropriate connections for the feeding tube and other embedded lines. Once all the connections were set up, which happened surprisingly quickly, the patient was slid into the cylinder like a rocket being loaded into a launcher.

Before Lynn and Michael could respond to what they had just seen, the conveyor system noisily repositioned itself seven rows away from where it had deposited the first patient, and rapidly extracted a second patient from a different cylinder. Once this second body was completely in the open, the robotic arms went to work disconnecting the various lines. Then, following a reverse route from that of the first, the second patient was zipped out of the room. Everything was accomplished in just a few minutes.

"Good God!" Lynn exclaimed when she could find her voice. "This is obscenely mechanized. There's no humanity, no dignity! It's against everything medicine stands for."

"Where the hell do you suppose the bodies are going?" Michael asked.

"God only knows," Lynn said. At that point they were treated to a repeat of the sequence, with another body coming back from parts unknown. After that, another body was taken away. The students soon got the impression that what they were witnessing was a constant process, maybe even 24/7, of bodies coming and going.

Being careful to steer clear of the huge and very active business end of the conveyor system that unpredictably moved back and forth on its oversize tires and up and down in front of the cylinders, the two students approached the last stack. Despite their horror, they felt a morbid curiosity. The cylinder at waist level was numbered 100. The one immediately above it was 99. Approaching the mouth of the hundredth cylinder, they looked inside. The patient was female, lying on a series of moving rollers to keep pressure off any given spot. While they were watching, a sprinkler system was suddenly activated inside the cylinder, rinsing and disinfecting the woman. A sucking sound came from the base of the cylinder as the fluid was drawn off. From their vantage point, they could appreciate that the container was angled down at an incline of something like fifteen degrees.

"It's like a freaking car wash," Michael commented with a mixture of disgust and admiration. "Somebody's put some real thought into all this."

"I suppose that's why their survival rate is so good."

The monitor to the side of the cylinder showed the patient's home page, which included her name, Gloria Parkman; her age, thirty-two; her location, Cluster 4-B 100; RANIBIZUMAB 3+ ACTIVE; and a long list of real-time vital signs and other extensive monitoring data. The monitoring was so extensive that the students intuitively understood that the patient had to have sensor chips implanted to make it possible. There were even real-time electroencephalogram tracings.

"Hey, I just remembered something," Michael said. "Ranibizumab was in the ophthalmology lecture yesterday. It's used for macular degeneration and is well tolerated without allergic problems."

"If it is already an established drug, I wonder why they are giving it to her?"

"Good question," Michael said. "Maybe there are still some allergic issues that the lecturer didn't mention. But one way or the other, I'm beginning to think coming here might raise more questions than give answers." Ducking his head, he moved down alongside the cylinder, between the cylinder and the wall. He was impressed the constantly moving roller system that kept the patient's b motion while avoiding pressure point problems. It was massage system in a tube that encouraged circulation the integrity of the skin.

"Hey!" Michael yelled to Lynn. "Come here was still captivated by the monitor. She w of physiological data that was being fol bly continuously run through a su

Lynn squeezed in beside Michael. In the restricted space, the noise coming from the machinery in the room seemed even louder. Lynn tried to follow Michael's line of sight and pointing finger. She was as impressed as he was with the roller system. "What am I supposed to be looking at?" she yelled.

"The catheter embedded in the abdomen! What do you think that could be for?"

"No idea. Do you?"

"No! But it looks to me like the abdomen is a bit distended. What's your take?"

"Now that you mention it, it does look a bit bloated. You think they are running fluid into the abdomen? That's not unheard of. The peritoneal cavity has quite a surface area and can even be used for dialysis."

"True! Maybe she's got a kidney problem. Let's go back and look at the monitor and see if the kidney function is normal."

Lynn backed out of the confined space first, followed by Michael. When they looked at the monitor, they could see that the kidney function was perfectly normal, including urine output. Then something from the long list of thi_____ _____ _____ vation caught Lynn's
_____ _____ ne of the stats gives
_____ _____ g anything into her
_____ _____ out."

_____ Michael said, look-
_____ se of ascites is liver

_____ d protein, but hers

_____ k into the cubby-

_____ e tires, suddenly
_____ oor tremble and

_____dy in
_____a kind of
_____nd protected
_____. Look at this!" Lynn
_____s marveling at the range
_____owed in real time and possi-
_____ercomputer.

momentarily trapping them in alongside cylinder 100. In the adjacent stack, a body was extracted, robotically disconnected from its various lines, and whisked out of the room. Then the conveyor system trundled away for its next assignment.

A moment later, when they emerged from their shelter, Lynn surprised Michael by climbing the ladder to peer into several of the upper cylinders.

"I think we better move on," Michael yelled up to her impatiently. "We are pushing our luck. With all this mechanical activity in here and bodies coming and going, somebody's got to be minding this place with video surveillance."

"I just wanted to check to see if any other patients have an intra-abdominal catheter," Lynn said, already climbing back down. "And they all do in this stack."

Michael stepped over to the next stack and peered in at the patient in the lower cylinder. "You're right. Seems they all have it."

"That's got to mean something, but what?"

"Good question," Michael said, "but we've got to break out, girl."

"I'm not leaving until I see Carl," Lynn said with a tone that brooked no argument.

"My personal opinion would be to let it go," Michael said, placing his hand on her shoulder in hopes of restraining her. "Seeing Carl here is not going to help you or him. You know what I'm saying."

"I don't care," Lynn said. She shrugged off Michael's hand and started down the line of cylinders.

For a moment Michael hesitated, wondering if it was best that she go by herself for a bit of privacy with her stricken lover. But he quickly decided otherwise. It was hardly the proper environment for any attempt at intimacy, and he didn't want to risk her getting emotional, which he thought was a significant possibility, knowing how he would feel if the situation were reversed and his girlfriend, Kianna, was one of the patients. He quickly caught up with her. As he did so, the forklift-like mechanism that pulled the patients in and out of the cylinders suddenly came in their direction.

The students had to flee back to the walkway that ran the length of the room against the wall opposite the bank of cylinders. The conveyor track taking the patients in and out of the room arched overhead.

After a patient was deposited in a cylinder close to where Lynn and Michael had been, the whole apparatus began moving to the opposite end of the room to pick up another.

"For the life of me, I can't imagine why they are constantly moving these patients," Michael yelled, going up on his tiptoes to try to get a peek into the black hole into which the conveyor track disappeared. "Or where the hell they are going." When he turned back to Lynn, he saw that she was well on her way to cylinder 64. By the time he caught up to her, he could tell she wasn't happy.

"He's not here," Lynn yelled over the continuous noise.

A quick glance confirmed for Michael that cylinder 64 was empty, although the monitor displayed Carl's home page, so it was where he had been or was to be.

"Just as well," Michael yelled back.

"Do you want to see if Ashanti is here?"

"I don't see any point," Michael said without hesitation. "For the tenth time, let's get a move on."

"All right," Lynn said, but still she hesitated. She had suggested seeking out Ashanti as a way to stall. Her irrational side wanted to wait for Carl to be returned as part of the continuous stream of patients coming and going on the conveyor system. At the same time, Lynn's rational side agreed with Michael that they needed to leave. For a moment she struggled with her indecision, and as she did so her eyes caught the various color-coded and labeled lines that would be robotically connected to Carl when he was brought back to monitor him and keep him alive. There was the intravenous line in blue, an arterial line in red, a gastrostomy line for nutrition in green, and an intraperitoneal line in yellow.

Michael grasped Lynn's upper arm. "I know it's tough for you to leave, but it isn't going to be any easier if you see him. We have to go!"

"I know," Lynn shouted with a degree of resignation. "But look! Carl already has an intraperitoneal line!" She pointed to the yellow connector. "Why? He certainly doesn't have ascites. Not yet, anyway."

"We can debrief when we get out of this freaking place. We've got a lot to process."

"You know what I think?" Lynn said with sudden urgency and a renewed degree of horror.

"I don't, but I can tell you are about to tell me. But tell me out in the hallway, where I can hear you. This racket in here is driving me crazy."

"All right!" Lynn yelled. The noise in the room was beginning to get to her as well. She let Michael pull her toward the walkway. It was just in time, because the conveyor system suddenly lurched in their direction again. When they reached the walkway, Lynn turned back to make sure the patient that was being brought in was not Carl, as the machine positioned itself in front of Carl's stack. But the patient went into cylinder 62, not 64.

Quickly, they retreated to the door they had used to enter the room. When it closed behind them, their ears were ringing in the comparative silence. Immediately Lynn blurted out, "I think I know what the hell Sidereal is doing. They're not experimenting on these patients, like we thought. They are fucking using them in a much more perverse way!"

"Okay, okay," Michael soothed. "What do you mean?"

"You remember how monoclonal antibody drugs like ranibizumab are made."

"Sure!" Michael said. He was taken aback by Lynn's sudden passion. He could hear it in her voice and see it in her eyes. "They are made by mice tumors called hybridomas."

"Which are?"

"What is this, a freaking test? Tell me what you are thinking."

"Answer my question! What are hybridomas?"

"A kind of cancer made by fusing mouse lymphocytes with mouse multiple myeloma cells and injected back into mice."

"And where are they injected?"

"Into the abdomen."

"And why are pharmaceutical companies required to jump through so many hoops to humanize the mouse-generated drugs?"

"To lower the chance of allergic reactions when they are taken by humans."

Lynn stared at Michael without blinking, waiting for him to connect the dots. It was all there, hanging in the air.

"Mothafuckas!" Michael snapped after a moment when all the pieces of the puzzle fell into place in his mind. He shook his head with repugnance.

"It all fits," Lynn said with equivalent disgust. "All of it. Sidereal Pharmaceuticals and Middleton Healthcare are in bed together. It's why so many people going into Middleton Healthcare hospitals are getting gammopathies. It's why their patients have such a sky-high incidence of multiple myeloma. And here in the Shapiro it's one hundred percent. They must be using all thousand patients to make truly human monoclonal antibody drugs, which don't have to be humanized. They are already human!"

"And, worse yet, they must be behind these anesthesia-induced comas," Michael said. "It must be a new method of recruiting healthy bodies they can tap twenty-four/seven. I'm sorry I have to say this, because of Carl."

"I'm afraid you're right," Lynn said. Her voice reflected both anger and loss. She took a deep breath to stay in control. "Carl's vegetative state wasn't an accident. I was afraid as much when I found the looping. Now I know for sure. What I can't understand is why we didn't see all this earlier. When I think about it, it's been staring us in the face."

"The question now becomes what to do," Michael said. "Who do we turn to?"

"This is a major conspiracy," Lynn said. "We can't go to anybody here in the medical center. There is no way to know who is involved and who isn't. We've got to go to Carl's father, Markus Vandermeer, and we have to do it tonight. In fact . . ." Lynn pulled out her cell phone. When she turned it on, she immediately saw there was no service. "Damn! I'll have to call him as soon as we get outside."

"Let's go!"

"Wait! As long as we're in here, I want to at least glance into the so-called recreation space. That's sick humor if I ever heard it. There can't be anything recreational about this place, but my thought is that maybe Carl is there." Lynn pulled out the floor plans and quickly studied them. "Okay! I see where we have to go. It's really close, and will only take a minute."

46.

Misha had to knock to get the pocket door into the SCC, or Shapiro Central Control, to open. For security reasons, the only way it could be operated was from inside. He gestured for Fyodor and Benton Rhodes to precede him into the highly air-conditioned room. He followed. Five armed security men in hospital security uniforms brought up the rear. All were Russian expatriates and took orders from Fyodor. Fyodor had personally recruited them from Saint Petersburg when he'd taken over the hospital security department. He considered them his shock troops.

The technician manning central control was called Viktor Garin. He was dressed in Shapiro coveralls, in contrast to the newcomers. He remained standing as the others crowded around the bank of forty monitors that were alternately displaying security feeds from all of the hallways and a number of the rooms from all six floors of the Shapiro Institute.

Although part of Viktor's job was to keep his eye on the security monitors, the vast majority of his time was spent on the other side of the room, in front of the feeds coming from the Shapiro automation equipment. It was with the machinery that most problems occurred. In the eight years he'd worked in the Shapiro, there had never been a security breach. The only infractions had been when several of the Shapiro staff members were caught sleeping.

Despite his being in the company of Benton, Fyodor spoke to Viktor in Russian, asking where the intruders were and what they had been doing.

"At the moment they are on floor four, heading for the recreation room," Viktor answered in Russian. "So far they have only visited the NOC, where they used a terminal to access the data bank, and then went on to Cluster 4-B, where they spent most of their time. As I said, at the moment they are heading for the recreation room." He pointed to the monitor that was tracking them in the fourth-floor hallway.

"What kind of data were they looking at in the NOC?" Fyodor asked.

"Mortality and discharge statistics and the file for the new patient."

Switching to English, Fyodor related to Benton what he had learned, including where Lynn and Michael were headed at the moment.

"They certainly are nosy fucks," Benton said irritably. "It's going to be a relief to get rid of them."

"You have to give them credit for being resourceful," Fyodor said.

"I'm not inclined to give them credit for anything," Benton said. "And I certainly don't like them going in the recreation room. Who knows what potentially infectious agents they could be carrying?"

"As you can see, they're wearing Shapiro scrubs, hats, and masks," Fyodor said, pointing to the proper monitor for Benton's benefit.

"Where did they get them, and how clean are they?" Benton questioned. "It's going to be a major disaster if these two jerks cause an outbreak in our patient population. As medical students, they are exposed to all sorts of illness. It's going to be an enormous setback if we lose even one patient producing a truly lucrative drug."

"We'll stop them as soon as we can," Fyodor said. "I think there is a good chance they won't try to go out onto the floor."

"We can hope," Benton said. "The only thing for sure is that they are going to be shocked, and who's to know what they might do?"

"They're not going to do anything," Fyodor said. "They can't. The whole institute is in full lockdown. They're not going anywhere and can't communicate out with their phones."

"Regardless, let's take care of them ASAP," Benton said. "The sooner the better."

"Agreed," Fyodor said cheerfully. "Frankly, we have been waiting for you. Did you bring the tranquilizers?"

Benton produced two syringes preloaded with large doses of midazolam.

Fyodor took the syringes. "Can we be sure this will completely tranquilize them?"

"Without doubt," Benton said with a laugh. "They will be completely zonked out for way longer than what we need to get them over to the OR. For your information, the diagnosis is going to be subdural hematomas. The official cause is going to be head trauma suffered during their unauthorized break-in. Norman Phillips, a neurosurgeon who is friendly to the program, will be surgeon. I'll be doing the anesthesia to make sure they don't wake up."

"Is the surgeon already in the hospital?"

"He's on his way," Benton said.

Fyodor turned to his enforcement team and handed the leader the syringes. Speaking in Russian, he told them to get it over with quickly and haul the tranquilized students up to the patient viewing room A. From there they would be helping to transport them one at a time over to the OR when the OR was ready.

47.

It took Lynn and Michael longer than they had expected to get into the recreation room. The entrance door had been different from all the others. It was as heavy as the door into Cluster 4-B, but instead of operating with a generic touch pad, it had another thumbprint security system like the one on the external door. Similar to their experience with the exterior door, it took several tries. Once again, Lynn had to warm the fake fingerprint by using her breath.

A small green light finally flashed above the touch pad, indicating success, and the door started to slide open. As with the cluster room, the first thing they were aware of was noise issuing forth. It was mechanical again, but not nearly as loud as in the cluster room. As the door opened farther, giving them a view of the interior, both students sucked in a breath and stepped back in shocked surprise.

The room was much larger than the cluster room in all respects, with a ceiling about fifty feet high. The level of illumination from a mixture of LED and ultraviolet recessed ceiling fixtures was intense. Also built into the ceiling was a maze of tracks supporting a

number of large grappling hooks, each with long, curved tines. The
grappling hooks resembled the claw cranes found in old-fashioned
gaming arcades that, for a quarter, allowed players to try to pick up
a prize. But here in the Shapiro the claws weren't picking up prizes
but rather ambulating people and dropping others off.

Massed on the floor were hundreds of naked patients, in either
a vegetative state or a coma, each wearing his or her helmet and,
incredibly enough, walking aimlessly about in a jerky, slightly hesitant, stiff manner, often bumping into each other as well as the
walls. Their hands and arms hung limp at their sides.

"My good God!" Lynn cried. "I'm not prepared for this. This is
worse than the cluster room. The helmets are not just for sensors."

"You are so right," Michael said, completely transfixed at the
spectacle. "The helmets have to be stimulating the motor centers in
coordinated ways to cause them to walk."

Lynn shuddered. "They are like zombies, only not dead."

Just inside the open doorway was a metal wire cage, six feet on a
side, to keep the patients from approaching the door to the hallway.
Some bumped into the cage just as others were bumping into the
walls. The students could see that most of the people had their eyes
closed, although a few had them open. Those who had them open
had a distant, non-focused look, suggesting that whatever their eyes
were seeing was not being registered in their brains. Their mouths
were generally closed, although a few were open and drooling. Their
expressions were totally blank. The patients made no sounds, even
when they collided with one another. The noise in the room came
from the grapplers as they brought patients in and deposited them
into the crowd and snapped up others and took them off to the side.

Lynn stepped forward into the cage, propelled by her morbid
curiosity. It was a sight like none she had ever seen or imagined in
her wildest dreams. Michael joined her. Neither of them spoke.
Suddenly a torrent of scented disinfectant liquid rained down from
an elaborate high-pressure sprinkler system far up on the ceiling.

Although it was short-lived, it was enough to drive both Lynn and Michael back into the hallway for a moment to keep from getting soaked. The patients ignored the sudden gush and kept up their endless, mindless wandering.

Stepping back into the cage area again, the students continued their marveling at the drama playing out in front of them. Informed by their neurology training, they knew how complex an activity such as walking was from a physiological perspective. It wasn't enough to stimulate a specific muscle. There had to be a host of muscles stimulated to varying degrees as well as simultaneous, partial inhibition of the opposing muscles for a human to stand upright much less walk, and it all had to be coordinated through the part of the brain called the cerebellum. It was complicated enough to challenge a supercomputer.

"This is how they manage to keep these people alive," Michael said, unable to take his eyes off the shuffling assemblage of brain-damaged patients. "This is why they don't have trouble with pneumonias or the cardiovascular systems. People have to be mobilized or they degenerate. And the UV light provides vitamin D and antisepsis."

"Oh, no!" Lynn cried suddenly with great anguish.

Michael's eyes shot in her direction. "What's wrong?"

"It's Carl," Lynn cried, pointing off to the left.

Michael tried to follow her line of sight. It was difficult in the sea of people, jerkily staggering about in chaotic, unpredictable directions, reminding him of the Brownian movement of molecules. To make matters worse, it was hard to fixate on any given face, as they all looked remarkably the same with their blankness.

"Where, exactly?" Michael asked. He went up on his tiptoes, his eyes jumping from face to face, searching for a familiar one.

"I lost him," Lynn said. She, too, was straining to see better.

"Are you sure you saw him?" Michael asked. "Or might it have been your imagination?"

"I saw him!" Lynn snapped angrily.

"Okay, keep it cool, girl."

"I'm going out there," Lynn announced with determination. The cage had a door made of the same wire mesh as the rest of the structure. It was secured with a normal throw bolt. Lynn gave it a twist. The door opened a crack.

Michael grabbed the door to keep it from opening more than a few inches. Several of the patients bumped into it. "I don't think that's a good idea," he said, trying to be calm yet sound forceful.

"I don't care what you think," Lynn said. "I'm going out there and find him."

"And do what?" Michael demanded. "Seeing him in here is going to be worse than seeing him in one of those damn cylinders, which would have been bad enough. Don't do this to yourself! Be smart!"

Lynn pushed on the door. Michael kept ahold of it. It was a bit of a tug-of-war. Another patient bumped into it and then veered off like the others but not before hitting up against Michael's fingers. By reflex of having been unexpectedly touched by one of the ghoulish ambulating inmates, Michael let go of the door. Before he could reach out and grab it again, Lynn had it open enough to squeeze out onto the main floor of the room.

"Shit, Lynn!" Michael yelled after her. "Get your ass back here! You're acting crazy, girl! Fucking A," he fumed under his breath. He pulled the door back into its jamb as another patient careened into it. It clicked shut. Michael went back up on his tiptoes. He had already lost sight of Lynn in the jerkily roiling mob. For a brief moment he debated what to do, wondering if he should just wait her out or go after her. It wasn't as if he thought she could get hurt except emotionally. What he really wanted to do was get the hell out of the Shapiro.

Michael's momentary torment was suddenly interrupted by the sounds of footfalls and voices in the hallway. He leaned back out through the open door into the corridor and shot a quick glance back up the way they had come. Approaching at a jog was a bevy of uniformed and armed hospital security people.

By reflex, Michael leaned back into the cage and hit the electronic door closer. On the outside was a thumbprint-activated touch pad, but on the inside there was a normal one. The door activated and slid closed, but before it could close completely, a hand shot in and halted it. Michael lifted a foot and gave the intruding fingers a significant kick. With an audible cry of pain, the fingers disappeared and the door sealed shut with a thud.

Faced with this new situation, Michael quickly ended his debate about what to do. He assumed the door to the hallway would not be a significant impediment to those out in the hall. Without further hesitation he opened the wire door and started in the general direction Lynn had gone. Within seconds he was completely surrounded by ambulating patients in various states of coma.

As Michael dodged the erratically plodding people, he experienced a weird déjà vu from having been a high school and college running back. Since he was plainly more eager than they to move quickly and cover ground in a specific direction, he bumped into a few with more force than he would have liked. To his astonishment, none of the patients fell down, a fact that impressed him. He guessed that the computer programs that were directing their walking were able to deal rapidly and appropriately with sudden changes in feedback information and recover enough to keep the patients on their feet.

After progressing twenty or thirty feet from the cage, Michael slowed and stopped, again going up on tiptoes. He had thought it would be relatively easy to locate Lynn since he was looking for the only person in the crowd with clothes, and in white, no less. But there were just so many people. The good side, he thought, was that it was going to be equally hard for the security guys to find them.

All at once Michael caught a momentary glimpse of Lynn's white hat. Quickly moving in that direction, he came up behind her. She had found Carl and put her arms around him in a hugging embrace. Of course Carl wasn't able to respond in kind. His arms were limp at his side, his face a tabula rasa, and his legs were continuing their walking motions even though Lynn was holding him in place.

Michael went behind Carl so that he could look into Lynn's face. She had her eyes closed.

"We've been discovered!" Michael said to her. He shook her arm to break her trance.

Lynn's eyes popped open.

"A bunch of hospital security appeared out in the hall," Michael said anxiously. "Luckily I got the door closed before they could come in, but they are probably in now."

Lynn nodded understanding, her face reflecting the same panic Michael was experiencing. She let go of Carl, and like a wind-up toy, he immediately veered off aimlessly.

"There is another entrance at the opposite end of the room," Lynn cried.

"I'm sure that is what they expect," Michael said. "They will catch us for sure. We have to do something unexpected."

Despite the ambient noise from the grapplers and the conveyor systems, they could hear the unmistakable sound of the door to the cage being thrown open, clanging against the cage's wall. Their pursuers were coming into the recreation room.

Both looked up at the grapplers, which were continuing their ceaseless operation. "No, that's not going to work," Lynn said. She sensed Michael had also briefly wondered if they could somehow use the grapplers to get out. "But maybe the conveyors."

The duo had been aware that the grapplers were depositing and bringing back people from beyond an eight-foot-high barrier on either side of the room. Without even discussing the issue, they started off toward the right side. Lynn got behind Michael and held on to him as he forced his way through the crowd. Behind them they were aware of a major disturbance and assumed the security people were trying to force their way in their direction through the wandering, blank-faced patients.

Hoping they had an advantage of being only two and working in tandem, Michael and Lynn reached the barrier wall that ran along the right side of the room. Sensing the security people were closing in on them, they searched frantically for a door. When they found one, they discovered it had no electrical lever on the wall to open it, apparently for fear the patients would bump into it. A quick inspection revealed there was a handhold depression on the door itself. Lynn put her fingers into it and pulled. The door slid open with relative ease.

Shoving patients away to keep them from following, Lynn and Michael quickly stepped through the door and pulled it shut behind them. As they had assumed, they found themselves in the terminus for the conveyor systems for Clusters 4-B, 5-B, and 6-B. Each was conveniently labeled. Lined up like duckpins were three lines of patients waiting to be either returned to their respective cylinders or lifted and placed out in the recreation space. As in the cluster room they had visited, the handling of the patients was done by robotic machinery. The ambient noise from the conveyor systems was significantly louder than on the recreation-room floor.

"If this is going to work, we should try the conveyor belt for Cluster 5-B," Lynn shouted over the din of the machinery. "We'll be on the same floor as the exit door."

Michael flashed a thumbs-up. As quickly as possible, they worked their way around the crowd of patients who were lined up, waiting to be sent back to their respective cylinders. In contrast to the other patients out on the floor, these patients were standing motionless, a feat as difficult from a programming perspective as making them walk.

Pushing on, Lynn and Michael skirted the robotic arms that placed the patients on the conveyor system for Cluster 5-B when cued. For the moment they were at rest, having just placed a patient. It was, the students thought, an opportune moment for them. Michael climbed up onto the belt on all fours. He motioned for Lynn to do the same.

Lynn cast a quick look behind her. Several security people were coming through the same door that she and Michael had used. Catching sight of Lynn, they yelled for her to stop.

Lynn ignored them and, mimicking Michael, leaped up onto the moving belt on all fours. The surface was a smooth and pliable silicone material, which afforded good traction. With Michael about ten feet in the lead but already out of sight, Lynn ducked her head as she was drawn into a four-foot-high tunnel.

About six feet past the entrance, the conveyor abruptly angled upward, and the tunnel progressively became darker. After Lynn was taken about twenty feet up the incline, the entire system came to a sudden halt.

"Shit!" she heard Michael's voice say somewhere ahead. "Why did the fucking thing stop?"

"The security people saw me get on," Lynn said. She began to crawl upward. She sensed Michael was doing the same, yet after only a short distance she bumped into his feet.

"Why did you stop?" Lynn asked. She could barely make out Michael's form in front of her. She knew they had to hurry. She could hear voices behind them.

"We're not alone in here," Michael said. "There is a patient in front of me. We're going to have to climb over. Are you okay with that?"

"We don't have any choice. There should be enough room." Lynn reached up and touched the ceiling. The tunnel was like a tube, with seemingly more than enough room to scramble over a body.

"I don't think it is going to be difficult, but it sure as hell ain't gonna be pretty."

"We'll manage," Lynn said, although she wasn't sure she believed it herself. She couldn't think of too many experiences worse than climbing over a naked, comatose patient in an upwardly angled, dark cylinder.

Lynn heard Michael say, "Sorry, bro," as he struggled forward. Lynn waited. Looking straight ahead and to the side of Michael's dark form, she could see a bit of light, giving her the confidence there wasn't that much farther to go.

"Okay," Michael said a minute or so later. "Your turn! I'm sure this poor bastard is going to think you are a picnic after me."

Getting past the patient was physically easier than Lynn had anticipated but psychologically more trying than she'd imagined. She struggled not to put any weight on the comatose person but wasn't totally successful. The fact that he was supine rather than prone made it worse.

"Okay," Lynn said breathlessly once she was past. She had been holding her breath while in close contact with the individual. Michael was waiting impatiently.

"Let's get a move on!" Michael whispered urgently as he began crawling forward. They could hear voices behind them more clearly. "They might reverse the direction of the belt."

After another fifteen feet of their racing on all fours, the belt leveled off and the ambient light increased dramatically, especially after the belt made a ninety-degree turn. After another ten feet they emerged into Cluster 5-B, which was a mirror image of Cluster 4-B. Relieved at having made it, both stood and climbed over the side. As they did so, the belt suddenly resumed operation, with the rollers moving in the opposite direction, as Michael had feared.

With a sense of partial relief from having avoided being pulled back into the clutches of the people chasing them, they used the conveyor superstructure to swing down and drop onto the walkway. With all conveyor machinery shut down, the room was quiet. The only real noise was from the intermittent flushing process in various cylinders.

The students lost no time. They rushed to the door leading out of the room and, once they determined the hallway was clear, made a mad dash for the exit. They ran past the NOC and soon skidded to a stop at the door to the outside. Michael snapped up their raincoats and handed Lynn hers, and they pulled them on quickly. They didn't want to have to explain themselves if they ran into anybody on their way to the dorm or in the dorm itself.

"Ready?" Michael asked. His hand was poised above the door lever.

"More than ready," Lynn said, glancing back over her shoulder. "Come on! Let's get the hell out of here!"

Michael hit the lever, but to their horror nothing happened! He hit it again several times in a row with the same effect. Then he pressed on the lever as hard as he could and held it. Still nothing. The door didn't budge.

Lynn folded her arm against her torso and lunged at the door with her right shoulder. She hit it hard, but it wasn't going anywhere. Michael did the same with the same result. The door was made of steel, with a solid core. It was meant as a significant barrier, and both of them knew it.

The two students eyed each other in desperation.

"What are we going to do?" Michael barked.

Lynn didn't respond. Instead she whipped out the stapled bundle of floor plans and rapidly flipped through them.

"Come on, sis!" Michael snapped breathlessly. "We have to run. Our only chance is to cross over to the hospital. Are you looking for the best route?"

At that moment both heard the unmistakable sound of a door bursting open. They couldn't see it and assumed it was the stairwell door.

"This way," Lynn said hurriedly. She started forward in the opposite direction from the hospital.

Michael ran after her, trying to tell her they were headed in the wrong direction, but she ignored him. After turning a corner, Michael again tried to talk to her. Behind them they heard the sound of men running in their direction.

Lynn turned yet another corner, entering a long hallway that stretched out like a study in perspective. She was running at full speed, with Michael a few steps behind. They were passing doors on either side.

"Where the hell are we going?" Michael gasped.

Lynn continued to ignore him. Suddenly she stopped in front of one of the doors along the main corridor. She did it so precipitously that Michael plowed into her. He had to grab her with both hands to keep both of them from falling. She struggled out of his arms and hit the door's opening lever. The moment it slid open, she dashed inside.

Michael followed. He was confused as to what she was doing. Before the pocket door had opened, he'd seen the block letters on the door that identified the room as PHARMACY AND GENERAL SUPPLIES. Once inside, he turned around and closed the door. Facing back into the highly air-conditioned room, he saw that it was filled from floor to ceiling with rows of shelving, crammed with all manner of drugs and associated supplies. To his further surprise, Lynn had disappeared.

Michael ran up the center aisle, glancing down each cross aisle, looking for Lynn. Her behavior had him baffled. He found her at the very back, on her hands and knees, in front of a relatively large metal latticework screen some two feet high and three feet wide that was positioned just above the baseboard and painted the same color as the wall. She had her screwdriver out and was madly removing the sheet-metal screws holding it in place.

"What the hell are you doing?" Michael demanded. "They are going to be in here in a flash and the ball game's going to be over."

"And we won't be here," Lynn said confidently.

"Are you suggesting . . ."

"That's exactly what I'm suggesting," Lynn said quickly. She took out the last screw and then struggled to remove the grille. It wasn't cooperating; dried paint was holding it in place. "When I was at the building commission today, I learned that the Shapiro shares infrastructure with the hospital, including the HVAC system. This return duct will take us back to the hospital."

"I ain't going in there, no way," Michael said.

"We don't have much of a choice," Lynn said. She was now frantically using the screwdriver to scribe the periphery of the lattice. A moment later she was able to break it free from the wall. "Finally," she voiced. She leaned the screen against the wall to the side of the opening and put down the screwdriver.

"How do you know you won't get lost?" Michael said.

"Easy," Lynn said. "We'll follow the airflow. The good thing is that the ducts have to get larger and not smaller."

"How come you picked this room out of all the rooms we passed?"

"I knew a pharmacy would be kept cooler than other rooms, meaning bigger ducts. And we are in luck. I don't see any video cameras in here."

With mounting panic, Michael glanced up at the ceiling. She was right. There were no cameras. Then he bent down and stared into the duct. Compared with this dark, narrow duct, dealing with the conveyor system had been a comparative picnic. Considering his size, he wasn't sure he'd even fit.

"We got to do this, bro," Lynn said. "It might take us a while, and I hope you are not claustrophobic. You want to go first or second? Whoever goes second has to try to reposition the grille."

"You first," Michael said.

"Okay," Lynn said, trying to bolster her courage. Despite what she had said to Michael, she had serious misgivings about what they were about to do. At the same time she knew they had to either try it or give up. And with the enormity of what they had discovered on their visit, she wasn't eager to put herself and Michael into the hands of Sidereal Pharmaceuticals or Middleton Healthcare.

Taking a deep breath, Lynn stretched out her arms in front of her and then, using her feet, pushed herself headfirst into the duct. By slithering like a snake, she found moving on the metal surface was actually easier than she had envisioned. She'd gone six or seven feet into the steadily growing darkness when she heard the metal grate hit against its housing. She sensed Michael was not behind her. Without being able to turn around or even see behind her with ease, she called out to Michael. "What the hell are you doing?"

"I'm replacing the grille," he called to her. "You go get the Marines. I'll duke it out here. Who knows? Maybe they won't find me, at least right off."

"Michael!" Lynn yelled loud enough to hurt her ears in the confines of the duct. "That's not fair. You tricked me!"

"For good reason," Michael said. "If they found this grille detached, they would know what we were up to. This way you have a fighting chance, not that I envy you. Go to it, girl!"

"Michael," Lynn yelled again, but with a bit less volume. "Don't do this! We are a team. Those were your words."

"Sorry," Michael said. "The ball's through the hoop and the game's over. Good luck!"

"Michael, please!" Lynn yelled, but he didn't answer. "Michael, are you still there?" Silence reigned.

"Holy shit," Lynn murmured. For a moment she debated trying to back up and see if she could kick the grate off. The reality was that she didn't think she could. Instead, after taking another breath, she began crawling forward, going deeper into the confined, utter darkness.

48.

Benton Rhodes clicked off his smartphone and slipped it into his pocket. He had been playing Angry Birds to entertain himself but he had run out of patience. He checked the time. More than two hours had passed since the security team had gone after the students. Although they had quickly cornered and tranquilized one of them after a relatively short chase, the other was irritatingly still at large.

"That's it," Benton said. He pushed back his chair and stood up to stretch. He, Fyodor, and Misha were still in the control center. Viktor had been busy supervising the Shapiro staff to get the automation equipment on floors four through six that had been shut down back online.

Fyodor and Misha turned to look at him. They, too, had been killing time. Everybody was tired and on edge.

"I think we should go ahead with the mock surgery on the male," Benton said. "There is no reason to wait to find the female, and Dr. Phillips has been ready for almost an hour."

"Fine with us," Fyodor said.

"When do you think you'll find the female?" Benton asked. He couldn't keep derision from his voice.

"It should be soon," Fyodor said. "We have brought in more personnel, and we are going to be systematic about it, starting from the sixth floor and working down. Frankly we are surprised she has eluded us this long. Obviously she's found somewhere to hide. We didn't expect that they would split up."

"Can one of you get me to the patient viewing room A?"

"Of course," Fyodor said.

49.

Lynn could tell she was nearing the end of what had been an arduous journey, both physically and psychologically. The first hour had been the hardest, as the size of the duct remained small. She had come to multiple junctions, some of which were hard for her to negotiate. At times she had to squeeze forward on her side and bend at the waist to get around sharp corners. As difficult as it was in places where she had to negotiate what seemed initially like insurmountable barriers, she seriously questioned whether she would be able to back up. A few times she used the flashlight app on her phone to help, but otherwise she remained in absolute darkness. Purposefully, she mostly kept her eyes tightly closed. With them open, she felt more claustrophobic and frightened. She was thankful there was a constant and gradually increasing breeze moving through the duct, assuring her she was moving in the right direction, particularly at junctions. The draft also kept her from feeling suffocated in the tight space. As difficult a time as she was having, she tried not to think about Michael and what he might be facing.

After the first hour of worming her way deeper and deeper into the system, the dimensions of the duct increased in a progressive, incremental fashion. Eventually she was able to make significant headway when the duct became large enough for her to crawl on all fours, as she and Michael had done in the conveyor tunnel. When the duct angled downward, she adopted a sitting position to slide down on her backside, as if she were on a slide in a children's playground. But out of fear that she might collide with something at the bottom, she inched along, keeping her feet pressed against the sides.

Once the duct again became flat and she could walk bent over at the waist, she made better time. To help orient herself, she ran her hands lightly along the metal sides. As she continued forward, she became more and more aware that the noise level and the turbulence of the moving air were increasing. She guessed they were coming from fans, which she assumed had to be large and powerful to move so much air over so great a distance. It dawned on her that she was getting close, and she began to worry that in the dark she might stumble into one of them.

Such concerns forced her to turn on her flashlight app before proceeding, yet she soon realized that using such a bright light would quickly exhaust her phone's battery. Instead of the flashlight app, she just used the light from the screen, which was more than adequate. The only problem was that the phone kept turning off.

A hundred feet farther on, the duct suddenly enlarged significantly, and ten feet beyond that, the passageway was completely blocked by a large dark gray filter screen. From the noise and vibration, Lynn could tell that the fan or fans were just on the other side.

With a new concern that she might be trapped by the filter blocking the duct, she approached it and reached out to see if it would hinge or somehow open. It didn't move. With the battery clearly weakening, she went back to the flashlight app and shined what light it was producing around the filter's border. That was when she noticed a narrow band of exterior light along the right-hand edge.

Lynn turned off her phone. The line of light along the filter's border was easier to see, and stretched from the duct's floor to its ceiling, giving her the idea that the filter slid in at that point from the outside. She tried again to move it by pushing in that direction. With some effort it moved this time. She pushed it out a few feet, noticing a dramatic increase in the airflow moving past her. To look beyond the filter, she went to turn on her flashlight again. But just before doing so, she noticed an additional, less intense vertical line of light coming in through the wall of the duct to her right, a few feet back from the filter.

Suddenly encouraged, Lynn turned her flashlight back on and shined it in the direction of this new line of light. What she saw was a hinged access panel and, most important, it was fitted with a handle. Pocketing her phone, she tried the handle. A moment later she was able to crack open the panel enough to see that beyond was a lighted machinery space.

As much as she wanted to burst out and escape the claustrophobic confines of the duct, Lynn forced herself to be slow and careful. Despite the noise and vibration of the fan or possibly fans, which had to be close beyond the filter, she tried to listen for any sounds of life in the machinery room. Quickly realizing it was impossible to tell, she carefully opened the panel farther, slowly and noiselessly, to afford herself a gradually expanding view of the room beyond. At that point in her ordeal the last thing she wanted was to run into someone and have to explain herself. Luckily she saw no one, even when the panel was wide open.

Being reasonably sure she was alone in the room, which was not surprising since it was past four-thirty in the morning, Lynn scrambled out through the opening and lowered herself to the floor. She had no idea where she was and just hoped she was in the hospital mechanical spaces, and not still somewhere in the Shapiro.

The first thing Lynn did was check for service on her phone. Now that she was out, her first thoughts were for Michael and how he was faring. Unfortunately there was no phone service, at least not in the hospital basement, where she hoped she was. Without being able to make a call, she quickly scanned the room for the exit. She was about to run to it when she became aware of how filthy she was. Looking down, she could see that the once-white Shapiro coveralls were almost black on her chest, abdomen, the front side of her legs, and the underside of her arms. She'd been totally unaware of how much dust there was in the air-conditioning ducts. Now she worried her face might be equally as soiled.

Lynn did not want to draw attention to herself, particularly from security. Understanding the apparent complicity of Sidereal Pharmaceuticals and Middleton Healthcare, she was not willing to trust any authorities. Despite the hour, she thought the chances were good she would run into some people in the hospital even if she tried to avoid it. Although the hospital slowed at night, it never completely slept. She had to do something about her appearance.

Lynn tore off the Shapiro hat. She did the same with the mask, which was still tied around her neck. The hat was soiled but not as much as her scrubs. She tossed the hat and the mask into a waste container, and ran over to a sink. Cupping her hands, she rinsed her face and then quickly dried it with paper towels.

As dirty as the towels were after drying herself, she knew she had been right about her face. There was no mirror to check, so she rinsed her face yet again. This time the paper towels were only slightly dirty. She tried to use wet paper towels to clean her scrubs. It was useless. She wished she had not abandoned the raincoat in the duct as soon as she had been able to get it off.

Frantically she looked around for some other, more normal coveralls, anything she could possibly use to cover herself, but there was nothing. It was clear that what she needed to do was to get up to the women's changing room off the surgical lounge and get a clean set of normal hospital scrubs. She didn't think it would be a problem at that time of the night, as the ORs were generally quiet, and the changing rooms even more so. She also knew it would be a convenient place to use her phone, as there was a good signal. What she wanted to do more than anything was call Markus Vandermeer. She wanted the FBI and the CIA or even, as Michael joked, the Marines. As far as she was concerned, she couldn't even be totally confident of local law enforcement. Middleton Healthcare was a powerful and important player in local politics.

Lynn cracked the door, which she assumed would lead out into a basement corridor, but it didn't. Apparently the huge HVAC system had its own space. The door led into an even larger machinery area. Here Lynn saw some hospital workers facing a large console filled with all manner of gauges. Like the main HVAC room, the ambient noise was significant and the lighting equally bright.

It wasn't difficult for Lynn to see what was undoubtedly the main door out of the area, as it was a pair of doors rather than just one. To further corroborate her suspicion, while she was watching, a worker came in, offering her a brief but encouraging glance out to what looked like a more typical hospital corridor.

Lynn watched for a short time. The workers seemed intent on their respective jobs, alternately checking gauges and writing in logs. No one, it seemed, paid much attention to the main exit except when they used it. Finally Lynn decided to take a chance.

Walking quickly, but not so quickly that she would draw attention, Lynn traversed the industrial-style setting. She felt terribly obvious but accepted that there was little she could do about it. She had no idea what she was going to say if someone stopped her. Luckily no one did. She went out through the double doors and sighed with relief.

Taking her phone out yet again, Lynn checked for a signal as she ran down the hall. There was still none. The battery power was less than five percent, so she switched the phone off. She entered the first stairwell she came to, fearful of eventually running into someone in the main hallway. There was no way she was going to use the elevator.

She took the stairs by twos and threes, hardly pausing on the landings. Passing the first floor, she continued up at the same pace until she reached the second. There she paused briefly to see about the phone signal. Finally there was something, but it wasn't much. But at least now she knew she was close to her goal, the women's surgical locker room.

The stairway opened up in a section of the second floor across from the Surgical Pathology Department and not far from the Anesthesia office where she and Michael had spoken with Sandra Wykoff. Lynn hurriedly passed through the area and reached the main bank of elevators, where she slowed. She saw no one, although she could hear the TV in the surgical lounge. Pausing at the open door, she carefully glanced inside.

Two orderlies were enjoying coffee and newspapers. There were no nurses. Lynn took it as an opportune time to pass through, which she did at a pace that wouldn't garner attention. She went directly into the women's changing room. Luckily it was completely empty, as she had hoped.

The first thing she did was tear off the Shapiro scrubs, roll them up, and push them down into the bottom of the trash bin, making sure they were completely covered. Once she had pulled on a new set of normal scrubs, she took out her cell phone, and now the signal was fine as she anticipated. From her contacts she pulled up the Vandermeer home phone number and pressed it. While waiting for it to go through, she checked the time. It was going on five o'clock in the morning.

It was Leanne who answered. After apologizing for the hour, Lynn asked to speak to her husband, explaining that it was important. When Markus came on the line, Lynn didn't waste time. At the moment, her main concern was Michael.

"Sidereal Pharmaceuticals is not doing unauthorized drug testing on patients," she said in a rush. "It is much, much worse. They are using the patients to make drugs and causing them illness and even death in the process."

"Okay, slow down!" Markus said, trying to wrap his sleepy mind around what Lynn had said. "Come again?"

Somewhat slower but with even more conviction and passion, Lynn repeated herself.

"How do you know this?" Markus demanded. Lynn could hear the sudden seriousness in his voice.

"Michael Pender and I broke into the Shapiro Institute tonight," Lynn said. "You are aware that it is run a bit like Fort Knox."

"Of course," Markus said. "It is for the benefit of the patients, keeping them from various diseases."

"That might be true to an extent. But from what we have found, we think it is more a cover for what they are really doing, and that is putting the patients at risk to produce monoclonal antibody drugs. And it is not just the inmates of the Shapiro. They are doing it with many ambulatory patients hospitalized in Middleton Healthcare hospitals. It is a massive conspiracy between Sidereal and Middleton. We are sure, as sure as we can be. And there's more. This is the worst part, especially for you and your wife and me personally. Carl's condition was deliberately caused so that he would be moved into the Shapiro to produce a specific drug. It wasn't an accident! It was a recruitment."

For a moment there was silence. Lynn thought that perhaps they had been disconnected. "Markus, are you still there?" she asked.

"I'm here," Markus said. "I'm trying to process all this. It is overwhelming."

"I know it is horrendous," Lynn admitted. "And there have to be a lot of top people involved. Otherwise it couldn't happen. I think they are making billions."

"Are you and Michael still in the Shapiro?"

"I'm not. We were discovered in there and chased. I got out through the HVAC system. Michael covered my tracks and is still in there. I have to assume they caught him and are still looking for me. Something has to be done, and done immediately! They could kill him."

"Okay!" Markus said. "I will immediately call the federal authorities, the FBI specifically. Where are you at the moment? Are you safe?"

"I'm in the women's surgical lounge in the main hospital."

"Have you spoken with anyone else?"

"No one. I don't know whom to trust."

"Smart! Maybe you should just leave. Get away from there."

"I still have Carl's car."

"Drive it away. Come here!"

"Okay," Lynn said. "But Michael? What's going to happen?"

"We will put it in the hands of the federal authorities. Perhaps a state SWAT team can be immediately mustered. For the moment I would prefer to keep the local police out of it, just in case."

"I agree," Lynn said.

"All right, get yourself over here. By the time you're here I'll know more."

50.

After pocketing her phone and taking a deep breath, Lynn looked at herself in the mirror over the sink. She was glad she hadn't run into anyone since climbing out of the air-conditioning duct. Despite having rinsed her face, Lynn saw it was still streaked with dirt, which made her look somewhat like a raccoon. Recognizing that she would undoubtedly run into people, she knew she had to make herself appear more presentable. With a bit more effort and a little soap, she was able to improve her appearance dramatically. She even straightened her hair, using her fingers as a comb. Accepting that she wouldn't be able to marshal much more of an improvement, she at last gave up.

Her plan was to try to avoid everybody as much as possible. If approached or questioned, she'd be pleasant but self-contained. The place she was most concerned about was the parking garage, as it was patrolled by hospital security after a recent episode with a nurse being confronted in the wee hours of the morning. She wanted to steer clear of all security people.

Coming out through the door of the women's lounge, she noticed that a nurse had appeared and was helping herself to coffee. Lynn started for the exit to the main hall feeling like a cat with its ears back. She avoided so much as glancing at the nurse, hoping to elude attention. Instead she looked off to the side, and because of this, her eye happened to catch a glimpse of the monitor on the wall, which indicated there was a neurosurgical case in progress in OR 12. The surgeon was Norman Phillips. It was what explained the paucity of people in the surgical lounge.

Lynn did a double take and stopped dead in her tracks. She blinked, hoping her eyes were playing tricks on her. The patient's name was Michael Pender! The diagnosis was subdural hematoma, and the planned procedure was an emergency craniotomy.

A short, involuntary cry—more like something a tortured animal might make—escaped from Lynn's lips. Frantically, she looked to see what the timing was. The case had started only a few minutes before, at 4:58 A.M.! "No!" she cried with enough volume to shock the three people in the surgical lounge.

Lynn spun around, her eyes stretched open to their limits. "No! No! Not again!" she yelled to no one in particular. The people in the room stared at her and didn't move. They were frozen in place, gaping at her unblinkingly, fearing she was mentally unbalanced.

A second later, Lynn was out the door in a headlong rush toward the paired swinging doors leading to the OR proper. As she ran, she pulled out her phone. Just inside the OR's doors, she paused briefly to bring up onto the screen her last call. Quickly she reconnected it, holding the phone to her ear as she began to run again. Behind her she heard the nurse from the surgical lounge yell for her to stop, saying she was not allowed in the OR. The nurse had burst through the swinging doors right after Lynn and was now chasing after her.

Coming to a halt outside of OR 12, Lynn was relieved to hear Markus's voice. Breathlessly she told him Michael was in surgery. "This has to be stopped. It can't be allowed!" Lynn cried. "He's not going to wake up. I know it! The same thing that happened to Carl is going to happen to Michael!"

The nurse who had chased Lynn ran up to her. "What the hell are you doing?" she demanded shrilly.

Lynn ignored her, concentrating on talking with Markus. "You have to get someone here now! The police, the FBI, anybody! Please! He is in OR Twelve! You have to stop this!"

"Hello?!" the nurse yelled, extending the word in the form of a question while she tried to get the phone out of Lynn's hands. "You can't be in here!"

Lynn disconnected from Markus and roughly pulled the phone away from the nurse's grasp. For a brief instant she eyed the nurse, who was looking at her as if she were a crazy person.

"Let's not cause trouble," the nurse said, trying to speak as calmly as possible. She reached out to grab Lynn's arm to lead her back out of the OR.

With a blow as forceful as a karate punch, Lynn knocked the nurse's hand away. Spinning on her heels, Lynn pushed through into the operating room. Inside, there were five people: anesthetized the patient; the gowned and gloved surgeon; a similarly attired operating nurse; the anesthesiologist; and a circulating nurse. Initially, no one looked in Lynn's direction, and everyone continued their banter. Benton, functioning as the anesthesiologist, and Norman, the neurosurgeon, were talking about golf while Norman operated. The scrub nurse and the circulating nurse were discussing scheduling. It wasn't until the second nurse burst in behind Lynn and loudly ordered her out of the operating room that activity and conversation in the room stopped, and everyone's attention galvanized on Lynn's sudden presence.

Lynn ignored the nurse as she had out in the hallway. Any vestigial hope that the patient might be some other Michael Pender vanished the moment Lynn could see him. It was definitely her dearest friend. She was absolutely sure even though part of his face and his body was covered with surgical drapes. Michael was in a sitting position, with an endotracheal tube in place and his eyes taped shut. The breathing bag on the anesthesia machine was rhythmically expanding and contracting with his breathing. The cardiac monitor was beeping a steady signal. The surgeon had already turned a scalp flap and was preparing to drill a burr hole.

Without a second's hesitation, Lynn stepped over to the anesthesia machine and bent down to look at its side. She wanted to see the number. As she feared, it was machine 37. She straightened up. The nurse who had run in after her again loudly ordered her out of the operating room, telling everyone that Lynn was apparently deranged.

Continuing to ignore the nurse, who was again trying to get ahold of Lynn's arm, Lynn turned to the circulating nurse. "You have to get another anesthesia machine stat! This one's trouble! People don't wake up."

"Please!" the first nurse said, resorting to begging. "You must leave!"

Benton recovered his shock and, after fumbling on the surface of the anesthesia machine, came up with a filled syringe. Without warning he came at Lynn like a bull in a china shop, causing another similar syringe perched on the anesthesia machine to fall to the floor. The nurse who had come in behind Lynn let go of Lynn's arm and stepped back in fright.

Thanks to Lynn's inherent and honed athleticism from her years playing lacrosse, she easily eluded Benton, effectively ducking under his arm and running around the operating table with the idea of keeping it between herself and the enraged anesthesiologist. When Benton started one way, Lynn went the other. While they were jockeying for position, Lynn again urged the circulating nurse to get another anesthesia machine. "If you do that, I will leave," Lynn yelled. "Otherwise I'm going to stay in here until you do." Her voice echoed off the tiled walls.

The circulating nurse was confused as to what to do and looked toward Benton for direction.

"I'm getting hospital security," the first nurse declared. Without waiting for a response from the operating team, she disappeared out the door into the OR hallway.

Dr. Norman Phillips, who had been momentarily paralyzed by this unexpected spectacle during his case, quickly recovered. He handed off his craniotome, which he had been about to use, to the scrub nurse and stepped back from standing directly behind Michael. Obviously willing to break scrub—contaminate his gloves and gown—by holding his arms and gloved hands out in front of himself, he threatened to block Lynn from moving in his direction so that she couldn't continue circling the operating table.

Lynn immediately took the neurosurgeon up on his offer to join the confrontation. She wanted to be as disruptive as possible, knowing that if the surgeon broke scrub he'd have to start all over again, wasting significant time in the process. Her hope was to maximize the delay in order to keep anything from happening to Michael until help, in the form of Markus Vandermeer, somehow got there. The problem was, she didn't have any idea of how long that might be. What Lynn didn't want was to have both Benton and Norman get ahold of her at the same time. She could well imagine what was probably in the syringe.

Pretending for the moment she was on a lacrosse field and that she was playing men's lacrosse and not women's, she body-checked Norman at full speed, hitting him with her shoulder and driving upward. She had seen Carl do it in old films he had from his college days. It worked superbly, catching the neurosurgeon completely off guard and knocking him off his feet to sprawl on the floor. She knew that was breaking scrub about as much as humanly possible.

Benton, rushing up behind Lynn, caught sight of this impressive display and skidded to a stop. Lynn took the opportunity to give a sharp chop with the edge of her hand to Benton's outstretched forearm with the hand holding the syringe. The syringe flew from his grasp, and falling to the floor, it spun safely under the operating table.

Lynn ran back around to the other side of the room after leaping over Norman, who was struggling to catch his breath. Spinning around, she waited for the next attack. Benton went back to the anesthesia machine, pulled out a small drawer, and struggled to get a new syringe filled with a mammoth dose of midazolam. Norman picked himself up off the floor, checking to be sure he had no broken bones.

"A different anesthesia machine!" Lynn yelled yet again to the circulating nurse or anyone else who would listen. "That's all I'm asking. I'll leave if you get it and use it." She didn't know if the planned surgery was indicated or not. Her guess was that it was not, but the surgery per se wasn't her main concern. It was the number 37 anesthesia machine.

"Dr. Rhodes?" the circulating nurse said. "What should I do?"

"Nothing," Benton sneered. He got the syringe filled and tossed aside the vial. Again prepared, he looked over at Norman, who'd now totally recovered. Both nodded and turned their full attention to Lynn. They then started around the OR table in opposite directions with the idea of trapping her.

Having been successful using the body check with Norman and still definitely reluctant to deal with both men at once, Lynn immediately launched a similar attack on Benton as she had done on Norman. Accelerating to near full speed, she ran at him. And once again, just before impact she crouched slightly so that when she hit him she could lunge upward with the point of her shoulder. At the last second before contact, Benton reared back defensively, having witnessed the effect on Norman. The ploy managed to cushion the collision significantly. But it also meant that both he and Lynn lost their footing with her momentum.

Lynn fell directly on top of Benton. She could hear the wind whoosh out of his lungs, and then she felt him struggling vainly to catch his breath even more than what Norman had experienced. Scrambling to her feet, she realized he had managed to stab her with the syringe, whether he meant to or not, when they when they met head-on. Buried almost to the hilt, it was still sticking out of her forearm.

But she didn't have time to worry how much of the contents might have been injected or whether it had been enough to compromise her. There was a more pressing problem. Norman had come around the operating table and was rushing at her like she had done to him, and as close as he was at that moment, there was no chance for her to be offensive. Instead, like she had done hundreds of times while playing lacrosse, she stepped aside at the very last moment like a matador, and the man mostly missed her. Yet he was able to grab a handful of her scrub top as he sailed past, and because of it, managed to keep his feet.

With as much force as she could muster, Lynn tried to tear herself free from Norman's clutches, but he held on and even managed to get a ahold of her left wrist with his other hand. Lynn reached up with her free hand and grabbed his face mask and gave it a fearsome yank, snapping his head forward before the elastic broke. But he didn't let go of either her clothes or her wrist. She struggled madly to get away, but no matter what she did, Norman held on.

Having caught his breath, Benton came to Norman's aid. After suffering a few significant slaps in the face, he was able to get Lynn's still-free arm. But that still left her feet and legs free.

Lynn struggled as much as she could, kicking both of them in the legs at least once. She was aiming higher but unable to manage it.

When the men thought they had the wild woman under a semblance of control, as she seemed to be tiring, they started toward the OR door with the intention of getting her out in the hallway. But that was easier said than done. Lynn made it as difficult as possible, particularly by getting one foot or the other on the doorjamb on each attempt and lunging backward with as strong a kick as she could muster. From her kickboxing, her legs were powerful.

"Can you hold her while I get more Versed?" Benton squeaked.

"To be honest, I don't know," Norman said hoarsely. "What a vixen. Who the hell is she?"

"I'll tell you later," Benton said.

"I'll tell you who I am! I'm a fourth-year medical student. The patient is my friend. I want a different anesthesia machine!"

Without warning, Benton balled his fist and struck Lynn in the face, bringing blood from her already injured nose. The blow caught Norman by surprise and for a second he loosened his grip on Lynn's arm. Lynn took advantage of this and snatched her right arm free. Mimicking Benton, she formed a fist and hit him with a blow surprisingly similar to his, bloodying his nose, as he had done to hers.

At that moment, directly in front of the three struggling people, the door to the hallway burst open. It was the original nurse. She rushed in. Following her and wearing surgical gowns pulled on like bathrobes over their hospital security uniforms were the same five men who had been chasing Lynn and Michael inside the Shapiro Institute. Lynn didn't recognize their faces, just their uniforms, as they were slightly different from the normal uniforms worn by hospital security.

"No!" Lynn cried. "I don't want to go with them."

"I think you should have thought of that before you burst in here," the nurse said triumphantly. She stepped aside so that the sizable men could rush in and take hold of Lynn. Still she struggled, but it was no use. In a moment they had her out in the hallway.

"Get her on a gurney!" Benton shouted to the security people. "I'll be out in a second with some medication." He exchanged a glance of incredulity and disgust with Norman. "You're right! What a fucking vixen!" he said as he quickly went back to the anesthesia machine. He wanted to get yet another syringe and another vial of midazolam.

"This will go down as my most unique craniotomy," Norman complained as he began peeling off his contaminated surgical gown and gloves. He looked back over at Michael, who had remained unconscious in the midst of the melee. "Is he all right through this?"

"He's all right," Benton said with a wave of his hand. He looked at the monitor. "The guy's as healthy as an ox."

Benton drew up the drug, purposefully going a bit overboard on the dosage. He didn't want any more scenes. While Norman went to scrub again, Benton went out to the gurney in the hallway. The security guards had Lynn pressed down on its surface. All five men had ahold of her. Confident that the men had her adequately restrained, he decided to go the IV route, with enough of a dose that he was confident would keep her in never-never land for hours.

"I refuse any medication," Lynn cried, trying to be authoritative.

"As if I care," Benton sneered.

"Is this the woman we were searching for in the Shapiro?" one of the security guards asked. He had a mild but definite Russian accent.

"This is the one," Benton said as he applied a tourniquet around Lynn's upper arm and swabbed the crook of her elbow. "Now you realize why it would have been far better if you had nabbed her when you should have."

From force of habit before making the injection and with the idea of eliminating any air, Benton held up the syringe in front of his face, the needle pointing toward the ceiling. As he did so he caught sight of the double doors at the very end of the hall bursting open and what looked like a line of people surging into the OR suite. Benton moved the syringe out of his line of sight and focused to get a better view. He was mystified. It was a lot of people, a lot more than should be coming into the OR at that time in the morning.

Transfixed and not a little confused, Benton watched as this long line of people approached at a run. He could see that they were mostly men, which was also perplexing because he knew that the majority of the OR staff was female. And stranger still, like the hospital security men who were beside him, holding Lynn down on the gurney, these newcomers were wearing hospital gowns pulled on backward, with the opening in the front, not the back.

As this new group neared, Benton's confusion began to metamorphose to fear. With each running step he got a glimpse that they were wearing uniforms, again like the hospital security men next to him, but with a difference. Benton could see that the color wasn't brown, like the color of the uniforms worn by hospital security, but gray like the South Carolina Highway Patrol. Worse still, most had their service revolvers clutched in their hands. . . .

EPILOGUE

Lynn Peirce tried to look on the bright side, as it was a bittersweet moment. A beautiful day had dawned, even though a week earlier the forecast had been for possible rain. If it had rained, it would have been a disappointment, since it would have forced Mason-Dixon University School of Medicine to hold its commencement ceremony indoors instead of in the glorious sunshine of the flower-filled medical center quadrangle. After four years of study, perseverance, and hard work, particularly in light of the horrific tribulations of the last month and a half, it seemed appropriate to be outside, in view of the hospital, the basic science building, the clinic building, and the Shapiro Institute just to be reminded that all these institutions were back to fulfilling their originally intended altruistic health care roles.

The investigation involving the mind-boggling malfeasance of Middleton Healthcare and their partner in crime, Sidereal Pharmaceuticals, was still ongoing, and the resultant indictments were continuing. So were the malpractice lawsuits, causing Middleton Healthcare to declare bankruptcy. As such, the scandalous affair continued to dominate Charleston's *Post and Courier* newspaper and to be the talk of the town.

Lynn and Michael's role in uncovering the shocking conspiracy had eventually leaked out. Ever since that fateful morning when she had been able to prevent the sham surgery on Michael, reporters had been trying to interview her, claiming she was a hero.

Lynn did not think of herself as a hero. She couldn't, not in the face of the terrible personal losses that she had suffered and felt she had helped cause. If anything, she chided herself for not figuring out what was happening sooner than she did. In retrospect, she wished more than anything that she had not involved herself in Carl's surgery, even though, had she not, the conspiracy would still be ongoing. She also wished she had been stronger and had not involved Michael, considering what happened to him because of her. Now, looking back, she wished she had not sought him out in a kind of Pavlovian reflex immediately after first seeing Carl comatose in the neuro ICU.

At that exact moment, 11:20 A.M., May 22, Lynn was standing at the foot of three steps leading up to the temporary stage that had been erected at the far end of the quadrangle lawn. It had a podium and three chairs, one of which was currently occupied by the commencement speaker. Standing behind the podium at the microphone was the dean of students. She was reading the names of the graduates, who had been organized alphabetically for the ceremony. Each time she read the name, the student mounted the steps and was given his or her diploma by the dean of the school. To expedite the process, the five students soon to be called were waiting at the steps so that they would be available instantly. Lynn was next, as Harold Parker, the classmate alphabetically ahead of her, was just being handed his certificate.

Lynn turned to look out over the audience. Hundreds of folding chairs had been placed in rows in front of the stage. All were filled.

There were even people standing at the very rear. From where Lynn was standing, she could see her mother, two sisters, and all four grandparents in the row immediately behind the first two rows reserved for the graduates. When her mother saw her glance in her direction, she waved. Self-consciously, Lynn half waved back. She was pleased they had all come to Charleston to celebrate her achievement, but she knew it was going to be a strain after the ceremony because all the fanfare was magnifying her sense of personal loss. After all that had recently happened, she didn't feel like celebrating.

"Miss Lynn Peirce," the dean of students announced, "Academically first in the class."

Dutifully, Lynn climbed the few steps and approached the dean of the school. There was a smattering of applause and even a few whistles, even though the audience had been asked to hold applause until all students had been given their diplomas.

"Miss Peirce!" Dean English said sternly, far enough away from the microphone so that no one else could hear. Then her face brightened. "Congratulations!" She handed Lynn her diploma, but then held on to it, reminding Lynn of Siri Erikson, who currently was one of the people indicted as a key player in the conspiracy. It had been uncovered that she had been behind perfecting the method of creating human hybridomas with herself as a test subject and then using the technique on dozens upon dozens of Mason-Dixon inpatients and the entire population of the Shapiro Institute.

"There is a proverb," the dean continued, "about curiosity killing the cat, which I personally have never supported. You have succeeded in justifying my position by totally debunking it. Myself, the school, the Medical Center, and the profession of medicine thank you for what your curiosity uncovered."

"You're welcome," Lynn said, nonplussed. She had not expected the dean would say anything other than "Congratulations," as she had done with the other students.

The dean continued to hold on to Lynn's diploma, surprising Lynn further. "I've made some calls to colleagues up north on your behalf," she went on. "Although we will be honored to have you as a resident here, I've been told that you might prefer Boston. If that is something you are interested in, please come and see me." She then smiled and let go of the diploma.

"Thank you," Lynn said simply, even more taken aback. She started off the stage as she heard the next student's name called out over the loudspeakers. "Michael Pender. Number two academically and the other twin."

Again there was a bit of applause and even titters, coming mainly from the fellow graduates in response to the inside joke about he and Lynn being twins, as it was hard for two people to look more different.

Lynn descended the steps on the other side of the stage, and turned around to watch as Michael approached the dean. He looked immense in his graduation gown, and his lock-twists that hadn't been shaved at his planned craniotomy stuck out from under his cap.

Lynn felt shell-shocked. She could not believe what the dean had just said to her. Could it be true that there was a chance to go to Boston for her residency, and if there was a spot, could she leave Charleston? Initially Carl had been moved out of the Shapiro after the revelations of abuse by Sidereal Pharmaceuticals, but, having shown no change in his status and since the Shapiro was so good at taking care of people in a vegetative state, Carl's parents were considering moving him back. If that happened, there would be limited visitation for Lynn.

Lynn could not help but smile as she watched Michael with the dean. The dean was holding on to Michael's diploma and talking with him above and beyond a mere "congratulations," just as she had done with her, surely thanking him for his role in the exposé. But as she watched, she saw Michael's eyes dart momentarily in her direction, making Lynn suspicious that something was being said about her and possibly about Boston. Instead of immediately heading back to her seat, as she had been instructed to do, she waited for Michael. As he approached, diploma in hand, she could tell he looked guilty. She knew him that well.

"Did you say something to her about my wanting to go to Boston?" Lynn asked.

"Who? Me?" Michael asked innocently. "Now, why would I say something like that?"

"I don't know. That's why I'm asking."

"Maybe because it would be the healthiest thing for you to do," Michael said. He gestured for them to head back to their seats. With Lynn in the lead, they started. "And maybe for me, too."

Lynn stopped, turned around, and gave Michael a quick hug and a peck on the cheek, despite being in full view of everyone. Lynn had never been demonstrative in public. The gesture resulted in a bit more applause and whistles from their fellow students. By then, everyone in their class knew of the role they had played in bringing to light the unethical and even murderous conspiracy that had engulfed the medical center. Lynn and Michael might not have thought of themselves as heroes, but just about everyone else did.

Are those the two?" Leonid whispered in Russian as Lynn and Michael took their seats.

"Yes," snarled Darko. He and Leonid were standing at the very rear of the audience. They were dressed casually but smartly in white dress shirts, leather jackets, and jeans. Neither had been caught up in the wide-ranging dragnet instigated by the FBI while investigating and dismantling the Middleton-Sidereal conspiracy. As hit men, they were off-the-books employees, and none of the co-conspirators wanted to risk implicating them, in fear of their reputation and

certain reprisal. "Why don't we just do them and forget about it,"
Leonid said. Neither man thought of the two students as heroes.
Quite the opposite.

"I'd love to, but we have to wait until we hear from Sergei,"
Darko said. "Let's get out of here! I've seen enough!"

The two men started off toward the parking garage. Darko had
wanted to see the students once more to make sure their faces were
engraved in his memory after his brief, violent, but unfortunately
inconclusive encounter with them.

"Why haven't we heard anything from Sergei?" Leonid asked
when they climbed into their car. "It's been more than a month."

"He has got a lot on his mind," Darko said. "Especially after In-
terpol chased him and Boris out of Geneva back to Moscow. We'll
hear from him. I'm sure he is going to want us to do something.
Those two students created a hell of a lot of havoc and lost time,
making Sidereal temporarily halt biologics production until a new
hospital chain partner is found. I can't imagine he's going to be willing to let them fly off free as birds. Nor am I . . ."

extracts reading groups
competitions books new
discounts extracts extracts
competitions extracts
books new discounts
events reading groups
books books extracts events
new new title reading groups
interviews
events extracts
discounts
new books events
events new
discounts extracts discounts
www.panmacmillan.com
extracts events reading groups
competitions books extracts new